The Long Game

An Alexis Parker novel

G.K. Parks

Copyright © 2019 G.K. Parks

A Modus Operandi imprint

All rights reserved.

ISBN: 1942710151
ISBN-13: 978-1-942710-15-8

For my mom and dad

ONE

"Shots fired."

I didn't need the voice in my ear to say it. The evidence of the event lay before me. A man choked and gasped, struggling to breathe. Two bullets had torn through his torso.

Warily, I glanced out the front entrance. I didn't see the shooter. Aiming in the direction from which the bullets came, I exited the building and grabbed the dying man by the collar and dragged him behind the decorative, cement planter. Kneeling next to him, I hoped more gunfire wouldn't follow.

"You'll be okay," I said. "Just hang on." Pink foam had already started to form in the corner of his mouth. I tapped the button on my radio. "We need an ambulance. Does anyone have eyes on the shooter?"

"Negative," a response came back.

The man made a gurgling noise, frantically clutching my hands which were doing what little they could to stop the bleeding. We both knew he wasn't going to make it. The wild, frightened look in his eyes searched for hope and comfort.

"I'm here. It's okay." I didn't even know his name.

He squeezed my hand as a final tremble coursed through him. His entire body tensed, and he emitted one last wheeze. A river of blood flowed from his mouth. His eyes dulled, and he was gone.

The radio calls continued back and forth as the security team searched for the shooter. I remained beside the dead man, listening for updates, but the team didn't have any. The shooter was in the wind.

Blinking, I slowly pulled my hands away and stared at the blood. His blood. Errant images ran through my mind, but I shook them away and wiped my hands on the dead man's shirt. This wasn't supposed to happen.

Sirens filled the air, quickly followed by flashing lights. A single patrol car pulled to a stop inches from me. The driver's side door opened, and a woman took cover behind the vehicle, aiming her weapon over the roof of the car.

"Hands in the air," the officer commanded.

I did as I was told. My gun was on the pavement next to my left knee. Predictably, the officer approached and kicked it away before she even bothered to ask who I was.

"Alexis Parker, private investigator," I said. "CryptSpec hired me, well, Cross Security, but I work for them."

She crouched down and felt for a pulse. Shaking her head, she pressed her radio and called it in. "Who is he?"

"I don't know."

"You don't know? I thought you said you're a private eye."

"The irony isn't lost on me."

She picked up my gun with her thumb and pointer finger and gave it a sniff. "Did you shoot him?"

"Does it look like I shot him?"

"In that case, you better tell me what happened."

"I wish I knew." It was against Lucien Cross's rules to speak to the police. Then again, it was also against my boss's wishes to involve oneself with murder investigations. As usual, he would not be pleased. "One of CryptSpec's programmers got canned. The CEO feared he might lash out, so Cross sent a security team to remain on standby. We were supposed to stop the situation from escalating."

"This isn't the programmer?" the police officer asked.

"No."

By now, several other units had arrived, along with a few detectives I recognized. They went to work, conducting a search of the area and roping off the crime scene. A detective and three officers entered the building. I spotted two patrolmen speaking to one of the members of the security team. The rest were elsewhere, either assisting or being questioned. Any minute, a few town cars would arrive, and this party would come to an end.

"Miss Parker, do you believe the programmer is the shooter?" the officer asked. "Could this be one of his coworkers?"

I blew out a breath, desperate to recall the proper order of events. By now, I could practically feel the blood drying on my hands. "I don't think so. I don't recognize him. And Ian Barber, the programmer, wouldn't have had time to do this." I pointed. "The shots came from that direction. They were fired before I exited the building. I didn't see who fired, so the shooter wasn't close." I looked down at the body. "Based on the wounds, I'm guessing he took rifle fire."

"I didn't realize PIs came into contact with a lot of GSWs," she replied skeptically.

"Parker used to be FBI," Detective Derek Heathcliff said from behind. "You can trust whatever she says. She knows what she's talking about."

"Detective," the officer spun to face him, "she was kneeling over the body when I arrived."

Heathcliff shrugged. "Of course, she was. Where else would she be?"

"Sir?" the officer asked.

"I'll take it from here." He sent her to assist in the hunt for the shooter and stared at me, taking everything in. "Are you okay, Alex? You look like you're about to pass out."

"I need to wash my hands."

His eyes narrowed, and he nodded down at the body. "Is that his blood?"

"Uh-huh."

"Okay, come on." Heathcliff led me into the building

and located the restroom just off the side of the lobby. He pushed the door open to the men's room and turned on the nearest faucet. "Do you want to tell me what happened?"

I rinsed my hands before soaping them up. More images flooded my mind. *So much blood.* I swallowed uncertainly. "CryptSpec believed they had a breach. The CEO thought it was internal. He suspected someone was copying their programming and selling it to a competitor. For the last couple of weeks, I've been investigating under the guise of human resources manager. The party responsible was fired a few minutes ago. Given the circumstances and CryptSpec's lack of security, Cross sent a team to make sure everything went smoothly."

"Great job," Heathcliff said sarcastically.

"The programmer didn't open fire. I'm not sure he even left the building yet." I turned off the water and took the offered paper towel. "I don't know who was killed."

"You didn't get an ID?"

I shook my head, feeling a layer of sweat coat my skin. My mouth tasted salty. "The man had already been shot by the time I made it to the door. Someone, Hoover, maybe, noticed something strange outside. He didn't give details. Then it was shots fired, and," I braced myself against the sink as I fought against the beginnings of a panic attack, "he died right fucking there."

"Hoover? Is he part of Cross's security team?"

I nodded, finding it increasingly difficult to remain upright.

"Slow, deep breaths." Heathcliff pulled me into his arms.

We'd worked together several times. We'd even been undercover a time or two, but we hadn't spoken in months. The case that ended my career as a federal agent had nearly cost him his job. Neither of us had been at fault, but most days, I was convinced I was cursed and tried to keep my distance before I brought more difficulty into his life.

"I'm okay," I said.

"Are you sure?" He took a step back and assessed me for signs of injury.

"Yes." I took a deep breath. "We need to find the

shooter, and we need an ID on the vic."

"Actually, Parker, I need you to answer a few more questions. We'll get statements from the rest of Cross's people, and we'll talk to CryptSpec. Other than that, there's not much for you to do."

"A man died."

"I know. I have to do this by the book."

A tiny smile crept onto my face. "It's good to see things are finally back to normal, Detective."

He nodded and led the way back to the lobby. As predicted, Lucien Cross arrived with a team of lawyers. And to think, ten minutes ago, I didn't think my day could get any worse.

"Alex," Cross eyed Heathcliff as if he were evil incarnate, "what the hell happened?" Before I could get a single word out, Cross changed his mind. "Don't say anything without counsel."

"She isn't under arrest," Heathcliff retorted. The detective led me past Cross and to the command center the police set up in a back office. "Take me through it."

For the next half hour, I laid everything out. Nicholas Mansfield, CryptSpec's CEO, had been denied a patent on their latest software innovation. A competitor had already claimed proprietary rights to the same technology. After careful examination, Mansfield realized the programming code was identical. He reached out to Cross Security to determine the source of the leaked information. After a thorough review of personnel files, background checks, and speaking to most of the employees, I determined Ian Barber, the head programmer, was responsible.

Cross Security sent a team to search Ian's desk and office while Mansfield and I spoke to him. Barber had just been fired and told to clear out. Mansfield asked us to search Barber's belongings to make sure he didn't steal anything else or try to sabotage CryptSpec's current projects now that he got the boot. Two members of the security team accompanied Barber back to his office while the other two covered the exits.

"Do you have any reason to believe Barber might be violent?" Heathcliff asked.

"I don't think he is."

Derek thought for a moment. Barber and Mansfield were being questioned by other detectives. "Where were you when the shooting happened?"

"Here. I just finished signing some paperwork regarding Cross Security's contract. I don't know how this happened or why."

"Did anyone know Barber was getting the axe today, besides CryptSpec management and Cross Security?"

"Not that I know of. You'll have to ask Barber's coworkers."

Heathcliff made a few more notes and clicked his pen. "Okay. You know how this works. If I need anything else from you, I'll be in touch. You remember something, you call me." He gestured to someone at the door who returned my nine millimeter. "Try to stay out of trouble, Parker."

"Easier said than done." I stopped in the doorway. "Hey, Derek, I won't get in your way on this. You have my word."

"That would be a first. Are you sure you're feeling okay?" A teasing smile pulled at his lips, and he winked. "Check with the officers outside before you leave and make sure they don't have any more questions."

"Will do."

When I exited the office, Cross was huddled next to Mr. Mansfield. Spotting me, he excused himself and grabbed my elbow before I could make it safely to the door. "Why is there a dead man outside the building?"

"I don't know. Isn't your security team supposed to handle the dangerous situations?"

"The threat did not come from Barber or anyone inside CryptSpec. We were practically ambushed. What's going on?"

"How would I know?"

His icy glare was supposed to intimidate. Instead, it pissed me off. "What did you tell the police?" he asked.

I jerked my arm free. "Everything they wanted to know."

"Miss Parker," he warned.

"Talk to your security team. Two of them were outside. They should know what happened. I don't." I shoved the door open, but he followed. A bloody sheet now covered the body, and I averted my eyes. "You want to know what happened? That man died before my eyes. I watched him drown in his own blood." Flashes of long-buried events coursed through my mind. "I can't be here right now."

"We'll be meeting in the conference room to address these matters. Go back to the office and wait for me there."

Nodding, I headed in the direction of the responding officer. After a brief exchange, I climbed in my car. A million questions went through my mind. What happened? Who was the dead man? Why was he shot? Did it have anything to do with CryptSpec or Barber?

Cross Security would deal with the last part. That was where our job began and ended, and I gave Detective Heathcliff my word that I wouldn't interfere with his investigation. Still, watching someone die wasn't something I could easily forget. And it dredged up a lot of bad memories. The last place I needed to be was the office.

TWO

"Stuart Gifford, age twenty-nine, five foot ten, one hundred and seventy-four pounds. A graduate of MIT with a degree in engineering." Cross continued to read the profile. "Does any of this sound familiar?"

"No." I glanced at the security team. The four men remained standing, practically at attention. I rolled my eyes. "Did he work for CryptSpec?"

"He's not a regular employee." Cross hit the print button and turned his attention to me. "He could have been a consultant or a temp of some sort. You were in the HR office. You had access to CryptSpec's records and personnel. You should know if he worked there."

"I didn't exactly memorize everyone's name or file."

"You should have."

I worked my jaw for a moment. "I never claimed to have an eidetic memory. Perhaps a robot would be better suited to meet your needs. I suggest you hire one."

He plucked the sheet of paper off the printer and held it out. "I want a full work-up on Gifford. Get to it."

For a moment, I stared at Lucien. It took every ounce of self-control not to tell him what he could do with this job. He returned my gaze, seemingly oblivious to my barely contained rage. He waited for me to take the paper before changing gears and grilling the security detail on what happened. Two of them had remained inside, providing an alibi for Ian Barber. However, the two stationed outside were getting ripped a new one for failing to notice and neutralize the threat.

Once inside my office, I slammed the door, balled up the paper, and threw it across the room. "Dammit," I cursed. "Dammit all to hell." I wanted to scream, to cry, to escape the images, the turmoil, the guilt. At least I was smart enough to realize this wasn't about Stuart Gifford. It was about the people I lost or nearly lost. I'd only been close enough to death to look it in the eye twice before. Once was when my first partner died. The second time was when I nearly lost James Martin.

Looking down at my hands, I could still feel the sticky blood. I had to wash it off. I needed to get it off my skin and clothes. More importantly, off my mind. I grabbed my go-bag and went down the hall. Cross Security was state-of-the-art, and the locker room and showers weren't half bad either.

After scouring my skin raw, I changed into some clean clothes and took a breath. A man was dead. That had to take precedence. There would be time later for my inevitable meltdown.

I returned to my office to do as my boss asked. Stuart Gifford. No criminal record. Outstanding student loans, sizable credit card debt, but nothing out of the ordinary given his socioeconomic status. He had a job as a civil engineer. After a quick call to his supervisor, I was made aware he was working on constructing a new bridge. As far as I could tell, he had no reason to be at CryptSpec.

Pulling my fingers away from the keys, I resisted the urge to continue digging. Frankly, we shouldn't even know the victim's name. Cross just happened to overhear it while he was giving his statement to the police. Since Gifford had no known connection to CryptSpec, this wasn't our case. For once, I was convinced that I just happened to be in the wrong place at the wrong time.

I checked for a connection between Gifford and Barber,

but I didn't find one. In a last ditch effort, I went to the filing cabinet and searched through the information CryptSpec provided when they hired us and the intel I gathered since I was assigned the case. No mention of Gifford, engineering, or bridges.

A gentle knock sounded at the door. Lucien stood on the threshold, waiting for permission to enter. My boss never stood on ceremony, and he made it clear from day one that he owned everyone and everything in this office.

"I'm sorry I snapped at you," he said. "I don't enjoy dealing with the police."

"You should get used to it, sir."

"I spoke to Dryer and Weston. They told me about the radio calls. You watched Gifford die. Based on what I've heard of his injuries, there was nothing you could have done to save him."

"It doesn't matter."

"Shall I assume that's the reason you're being particularly abrasive this afternoon?"

"What do you want, Lucien?" He hated when people beat around the bush, and I could see why.

He cleared his throat. "Have you completed the work-up on Gifford?"

I showed him what I had so far. "Why don't you just call Mansfield and ask? It would save us a lot of time and effort."

"I may just do that." He left without another word.

Pushing away from my desk, I circled the room. It would have been nice to have a window to look out. The drab walls were oppressive. I checked the time and went across the hall to Kellan Dey's office. He was another of Cross's private investigators. Unlike me, Kellan had come to Cross from the DEA.

"Are you busy?" I asked, brushing my hair out of my face.

"No more than normal. What's up, Alex?" He studied me for a moment. "You look like you could use a drink."

"I could use a lot more than a drink. Look, I know it's Friday afternoon and we all want to get the hell out of here, but I'm about to lose it. Will you cover for me?"

"Sure." His brow furrowed. "What's going on?"

I didn't want to talk about it. "Lucien has me researching Stuart Gifford in connection with CryptSpec. I don't believe there is a connection, but the man was killed right outside their front door."

"Shit." He picked up a pen and wrote down the name. "Anything else I might need to know?"

"That's pretty much it. I told Cross what I found, which was nothing, but in the event he comes up with some other ridiculous theory, I was hoping you could deal with it."

"No problem."

"I owe you."

"Make it up to me. Lunch Monday. Tequila and tacos."

"I don't drink tequila."

He laughed. "That's okay. You don't have to drink it. You just have to pay for it."

Escaping the confines of Cross Security, I took a cab across town to the Martin Technologies building. It was four o'clock when I stepped foot inside, and I smiled at the person manning the security desk. Since I didn't recognize him, I figured he must be new.

"May I help you?" he asked.

"I'm here to see Mr. Martin. Is he busy?"

The guard clicked a few keys. "Do you have an appointment?"

"Not in those precise terms. It's more of an open invitation." I turned up the charm and leaned over the desk. Perhaps I should have left a few buttons open on my blouse, but I wasn't expecting things to be this complicated. "If he isn't in a meeting, can you just call up to his office and ask if he has a few minutes for an attractive brunette?" The guard looked utterly bewildered. "Just check. I'll leave if he says no."

"One moment, ma'am."

I cringed as the term caused another barrage of negative memories to flood my mind. The back of an ambulance. The frantic warning beeps on the monitors. The EMTs rushing around. Michael Carver flatlining. I gasped, unraveling at the seams.

He put the phone down. "My apologies, Miss Parker. I'll

take you upstairs."

I clung to the elevator rail. As soon as the doors dinged, I pushed my way out of the tiny metal box. "I've got it from here." I didn't wait for a response as I went down the short hallway.

The glass wall that lined the exterior of James Martin's office was currently set to clear. He was behind his desk with an amused look on his face. When I reached the door, he pressed the remote unlock, and I stepped inside. Immediately, the clear wall became opaque.

"This is a pleasant surprise. Wasn't I supposed to pick you up at your apartment tonight?" Martin asked.

"Were you?"

"Sweetheart, what is it? What happened?" He came around the desk and reached for me.

I melted into his arms, pressing my ear against his chest until I could hear his heart beating. "I shouldn't bother you with this."

"Alexis, this is why I'm here. Bother me, please." His desk phone rang. He pulled back, and I stood on my tiptoes and kissed him. "Hold that thought."

While he spoke on the phone, I went into his private washroom and scrubbed my hands again. "You're losing it, Parker." This was ridiculous. I knew it was, but watching Gifford die triggered something that I thought I made peace with years ago. Right now, the wounds felt fresh. And if I wasn't careful, they'd become debilitating.

Martin appeared in the doorway. "What's going on?" he asked gently.

"Someone died." I let out an ugly laugh. "I didn't know him. I didn't even know his name until Cross weaseled it out of the police. But I was there. I held his hand. I watched the life leave his body. I've only seen it happen twice before, which is crazy considering the number of people I've killed. God," I inhaled a shaky breath, "I'm a horrible person. This man died, and I'm stuck thinking about..." My voice trailed off.

He ran his thumb against my cheek. "Alex, I'm okay."

"You had the same look when you were shot, when you were bleeding out. I can still feel your blood on my hands and see the growing stain on the carpet. I thought I lost you."

"I'm right here. You won't lose me."

But I saw the look in his eyes. It scared him when I got like this. We'd dealt with this issue and the aftermath of my worries and nightmares several times. It had nearly ended our relationship.

"I know. I just had to see you like this and not the way I remember that day going." I stepped away from him. "I should let you get back to work. You probably have more meetings."

"I don't." He watched me uncertainly, sensing I needed some space. "You should stay. I'd like to have something beautiful to look at while I finish going over the projections. Plus, it'll save me a trip to pick you up."

I stopped in front of the floor-to-ceiling windows and stared out at the city. Martin had a fantastic view. The entire world was spread out before me. "Would you mind terribly if we stayed in tonight?"

He hesitated, and I glanced over my shoulder as he fidgeted with his tie, finally getting annoyed with the knot and taking it off. "We promised Luc and Vivi. If the Guillots weren't hosting a dinner for the new board members, I'd cancel without a second thought. But I have to be there. I'll duck out early and meet you back at our place if you don't feel up to socializing. Or your place. Whatever you prefer."

"That's okay. We should be there. It's important." I moved to the bar in the corner and spun a few bottles. Finally, I cracked open a can of seltzer and took a seat on one of the leather couches. Kicking off my shoes, I pulled my knees to my chest and sat in the corner in order to face his desk. "I ran into Derek today."

Martin clicked a few keys, alternating his gaze from the monitor to me. "How is Detective Heathcliff?"

"Embroiled in a homicide, which I vowed to stay away from."

"Really?"

I took another sip. "Yeah, well, you know Cross's stance on murder investigations. And after everything, I don't think Derek's career can afford any more complications."

Martin made a sound, indicating he was listening, but I knew something on the screen had caught his attention. I kept my mouth shut and worked through some of the exercises various shrinks had suggested to deal with these unwanted memories. As usual, I didn't find them helpful. The only thing that ever worked was the realization that I had two options — live in the present or sacrifice everything for the sake of the what ifs.

I made my decision. I chose to have Martin now and for as long as I could instead of dwelling on the possibility that his proximity to me would result in his untimely demise. Ultimately, he would decide if the danger was too great, and I would respect it.

I watched him work. He rolled up his sleeves, exposing his forearms. He had already taken off his tie and unbuttoned his vest. His jacket was hanging neatly behind him. This was his passion. Apparently, life went on. At least for most of us. Stuart Gifford couldn't say the same.

I wondered how long Martin would stay immersed in the paperwork before realizing I was still in the room. Truthfully, this was why we worked. He understood my obsessive workaholic tendencies because they mirrored his own. Long ago, we swore we'd put our careers first and relationship second, but that wasn't true. Even though he said he had to go to Luc's tonight, if I remained at home, he would duck out before the main course was served. We'd been through too much for it to be any other way. I just wondered if he would end up resenting me because of it.

Inevitably, my mind went back to the events of the morning, but I was calmer now. Seeing Martin alive and well kept the more painful memories at bay. Slowly, I recalled everything from this morning — my meeting with Mr. Mansfield to the sound of the gunshots. The shots had come from a distance. I heard them, and so did the security team, which led to one glaringly obvious discrepancy. Gifford had been shot twice in the chest. He wasn't shot in the back.

"Holy shit." I dug into my bag for my phone. "He was leaving CryptSpec."

"What?" Martin looked up.

"Never mind." I dialed Heathcliff and started to pace in front of the windows, aware of Martin's gaze following my every move.

"That was quick," Heathcliff answered. "I figured you would at least wait until tomorrow."

"This can't wait. Gifford was shot in the front."

"Thanks, Sherlock. I believe the medical examiner might have mentioned that, or y'know, I picked up on it from being at the scene."

"Yeah, but I moved the body."

"You what?"

"Well, he wasn't a body when I moved him. I pulled him into cover. He was shot in the chest and fell backward. His head was closest to the door, and his feet were facing the parking lot."

"But you moved him." Heathcliff blew out a breath. "You're telling me he was leaving CryptSpec."

"Uh-huh."

"Son of a bitch." Derek yelled something to someone in the background. "This changes things."

"I thought it might. I just wanted you to know. I'm sure you already pulled CryptSpec's footage, but if everyone inside claimed not to know him, then someone's lying."

"Anything else?"

"That's all I have. I promised you I'd stay out of this but figured you'd want to know."

"What about Cross? Is he staying out of this?"

"Your guess is as good as mine."

THREE

"Did you catch the news?" Bitsie asked. "Another office shooting. I really don't understand why this keeps happening. Doesn't anyone remember what it's like to be civilized?" She looked at her husband, Charlie Roman, and lowered her voice. "I worry about him at work. It shouldn't be that way. It's not like he's stationed in Fallujah." She lifted her glass and took a sip. By my calculations, she should have been cut off after cocktail hour. "Don't you worry about Luc?"

Vivi Guillot blushed slightly. The hostess was embarrassed by her guest, particularly since the woman was having this discussion in front of me. "Bitsie, there is no need to worry. The building is secure."

"Of course you would think so. Luc wasn't at the company when the explosion happened."

"I can assure you, Mrs. Roman, the Martin Technologies building is one of the safest offices in this city. The security guards are well-trained. The protocols in place are on par with those of federal law enforcement agencies," I interjected. "You have nothing to worry about."

Martin rubbed my thigh. Despite the conversation he was having with the other end of the table, he must have been paying attention. I wondered if he'd chime in.

"How would you know?" Bitsie asked, her volume increasing on account of her drunkenness.

"I helped establish them." I turned my attention to the grilled asparagus and sliced through the spears with my knife more forcefully than necessary.

Bitsie opened her mouth to say something, but Vivi intervened, holding up a basket of bread. "Have you tried the brioche?" With Bitsie occupied, Vivi changed topics, focusing her attention on me. "How do you like working for Cross Security?"

I chuckled and put down my silverware. It was clear I couldn't win. "It's fine."

Bitsie swallowed the mouthful of bread. "Oh, so you're some big shot security whatsit?"

"I think I'm a whosit instead of a whatsit. Y'know, since I'm a person and not a thing."

Martin squeezed my leg before I said something one of us would regret. "Alex has done incredible work to safeguard Martin Technologies. She used to work for the Office of International Operations, an elite branch of the FBI, and now she's at the best investigation firm in the city. I understand your concern, Bitsie. But you have my word, Charlie is safe."

Charlie, who was seated on the other side of his wife, mouthed an apology. At this rate, they might be divorced by dessert, not that I would object. I always liked Charlie. He was a couple of decades older than Martin, but he was sharp and funny. His wife, on the other hand, was quickly becoming one of my least favorite people. And I'd dealt with Lucien Cross and an unknown shooter earlier today, so that was saying something.

To avoid further incident, Charlie introduced Bitsie to the two women sitting diagonally from him. I finished eating and asked Vivi about her son and his future plans. He would be starting his junior year in the fall and was in the beginning stages of choosing a university.

"He's been talking about going back to Paris," Vivi said. "We visit home frequently, but still, it's an ocean away."

"What does he want to be?"

She laughed. "It changes by the day."

"He's young. He has time to figure it out."

"Absolument," she replied, forgetting herself for a moment.

Before I could think to say anything else, my phone rang. "Pardon." I dug into my bag. It was Heathcliff. "I have to take this." I pushed away from the table.

Since dinner had been served on the piazza, I stepped down from the covered patio and wandered along the lighted path. The Guillots had a finely manicured lawn and garden, and in the center was a fountain. I rested my hips against the ceramic edge and answered the dozen questions Heathcliff asked.

He'd spent most of the evening reviewing CryptSpec's security footage. "Stuart Gifford had a meeting with a few software developers this morning, including Ian Barber. Is there anything I should know about the others?" Heathcliff read their names, and I did my best to recall details. But after I cleared them of corporate espionage, they fell off my radar. "You're not much help, Parker. I expected more from you."

"Sorry, Detective."

"It's okay. I just thought your research might have saved me a couple of hours. Turns out I have to perform my own due diligence. But considering they came up clean on your investigation, I'm not counting on finding much."

We disconnected, and I glanced back in the direction of the dinner party. Servers cleared away the plates, and the guests milled about while caterers set up a dessert buffet. This wasn't my scene. On my best day, I felt like an imposter, but today, I feared I might just snap.

Martin took a seat beside me, taking off his jacket and draping it over my shoulders. "Let me guess. You're thinking up some emergency in order to get the hell out of here."

"Am I that predictable?"

"Not in the least." He ran a hand through my hair. "Where do you want to stay tonight?"

"Not here."

He laughed. "You know what I mean. Given the circumstances, if you'd be more comfortable sleeping at your apartment, I'll have Marcal pack a bag for me." Predicting my next statement, he added, "I'm not leaving you alone tonight or any night in the foreseeable future."

"Are you hoping to get lucky, mister?"

He kissed me long and slow. "I've been thinking I should sell my place."

"Martin," I objected, but he put a finger to my lips.

"No, just listen. You haven't stepped foot inside since we got back together. You've been hesitant to come back, and I know that has more to do with our break-up and reconciliation rather than what happened years ago. But that day still bothers you. That house was my connection to my mother, but now I have her sketches. And honestly, I realized the memories I have inside that house have nothing to do with my mom and everything to do with you. We can make new memories in a new house."

"Okay, now you're creeping me out. That's rather Oedipal or Freudian." I grimaced. "Either way, it's just icky."

He rolled his eyes. "That is not what I said." The voices of other guests grew louder, and I feared someone was about to find us and rope Martin into another business discussion. Didn't these people get enough of that at work? "I think we should start looking for a place. The apartment we bought is okay for the short-term, but we don't have much space. We need something bigger." He nudged me. "On days like this, I know how badly you need a treadmill."

"What can I say? I like to run away from my problems." I noticed someone quickly approaching. "And right now, I believe that means faking an emergency before I get into an altercation with Bitsie." I shrugged out of Martin's jacket as Don Klassi, one of the new board members, approached.

"James." Don held out his hand, and they shook. He turned to me. "I don't mean to interrupt, but I couldn't help but hear the conversation you were having with Bitsie and Vivi earlier." He glanced at Martin. "Would you mind terribly if I borrow your lovely companion for a few moments?"

Martin tensed slightly. "It's okay with me, if it's okay

with Alex. But didn't you just say you had to leave, sweetheart?"

"Just a moment of your time, please," Don said. "I'll make it quick."

"It's okay," I relented. "What can I do for you, Mr. Klassi?" Martin gave me another uncertain glance and slowly headed back to the party.

"Don," Klassi corrected. He took a seat beside me and stared at the fountain while he rubbed a finger against his chin. "I heard James say you're a private investigator." He looked toward the piazza to make sure we were alone. "Does that entail any type of privacy protection?"

"Not exactly. I'm not a doctor or lawyer."

"But cases can be kept confidential, right?"

I didn't like where this conversation was heading. "It depends. Crimes should be reported to the authorities."

"What if there's no proof?"

"Do you want proof?"

After a pregnant pause, he said, "May we speak in hypotheticals?"

"My favorite."

He shook off his bewilderment. "Say a scam artist took a substantial amount of money from someone, is there anything that can be done to rectify the situation?"

"The fraud unit would deal with that. I can get you a number. Hypothetically."

"No. There's no proof. The money isn't traceable."

I raised an interested eyebrow. "Is it dirty money?"

"Not exactly. It's complicated. The situation is complicated. And given my reputation and position, it would be highly detrimental if these circumstances were to get out. Police or FBI involvement would trigger a media storm. I was hoping someone in the private sector could get my money back with minimal questions."

"Someone probably could," I said. "And you mean your hypothetical money."

"Right. Does that mean you'll take my case?"

"I don't even know what your case is, but feel free to set up an appointment with Cross Security. I'm sure Mr. Cross would be more than happy to assist you." Particularly since my boss had a weird obsession with Martin and everyone connected to him.

Klassi hesitated and lowered his voice. "Actually, I would prefer if someone I knew would handle this personally and quietly."

It was true I'd been known to moonlight and had the non-compete struck from my contract with Cross Security, but whatever Don Klassi had gotten involved in didn't sound legal. "Are you asking for my help?"

"I was hoping you'd volunteer, given my position with Martin Tech."

Standing, I exhaled slowly. "Mr. Klassi, I don't respond well to blackmail or extortion. That being said, your presence this evening indicates that you are a valued board member. Should I be concerned that the unfortunate circumstance that you have found yourself in would negatively impact Martin or his company?"

"Truthfully, I don't know. But if I can't find a way to get back my money, I will be forced to pull funds from other sources. I'm not saying that to blackmail anyone. I'm not trying to force your hand. I'm just desperate. I need help, and the authorities can't provide it. There is no proof. No way to trace my money or what happened to it. I've heard horror stories of people who've suffered from identity theft. Their cases remained open for years before anything was resolved, and even then, the damage was already done. This has to get fixed now. Before it's too late. I hope you'll at least think about it." He put a business card on the edge of the fountain and wandered back to the party.

On the bright side, at least I had something else to think about besides Stuart Gifford's dying breath.

FOUR

As predicted, I didn't sleep well. Surprisingly, I wasn't plagued by nightmares. It was the general sense of unease keeping me awake. A storm was brewing. I could feel it. Maybe it was a self-fulfilling prophecy, but every time I had this feeling, something bad happened. And bad usually meant catastrophic.

My finger traced the scar on Martin's shoulder. It didn't look like much. The surgeons had done an excellent job. It was just a single, pinkish-white streak against his otherwise unmarred skin. He was lucky.

Lazily, he reached for my hand. "Is it morning?"

"Almost. Go back to sleep. I didn't mean to wake you."

He opened his eyes and yawned. "It's Saturday. We can stay in bed all day. I'll sleep later. What's on your mind?" Martin was a morning person. He could go from sound asleep to pleasantly awake in a matter of moments. I had no idea how that was possible. He should probably donate his body to science, so someone could study that phenomenon.

"Don Klassi."

"Really? Why?"

"I told you about our conversation. Aren't you worried

what kind of blowback this might have on your company?"
He snickered. "You're worried about my business. That's a first."

"It is not."

"It kind of is." He rolled over and propped himself up on his elbow. "Don has a seat on the board. He has substantial shares in my company, and he voiced his approval of our recent R&D. However, MT will be fine without him. If he wants to cash out, I don't mind. I've done the math. Regardless of who buys him out, I'll still have majority control. This can't hurt me. I'm not worried, and you shouldn't be either."

"How did he amass his wealth?"

"Real estate, I think. Property development or something like that."

My mind went through all the illegal possibilities. "Has he tried to bring anyone else in on some vague venture?"

"Like a Ponzi scheme?"

"It crossed my mind."

"Alex, just say it."

"Say what?"

"You want to take his case." He gave me that infuriating, know-it-all look of his. "But you think you need my permission."

I scowled. "I hate to break it to you, handsome, but that's not how this works."

"Permission might have been too strong a word. Blessing might be more accurate."

"Does that mean you want me to stay away from this?"

He thought for a moment. "No, but I don't want you to investigate out of some misguided sense of obligation to me."

"You think rather highly of yourself, as if my actions are intended entirely to please you. Despite popular belief, you are not the center of the universe."

"Are you sure?" He pinned me against the mattress, his weight resting on one forearm while his free hand ran through my hair. "I think I might be the center of your universe." He kissed me, continuing downward as his lips trailed along my collarbone. "Tell me I'm wrong." I didn't say anything. Instead, I arched into him. He stopped what he was doing and looked me in the eye. "You should know, you're the center of my universe. And I will do anything to please you."

We made love until the sun came up, and then I slept until the early afternoon. Martin was beside me, perusing some official looking files. I scooted closer and kissed his chest.

"Morning, gorgeous." He put the files down. "How did you sleep?"

"Like a brick." I stretched. "What are you doing?" I scrunched my nose and looked around the room. "Where did you get those? Did you stash them inside my apartment one day when you were picking me up?" With the exception of last night, Martin hadn't slept over since that one night while we were still broken up. We normally stayed at our place, not my place. So I couldn't understand where he would have gotten files from work. "Did Marcal pack those for you?"

He laughed. "These are for you. I had a courier deliver them this morning."

"What are they?"

"Everything MT has on Don Klassi." He watched with predatory fascination as I got out of bed and went in search of some clean clothes. "Since he's who you were thinking about at five a.m., I thought I should indulge your little fantasy."

"It was six a.m. when you were indulging my fantasy," I corrected, flashing him a wicked smile over my shoulder. I headed into the bathroom. "Did you find anything interesting?"

"Not really." Martin's voice grew louder, and I knew he was outside the door. "We ran a credit and basic background check when he first joined the company. Everything looks good."

I brushed my teeth and turned on the shower. "He said the money he lost was untraceable."

"Like cash?" Martin asked.

"Maybe. He said it was complicated." I opened the bathroom door and found him in the midst of shedding what little clothing he was wearing. "Someone's confident," I remarked.

He smirked. "I have every reason to be." He stepped past me and into the shower. "The source of the cash could make it complicated."

He waited for me to join him before grabbing my shampoo bottle and squeezing some into his palms. Then he proceeded to soap my hair and massage my scalp and neck. A girl could get used to this.

"Any idea what kind of sketchy people he does cash-business with?" I turned around and leaned my head back to rinse the shampoo.

"No. His background came back spotless." He let his eyes travel the length of my body. "What was I saying?"

I chuckled. "That's enough shoptalk for this early in the day. I haven't even had my coffee yet."

"There's something that I haven't had yet, either."

*　　*　　*

"You don't have to do this." Martin lingered near the front door. He was stalling. "It's entirely up to you."

"I know. I heard you say it the first four times." I handed him a duffel bag filled with my workout gear and my rolled up yoga mat. "Until we figure out the treadmill dilemma, take these with you. I'll head over as soon as Don leaves."

He slung my bag and mat over his shoulder. "I could stay and help."

"How's your note-taking?"

Martin smirked. "You stole my line."

"Deal with it." I jerked my chin at the door. "Now move your ass. My client is on his way."

Martin left without another word, and I tidied up my apartment. Ten minutes later, someone knocked on my door. I opened it, and Don's eyes went to the nine millimeter holstered at my side. Ignoring his stare, I invited him in and shut the door.

"Thank you for agreeing to see me," he said.

"Take a seat." I gestured to the dining room table. "There's no need for pleasantries. You were desperate for my help last night, so let's hear it. What's going on?"

He hesitated, still eyeing my gun which was making him uncomfortable. Admittedly, that's why I was visibly armed. He fidgeted with one of my placemats and blew out a calming breath. "Someone took a lot of money from me. You have to find some way of getting it back. And I'd appreciate it if you didn't share these details with anyone."

"I'll make you a deal. You explain the entire situation. In the event I refuse to take your case, I'll forget we ever spoke."

He was between a rock and a hard place. He didn't have much of a choice. "Noah Ryder stole ten million dollars from me."

"How?" I asked, somehow managing to keep my jaw from hitting the floor.

"Are you familiar with cryptocurrencies?"

"Let's pretend I'm not."

He chuckled. "I wasn't either. I knew the basics, but it's ridiculously complicated. I'm not entirely sure how it works. But it's supposed to be secure, private, and decentralized. Basically, beyond the reach of government control."

"Were you trying to avoid taxes or alimony?"

He snorted. "Both."

"Gaming the system doesn't always work out so well."

"Gaming the system is how I made my money. That's how James made his. It's how the big dogs become the big dogs. You're naïve if you believe otherwise."

My expression turned stern. "People who break the rules inevitably get caught. I don't think I can help you, Mr. Klassi."

I moved to the front door, but Don didn't budge. He studied me for a long moment. The desperation I saw last night returned to his face. He wasn't accustomed to asking for help. But in this instance, he was willing to beg.

"Please. I get it. You like law and order. You're one of them. You believe in the system. Checks and balances and all that." His gaze swept the room. "What I did was wrong, but who did it hurt?" He rubbed his face. "No one. But I end up getting screwed. I found someone who was trading cryptocurrency for cash." Klassi removed a USB drive from his pocket and slid it across the table. "That's supposed to be the coin created from my last transaction. Without a miner confirming the transaction, it remains pending, and anyone can forge it. I'm guessing the transfer was never verified, and Ryder transferred the cryptocurrency elsewhere."

"A miner?"

"Think of them as bankers."

"It sounds risky," I said.

"It's supposed to be the complete opposite. I found Ryder through a financial consulting service an acquaintance recommended. I started with a few small transactions to test the waters, and it was great. So I did it again and again. I've been exchanging cash for coin for a few months now. Noah Ryder's been my guy all along. I was shocked when he ripped me off."

"So you lost the ten million over time?"

"No. It happened last week."

"Tell me everything."

"Noah contacted me, said he just mined a ton of coin, and knew I was looking to cash out some of my accounts. He asked if I'd be interested or knew anyone else who was looking to expand their economic portfolios. He was trading coin for cash." Don swallowed. "Stupidly, I jumped at the chance and asked if he could cover the full ten mill."

I'd heard of similar stories in the past, just nothing as up-to-date as a cryptocurrency scam. "Did you confront him?"

"I tried. He said the coin was on that drive. When I told him it was blank, he said I was lying. He hasn't answered any of my texts or e-mails. He disappeared."

"Did you ever meet in person?"

"We always met in person. The first time was at his office. After this happened, I drove straight there. The place was cleared out."

"Figures." I thought for a moment. Noah Ryder was a grifter, running the long con, and it worked. "Okay, but you transferred physical money to Noah. If it came directly out of one of your accounts, we can trace that. It shouldn't be a problem."

Klassi's cheeks flushed. "The ten million came out of a numbered account. By the time I realized I'd been swindled, there was no way to recall it. I have no idea where it went. I had several bankers, accountants, and even hackers look into it. It's gone."

I grabbed a pad of paper and a pen and put them in front of him. "I need the account number, Noah's office address, phone number, e-mail, whatever you have on him, and the acquaintance that introduced you in the first place."

Klassi neatly printed most of the information, double checking it was correct before sliding it back to me.

I skimmed it, realizing he left off his friend's name. "I need to know who introduced you to Noah."

"I'm not comfortable saying. I don't want anyone else to get in trouble."

"Why didn't you report Noah?" I asked.

Klassi didn't speak, and I dropped into the chair across from him. It was time this meeting turned into an interrogation. Too many things didn't make sense.

"Come on, Don," I coaxed, "you know I'm not an idiot. Why don't you want the authorities to know about this? Where did your assets come from? And don't tell me it's from gaming the system." Cryptocurrency might be gaining traction with the world's richest tycoons, but it was also commonly used as black market currency because it was used pseudonymously and entirely untraceable. There had been various iterations; most faded into obscure nothingness, becoming devalued and worthless. Only a few remained strong, but I wasn't sure how any of them would fare in the long-term.

Klassi licked his lips and shook his head. "It doesn't matter. I just want the coin I was promised."

"That's the wrong answer." Despite Martin's wishes, my instincts would always be geared toward protecting him. It's how I was wired. "I need to know what we're up against. And knowing where your dirty money came from might be key."

"Let's just say my money came from the proceeds of an

investment club."

"Real estate fraud?"

His cheeks turned a deep red. "No. It's nothing like that. What I've done is not illegal, but I can't exactly go to the authorities either. My business associates would not be happy with this kind of negative publicity. They wouldn't want the attention, particularly when we have something big in the works."

My eyes went hard. "Why are you invested in Martin Technologies?"

"I needed to diversify my portfolio."

"Or you were looking for new investors and building opportunities."

"I'm not admitting to doing anything wrong. The market dropped. I can't control falling property prices."

I reached for the paper he had written on. "I'll look into this on one condition."

"Anything."

"Sell your shares of MT and stay the hell away from there."

He extended his hand. "I can do that."

FIVE

"Are you mad?" I asked. Martin hated it when I overstepped, but it had to be done. I just didn't know if he'd see it that way.

He continued to flip through the paperwork his human resources and legal department had compiled on Don Klassi. "I'm fucking furious."

"Martin," I began, but he held up a hand to silence me.

"Not at you." He graced me with a grim smile. "Him. Them. Myself." He gestured at the pages. "We have a careful vetting process for employees. But when a shareholder invests enough, he automatically gets a seat on the board. It's ridiculous. It needs to be changed. Maybe I shouldn't have investors and shareholders. Perhaps there's a way I could buy them out."

"Obviously, your company needs the added revenue."

"Yeah, but we're not hurting financially. Our investors mostly cover new projects and the expansion of existing lines. When Klassi bought enough shares to earn a seat on the board, someone should have done some checking. There must be a way to prevent people like him from potentially sullying the reputation of my company." He took a breath. "At least he didn't have any real input, but," he rubbed his eyes, "I'll need to get on the phone with legal and figure out what we might be facing."

"Possibly nothing. He'll sell off his shares, give up his seat, and that might be it."

"That's not the problem. Figuring out how to prevent similar issues in the future is." Martin looked at me. "Don's actions can't hurt me. At least, they shouldn't be able to. But he wanted to use my company to further his own interests. And based on what you suspect, he's hurting other people with his real estate schemes. He shouldn't be allowed to get away with it."

"Damn, you're noble."

Martin grinned. "Like a knight in shining armor."

"My hero. Should I swoon?"

"Only if the mood strikes."

I hid my smile. "Maybe later." Taking a seat beside him, I reviewed the information again. "Klassi doesn't want this to get out, which is why I'm assuming it's illegal, but it's possible he's operating in a grey, legally ambiguous area. He doesn't have a criminal record, which is a good sign. We might be jumping to worst case scenarios. I'll have to do more digging to figure out exactly what's going on. But he's desperate to get the coin he paid for, not that I blame him. Still, with that much at stake, I'd go to the cops."

"I'll prepare for the worst and hope for the best." Martin pushed the files closer to me. "I appreciate any advance notice you can give me on his illegal activities."

"Yeah, well, that's probably up to Mark." I glanced over my shoulder at my former boss. SSA Mark Jablonsky stood on the balcony, animatedly speaking into his cell phone. As soon as I realized just how far-reaching the financial ramifications of Don Klassi's case were, I called Mark for help. Klassi wanted this kept quiet, but he didn't need to know the details of how I conducted an investigation. "Mark will know when and if Klassi will be investigated. Luckily, that has nothing to do with you."

"No, but we're assuming it was dirty money. He might have been funneling his dirty money into my business and getting back clean returns. Maybe that's why he bought the shares. We performed our own internal audit, and the SEC checked our findings. This really shouldn't bite me in the ass." It sounded like he was trying to convince himself.

"You're not responsible," I said.

"She's right." Mark stepped back inside, closed the door, and fixed the curtains. The wind had blown his tie over his shoulder, and as usual, his suit was wrinkled. He had been at work when I phoned for a favor, and after running the details by the guys in fraud and financial crimes, he met us at our apartment. Mark dropped into a seat and fixed his tie, brushing off some crumbs that were stuck on his shirt in the process. "Any reason Cross Security couldn't handle this?"

I glared at him. It was no secret my mentor despised my new boss and my current job. "Cross doesn't know everything I work on. I am free to moonlight."

"Sure, just keep telling yourself that," Mark said. He reached for a beer and took a swig. After wiping some foam off his mustache, his eyes narrowed. "What's your game plan here, Alex? Are you really going to help this asshole?"

"I told him I'd look into it." I circled the island and pulled a bottle of water from the fridge. "I don't know what Klassi's deal is, but Noah Ryder is obviously scamming people. Ten million is a lot of money."

"Klassi made a good mark," Jablonsky said. "He's hesitant to go to the authorities, and if Ryder's been dealing in cryptocurrencies, he's probably ripped off a lot of other questionable people. Assuming he's still breathing, he's smart enough to only screw with these white collar fuckers instead of actual hardened criminals."

"Ten million is a huge score," Martin said. "Wouldn't Ryder have moved on just in case?"

"It depends how many other big fish he had on the hook," Jablonsky said.

I thought for a moment, not sure I was particularly committed to this case beyond the scope of removing Don Klassi from MT. "I doubt there's anything I can do, which is why I gave it to you." I looked at Mark. "Did anyone at the FBI recognize the name?"

"You know what the fraud department looks like. These bastards frequently change their names. It's why it's so difficult to track them, but Ryder's a new one or at least a new alias. They're opening a file on him now, and we're looking into other scammers known for dealing in cryptocurrencies. Assuming Klassi told you the truth, Ryder could be a miner. Cybercrimes will help investigate. Maybe someone on the dark web knows Ryder or heard about this scam."

"That's a lot of ifs." I leaned against the counter. "Any helpful suggestions on how to get answers faster?"

Jablonsky's look spoke volumes. "For starters, you could be working at some government agency instead of parading around town like Lucien Cross's trophy. Don Klassi is precisely the type of client Cross takes. This isn't you, Alex. You like knowing you're on the right side of things. In this instance, you can't say that."

Before a biting remark could leave my lips, Martin intervened. "She's doing this for me. This is my fault. Don approached her last night at a dinner party. I put her in this situation, not Cross."

Jablonsky grumbled to himself. "It's still a waste of talent." He sighed and shook his head. "The two of you attract trouble like magnets to a fridge." He finished his beer. "I'll let you know if I hear anything. I just hope you're happy, Parker. Lord knows I've caused you more heartache than anyone. You needed out of the job, and you're out. But I will always have your back, even if you are Lucien's lackey." He gave me a hug, shook hands with Martin, and bid us goodnight.

"Why does he always have to be so tough on me?" I asked, more to myself than to Martin as I cleaned up the remnants from dinner.

"He loves you. He wants what's best for you, and we all have doubts about Cross."

"So true." I finished loading the dishwasher and got ready for bed. "I just hate that he sees my career choice as a disappointment."

"Do you want me to talk to him?" Martin joined me in the bedroom, stripping out of his t-shirt and jeans before pulling down the covers. "It might make my armor shinier in your eyes."

"We're back to the knight thing?"

"Knight, hero, god, whatever you prefer."

I threw a pillow at his head and got under the covers. We had just settled in when the phone rang. "Son of a bitch." I hit answer. "What is it?"

Lucien Cross cleared his throat. "The police are insisting on a second round of interviews with everyone involved in the CryptSpec case. Report to the office tomorrow by noon."

"I'll be there."

"Has anyone from the precinct contacted you since that morning?" Cross asked.

"I spoke briefly to Detective Heathcliff. Last I heard, he was trying to determine why Stuart Gifford was at the CryptSpec building that morning."

"You're positive Gifford was inside?" Cross asked.

"Yes."

"Why didn't you tell me this sooner?"

"I didn't remember. And when I did, I told the person in charge of the investigation. You made it clear this wasn't our job."

"Tomorrow at noon. Don't be late." He clicked off before I could respond.

Martin rubbed my arm as I placed the phone back on the nightstand. "What is it?"

"We said his name one too many times. He's like Beetlejuice." I turned off the light and fought away the images that ran through my mind. "The police have more questions about the murder. Cross is having everyone meet at the office tomorrow. It's not a big deal."

Unfortunately, this reminder right before bed ruined my night. After hours of twisting and turning, I woke up panicked and covered in sweat. The bedroom felt too small. The dark was too dark. I grabbed my pillow and went into the living room, turning on the small kitchen light along the way. Martin found me thirty seconds later and stretched out beside me on the grey suede. He calmed my frantic breathing with his guided, steady breaths.

When I awoke the next morning, I felt like I'd been hit by a truck. Images and memories flooded my mind, causing something far worse than any hangover. The last thing I wanted to do was go to work. My eyes fixed on Martin, who was transitioning from upward dog to downward dog. At least someone was putting my yoga mat to good use.

He lifted his feet slowly off the floor and floated them to where his hands were supporting his weight before standing up and moving through some sun salutations. I hated yoga, probably since I was a failure at inner peace. The few things I did like about it were the emphasis on strength training and flexibility; both of which Martin had in spades.

After executing a perfect flying crow that made me jealous, he transitioned into a handstand and did several vertical push-ups. When he finally stood up, I said, "I didn't know you were into yoga. Do the other ladies know about this?"

He reached for a towel and wiped his face. "Since my home gym is at home, it's the best workout I can get without any equipment." He wiped off my mat and rolled it up. "Did I wake you?"

"No. Thanks for sleeping out here with me last night."

He leaned down for a kiss. "You're welcome." He stretched his arms, wincing when his shoulder popped. "We never got a chance to finish the conversation we started the other night." He put a pan on the stove, added some oil, and cracked a few eggs. "You never gave me an answer to my question about selling my house."

"I can't answer that."

"Yes, you can. I just want to know if you're comfortable there. I think I already know the answer, but I don't want to sell the property if that's where you want to live or where you want to live one day."

"Can we please not talk about this now?" I climbed off the couch. "I have to get ready for work, and I'm having enough trouble keeping my mind off of you getting shot." My eyes went to his shoulder, which he was absently rubbing. Martin was on his best behavior. He wanted to comfort and support me in the hopes I wouldn't push him away or hide. Unfortunately, every part of me wanted to run, but running would hurt him. It wouldn't save him or protect him, even if my inner voice loudly and vehemently disagreed.

"You should try yoga. It's supposed to be a great way to get centered."

"Or to show off," I quipped.

He popped a mushroom cap into his mouth, a devious twinkle in his eyes. "I must admit, I also enjoy it as a spectator sport."

"To watch or be watched?"

"Both, but only when it comes to you." He left the eggs cooking and moved closer, brushing my hair out of my face. "You have to stop reliving the past. I understand that watching someone die is going to affect you, but you can't let it destroy us. Life's too short, sweetheart."

"Carpe diem." I searched his eyes. "Do you trust me?" That was our biggest obstacle. I'd lied to protect him before, and that had caused a chasm between us that we'd only recently bridged.

"I do, and I want to make it perfectly clear that I'm here. You don't have to deal with this alone."

I nodded; the words stuck in my throat. I could use a break from the emotions and feelings. Perhaps going to the office on a Sunday wouldn't be such a terrible thing after all.

SIX

Lucien silently observed the follow-up interview from the corner of the room. Surprisingly, he didn't have any of the city's elite defense attorneys sitting in on the meeting. Perhaps they were all golfing.

"Thanks for your time." Detective Heathcliff flipped back the pages in his notebook. "That's all I needed."

The security team looked to Cross, who gave a slight nod. As if on cue, the four of them filed out of the conference room. Cross moved stiffly away from the wall. "This unfortunate homicide had nothing to do with my team or our investigation. Today was a courtesy. I hope you realize that."

"We appreciate your cooperation," Heathcliff replied in a mechanical tone.

"Parker," Cross said, "see him out."

"Yes, sir." I swiveled my chair back and forth, alternating between watching Cross storm down the hall and Derek making a few final notes. "You're a detective. Tell me you aren't that oblivious."

Heathcliff looked up from his notes. "I'm just making sure I have the facts, ma'am."

"Don't you dare start that. I'm not nearly as diplomatic

as Lucien."

He tucked his notepad into his jacket pocket along with his voice recorder. "You are when you want something." He looked around the conference room. "Are we under surveillance?"

"Honestly, I have no idea."

"How about I buy you a cup of coffee?"

"That would be nice." I led the way out of the conference room and back to the elevator. A temp was working at reception, and a couple of guys were working investigations inside their closed offices. But for the most part, the place was dead, just like Stuart Gifford. "Maybe next time you stop by, I'll give you a tour. It just depends on Cross's mood."

"I won't hold my breath." Derek led the way to the café at the end of the block. Once we were situated at a table, he asked, "Were they straight with me?"

"As far as I know." I blew on the steaming liquid inside my cup. "Do you have any leads?"

"I thought you were staying out of this."

"I am, but you invited me to coffee. And something tells me it wasn't because you had an extra five bucks in your pocket and no idea what to do with it."

He leaned closer. "From what I have deduced, Gifford's computer was hacked and held hostage. A friend of his suggested he visit CryptSpec. They run a side business overriding ransom software. I have a few leads."

"So you wanted to know if Cross Security knew anything about CryptSpec's side hustle." I thought for a moment. "I didn't come across anything related to it. CryptSpec's in the software business. They make a lot of training and simulation programs and apps. Are you sure removing ransomware is actually a service CryptSpec offers and not just something one of the programmers does on the side?"

"Hard to say for sure." Heathcliff grinned. "Didn't you promise me a copy of your files?"

"Ah, so you were just bribing me with coffee. Why the mind games to make me think I was going to ask you for a favor?"

Heathcliff shrugged. "I thought you'd be more willing to

help if you thought it was your idea."

I laughed. "Derek, it was my idea." Cross might fire me for it, but I owed Heathcliff. "Hang here. This may take a few minutes."

"Not a problem." He studied the menu written on the chalkboard. "I'll just get some lunch."

When I opened my office door, I half expected Lucien to be waiting on the other side. Thankfully, he wasn't around. Maybe he had somewhere else to be this afternoon. After running the files through the copier, I stuffed everything back into the cabinet, put Derek's copies into a manila envelope, and locked my office.

"Where are you going?" Lucien asked.

I spun. "Excuse me?" The bastard always popped up at the most inopportune moments. He was a human Jack-in-the-box.

He nodded at the envelope. "What is that?"

"Research."

He narrowed his eyes. "On?"

"A case I'm working."

"What case?"

"It's private."

He wasn't buying it. "I see." He stepped into the elevator with me. "Show me."

"Don't you trust me?"

"Not particularly." He moved closer. "I could take that from you and open it, but I'm pretty sure I know what I'll find. It's probably the same thing I would discover by printing the last page from the copier's memory. And I'd really hate to have to draw your loyalty into question."

"You told me you didn't require my loyalty."

"Why does the detective want our files?"

"He doesn't want our files." Just mine.

Cross took a step back. "Who's the client?"

"I don't want to say."

"You either tell me who your new client is or I'll be forced to find out myself, starting with whatever you just photocopied."

"Don Klassi." It was the only name that came to mind.

Cross gauged my reaction, but it wasn't a lie. "He's on

the board at Martin Tech."

"How do you know that?"

"I make it my business to know things. You should realize that in a security firm, my security firm, I'm not going to risk data breaches with subpar office peripherals. The copy machine erases data after printing is complete and has a routine built in to overwrite deleted data."

"Bastard," I mumbled.

"However, I do not want to learn that any Cross intel was passed over to the police department without my express consent or the consent of our clients. Is that understood?"

"Yes, sir." I would just make sure he never found out. That seemed to be the main takeaway to his statement.

"Very good. We'll discuss Don Klassi's case tomorrow morning."

"We can't. He came to me personally. He wants his problems kept secret. He hired me, not Cross Security."

"Undoubtedly, a favor for James Martin." Cross waited for the doors to open. "Don't worry, Miss Parker. I can keep secrets just as well as you can." He exited the building, climbed into a waiting town car, and disappeared.

When I returned to the café, Heathcliff had consumed three-fourths of his sandwich. He dipped the final piece into some au jus and stuffed it into his mouth. I took a seat after making sure none of Cross's minions were spying on me and slid the envelope across the table.

"I hope that helps."

"Probably not, but I won't know until I look at it."

"Do me a favor and pretend you don't know where it came from."

Heathcliff wiped his mouth on a napkin and watched me drink my coffee. When I didn't offer any additional explanation or idle threats, he pulled the pages out of the envelope and flipped through them. "The financials will be helpful, as will their CVs."

I wasn't sure how, but I refrained from asking. Instead, I picked up a chip from the corner of his plate and took a bite. "Have you heard about anyone trading in cryptocurrencies?"

Heathcliff's brow furrowed. "Why?" That wasn't an intrigued why; it was a *how do you know about that* why.

Klassi made me promise to keep this quiet, and so far, I'd blabbed to Martin, Jablonsky, and Cross. Hell, at this rate, I might as well tell Heathcliff too. "Some guy at MT got taken for a lot of money."

"That sucks." Heathcliff tucked the pages back into the envelope and looked at his phone. "I need to get going. Us civil servants don't get the weekends off."

"No rest for the wicked," I said.

He saw the dark circles under my eyes. "You'd know better than anyone. Hey, if you need someone to talk to about anything, you know I'm around. I've got a bottle of bourbon dying to be opened."

"Thanks, but Martin already offered."

"Well, his booze is top shelf."

"Yeah, except when he offers to talk, he actually expects a meaningful exchange of words, not just pouring and drinking."

Heathcliff put on his jacket. "Yeah, but we both know you're not always so great with the word thing."

"Fuck you," I retorted.

"Case in point." He tapped the envelope against his chest. "Thanks again, Parker. I'll see you around."

After I finished the chips Derek left on his plate and the last drops of my now cold coffee, I went back to the office. I had a lot of decisions to make in a short amount of time. It would help if I had some idea what I was doing.

For starters, I ran an extensive background check on Don Klassi. He was clean. As far as I could tell, he wasn't on any government agency's radar. That was a good thing. Maybe I misjudged him, but I doubted it. Even if his moneymaking schemes weren't illegal, they were morally questionable.

"You're one to judge, Parker," I muttered. I'd committed a few atrocious acts in the past. Sometimes, the only way to fight fire was with fire, but that didn't make looking myself in the mirror any easier. I just didn't want to add more bad acts to my ledger. On the cosmic balance sheet, I was losing. I'd need to spend the rest of my life helping orphans and rescuing kittens from trees, and even that wouldn't be enough. Nothing ever would, but I was tired of taking on questionable clients. Dammit, Jablonsky was right, as usual. That was the price I paid for a job at Cross Security with its top of the line facilities and practically limitless resources.

I rubbed my eyes and circled the room. Klassi had nothing to do with Cross. He had everything to do with Martin, and since I was stuck on another "save Martin" kick, this was the best and least destructive way to do it. I'd look into it, and Don would walk away from MT. It was an easy win for everyone.

"Nice digs," someone said from the door, and I practically jumped out of my skin. Luckily for Jablonsky, my nine millimeter was in my desk drawer. If it hadn't been, I might have shot him. "Did you have to sign the contract in blood?"

"Don't be a dick."

He cocked an eyebrow and entered, pulling the door closed behind him. "Marty told me you were here. I was hoping to run into Lucien. It's about time that pompous prick and I had it out."

"Mark," I warned, giving him my no-nonsense look, "I'm already in enough hot water. Don't make it worse. Please."

He dropped onto the couch and put his feet on the glass coffee table. "This really is nice."

"Why are you here? How did you get in?"

"Didn't I teach you everything you know?" But he didn't answer the question. "I wanted to talk to you about Don Klassi."

With my annoyance immediately forgotten, I asked, "What do you know?"

"Not a lot. However, you need to think this through. Assuming what you've been told is true, this con artist is targeting a specific type of mark. He's playing the long game. To empty out an office, dump his phone and e-mail, and disappear without a trace, he must have done it before. Have you checked out the alleged address yet?"

"I haven't done anything except run Klassi's name

through the system."

"I did the same. From what we can tell, he gets close to the line but hasn't crossed it. His actions are legal, at least on the surface."

"What about Noah Ryder?"

"Like I told you last night, we got nada on him. Fraud hasn't received any similar complaints. Ryder isn't in the database. I went through DMV records, social security, everything I could think of. It's unlikely that's his real name."

"What about cybercrimes?" I asked.

"They're still digging. Honestly, we have next to nothing to go on. I don't believe they are going to find him either."

I went to the computer and typed in Noah Ryder. Several entries popped up, but none of them matched the description Klassi provided, not that I expected them to. No one was stupid enough to run a ten million dollar con job and use his real name. Next, I tried the office address, finding it vacant and available to rent. That same space had been rented several times in the last year, but none of the tenants lasted more than a couple of months.

"Did you run the other businesses and companies that rented the property?" I asked.

"Yes, but nothing popped."

I resisted the urge to do it again. Cross had access to several useful databases, but I didn't see any reason to double-check Mark's work. Instead, I keyed in the phone number and e-mail address. The phone was an unregistered burner. It had been paid for with cash and had been disconnected for weeks. The e-mail was an automated box. Someone upstairs might be able to gain some useful information on it or link it to websites or social media profiles.

"Alex," Mark crossed the room and rested his hips on the side of my desk, "we need to talk about this."

"What?"

He pressed his lips together. "Marty told me what happened Friday morning. He also mentioned that Klassi practically blackmailed you into helping him."

"Is it blackmail? I only agreed on the basis that he sell

his shares of MT and stay away from Martin." I swallowed. "Is that why you want to talk about this? Did Martin say something to you? Is he angry I'm influencing factors that affect his life and livelihood?"

"No, he's not afraid you'll fuck up again." Mark gave me that knowing look of his. "But apparently you think you might."

"I don't have time for this. Just spit it out."

"Assuming we don't find anything solid on Noah Ryder, the FBI won't be able to conduct much of an investigation."

"Well, Klassi didn't want me to tell anyone, so he should be relieved, unless of course the FBI decides they should start investigating him instead."

"As a courtesy to you and Marty, I've kept the details of Klassi's involvement to a minimum. If we find more on Ryder, that will change. But if we don't, I'll keep it quiet and let Marty do whatever he wants once Klassi is no longer earning dividends from MT. That being said, I want to know what you are doing about Klassi? Are you going to follow through? Or is this a bluff?" Mark gave me a pointed look. "Your word used to mean something."

"It still does."

"That's what I figured. Too bad Cross hasn't knocked that out of you yet."

I ignored the jab. "Are you trying to tell me what to do?"

"What would be the point? You never listened when you were under me. Why would you listen now?" He licked his lips. "I'm just here to say if you plan to pursue this, you're going to need resources. More than the few favors I can provide. And more than whatever spare change Marty might have in his couch cushions. You're going to need a solid, planted identity and money. Lots of it." He looked around the office. "Guess you're at the right place after all."

"I don't want Cross involved."

"Then you need to come up with some irrefutable evidence. Something solid. Airtight. That way, I can persuade the Director to sign off on providing some assistance. Let's call it a joint-op of sorts."

I scoffed at the notion. "I burned that bridge. We both know it. When I resigned the last time, Director Kendall told me there was no going back and no consulting work. My ties to the Bureau were irrevocably severed. He won't authorize it. He'll just laugh in your face."

"Then what the hell are you going to do?"

"I don't know yet."

SEVEN

"Have a seat." Cross gestured to the leather couch. "I'm sure you noticed I didn't assign you a new case this morning."

"I'm aware." So was every other investigator at the Monday morning meeting. I'd gotten several funny looks from Kellan Dey and Bennett Renner. "Are you planning to terminate me?"

Cross let out a barking laugh. "Do I look like Schwarzenegger?"

"Not really." My boss was in a good mood, which meant he didn't know I'd given intel to the police or was intentionally pretending he didn't know. My money was on the latter. "So why the special treatment?"

His eyes lit up. "You know what I want."

After the discussion I had with Jablonsky yesterday, I knew I'd need Cross Security's help to investigate Don Klassi's case, so I told Lucien everything Don had said. I left out my arrangement with him, where we met, and Martin's sudden dislike for the man. Those things were irrelevant, even though Lucien asked three times if this was a favor for Martin.

Cross had an unhealthy obsession with my boyfriend and had recently approached Martin about producing a line of tactical gear. I didn't think Martin wanted to move forward on any such endeavor, but Cross thought I was his ace in the hole, which gave me a bit of leeway.

"Ten million," Cross murmured. He went to the intercom and pressed a button. "Set up a meeting with Don Klassi for this afternoon. Tell him Miss Parker requested it. And find out if the gallery is still available. If it is, have Amir draft a profile for a wealthy art dealer."

"What are you doing?" I asked when he returned to his chair.

"Getting the ball rolling. I'll be sitting in on your meeting with Mr. Klassi to discuss revising whatever payment scheme you have worked out. Cross Security can cover the expenses and incidentals in exchange for a finder's fee. Ten percent is the industry standard, and given the circumstances, it seems reasonable, particularly when the probability of a recovery is quite low."

"You think he's going to pay you a million dollars to take his case?" Cross must have suffered a massive brain injury without my noticing.

"Without us, he's out ten. He should leap at the chance, especially when he realizes he won't have to pay unless you make a recovery."

"That's insane."

"He's lost enough money. He'll jump at the chance." Cross cocked an eyebrow, clearly confused why I wasn't more excited by this prospect. "Don't worry, Alex. We'll split the finder's fee fifty-fifty after expenses. I have no intention of overstepping, but surely, you realize this case is beyond your sole capabilities, unless you have a benefactor to which I'm unaware."

"I don't."

His eyebrows rose and fell. "Not to mention, per the terms of our agreement, any work you do for James Martin automatically makes him my client."

"This isn't for Martin."

Cross didn't argue. He simply went back to his desk. "I'll make arrangements. Conduct your research in preparation for our client meeting. We will present this offer to Mr. Klassi as a united front."

"Sure thing." I stood, figuring I needed to explore the office space Noah Ryder had used and give the techs the information on the e-mail address and phone number. This was happening, and it was happening fast. Maybe Klassi would object, but something told me he wouldn't. If anything, I needed to run damage control. Don Klassi knew too much about my relationship with Martin, and I didn't want him to spill the beans to my boss on the off chance Lucien didn't already know.

On my way across town, I called Klassi. Our meeting was scheduled for two, but I didn't want to blindside him or be blindsided. I explained the problems I'd encountered, detailed Cross's insistence on maintaining a client's privacy, and hinted that the terms of our agreement remained intact and Cross need not know about them. Klassi agreed, assuring me he was in the midst of selling his MT shares. That deal would be done by the end of business today, which meant he'd sign the contract with Cross Security and his problem would officially become mine.

We disconnected, and I entered the office building. Individual spaces were available for sale or rent, making the building a total hodgepodge. There was no central reception area. The few directories listed current occupants only. Noah Ryder had done an excellent job masking his true intentions and concealing his identity.

The office he used remained vacant. I spoke to a few of his neighbors. Surprisingly, most of them recalled the man, but they didn't know much about him. Some believed he was a hedge fund manager. Others figured he was a financial consultant. A few thought he was some techie with a start-up, and the woman with the corner office thought he was a freelance graphic designer. The office door was locked, so I didn't get a chance to look around. But from what I could see by peering into the window, it was empty. If Ryder was as clever as I had been led to believe, he wouldn't have left anything behind.

Still, I dialed the number listed on the door and left a

message for the building manager to call me back. It was possible the people I questioned about Ryder had been thinking of one of the other tenants that had come and gone. Then again, if Ryder was playing the long game, he might have introduced himself to his neighbors to add some legitimacy to his persona. He would want a trail, just not one that would link to his real identity.

While I waited for the building manager to call back, I thought about the rest of the details. Jablonsky said no one had reported any similar crimes to the FBI, but I wasn't sure if the same was true for the local police. Based on Heathcliff's tone yesterday, I suspected he knew something, so I called the precinct.

Derek blew me off quickly, but he promised to keep his ear to the ground. In return, he wanted more information on CryptSpec. While answering a few questions concerning the documents I gave him the previous afternoon, I heard the telling beep of an incoming call.

"I have to go. Good luck with your case." I switched the call over. "Hello?"

"Hi, may I speak to Alexis?"

"You've got her." I glanced at the caller ID to make sure it matched the number posted on the glass door. "I have a few questions about an office for rent. Unit 39D. I was hoping to see it."

"That can be arranged. Let me check my calendar."

"How about now?"

"How long will it take you to get here? I'll be leaving for lunch soon."

I held back my laugh. "Not long. I'm actually standing right outside."

"I'll grab the key and meet you outside the office." The building manager disconnected without asking any other questions, and I wondered just how desperate he was to rent the empty space. With the current turnover rates, he probably wanted to fill as many offices as possible as quickly as possible.

The elevator opened twelve minutes later, and a balding gentleman stepped out. His pallor wasn't good, and his clothes were too big. He looked sickly.

"What's your name, honey?"

"Alex," I replied, dismissing the honey as a generational faux pas.

"I'm Lem. Pleased to meet you." He unlocked the door and held it open for me. "Ladies first."

I stepped inside. The office wasn't much, just a glorified cubicle with a tiny waiting area. The walls around the main office were thin, frosted glass. The rest were painted bright white, starkly contrasted by the dark holes from removed nails.

A modern looking glass and steel desk filled the cubicle. It had been bolted to the floor. Everything else was gone. "Is the desk included?" I asked.

"Yes. We used to have a few leather chairs in the reception area and a rolling desk chair, but the first tenant took them when he left. After that, I decided not to replace them. Is that a problem?"

"No." I narrowed my eyes at the desk, crouching down to check for fingerprint smudges. "Do you have a record of previous renters?"

"Yeah," Lem replied suspiciously, "why do you ask?"

"What can you tell me about the last guy who rented this place?"

"Who did you say you were?"

I smiled warmly and stood up straight. "Sorry, I get a little obsessed with things sometimes, and when you said the furniture was stolen, I wondered if you knew who took it or considered taking legal action for damages. Do thefts often occur in this building?"

Lem shook his head, suddenly more concerned with scaring off a potential renter than wondering why I was being so nosy. "Nothing out of the ordinary."

"That's good."

"Are you interested?"

"It depends. How long is the lease?"

"We rent on a monthly basis."

"Great. I'll take it." The asking price was $800. Considering it was smaller than Martin's walk-in closet, that seemed steep. But with real estate, it was all about location. And since it was Noah Ryder's last known location, that made it valuable, at least to me.

Lem was pleasantly shocked. After a lengthy elevator ride, he let me into his office. It was twice the size of 39D. It had a tiny love seat and a television. A row of grey, metal filing cabinets lined the back wall and part of the side wall. A large, cluttered wood desk took up the rest of the space. I sat across from Lem in one of the two chairs while he went through the cabinets in search of the records for 39D.

While he was searching, I scanned the documents on his desk. "When was the last time someone occupied that unit?" I asked. "The last time I rented office space, I kept getting the previous guy's mail. Just wondered if that might happen again."

"I think it's been empty for a while. I'm not entirely sure. I've been ill, and I had a temp covering for me. She wasn't exactly the best at keeping records."

"I'm sorry to hear that."

He pulled out several files, one specific to that property and the rest were boilerplate rental agreements, information on the security deposit, a detailed list of fees, and parking information.

I looked down at the official documents. Cross said he'd cover expenses, and in the event Ryder left prints or some sort of evidence in the office, this would give us access. I didn't think we'd find anything, but I had to be sure. "Is it possible to have the locks changed. I've had problems with break-ins in the past."

He marked the signature box on the rental agreement and handed me a pen. "I can have someone from maintenance change them while you look that over."

As soon as I was alone, I rifled through the filing cabinets. Lem labeled everything by unit, and I pulled out the binder for 39D. The info I wanted was right on top, and I took photos of each page. The signature said Noah Ryder. Obviously, the grifter wanted a trail in the event Klassi checked into him before forking over the cash. On paper, Noah Ryder looked legit. Somewhere in the details, we'd find the man behind the mask. I just wondered if that would happen before Ryder disappeared for good. Perhaps it was already too late. He'd stolen Klassi's money a week ago. He could be across the world by now.

"Here's that key," Lem said, disturbing my pessimistic thoughts. Quickly, I signed the page and handed him the agreement. "How long do you think you'll be here?"

"Just a month." I wrote out a check and put it on his desk, hoping it wouldn't bounce. "Do you need a reference?"

He shook his head. "You're not going to be here long enough for that. Assuming your check clears, we won't have a problem."

EIGHT

"Did you forget something?" Kellan asked, entering my office.

"I don't think so."

After renting the office space, I sent a team of Cross's crime scene techs to analyze every inch of 39D, met with Klassi to officially acknowledge that I was taking his case and convince him to agree to Cross's terms, and spent the rest of the day doing research. The information Noah gave Lem was bogus. Noah's listed home address and telephone number tracked to a Chinese restaurant, and the account number from his check led to an empty bank account. Cross's experts were tracking the details on the account, hoping it would lead to something usable, but I hadn't heard back from them.

"Shouldn't you have gone home by now?" I asked.

Kellan laughed and eased into one of my client chairs. "Hi, I'm Kettle. Nice to meet you."

"Oh, shit."

He smiled. "There it is."

"I completely forgot I promised you lunch."

"It's okay. I'm easy, just as long as you're up for dinner and drinks."

I flopped back in my chair. "Sure. I'll meet you

downstairs. I just need to make a quick call."

Kellan raised an interested eyebrow. "Ooh, did you actually have a date? Why don't you have him tag along? I'd love to meet him."

"There is no him. I just have some follow-up to do before it gets too late. I'll be down in a sec."

"Fine."

Once he was gone, I closed my office door, dialed Martin, and organized the paperwork neatly into a file that I placed inside my top drawer. "Hey," I said as soon as he answered, "did Klassi follow through?"

"Yeah. He's out."

"You sound relieved."

Martin hesitated. "I didn't appreciate his cavalier attitude toward making money by gaming people. That isn't someone I want on the board of my company." He sighed. "I'm sorry, sweetheart. I didn't mean to get you roped into this."

"Lucien's elated. He's funding the investigation." I glanced down at the reimbursement check. Ten minutes after I handed the receipt over to accounting, I was issued a check. "If we recover Don's stolen funds, we're looking at a seven-figure payday."

"Shit," Martin dragged out the word. "Shouldn't you be overjoyed?"

"I'll let you know. There's something odd about the situation, but I'm having trouble putting my finger on it." I could practically hear Kellan tapping his foot thirty floors below. "Anyway, I promised a colleague lunch, but with the way my day went, it's turned into dinner. And I still have a few things to finish up here, so I'll be home late."

"You are staying at our place, right?"

"Yes."

Martin's tone relaxed. "I'll see you later. Enjoy your dinner."

I grabbed my bag and went downstairs to meet Kellan. As predicted, he wanted to go to the Mexican place down the street. It was a warm night, and most people were seated on the patio. Kellan and I remained inside with the more docile crowd. He ordered a few tequila shots and dug into the basket of chips.

"Are you sure you don't want one?" He held a shot glass in my direction.

"Not my thing." I took a moment to breathe. "What does Cross have you working on?"

Kellan downed the shot and reached for another. He let out a tiny growl. "CryptSpec." He tipped back the next mouthful and reached for a lime wedge. Cringing at the sourness, he put the finished lime in the glass.

"I thought we finished with CryptSpec."

Kellan shrugged. "You did. The security team did, but the police investigation has raised new questions. Mansfield wanted us to check everything again." He looked apologetic. "It seems pretty cut and dry to me. Ian Barber took suspicious payments and had access to the stolen programming."

"Does Cross think I missed something? Does it have anything to do with Stuart Gifford?"

Downing the last shot, Kellan reached for the chips. "You know Lucien's stance on murder investigations."

"We avoid them, but he assigned you to poke around. Why?" It didn't make sense, and then I remembered what Heathcliff said about Gifford's reason for being at CryptSpec. The suspicious payments into Barber's account could have been from his side business, removing ransomware. Maybe he wasn't the corporate spy.

"Barber's suing for wrongful termination, so Mansfield wants to make sure we did everything right. Since Gifford was killed the same morning Barber got booted, it draws a lot of things into question, which probably have nothing to do with the job you did. I think it was just bad timing."

Leaning back in the chair, I cursed. "What's happened at CryptSpec since Friday morning?"

Kellan gnawed on another tortilla chip. "It's hard to say. The police have barred us from interfering and have questioned most of the employees. I can't get access. I don't think you missed anything. I told Lucien that, but he just wants us to be thorough."

"When you do speak to Barber, you should ask where the payments came from. I couldn't track them. They were cash deposits he personally made. Initially, I assumed it was what the competition paid him for CryptSpec's secrets, but maybe I was wrong."

"Barber was, is, disgruntled. That was obvious from his evaluation reports and outbursts during meetings. CryptSpec's security footage even caught a few arguments he had with Mansfield over his paycheck and value at the company. His personality fits the type. Barber thinks he's smarter than the rest of them and wanted to prove it. Your conclusions are valid."

"Except there's a side hustle."

Kellan rubbed a hand down his face. "You never made any mention of it."

"I didn't know about it at the time."

"That was three days ago. What changed?" A knowing look erupted on his face. "That's what the police uncovered in regards to Gifford's murder."

"I don't have details, just that some guys at CryptSpec are repairing computers on the side."

"That doesn't sound particularly lucrative. There are a million repair shops that do the same thing."

"Like I said, I don't know much, but it has something to do with ransomware. People will pay just about anything to save their precious files."

"Even if Barber made his money doing that and not by copying the company's code, those are still grounds for termination. CryptSpec employees are prohibited from working on other projects." Kellan stopped eating, his mind working on the facts despite the three shots of tequila. "And it paints Barber as a possible murder suspect, if Gifford was there to have his computer fixed and threatened to out Barber to Mansfield." He reached for the laminated drink menu tucked behind the napkin holder. "I'm gonna need another drink because tomorrow morning I have to tell Lucien we're dropping CryptSpec and the reason why. He is not going to be pleased."

"Just blame me. I'm sure Cross will see this as my fault anyway."

"Well, you are quite friendly with several police detectives. Not even Renner's that nice to them, and he used to be a cop. You ever hook up with any of them? That O'Connell guy or what's his name, the one working Gifford's case?"

"Heathcliff." I shook my head. "I don't play where I work."

Something about Kellan's expression told me he didn't necessarily believe me. "Mai tai?"

"I don't want a drink."

"Tonight, we need a vacation from work. Bahama mama?"

"What?" I tilted my head to read the description. "No, I need to stay sharp. I have to check the want ads when I get back to the office."

"Come on, Alex. Dinner and drinks. You agreed." He continued reading. "Skinny martini?"

"Just drink enough for both of us. I have work to do."

He rolled his eyes. "So do I, but it's going to wait until tomorrow." When the waiter returned with our meal, Kellan ordered a pitcher of coconut rum mixed with some pineapple and lime juice. A few minutes later, the concoction was placed in the center of the table with two glasses outfitted with tiny umbrellas.

"I'm not drinking that," I protested, even as Kellan filled both glasses to the brim. "What happened to fearing I had an addictive personality? Now you're pressuring me to drink. Is this high school? Are you trying to get me drunk? Are you hoping to take advantage?"

He chuckled. "Sorry, sweetie, but you're not my type. And since you don't have a problem, what's the harm?" He took a sip and dug into his mushroom and chorizo quesadilla. After a few bites, he asked, "Why didn't you tell Lucien when you found out Barber might not be the mole?"

I blushed, feeling sheepish. To hide my embarrassment, I took a sip of the rum punch. It wasn't bad, but it would have been better if I was drinking it on a beach with Martin. "My mind's been on other things, and until you mentioned the possibility that I got it wrong, I never actually considered it."

Kellan snickered. "It's because you're that good. It is highly improbable the great Alexis Parker could be wrong about anything."

"Hardly."

However, he was buzzed enough at this point to continue the jabs. "No, seriously, you solved what was considered an unsolvable case at Cross Security. And Lucien's been kissing your ass ever since."

"Are we talking about the same Lucien Cross?"

"Yes." Kellan gave me a look. "Are the two of you boning?"

"God, no. Is that what people think?" From the look on his face, I was pretty sure the idea had just come to him at the spur of the moment, but I didn't like it.

"You have to admit our boss treats you differently than everyone else at the office. At first, I thought it was because you were new. He tends to break all the newest hires of their bad habits and makes sure they know how things are done at Cross Security, but you've been around for four months. He's obsessed with you."

"Any idea why?"

"Sex. Money. Sex and money." Kellan finished eating. "Except you said you aren't screwing. So money?"

"Cross obviously has plenty of that."

"That doesn't mean he doesn't want more." Kellan gave me another look. "Rumor has it you have a whale on the hook." I didn't say anything, but Kellan was an astute investigator. He could read between the lines. "You're lucrative for business, so Lucien wants to keep you happy. That's what this is. You're his ticket to the golden goose."

I shook off my annoyance and dug through my wallet for some cash to cover dinner and drinks. Kellan Dey might be easy, but he definitely wasn't cheap. "Thanks for covering for me on Friday, but had I known Lucien was so pliable to my whims, I wouldn't have bothered asking for the favor."

"Jeez, Alex, I didn't mean to offend you. I just want to know what the deal is."

"Sure, no problem."

He stood up, and we made our way to the door. "I'll walk you back to the office and grab a cab from there."

"I'm okay. Can you get yourself home?"

He snorted. "When I was undercover with the DEA, I regularly drank a lot more than this. I'm fine." He squeezed my shoulder. "Are we good?"

"Right as rain."

He nodded, but I wasn't sure he believed me. He stepped down from the curb and hailed a cab. In moments, a taxi stopped in front of us. He bid me good night, and the car drove off.

The office was only a few blocks away. The walk would give me time to clear my head. Honestly, I was annoyed, bordering on angry. I might have botched an investigation, which pissed me off. Seeing Stuart Gifford get killed also pissed me off, as did dealing with Don Klassi. Okay, so maybe the problem wasn't figuring out what made me angry since everything was making me angry. The real kicker was Kellan's questions about Cross. That bothered me more than anything else.

I never wanted special treatment. Never. Not here, not with Martin, and not at the OIO. But Kellan was right. Lucien did treat me differently, and I knew it had a lot to do with Martin. I just wasn't sure what to do about it. Working for someone like Cross wasn't what I wanted to do when I left the OIO, but I could barely make ends meet running a solo P.I. gig, which didn't leave me with much of a choice.

A rustling sound caught my attention. I continued walking, focusing on the reflections in the windows I passed. I didn't see anything out of the ordinary. Glancing behind me, I saw several people moving in the same direction, but no one was paying an inordinate amount of attention to me. They didn't appear threatening. Yet, the hairs at the back of my neck prickled. An alleyway was coming up on my right, and I slowed, carefully approaching the opening.

When I got to the mouth, I turned my head and peered into the dark, prepared to fight or run, but no one was there. I was on edge. It was probably a result of my mental irritation. Sighing, I continued toward the office. A few steps past the alleyway, the shrill sound of a car alarm caused me to turn around. That's when he struck.

NINE

My temple collided with the brick wall, but his grip remained firm on my upper arm. He spun me around. This time, turning me to face him. He slammed my back against the wall hard enough to knock the breath from my lungs. The knife against my neck was ice cold, sending a shiver through me. There was no space between my skin and the razor-sharp edge. One wrong move and I'd be dead.

"Scream, and I'll slice your throat," he growled. His voice was husky and deep.

I didn't dare take my eyes off of him. Surely, someone would notice us. He pulled me into the alley, not far from the mouth. People were walking on the street. Someone must have seen what happened.

He stepped on my feet, using his weight to keep me from moving. A dark mask concealed his face, making every detail about him impossible to determine. The first thing he did after shoving the knife against my throat was yank my purse off my arm and toss it away. It disappeared into the dark abyss. Obviously, this wasn't a mugging.

Pressing against me, he cautioned a glance at the street. The moment someone walked by, he pushed harder on the blade, reminding me to keep quiet. I did as he wished.

G.K. Parks

For what felt like hours, he held me against the wall with his body and the knife. Once he was convinced the coast was clear, he turned his focus to me. Now that he had me, he seemed unsure how to proceed.

"What do you want?" I hissed, contemplating how to subdue him without dying in the process.

He was calm. He didn't hurry or rush, nor did he act excited or aroused by the impending violence. He had complete control. He planned this carefully with no chance of failure. No surprises. Whatever was about to happen, he orchestrated. And he was confident. Too confident.

I swallowed, the blade digging deeper. My eyes shifted to the side, and I searched the dark recesses for my discarded bag. Did he know I had a gun? Or was my purse a hindrance? Think, Parker. What are your options?

He refused to answer me. The only words he spoke warned me to remain quiet. He expected compliance, and from the way he held the blade, he would get it. Or my blood would spill.

I saw it in his eyes; he was waiting for me to do something stupid. It would leave him with no choice. He'd be forced to act, and in some twisted way, his conscience would be clear.

I opened my mouth to speak, and he flicked the tip of the blade, just enough to draw blood. Despite the mask that covered everything but his eyes, I could read his expression. *Don't speak.* Something came over him then, as if he finally decided what he was going to do. He reached between us with his free hand and fumbled with my belt.

My mind went into overdrive. Weaknesses, find weaknesses. This wasn't the best position to be in. My gun and phone were too far away to be of any use. Based on his build and my aching and numb toes, he was heavy and strong. "Please," I whispered, "I'll do whatever you want. Just don't kill me." If I gave him complete control, he'd relax, and I'd take advantage.

He unhooked my belt and leaned back on his heels to work it free from my pants. His unyielding weight kept my feet glued to the ground. I tried to squirm away, and he grabbed my shoulder and pushed my back against the wall.

- 61 -

He dared me with his eyes, but I stopped moving. He'd slice me open before I could wrestle the knife away.

Instead, I focused on the soft, easy targets. His eyes and his groin. This was close quarters combat. I could handle myself. I just needed to get into position. The eyes would be more difficult since moving my arms would surely cause him to cut me. I needed him to take a step back.

Suspecting he wanted to get his rocks off, I'd give him a helping hand or a knee. "Please," I whispered, "I won't resist."

He tugged hard on one end of my belt, causing my hips to twist and knock against his. Without thinking, he turned to the side to pull the last length of belt free, and his foot moved almost entirely off of mine. Bingo. That was it.

I slammed my knee into his crotch, and he doubled over. The knife caught on my clavicle, and I yelped in pain. The blade wedged just behind the bone and stuck. But that didn't stop my retaliation. I kneed him again, this time in the chin. He stumbled backward, ripping the knife free as his back collided with the opposite wall.

"You sick fucker," I snarled, aware he still had the knife in his hand. I landed a roundhouse kick to his chest, afraid to get too close on account of the blade and his physical advantage. He fell back, dropping the knife.

In the dark, I couldn't see his hands. Was he going for a gun? Did he have another weapon? I screamed, hoping to attract as much attention as possible. He didn't pull a gun. Instead, he barreled toward me, intent on shutting me up.

My elbow cracked into his jaw, and I spun, thrusting the palm of my other hand upward and breaking his nose. His eyes teared so badly he probably couldn't see. He let out a vicious snarl, wiping at the tears. I slipped deeper into the dark, searching for my gun. Rushed footsteps echoed on the sidewalk, and I prepared for another attack.

It never came. The commotion caught the attention of several pedestrians. The attacker barreled past the first two men who came to my aid. He knocked one of them on his ass and darted across the street.

For a split second, I was torn. Should I pursue? He was injured. I might be able to subdue him, but it was a gamble.

His knife had clattered to the pavement, and he never reclaimed it. The asshole was probably in too much pain to think about it. And I knew whatever sick intentions he had were long forgotten. Who the hell was he? And what did he really want?

Despite my preference for enacting my own form of justice, I was in no condition to go another round either. Not without my gun. I found my purse amongst several garbage bags that had fallen out of an overstuffed trashcan. I picked it up, removed my nine millimeter, and stepped onto the sidewalk.

Dammit. Where did he go? The blood trail ended at the curb.

"Did you see a man running away?" I asked the closest guy. "He had his face covered and a broken nose."

"No shit," the guy said. "Son of a bitch nearly toppled over me." He glanced at his friend. "We called the cops. They should be here soon." His eyes went to my collar, but I didn't wait for him to say anything else.

"Hey, you." I pointed to a couple across the street. "Did you see a man with a mask?"

"He got into a car and took off," the woman said. She looked both ways and darted across the street. "Are you okay?" She didn't touch me, but she looked over my injuries and askew clothing. "Did he...?"

"No," I looked at her, "he tried."

"Good for you." She reached for her husband's hand. "Darren, call 911. Get her an ambulance and the police." She looked at me again. "You should sit down. That looks really bad."

"I'm okay." Cross Security loomed fifty feet away. Another few steps and I would have been inside. None of this would have happened. Yet, something told me the attack wasn't a coincidence, but my mind couldn't wrap itself around the inconsistencies. I had no idea what just happened. Was it an attempted sexual assault? I wasn't convinced that had been my attacker's intention. He wanted my belt, not inside my pants.

"The police are on the way," Darren said, showing more compassion now that his wife was insisting upon it.

"What are your names?" I asked, figuring they might disappear like the other two men who helped stave off the attack.

"Darren and Darlene Stone." Her eyes darted back and forth, as if we were in the middle of a war zone. Perhaps, in some ways, we were.

"Did you happen to get the license plate of the car?"

They shook their heads.

"What about make or model?"

"Um, it was that red car parked over there," Darlene said.

"It had four doors. Old, like from the early 1990s," Darren added. "The car alarm went off a few minutes ago. I didn't even think old junkers like that had alarms. Maybe you noticed it?"

"Figures," I muttered. It was the only thing that made sense. Whoever the asshole was, he had been waiting for the perfect opportunity. Except there was no perfect opportunity, so he made his own. I pressed a hand into my collarbone, hissing. Oh yeah, that would require stitches. "Shit."

A patrol unit arrived a minute later. I pointed them at the scene of the attack and gave the officers my name and information while one of them pressed some gauze against my clavicle. I introduced them to Darren and Darlene and asked if we could continue this inside. One of the officers accompanied me to the office while the other questioned my new friends.

"Are you sure you don't want to go to the hospital?" the officer asked.

"We have medical staff on duty. This will be faster."

"And you're certain he didn't touch you."

"Not like that." I gave the cop a look. "He had gloves on. His entire body was covered, head to toe. I can't tell you anything except his height and maybe his weight. He drove an old red car and triggered the alarm as a distraction. That's when he grabbed me."

"That's something."

I stepped out of the elevator on the thirtieth floor. "Do you want to call in the guys from evidence collection?"

"You said he didn't touch you. What do you think we'll be able to collect?"

"Look, I want this guy off the street. I want him caught, and I want him locked up. If he had attacked someone not quite as trained or prepared as me, things would have gone a lot differently. He also knew how to hold the blade, how to stand, how to act. He's probably done it before." Actually, I was positive he'd done it before.

"Any idea how many serial rapists are on the loose?" the cop asked.

I glared at him, unable to determine if that was rhetorical. "Why don't you tell me?"

"A whole hell of a lot more than there should be. We'll do what we can to find this one, but I can't make any guarantees. You were lucky. It could have been a lot worse. The thing is, when it comes to prosecuting, the charges won't be that steep since he didn't touch you."

"I'm not convinced this was a failed sexual assault. And let's be real. Assault with a deadly weapon or attempted murder comes with steep penalties. It's up to the prosecutor, the judge, and the jury. That's why you need to make sure the case will hold up. Get a team down here to check everything, or I'll have private sector professionals do your job for you."

He clicked his radio and requested a detective and evidence collection at our location. "Anything else I should know? Maybe you got some other helpful hints on how I should do my job."

"Actually, I do," I retorted. "You have the knife he used. Maybe he touched it before he put on his gloves. Perhaps you'll get prints. And you need to run the car. Check nearby businesses for security cam footage. You find the car, you'll find him."

"Sure. Easy peasy." He watched the bloodstain on my shirt grow larger. "Since you got all this useful information, you should realize hospital records speak volumes. Are you sure you don't want an ambulance?" He clicked his radio again, requesting an ambo to our location, even though I knew the medics here could testify just as easily as any ER personnel.

"The medics are upstairs." I grabbed my bag from behind the door and headed back to the elevator. "Do you know how chain of custody works?"

"Yes, ma'am." He was growing increasingly annoyed by my attitude, but I didn't care. "I watch those crime shows too."

"Great. When I take off these clothes, they're going into a sealed evidence bag, which is going into your custody. You are going to observe this happening and sign off on it to ensure that no shyster defense attorney can object to whatever trace they might find."

"Wonderful. Maybe we should record it too." We stepped out of the elevator, and the cop spun in a circle, suddenly realizing I wasn't full of shit. "Where the hell are we?"

"Welcome to privatized policing."

The techs Cross employed were the cream of the crop. They could find and analyze almost anything. Of course, when it came to pursuing legal grounds, I wasn't entirely sure how convincing the evidence they obtained might be. That's why I wanted the real police to handle this matter. However, they were bogged down in cases, and this wouldn't be a priority. The officer following me around had practically said as much.

A detective arrived, someone I didn't know, who asked the same questions as the patrol officers. She took my statement, my clothes, and photographs of my injuries. She had just left when Lucien returned to the office.

"Miss Parker, why are there patrol cars outside the building? Someone notified me the police were here."

I winced as the medic finished the last stitch, tying off the ends. I pulled my shirt up over my shoulders and buttoned my blouse while he dabbed at the scrape on my face with an alcohol-soaked cotton swab. I pulled away, wincing. That was enough of that. However, he remained undaunted and put a band-aid over the cut.

"Do you want a little something for when the lidocaine wears off?" the medic asked.

"No, I'm okay. Thanks for the patch job." I turned to face Cross. "I need whatever security camera footage you have for outside the building." And then I told Cross what happened, recalling just how mad I'd been when I left dinner.

"I'll get started on it." Cross studied me uncertainly. "Are you sure you're okay?"

"I'm fine."

His eyes narrowed, taking in every cut, scrape, and nervous tic. "Do you want a detail to follow you around until the police apprehend him?"

"No, and I doubt they will."

Cross picked up the phone and ordered a team to check for trace in the alleyway as soon as the police were finished. "We'll find the vehicle. Don't worry."

"This is a police matter."

"You're one of my investigators. That trumps everything."

"I don't want special treatment."

"Too bad."

Grumbling, I went down the stairs to my office. A thought hit me just as I reached for the doorknob. The attack wasn't random. It was supposed to appear that way, but the timing and location were too convenient. The assailant planned everything. That's why he set off his car alarm. It gave him the chance to grab me off the street without anyone noticing.

Who the hell was he? And what did he really want? I didn't think sexual assault had been the priority. He waited too long. He was too careful, too measured. Most random attacks were frenzied. This wasn't. He was calm, like he was waiting for something. Either I was being stalked, or I was targeted for another reason. I had to find out why.

TEN

The security cameras didn't catch the car's plates, and the view of the driver left a lot to be desired. That damn mask made him unrecognizable. Cross had done what he could with facial recognition, but it wasn't enough. Both the police and Cross Security were working on DNA analysis from the blood drops found at the scene, but DNA took time.

I wanted to know who the man was and, more importantly, why he attacked me. My gut said it wasn't a random act of violence. He chose me. If the point was to kill me, he would have sliced my throat. No, he wanted something else. The police were convinced it was a failed sexual assault, but he didn't rip open my blouse or yank off my pants. He just wanted my belt. Maybe it was a fetish, but I didn't think so. Like most adversaries I'd faced, he underestimated me, but if he hadn't, I wondered what he would have done.

Oddly enough, the attack actually had a positive effect on my psyche. Instead of falling deeper down the rabbit hole of death and mayhem, which was the direction I had been heading after watching the light leave Gifford's eyes, I was now invigorated. I'd been trained to survive, and I proved it. I was invincible. And even though the voice in my head reminded me how ridiculous that notion was, I couldn't shake it. I liked the high. Truthfully, I felt great, which was ironic.

Martin, on the other hand, didn't share my sentiment. He didn't exactly know the whole story, but he knew I'd been jumped on my way back from dinner and the police and Cross Security were investigating. As usual, the stitches concerned him.

"Miss Parker, Mark Jablonsky is here to see you," the receptionist said.

I hit the button for the intercom. "Thanks. Send him in." I grabbed a pen and sticky note and went back to what I was doing.

"Holy shit." Mark stood in the doorway with his mouth agape. "I've seen serial killers that weren't this crazed."

"I'm not crazed," I retorted, sticking my note to the wall. "Close the door before Cross sees you." I turned to Mark, eyeing the folder in his hands. "Did you bring it?"

He held it out, walking toward me while he analyzed my handiwork. "You're going to need more wall space."

"I'll manage." I placed the file on the coffee table and started dissecting it. "How many favors did you have to call in?"

"Not many. That's everything cybercrimes found on Noah Ryder." He bit his thumbnail and pointed at the post-it. "What's all this?"

"CryptSpec," I said dismissively.

"And this?" Mark asked, turning and striding across the room. He flicked a few of the photographs I taped beside my notes. "That's from the attack?"

"Uh-huh." I sorted the documents into workable piles. "Ryder has a specific profile he targets. Any idea if he's still active?"

"Your guess is as good as mine." Distracted by my macabre collage, he didn't elaborate further.

I threw a pencil and hit him in the back. "Hey, I need to know if the FBI is opening an investigation into Ryder."

He rubbed his head and glared at me. "Not at this time. Are you sure you're okay? Marty's concerned. And after seeing this, so am I."

"No reason to be." I grabbed a few pushpins and tacked the FBI profile and list of Ryder's possible aliases to the wall under his name. "I'm just busy, and this was the easiest way to keep things organized." I pointed to the back wall. "Stuart Gifford was murdered right outside the CryptSpec building. The police are investigating." I lowered my voice and looked uncertainly at my closed office door, afraid Cross might appear. "Detective Heathcliff believes a few of the people who work there have a side hustle removing ransomware. It might go to motive."

"You think they're causing the problem and fixing it?"

"That is the nature of ransomware. I assume Derek's thinking the same thing, but we haven't spoken about it directly. Blackmail and desperation are great motives for murder, and if Gifford figured it out, that would be reason enough to kill him." I shrugged. "Plus, I have no idea why Gifford was at CryptSpec unless it was related to the ransomware."

"Maybe it's more than a side hustle."

"It's possible their new app is being used to exploit security weaknesses on computers and devices. Maybe that's how the programmers are installing the ransomware. Then again, the competition could be responsible."

Mark raised an interested eyebrow. "Go on."

"I was hired to flush out an internal leak. I thought I did, but after Gifford was killed, other facts came to light." I finished updating the Noah Ryder wall and crossed to where Mark was standing. "See this," I pointed to a printed screenshot, "this is the information CryptSpec can access when someone agrees to the TOS. It would make finding targets easy, and with a bit of internal manipulation, some of the guys at the company could use the app to make a handsome profit by victimizing users."

Mark blew out a breath. "Technology. Gotta love it."

I had shared my theory with Kellan and Lucien, but the official company line was we had dropped the CryptSpec investigation. The civil engineer might have discovered what was going on or who was behind it, went to CryptSpec to confront the guilty party, and was murdered for his trouble. But that was just my working theory. Heathcliff's might be different.

"Perhaps you could find out how the police investigation is going," I suggested.

"Why don't you just ask?"

"I promised Derek I'd keep my nose out of it."

Mark snorted. "Oh yeah, that's exactly the vibe I'm getting."

I turned and pointed at the opposite wall. "Whoever jumped me did so because of one of my investigations. CryptSpec was the only Cross Security case I worked on before the attack, so I can't just leave it alone."

"Or you got knifed because of Noah Ryder," Mark pointed out.

That was a possibility, but I'd barely gotten started on that case. It would have been unlikely Ryder would have found out I was investigating him, especially since I hadn't even made contact or determined if he was still in the city. "I rented the office he used to meet Klassi and spoke to several of his neighbors and the building manager. So it isn't beyond the realm of possibility one of them tipped him off, but it's less likely."

"What about good ol' Don? Klassi didn't want to go to the police and has an unnamed associate who told him about Ryder. Maybe he ran his mouth and got you in trouble."

I pointed to a note asking the same question. "Can't rule it out."

"Could it be someone from your past? Maybe a case we worked?"

"Possibly, but the bastard knew to wait outside this building. Obviously, he knows I work here." I narrowed my eyes. "I'm not sure how anyone from my past would know that. Hell, I still haven't figured out how he knew I'd be returning to the office."

"What about the guy you went to dinner with? Did you check into him? Maybe he tipped off your attacker."

My eyes drifted to the window that looked into the hallway. If I squinted, I could see Kellan working at his desk. "I don't think he set me up."

"What about Cross? He likes to play games. You said he

tests people. Could this have been a test?"

I brushed my hair out of my face and tilted my neck to the side to reveal the stitches. "The guy would have killed me if he'd gotten the chance. I don't think Cross hired a killer."

Jablonsky let out an unsettling grunt but didn't offer a protest. "So what's your priority now? Case one, two, or three?"

"Heathcliff's got CryptSpec, so unless I hear something, I'll keep moving forward on Klassi's case. The plan is to bait Noah Ryder. Once we determine if he's still around, the next thing to do is take him down. I have a client's money to recover. I'll put this to bed while Heathcliff handles CryptSpec, and hopefully, the asshole with the knife gets caught by one of us." I tossed my alias's profile to Mark. "Quiz me."

He dropped into a chair and perused the paperwork. Pulling out his phone, he entered a few things and continued to search and verify. "It looks good. Stands up to a fair amount of scrutiny. That might be important." He flipped back to the first page. "Okay, tell me about yourself, Mrs. Alexandra Scott."

I ran through the background details, name, age, address, occupation. As usual, Jablonsky tried to trip me up on the minor details, but I'd done enough undercover work not to get confused. I knew my cover identity's alma mater, her major, minor, and the sorority she joined. I even knew the names of her sorority sisters, the annual parties they held, the frats they invited, and how much they made on fundraisers. The devil was always in the details.

"And your husband?" he asked, an amused grin on his face.

"Rich, stuffy, and old."

"Does he remind you of anyone?"

I gave Mark my death stare. "Conrad's a rich art collector. He's from old money. He was close with one of my art professors and introduced us at a gallery showing. At first, things were great. He paid attention, made me feel special, treated me the way no man ever had. The typical older man, younger woman routine. With age came wisdom, elegant taste, and expensive jewelry, but once we were married, his interest dwindled. I was just a trophy he showed off on special occasions but otherwise left on a shelf to get dusty."

"Plus, he's too old to get it up," Jablonsky commented. "Obviously, he can't keep you pleased. So you want out."

"Speaking from experience?"

Mark was in his mid-fifties and divorced three times. "That wasn't my problem, but I never dated anyone young enough to be my daughter. Keeping up is a younger man's game." He flipped to another page. "So what's the play? You plan to divorce the geezer, but you want to stash away as much as you can before you file the paperwork?"

"The prenup requires a minimum of ten years of marriage before I get a dime, and we've only been married six. He already has wifey number five lined up. He's been boffing her for the last year. He's left me with no choice. I can't possibly wait another four years before filing."

"Particularly when you're going to be too old to hook another wealthy sugar daddy in four years. Dare I say, you're probably too old now."

"Thanks," I said sarcastically.

"According to this, Conrad bought you a studio and a gallery. He saved you from the life of a starving artist. Your gallery hosts other artists, and you paint on the side. If push came to shove, can you back this up?"

I nodded. "Cross rented a gallery, backdated the paperwork, and set up the peripherals."

"I'd love to see you with a canvas and paintbrush. What's your specialty? Dogs playing poker?"

"Abstract art."

"Good call."

"Anyway, the techs upstairs have tracked Noah's online activity. He has a few financial and consulting sites and groups set up, so I've asked for help, suggestions, and advice on ways to move around Conrad's money."

"Have you gotten any bites yet?"

"A few, but we can't be sure it's Noah. I'm waiting to see if he responds to my follow-up questions. Klassi had Noah's e-mail address, so we ran that, but it's been shut down. I'm guessing he created it once he decided to target Klassi and got rid of it after he took Don's money."

"Have you called the provider?"

"We traced the owner and administrator, but it was registered outside the country to a foreign corporation that doesn't exist. Honestly, I don't know if we're going to get this guy."

"In other words, you're just hoping to get lucky."

"No," Cross said, stepping into the room. I didn't hear him open the door. "We're making Alex's cover as titillating as possible. If Ryder's around, he'll bite. Conrad Scott has hundreds of millions of dollars at his disposal. Just imagine how much Alex might be able to steal before Conrad realizes what's going on. Noah Ryder wouldn't miss another lucrative payday like that."

"You sound certain," Jablonsky said, standing and sizing up Cross. "You always were a cocky son of a bitch."

Cross didn't stoop to trading barbs. "I'm not cocky. I'm confident. And I have every reason to be." He turned his attention to me. "Alex Scott just received an answer to her e-mail. Noah is offering to help and wants to stop by the gallery tomorrow night."

"Are you sure it's him?" I asked.

"There's only one way to find out." Cross's focus bounced from wall to wall. "Make sure you're prepared. Should you require more space, I'll have someone roll in a free-standing corkboard."

"Enabler," Jablonsky muttered.

Cross turned to him. "I see your investigative tactics haven't changed since that seminar we attended years ago." Cross plucked at the intel Mark had brought for me. "I guess it's true what they say about old dogs. Remind me again what your rate of closed cases is."

"There's a right way and wrong way to do things," Mark growled.

For a moment, I wasn't sure what Lucien was about to say. But whatever it was, he decided against it. Instead, he gave a curt nod and walked out of the room.

"I should go." Mark gave me a hug. "Be careful." He sneered at the doorway. "I don't trust him."

"Most of the time, neither do I, but he comes through when it matters."

"Sure, because it makes him look good. Maybe he creates these situations just to manipulate you."

"Now who's paranoid?" I retorted.

"You taught me it's not paranoia if it's true." Mark grinned. "Guess I'm not such an old dog, after all."

ELEVEN

I was seated in the white leather chair behind the desk in the foyer. Alexandra Scott's art studio connected to the gallery via the rear hallway. The studio was a tiny workshop perfect for one. Despite being small, the rest of the gallery was exquisite, just like the diamond ring on my finger. It was obvious to even casual observers that the Scotts had money; Cross made sure of that.

The gallery was basically a loft. The upstairs had dark, hardwood floors. One of the walls was exposed brick, giving it a Bohemian, urban vibe. Currently, the walls and support pillars were covered in some trendy upcomer's latest creations. According to the brochure, the last showing had completely sold out with no piece going for less than five grand. The combined estimated worth of the pieces upstairs came out to a cool million.

The bottom floor was much more elegant. It had a museum feel with white and silver tile floors, glass doors, and a state-of-the-art security and fire prevention system. This was where valuable masterpieces were displayed. The security system was no joke with a laser-grid and pressure sensors. Currently, three masterpieces were inside, allegedly from Conrad Scott's private collection. However,

Conrad Scott didn't exist, and neither did Alexandra. I wasn't sure where Cross had gotten priceless paintings on such short notice, but I suspected they might be forgeries, albeit good ones. Since I couldn't be certain of their legitimacy, I hoped Ryder wasn't an art expert.

When I asked Cross about the gallery, he told me one of the museums wanted it as an annex to host private dinners and events for their exclusive patrons. However, it became too expensive to have a secondary site when the museum already had plenty of rooms that could be used, so the gallery went up for auction. After several failed attempts by aspiring artists to turn it into something profitable, it remained empty until now.

I clicked a few keys on the computer, continuing the ruse of searching for some way of hiding my husband's money where no attorney could find it. Movement on one of the monitors caught my eye, and I turned to look at the security feed. Four cameras covered the gallery. The one outside had a great view of the front of the building where a dark, luxury sedan had just parked. The man who stepped out looked perfectly coifed with his nice suit and fancy haircut.

He held his head high as he entered, not making any attempt to hide from the security cameras, which made me question the likelihood that he was the infamous Noah Ryder. Offering a polite smile, he strode toward me.

"Mrs. Scott?" he asked.

"Yes, how may I help you?"

He extended his hand. "Noah Ripley," he said. "I received your inquiry and thought it best to meet with you in a neutral location." He took a seat, glancing up at the security camera above my head. "Is your husband here?"

"No."

"Is it safe to speak freely?"

"Yes, of course."

He squinted with one eye, tilting his head to the side. "You expressed an interest in diversifying your assets."

"That's the polite way of putting it." I reached for a pen. "I'm sorry. I've reached out to so many firms and posted my contact information in a lot of different online groups.

Where did you say you were from?"

"R&P Asset Management. You requested additional information on alternative investments." He placed his briefcase on his lap and popped the top, removing several forms and pamphlets. He held out a page that was a printed version of the form I filled out. "You did contact us, right?"

It was a basic form. I might have filled it out, or he could have scraped my data from somewhere else and created the intake form himself. There was no way to tell, but it didn't matter. He was here. That was all I cared about.

"I guess so. I've been so scattered lately."

"Well, you have a lot going on." He opened one of the pamphlets and turned it around to face me. "As you can see, we offer advice on everything from precious metals to foreign investments. It just depends what your long-term goals are."

My expression soured. "My long-term goals were to marry the man of my dreams and live happily ever after, but things change."

"Is this an alimony situation? Obviously, you have ample means. Are you the primary breadwinner?"

"Hardly. This is Conrad's," I met his eyes, knowing that a certain amount of eye contact was key to selling lies, "my husband's, gallery. He purchased it for my use, but I imagine once I serve him with papers, it'll be gone. Just like everything else."

Noah frowned, digging deeper into his briefcase. "Look, R&P isn't in the business of hiding assets or subverting tax law. We don't do anything illegal, nor would we ever advise our clients to violate any laws. That being said, there are legal avenues worth exploring." He placed a business card on the desk. "I think I can help, but I'll need more detailed information on your financial situation and a breakdown of your assets and your husband's. I assume you're hoping to get a clear view of things before you dissolve your marriage." He licked his lips. "Have you consulted a divorce attorney? What did he say?"

"I haven't yet. I was afraid Conrad would find out, and I'm not ready for that. Our prenup is rock solid. The conditions haven't been met, so I will most likely get nothing. Only the assets I brought to the table will go with me. He gets everything else."

"Like this gallery." Noah looked around. "That doesn't seem fair."

"It isn't. I just want to make sure what's mine, stays mine, and he can't touch it. Is that so wrong?"

Noah shook his head and pulled out a checklist. He spun it around, marking a few items with a pen. "Get as much of this information as you can, and I'll see if there's anything I can do to help." He circled the phone number on his business card. "If I don't hear from you, I'll assume you've decided to pursue other avenues. Either way, I wish you the best of luck, Mrs. Scott. Divorce is hard."

"Speaking from experience?"

"Unfortunately." He made a show of looking at his watch. "Thank you for agreeing to this introduction." He glanced at the glass doors off to the side. "Do you mind if I take a peek inside?"

"That's what we're here for." I led him through the glass entryway. "This is Conrad's private collection. Upstairs we host new artists."

"I see he has a taste for the French masters."

"Actually, I chose these. I always loved impressionism. I'll miss seeing them every day. It's not like I could just stuff them in a suitcase and walk away with them." Noah laughed politely, but I couldn't get a read on him. "Would you like to see upstairs? We're planning a show, but you can have a sneak peek if you like," I said.

"Actually, I have another meeting to get to. Just think about what I said, and if you want me to come up with some options for you, let me know. I'm here to help."

"Thanks, Mr. Ripley." I shook his hand. "Perhaps you'll have time to tour upstairs next time."

"I intend to take you up on that."

I watched him walk out the door, get into his car, and drive away. The security camera had gotten a great view of his face, and the exterior camera caught his license plate. I rewound the footage, pausing and zooming in. Then I printed a hardcopy of his face and the plate, copied the footage to an external drive, and phoned Don Klassi.

"Meet me at Cross Security. I have something to show you." After hanging up, I phoned the office and requested someone run the plate, Noah Ripley, and R&P Asset Management. I didn't believe in coincidences or that Noah Ripley and Noah Ryder were two different people. "I found you. Now to find what you've done with the money."

I locked up and went outside. The hair at the back of my neck prickled, and an uneasiness settled over me. My eyes darted back and forth, and I unzipped my purse and reached inside for my gun. Was someone watching me?

I didn't spot anyone, but that didn't mean anything. I missed the assailant lurking in the shadows the night of the attack. Perhaps I was losing my touch. More than likely, I was paranoid. This was the first time I was walking alone at night since the attack. The bastard was out there, somewhere. Still, it was unlikely he would have located me a second time, particularly at a gallery that I'd never been to before today. Regardless, I kept my gun in my hand. If he tried again, he'd learn not to bring a knife to a gunfight.

I made it to my car without incident and drove to Cross Security. I parked in the garage and rode the elevator to my office. The information I requested was waiting on my desk, and Cross was seated on the sofa.

"How'd it go?" he asked. "From what I was told, it seems we've located Noah Ryder."

"Ripley," I corrected. "He changed his last name. I called Don. He's on his way. I want him to verify it's the same man."

"You think there could be more than one?"

"It's possible." But I didn't believe it. However, I knew Cross didn't have the same opinion on coincidences that I did. "Is there anything else I should know about the gallery, the paintings, or Conrad Scott?"

"You have everything you need. Why?" A sly suspicion played across his face. "Did something happen?"

"No, but this is my case. Autonomy, remember?"

"Fair enough. Once Mr. Klassi verifies it's the same man, it's your play. Do whatever you see fit. If you need additional resources or back-up, I will avail myself to you."

He stood. "Otherwise, I won't interfere. Let me know how things turn out."

"Will do."

That went a lot easier than I thought, but I had a sneaking suspicion Cross would find some way to insinuate himself into my case again. He always did. Sighing, I took a seat and read through Noah Ripley's extensive background. I made a few notes to call the Dean of Admissions at his alma mater to find out if he had ever been a student. It was easy to fake the paperwork. It was a little more difficult to convince complete strangers to lie for you.

I reviewed the business profile on R&P. It didn't stand up to scrutiny. It was a new establishment. Something that existed in name alone for five years before getting taken off the shelf, dusted off, and used as an actual entity. Noah Ryder/Ripley was a grifter, a talented liar who planned at least three moves ahead. He knew how to run a long con. As far as I could tell, he'd been doing it for at least half a decade.

"Is this the guy?" I asked Don when he entered my office. I held up the photo from the surveillance feed.

"That's Noah. How'd you find him?"

"I let him find me."

"Okay, so now what?" Don helped himself to the bottle of bourbon sitting on the cart in the corner. "When do I get the rest of the cryptocurrency?"

"That will be a little trickier, but I'm working on it."

"Then why did you call me?"

I chuckled. "I thought it might be important to make sure I had the right guy before I accuse him of stealing ten million dollars."

Don swallowed and looked around the office. "Wow, it's just like those crime shows but on steroids. I didn't think actual cops did this."

"They don't. In case you forgot, I'm not an actual cop."

"I didn't forget." He finished his drink, turning his focus to some of the other photos on the wall. "What's this about?"

"Different case," I said dismissively.

He stared at the red car for a long time. "That looks like

a Grand Prix, maybe a '92."

"Are you a car guy?" No one had been able to pin down a year given the crappy angle of the surveillance camera.

"No, but my first driving lesson was in one of those. It's weird. I haven't seen a car like that in years, and now they're just popping up all over the place. Who knew any were left on the road?"

"You've seen that car before?"

He thought for a moment. "I don't know. Maybe."

"Where?"

"Probably while I was stuck in traffic." He prattled on about crosstown traffic during rush hour, but I tuned him out and went to the computer. According to the DMV, there were less than fifty registered in the city. "Is that it?" he asked.

I looked up from the screen. "Yes, Mr. Klassi. Thank you for your time. I will update you as soon as I know something."

"See that you do." He put his empty glass on the edge of my desk. "I need that coin as soon as you can get it."

TWELVE

Finding the car shouldn't be this hard. It was old. Like Klassi said, not many were left on the road. I rubbed my eyes and closed the search box. I'd gone through every vehicle in the database that fit the parameters and cross-referenced that information with driver's license photos. Granted, I didn't know exactly what the assailant looked like, but male, 5'10 to 6'2, roughly 170-200 pounds, and between the ages of eighteen and forty-five provided a broad enough range to include my attacker. However, no one who owned an old red car fit that description.

"You've got to be kidding me," I growled at the screen.

"I didn't say anything yet," Kellan said from the doorway. We hadn't spoken much since the attack. He felt guilty, and I was still pissed he thought I would sleep with Cross for special treatment. "What's going on?"

"I thought I had a lead on the bastard with the knife, but it turned into another dead end." I gave him my undivided attention. "What do you want?"

"Since Renner and I are working late, we were going to order in from the Italian place. We wondered if you wanted anything."

"Zuppa Toscana and a garden salad."

"Okay." He hesitated to leave. "Is there anything I can

do to help?"

I shook my head and reached for the folder on Noah Ripley. When I glanced back at the door, Kellan was gone. Noah Ripley had an impressive CV listed on the R&P Asset Management website, so I dove deeper, checking everything I could find on him. Then I did another search on Noah Ryder.

On a hunch, I searched social media sites, specifically those geared toward professionals. The names Noah Ryder and Ripley returned several hits for what appeared to be nearly duplicate accounts, except the locations differed. Maybe our grifter was also an identity thief. The best cons always had the most truth behind them. So maybe Noah Ryder did exist, and this impersonator decided to use some of Noah's actual details in creating his backstory in order to ensure he'd pass muster should his fictitious persona come under scrutiny.

"You son of a bitch." The same was true for Noah Ripley, including his alma mater and alleged job history. Unfortunately, I couldn't find an actual photo. Surely, the real Noah Ripley, if there was a real Noah Ripley, must have been photographed at some point.

I went back into the DMV records, looking for Ryder or Ripley or any way to prove the man I met earlier this evening was not who he said he was. In the event I was forced to confront him, the more evidence I had, the easier it would be to convince him to return Klassi's money. Involving the authorities would be a nonstarter. It'd be years before enough evidence was collected, and who knew how many counts of identity theft and criminal fraud this man had committed. Don wanted his money now. He didn't want to wait, and he didn't want the cops involved. Cross would back that play. As usual, I was between a rock and a hard place.

Stop it, Parker. You're not a fed, I reminded myself, returning my focus to understanding Noah. The best way to resolve this for my client would be to out con the con man. That meant I needed to work on Alexandra's backstory and motivation and make sure she fit the mold for Noah's perfect mark.

The profile Cross's people created was decent. Alexandra Scott seduced her professor's rich friend and married Conrad as soon as she completed her MFA. Conrad whisked her off to Europe, where they lived for the first eighteen months of their marriage. Inevitably, they returned to the States. By then, Conrad had grown bored. Despite his wandering eye, the prenup said if the marriage lasted less than ten years, Alexandra got nothing.

The writing on the wall and the lengthy list of Conrad's ex-wives indicated he never planned on their marriage lasting a lifetime, let alone a decade. That made Alexandra desperate. Time was running out. Maybe I'd up the ante during a future meeting with Noah and tell him my husband already lined up wife number five.

I was just adding some final notes when Bennett Renner poked his head into my office. "Food's here."

"Thanks. I'll be right there."

I finished what I was writing and went to grab my dinner before one of the guys ate it. Bennett had a pizza box in front of him, and Kellan was rummaging in the fridge for a bottle of iced tea. Bennett gestured to the seat across from him where my container of soup and salad were sitting inside a plastic bag. Picking up the receipt, I reached into my pocket for some cash.

"Don't worry about it," Bennett said. "I got you."

"Thanks."

He jerked his chin at the chair. "Why don't you join us?"

"I have too much to do."

"Sit down," Kellan said, "unless you're freaked to eat with me again."

"Your table manners aren't that bad." Reluctantly, I took a seat and pounded the end of the flatware packet against the table until my fork broke through the cellophane. I studied Bennett. "What did Cross assign you?"

Bennett took a big bite of pizza. "Nothing really, just acting as a go-between," he said with his mouth full. "The boss wants to know what progress the police are making on the CryptSpec case."

I leaned forward eagerly. "Me too." I glanced at Kellan.

"I thought you told Cross we had to drop CryptSpec."

"Yeah, well, we did." Kellan found his tea and took a seat. "But if Barber isn't the mole, we haven't actually done our job. And now that the CryptSpec employees are under suspicion of installing ransomware on their customers' devices, Mansfield wants to find out if his people are involved or if it's just a weakness some unknown hackers have decided to exploit. Needless to say, Cross wants us to continue investigating the employees the cops have already cleared to see who's dirty, which is why Bennett has to call in his chits with his precinct pals."

Renner muttered something around another mouthful. "The techs are hoping once we get a look at the ransomware code, we'll be able to trace it to a specific programmer."

"Mansfield said the same thing," Kellan chimed in.

"Except we don't have access to the ransomware coding, and we have no way of knowing who the current victims are. It's a mess. The police issued an alert saying if anyone is targeted by ransomware to bring the affected device to the precinct, but you know what the public's like. Detective Heathcliff is not happy," Bennett said. "We're screwing around too close to his homicide case. And he's still not convinced the ransomware isn't connected to Gifford's murder."

"It sounds like a shitstorm," I mused, surprised I hadn't heard from Derek.

"It is. Suffice it to say, CryptSpec is doing some in-house cleaning. Anyone we even suspect is getting called in for questioning and forced to submit to a polygraph. Cross actually has our deception expert conducting the interviews. Mansfield was originally concerned with his code being sold to competitors, but now he's more concerned about the lawsuits his company may be facing if it's found that his product is enabling hackers to take control of their users' devices or that his programmers are responsible for the malware," Kellan said. "You should be relieved you found something else before Cross could put you back on this, Alex."

Renner grinned. "That's because she brought him a

seven-figure payday."

"How'd you hear about that?" I asked.

Bennett looked down at the two carat engagement ring and wedding band Cross had given me to wear as Alexandra Scott. "I hear things. And that is one shiny bauble. Lucien doesn't pull out the expensive toys unless we're looking at a big payday."

"Who's the client?" Kellan asked.

"Don Klassi," Renner replied before I could say anything. I quirked an eyebrow, waiting for an explanation. "I was speaking to Cross when you phoned earlier tonight. He clued me in on what you were doing. He figured since I was being so buddy-buddy with my old pals on the force, I might be able to find out if they had anything helpful to add on the scammer you're pursuing."

"Do they?" I asked.

"Nah."

"So what good are you?"

Bennett shrugged. "Well, I did buy you dinner."

"Now if only you could help me track down a shitty red car." I stabbed angrily at a piece of lettuce, annoyed that no one had gotten a hit on what should have been an easy identification. "Actually," I put down my fork, "the two of you can do something for me. See if the car connects to anyone at CryptSpec. Check the surveillance footage from the morning of the murder. Let me know what you find."

I closed the lid on my salad and put it into the bag with my soup and took my dinner back to my office. I didn't find a connection between the car and CryptSpec, but it wouldn't hurt to have someone double or triple-check. In the meantime, there was one glaringly obvious clue that I ignored. Klassi recognized the car. He wasn't sure where he'd seen it, but he'd seen it. That meant the bastard with the knife was linked to Klassi's case. The timing couldn't have been more perfect.

The assailant could have followed Klassi when he stopped by Monday afternoon to sign the official paperwork. Perhaps the asshole saw me talking to Don, or he picked up my trail when I went to check out Noah's office. Either way, he would have known I was working for

Klassi. Shit. Was my cover identity already blown?

I closed my eyes and tried to think. It was hard to recall much about a man with a mask covering his face, but he didn't have the same build as Noah. Noah was rail thin. I'd be surprised if he weighed more than a buck fifty. Noah didn't attack me. That much was as obvious as the unbroken nose on his face, but maybe Noah had an accomplice.

For the next twenty minutes, I debated why Noah would take a meeting with someone he knew was out to get him. That didn't make any sense. Obviously, whoever jumped me knew I wasn't a cop. Therefore, if he was working with Noah, they'd both know I wasn't law enforcement, so Noah would have no reason to try to con me into tipping my hand. Private eyes didn't build those kinds of cases, and for Noah, who'd been doing this for several years, it wouldn't make sense to take an unnecessary risk, particularly when he just walked away with a ten million dollar payday.

The attacker and Noah weren't linked, which meant I was attacked because of my connection to Don Klassi. Despite the fact Mark, Martin, and I checked into Klassi, the things that Don said about his wealth and his insistence to avoid the authorities had immediately left a bad taste in my mouth. The FBI didn't find any criminal activity in his past, and neither did the resources at Cross Security. Still, Klassi was slimy. I was sure of it the first time we spoke. Even Martin picked up on that vibe. So what was Don involved in that had nearly gotten me killed half a block from the office?

I had to find out who introduced Don to Noah, and I needed to know more about the ten million dollars. The money might not have been Don's. Perhaps he was cleaning it for some scumbag. All I knew was the assault linked to Don. What the hell did I get dragged into this time?

Getting up, I removed my nine millimeter from the drawer, chambered a round, and put it into my shoulder holster with the safety off. Then I took the elevator to the lobby and went out the front door. The first time Don visited the office, he left his friend behind. I wondered if the masked man was on the prowl again tonight. Truthfully, I hoped he'd find me because I had a score to settle and questions that needed answering.

THIRTEEN

"Who is he?" I spat.

Klassi wasn't pleased that I found him at an upscale bar. He was even less pleased that I was questioning him in front of his business associate, Joshua Standish. "Joshua, this is Alexis. We met at a dinner party the other evening." Klassi painted a phony smile on his face. "Excuse us for a moment." Klassi slid off the chair and led me out of earshot. "What the hell do you think you're doing here?"

"A few days ago, I was attacked outside my office." I yanked on the collar of my shirt, exposing the stitches. "It turns out the bastard's connected to you."

"To me?" Klassi squeaked. "Are you sure?"

"You recognized the car. His car." I waved off a waitress before she could get close to us. "I need to know everything. And I'm not prepared to leave until you answer my questions." I shot a look in Standish's direction. "You might want to make it quick before your business partner gets curious. I'd hate to have to break the news to him."

"I'm sorry you were attacked, but I can assure you that has nothing to do with me."

"Who recommended you use Noah Ryder to trade cash for coin?"

"Miss Parker, please." Klassi turned. Smiling at Standish, he held up one finger, as if this would only take a moment longer. When he turned back to face me, the smile was gone. "No one important. It was a fellow businessman. Honestly, I can't even be sure who it was at this point. I speak to so many people every day."

"What's his name?"

"No, you've already interrupted my life by barging in here. I won't let you harass my friends. I have a reputation to uphold."

"Afraid I'll do something to tarnish the halo above your head?"

His eyes snapped to mine. "Tarnish my reputation, and I'll take you down with me. Or rather, I guess I'll take James down with me. It's up to you."

"Where'd the money come from?" I asked. "The ten million you gave to Noah, where did you get it?"

"I worked for it. I earned it." He glanced back at Standish. "Before you interrupted, I was just discussing with my partner a lucrative property expansion that we've embarked upon. Despite what you may think, I do work for a living."

"Is that what you call scamming people with your investment clubs?"

"It was no scam. I'm not the con man. Noah is. Property value is volatile. I can't help it if prices drop unexpectedly, just like I can't control when prices soar. Now, if you'll excuse me."

I grabbed Don's arm. "Watch yourself, Mr. Klassi. Someone's upset you hired me. It's either the person who put you on to Noah, or it's whoever you're in bed with. Either way, they aren't messing around. You better hope I figure out who it is before they decide to come after you with a knife. I don't believe you'd fare well in a close quarters situation."

Don swallowed. "Whatever happened to you had nothing to do with me. If it did, I'd tell you." He gave a slight nod to the bouncer standing beside the hostess station. This was a private bar for members only, and I was about to be reminded of that fact.

I shook my head and went out the door. Getting Don to crack would take time and leverage, and even then, I wasn't sure he'd cooperate. I'd have to figure this out another way. It was a good thing I worked at the best private investigation firm in the city. Phoning the office, I requested a complete work-up on Don Klassi's financials. If he had any unscrupulous associates, we'd find the money trail.

Walking away from the bar, I felt him. He was here. Watching. Poised to strike. I stopped and pressed my back against the wall. My hand went inside my jacket, gripping my gun. Despite the warm, summer night, I shivered.

At first, I didn't see him, but every fiber of my being went on high-alert the moment I stepped out of the bar. I searched the sidewalk, watching as people moved past me without any fear or hesitation. He was close, just not that close.

I scanned the other side of the street. Shrouded in darkness, he stared back at me. He was a barely visible shadow positioned between the streetlights, peering out from behind the railing to a basement shop. Our eyes met. His vision sharp and focused on his prey — me.

I couldn't tell if he was armed. Honestly, at this distance, I couldn't tell anything about him. He didn't wear a mask, but he concealed his identity beneath a hood, like a comic book villain.

Pulling my weapon, I darted across the street, dodging the cars along the way. He dropped from his perch, disappearing before I even hit the sidewalk. I raced down the steps, my gun at my side. He wasn't waiting at the bottom. He must have gone inside.

I twisted the knob and entered the establishment. The room was pitch black, except for strobing lights and a steady, pumping rhythm that made the floors vibrate. A blonde tugged on the leash hooked to a fat man wearing assless chaps, a nipple ring, and nothing else. She glanced at me, spotting the gun as the light strobed back on. She screamed, but I pushed past her.

Out of all the places the bastard with the knife could have disappeared, this was the worst. An underground sex club guaranteed plenty of rooms to hide in. The shitty lighting and thick velvet draperies provided ample opportunities to conceal himself in plain sight, and with the unspoken rule of anonymity and privacy, no one would remember seeing him.

Pressing against the right wall, I moved deeper into the dark, musky hallway. I heard a scream and spun, aiming at the sound. Another shriek followed, and I realized it was the wrong kind of scream. Dammit. He was somewhere in this labyrinth of sex and velvet. I just had to find him.

I peered into one room after another, the lights wreaking havoc on my depth perception. He could be anywhere. Hell, he could be right behind me, and as long as he moved in time with the strobing light and ducked behind the velvet curtains, I would never notice him. The hair prickled at the back of my neck. He was close. I could feel him.

He barreled into me from behind, knocking me against the wall. Darkness followed by blinding light. He was halfway down the hall now, taking a quick right as the hallway branched. Darkness. Light. I blinked, chasing after him. I caught a glimpse when the light strobed again. By the time the area lit again, he had vanished.

I slowed. This was a dead end. He had to be here. Somewhere. A few groans sounded to my left. Between the measured light intervals, I could see the curtain in front of me move. The next time the light came back, he was inches from me.

The first blow glanced off my shoulder. He tried again. His punches and moves appearing choreographed in the blinking light. He rushed forward, throwing himself against me. The door behind us gave out, and we toppled to the floor.

The couple inside scattered, fleeing past us as I flipped the guy over top of me. A commotion sounded in the hallway. Apparently, someone went to get help. In the dark, I lost sight of the assailant. Slowly, I turned, doing my best to survey my surroundings despite the uncooperative lighting.

I tried to listen, to use my other senses, but there was

too much noise and vibration from the music. Damn these lights. I blocked the door, wondering if there might be another way out. If he remained in the room, he was still and silent. The curtain rustled to my left, and I turned. That's when he clocked me and darted out the door.

"Son of a bitch." I chased after him, catching glimpses of someone moving faster than everyone else. It was a mad rush to vacate the premises before the police arrived. He turned a corner, and I followed. It led to a wider hallway and a door. He slipped through, and I burst into an all-out run.

The overhead lights came on, and I shielded my eyes from the sudden unexpected brightness. A moment later, he was out the door, leaving a confused woman sitting behind a desk at what must have been the main entrance.

I burst out the door, spotting him getting into a red car. I hauled ass, chasing after the car that was now speeding down the street. There was no light around the license plate, so I couldn't get a plate number. The bastard really thought of everything. I continued running, my legs cramping as I tried to keep up with the car's engine, but he was getting farther and farther away. Stopping, I aimed and fired, but he took a turn. My bullet impacted with the side mirror.

Dialing Jablonsky, I figured he'd have more pull in getting patrols mobilized at the police department than I would. I gave him my current location, the direction the car was traveling, and anything else that might be useful. Then I trudged back to the bar which was on a parallel street. Klassi couldn't deny this bastard wasn't after him, and I fully intended to point that out. But by the time I made it back to the bar, Klassi and Standish were gone.

With no other leads, I returned to the office. Before going inside, I walked the streets, checking every alleyway, hidden alcove, and dead end. I toured nearby garages and strolled past the rows of vehicles parked on side streets. I didn't find the bastard or his red car. He didn't come back here to finish the job. He was probably still licking his wounds from our first encounter.

I didn't believe the unsub expected to run into me

tonight. He wasn't prepared for a showdown, which is probably why he ran. Still, I couldn't be certain that he didn't tail me from the office to the bar. I didn't believe Don's claims of ignorance, but on the off chance I was wrong and the slimy businessman was right, I needed to be sure.

After nearly an hour of searching for signs of the unsub, I entered Cross Security, washed up, and reheated my soup. While I was finishing my dinner in the now empty breakroom, Kellan came looking for me. He reviewed the footage from CryptSpec but didn't spot the red car. I wasn't surprised.

"What are you thinking?" Kellan asked as he leaned against the fridge.

I shook my head, knowing it would sound stupid if I said it. "Just making sure we didn't miss anything."

"Can I ask you something?"

I looked up, feeling the mood shift. "What is it?"

"How do you know Don Klassi?"

"Friend of a friend. Well, more of an acquaintance of a friend."

Kellan thought for a moment. "You have some rather interesting friends. Care to elaborate on that?"

"Not in the least." I narrowed my eyes. "Why the twenty questions?" He'd been prying a lot into my personal life lately, and I didn't like it.

"I was just curious." He nodded at the clock on the wall. "It's getting late. Are you planning on calling it a night?"

"In a bit."

"Just remember, building security is around if you need an escort to your car."

I chuckled. "Yeah, thanks."

After speaking to Mark and learning the police had no luck locating the car or driver, I tried to let it go and grabbed the notes I made on Alexandra Scott. I needed to have a better grasp of my alter ego. All I really knew about her was that she didn't care about the asshole following me or his stupid car.

I wanted to contact Noah, but calling too soon might scare him off. I'd wait at least thirty-six hours before reaching out, as if I were actually considering my options or possibly even consulting other agencies. He needed to woo me. It was important he work for this. If it was too simple, he might realize it was a ruse.

When I completed filling in the tiny details of Alexandra's life, including her agenda to marry well and live a life of luxury, I reread the literature and questionnaire Noah had given me. After filling everything out and printing the documents he requested, I placed everything neatly inside a folder and turned off my computer.

The surveillance photos caught my eye, and I glared daggers at the red car. The unsub was smart enough to conceal his plates. The angle didn't provide any indication of the year or model. No parking passes, EZ Pass, or decal of any sort was visible. And obviously, the VIN was completely out of the question.

Maybe it was an out of state vehicle. That would explain the lack of DMV records, but expanding to a nationwide search would be time-consuming. I'd start with the tri-state area and go from there. Unwilling to give up, particularly after the unsub gave me the slip earlier, I copied down Klassi's home address and went for a drive. Since Don didn't want to speak to me at the bar, he'd have no choice but to speak to me at home.

FOURTEEN

Don lived in a concierge building. Getting inside would be tricky. After scouting the area for the red car, I parked in front of the building and gave my information to the doorman. He told me Mr. Klassi wasn't home, but the front desk called up to his apartment anyway.

"Sorry, ma'am. Would you like to leave a message?" the concierge asked.

"Yes, but it wouldn't be polite to ask you to relay it." I already had enough of Don for one day. Maybe the unsub found him and killed him. That would serve my client right, I thought bitterly before scolding myself for thinking such a terrible thing.

Seeing no need to waste my time, I left the building and circled around. Assuming the unsub was after Don, he might be lying in wait for Don to return home. But I didn't spot my target or his clunker of a car.

The neighborhood was upscale. The only aging automobiles were classics in pristine condition. Something from the early nineties would stick out like a sore thumb, and the police would probably be phoned immediately. I suspected even the help drove luxury cars provided by their employers. There was probably a public ordinance forcing anyone who couldn't afford a nice vehicle to take public transportation or walk.

Deciding this was yet another waste of my time, I headed home. My thoughts returned to the Scotts. Conrad was probably someone just like Don. Greedy, arrogant, and privileged. At least I'd know to act accordingly for my follow-up meeting with Noah.

As I turned onto a less residential street in what had morphed from a prestigious, gentrified area to yet another sketchy block in the city, I spotted the distinct taillights. Perhaps it was the late hour or my imagination, but I raced ahead, hoping to catch up to the car before it disappeared.

I turned onto the next street, but there were four cars between me and what might have been a red Pontiac. I maneuvered as best I could to keep the car in my sights, but by the time I made it to the stop sign at the end of the street, I lost it. Slamming my palm against the steering wheel, I studied the four possible directions it might have gone, picked one, and hoped to catch another glimpse of the car. No dice.

It was nearly three a.m. when I made it home. The image of the taillights was burned into my retinas. Was it even the same car? Was I hallucinating? And really, why did it matter? Klassi didn't care, so I had no reason to worry about his safety, just my own. I needed to pull it together and focus on Noah. That was my case. My priority. And something told me that would lead to the unsub.

"Alex?" Martin asked groggily. He flipped on the table lamp and rubbed his eyes. "Where have you been?"

"Don't ask."

He glared at me. "I just did."

"I'm not sure. I went on a wild goose chase and ended up at a bar and a sex club. Afterward, I just drove around, chasing ghosts."

"Yeah, you're right." He got off the couch and stretched. "I shouldn't have asked." He went into the kitchen to get a glass of water. "You know, you could have called." He looked at the glowing display on the microwave. "Amazing, I can actually get four hours of sleep before work."

"You didn't need to wait up."

"How could I not?" He gulped down the water and left the empty glass in the sink. His eyes came to rest on the diamond ring on my finger. "That's not the ring I gave you. Anything you want to tell me?"

"It's Cross's." I took it and the wedding band off and put them in my purse. "It's for Don's case."

"Great." He headed for the bedroom.

By the time I joined him, he was already asleep. I watched the gentle rise and fall of his chest. I should have come home hours ago. Instead, I spent half the night driving around for a car that was probably a hundred miles away by now. The police and Cross were looking into it. I had other things to worry about. But the unsub was out there. He wanted to hurt me or stop me. Probably both.

I was acutely aware of two things. First, I wasn't a victim. I refused to be one. My hand went to my collarbone, and I pushed down gently. The wound remained tender. I knew it could have been worse, and that thought scared me. Reality was finally setting in. I wasn't invincible, but it was nice while it lasted. Second, I knew the attack connected to Klassi's interaction with Noah, but I didn't know enough about the case yet to warrant being threatened. So why the hell did I get knifed in an alley outside work and stalked to the bar tonight?

Martin made a snuffling sound in his sleep, as if reading my mind and snorting at how ludicrous the entire thing was. After hours of twisting and turning, my thoughts in overdrive, I finally settled down and closed my eyes. This apartment was my sanctuary. The building had top of the line security. I had nothing to fear, but some nights, rational thought didn't mean a damn thing. Luckily, I was able to distract myself from any potential danger with questions about Kellan's curiosity. Since when did he take such an interest in my private life? It made no sense.

My thoughts wandered, and I fell into a deep slumber. It was a little after twelve when I woke up. I slept through the alarm. Shit. I left my phone in the kitchen when I came home, which explained why I didn't hear the four missed calls. Two were from Mark. The others were from Heathcliff and Cross. At least my boss only phoned once.

Hurrying to the office, I arrived just as most of the building was returning from lunch. The elevator remained crowded, but I was the only one who exited on the thirtieth floor. The receptionist glanced in my direction.

"Any messages?" I asked.

She shook her head.

"Thanks." I continued to my office.

No new casework had been slipped under my door or left on my desk. That was a good sign. Relaxing, I realized that, given the circumstances, there really wasn't any reason why I needed to attend the morning meeting. It wasn't like Lucien would assign me a new case when I was in the middle of something.

After listening to my voicemails, I called Detective Heathcliff back. We had a lot to discuss. I told him about the assault and the red car, but he was already up to speed on the situation, thanks to Jablonsky and Renner.

"I already checked every CryptSpec employee. It doesn't belong to any of them. I spoke to the officers who responded to the call that morning, but none of them remembers seeing the car outside. I assigned a few officers to check through nearby CCTV feeds, but I don't think it was there."

"Probably not," I admitted. "I'm guessing it has to do with a different case."

"The scammer with the cryptocurrency?" Heathcliff asked.

His question made me suspicious. "Yeah, why?"

"Any idea what type of cryptocurrency he's dealing?"

"Type?" I searched the papers hanging on the wall for the report. Since I'd given the information to the techs upstairs, they provided an elaborate breakdown. "It was something I never heard of." I found the page and read the name. "Does that mean anything to you?"

"It's worthless, not the intel. The currency," Heathcliff said. "Some of these coins never gain traction, and the value of the coin nosedives. It's not any safer than the fucking stock market."

"Did you invest and lose your shirt or something?"

He blew out a breath. "No."

"Then what's the deal?"

"You know how CryptSpec's CEO originally got his start?"

"Programming."

"And mining. His start-up had the processing power, so he and his partners put it to use. The coin he mined is worthless now, but according to blockchain ledgers, he still possesses a ton of it. It's how he financed the operation early on, before the currency went belly up. Without the cryptocurrency, he wouldn't have a business. He was lucky to have cashed out when he did."

"Do you think our cases are connected?" I asked.

"Hard to say, unless you name your client. You mentioned it was someone from MT."

I knew I should give up Klassi, but I already lost one case to the PD. I couldn't lose another one, particularly since I'd already invested my blood, sweat, and tears. "What happens if I tell you?"

"I'm in the middle of a fucking homicide investigation. What do you think is going to happen?"

"I'm close, Derek. I've already met with the con artist once. And my client was adamantly opposed to police involvement. He'll freak if you bring him in for questioning. Just give me some time to sort through this mess."

"Your throat was nearly sliced open, and anything could have happened last night. Why won't you play ball? What if the guy in the mask killed Gifford?"

"You said the car wasn't there."

"He could have walked or found another ride," Heathcliff growled. "For all I know, your client could be a killer. Are you sure you want to protect him?"

"He isn't the killer. He was in a board meeting when Gifford was shot."

Derek wasn't pleased that I was refusing to cooperate. "I could go to Martin and ask for names and figure it out from there."

"By all means, Detective, feel free."

He grumbled something I pretended not to hear for the sake of our friendship and hung up. Well, at least I remained true to my word. I wasn't interfering in his investigation.

However, the conversation did give me plenty to think about, and I researched the coin Klassi received in exchange for cash. Like Derek said, it was worthless. Don made several transactions over the course of two months. Didn't he realize he was being taken? And why was he so concerned about getting the ten million he spent back in worthless coin? If it was worthless, why didn't Noah just fork it over? Hell, I'd trade a bag of pebbles for diamonds any day. And in essence, that's what the scam artist was doing. By withholding the coin, he opened himself up to Klassi's wrath. This changed things.

I was in the middle of dialing Jablonsky when Cross burst through my door. "How long?" he bellowed, his voice reverberating off the walls.

"For what?" I asked.

He slammed my door, making the walls shake. "When did it start?"

I put my phone down. "What are you talking about?"

He was irate. The last time I'd seen him this angry was the night he fired one of the members of his security team. He stalked back and forth, swallowing and clearing his throat. He coughed again. "How long have you been seeing James Martin?"

Ice ran through my veins, but I did my best not to react. Martin thought Cross knew about our relationship all along and liked to screw with us. Obviously, that wasn't the case. "I don't see how that is any of your business."

He let out a huff and jerked the client chair away from my desk. He circled back around, coming to stand in the now empty space, and gripped the edge of my desk. "We had an agreement. James is supposed to be mine."

I stared at him as if he had six heads. "Excuse me?"

He straightened and stared at the ceiling, composing himself. "Before you started here, you worked for him. A condition of your contract stipulates that any future work you do for him falls under the scope of Cross Security."

"I told you our business relationship was over."

"Yeah, like I was going to believe that." Cross rubbed

both hands over his face. "How long have you been dating? Is that why he originally hired you over my firm?"

"How dare you?"

Cross shook it off. "No, I'm," he indicated that I should give him a minute while he organized his thoughts, "not implying that. Forget I said that. Shit." He crossed his arms over his chest. "I need to know what the situation is."

"You need to go to hell."

He licked his lips. "According to every media outlet, James Martin is single. He's listed as one of the city's most eligible bachelors. In an interview he gave six months ago, he said he wasn't dating. *He said it.*" Cross blinked rapidly, shaking his head. "Is this just a fling? Do the two of you hook up whenever you feel like it? Booty calls or whatever people are calling it now? Is that what the apartment is for?"

"We are not discussing this. This is none of your business."

His eyes narrowed. "I told you I thought he was interested in you. I was right." He watched me carefully. "But you already knew that. Dammit. Tell me how long this has been going on."

"Asked and answered," I growled, not understanding why Cross thought my private life had anything to do with him.

"That's why Don Klassi came to you. He's on the board at Martin Technologies. You might not work for James, but you're doing his bidding."

"Fuck you." Don must have decided to get payback for last night.

A million thoughts went through Lucien's mind. He hesitated for a brief moment before adding, "You own an apartment together. The paperwork went through months ago. Care to explain that?"

"Get the hell out of my office."

"Per the terms of your contract," Lucien began, but I stood up.

"I said get out." I pointed at the door. "Now."

"Fine. We will discuss this when you're calmer."

"When I'm calmer?" I balked. "Who the fuck do you

think you are?"

He didn't respond. He simply walked out of my office like his outburst didn't just happen. As soon as he was out of sight, I dropped into the chair. I was so angry my hands were shaking. Who the hell did he think he was to ask about my personal life? I ran through the things he said and the accusations he made, getting more infuriated by the second. Getting up, I slammed the door closed. If I wasn't careful, I might kill somebody. Preferably Lucien or maybe Klassi.

I reached for my cell to call Martin but decided against it. He had enough on his plate, and he didn't need to listen to me yell about my asshole boss. Instead, I rolled my neck from side to side, resisting the urge to heave heavy objects across the room. When I was slightly more in control, I dialed Mark.

"Hey," I said, figuring I could rant and rave to him, "you're not going to believe the day I'm having."

"Did you get my messages?"

"What's up?"

"Someone ran your details late last night. With everything that's been going on, I have you flagged, so I get an alert whenever anyone pokes around."

"I'm waiting," I said, already suspecting what he was about to say.

"Someone at Cross Security ran your credit history, phone, and property records. It was a little after eleven when they did it. It was probably just a work thing, but I thought you should know."

"Oh, I know."

Mark heard the tone of my voice. "I warned you about Cross."

"*I told you so* isn't exactly what I want to hear right now." I picked up a sharpened pencil and flung it across the room like a dart, wondering if it would stick in the wall. It did not. "My boss is an asshole. Any idea exactly who ran my records?"

"It just came from the office. That's all I know."

"Yeah." My eyes focused across the hall. "If you're not busy later, I'd like to talk through some ideas and theories.

Heathcliff mentioned some interesting things about cryptocurrency."

"Cryptocurrency or how to kill Cross." Mark chuckled. "Either way, count me in."

"Thanks. I'll see you tonight."

"Any other car sightings?" he asked before I could hang up.

"Not today."

"Good."

I stormed across the hallway and barged into Kellan's office. Unlike Cross, I didn't scream at him the moment I entered. Instead, I took a seat in his client chair and stared at him. Silent interrogation was usually the most effective. I just wasn't sure how much training a former DEA agent might have undergone to resist such tactics.

Luckily, Kellan cracked in less than a minute, probably since half the floor heard me arguing with Lucien. "Alex, you don't understand."

"Enlighten me."

"When you came aboard, Cross asked me to look into you. To find out everything I could about you and James Martin."

"That's why you were so friendly at first. You've been lying to me since the day we met."

"Alex," he insisted, but I held up my hand to silence him.

"That's why you've been asking so many questions lately and why you kept trying to get me drunk, so I'd tell you whatever you wanted to know."

"At first, I thought Lucien was just doing his due diligence. He likes to know everyone's secrets to avoid unpleasant surprises down the road. But you were clean. So I started thinking maybe he had a thing for you, but you made it obvious that wasn't the case. When Renner told me about Don Klassi, I recognized the name and ran your records. I'm sorry."

"What did you find?"

"The apartment. The regular phone calls."

"What did you find on Klassi?"

Kellan looked confused. "Nothing."

I bit the inside of my lip and gave him an icy stare. "My relationship with Martin has no bearing on anything, least of all my ability to work here. It is none of Lucien's business, and it sure as hell isn't yours. Just tell me one thing. Did you have anything to do with the attack?"

His mouth dropped in shock. "How can you even think that?"

"I don't know you. And I sure as hell can't trust you. Just answer the damn question."

"No. I would never."

"Fine." I stood. "Do yourself a favor, Dey. Stay the hell away from me."

FIFTEEN

"Why does it matter?" Martin asked. His eyes followed me as I paced back and forth. "Who cares if Cross knows we're together? I don't. And honestly, sweetheart, you knew when you signed the papers on this apartment that our secret was out. Frankly, I'm surprised it took him this long to figure it out." He pointed a finger at me. "That's the reason I didn't hire that prick in the first place. He's slow on the uptake. And you can tell him that the next time he asks."

"He wasn't supposed to find out. No one was." I met his eyes. "It matters."

Martin sat back and rubbed his palms on his thighs. "Explain to me why."

"It's not safe. Lucien's an issue, but the unsub with the knife is more of an immediate threat. You can't deny that."

"It's not any more dangerous today than it was yesterday, before he knew. You aren't a federal agent. The chances of someone seeking retribution have diminished. No one should actively be trying to hurt you."

I tugged on my collar. "Yeah, we see how well that's going, right?"

Martin wanted to pretend everything was fine. He hated

knowing I was at risk, and he knew how detrimental outside threats were to our relationship. He found the conversation vexing, and the vein at his temple jumped and pulsed. "We cohabitate eighty percent of the time. Y'know, I really thought this time would be different. I don't know why. It never is with you."

"Martin, I'm not saying this changes anything."

"Then what the hell are you saying?" He got up to pour a drink. "We live here. We've been living here. Anyone who feels like checking into property records will discover that. The cat's out of the bag. The ship has sailed. We can't put the genie back in the bottle."

"Any more idioms you feel like using?"

The beginnings of a grin formed at the edges of his mouth. "Give me a minute. I'll see what I can come up with." He swallowed a mouthful of scotch and let out a long exhale. "It's out there, and someone found it. What's the problem?"

"Someone found it, which means other people can find it. You have to be careful. We have to be careful."

"But you already knew that." He gave me a long look. "All or nothing. I told you I'm all in. I guess it's time you make a decision." He smiled. It wasn't nice or friendly; it was more of a gotcha smile. "Not so easy, is it?"

"I'm in. And if you didn't figure that out the day I signed the papers on this place, you're not paying enough attention." I took the glass from him and gulped it down. "However, that doesn't change anything. Cross wants you. At this point, it's not beyond the realm of reason to think that he's jealous I'm your girlfriend. Maybe he caught a gay vibe. You do wear a lot of pink and purple for a straight man."

"Lucien isn't gay," Martin said. He poured another splash of scotch into the glass, waiting to see if I'd make a move for it. "Even if he is, I don't swing that way. And nothing on *Page Six* or in the tabloids ever indicated otherwise. Your point is moot."

"No, it isn't. Maybe if you'd start paying attention to what I'm saying, you'd see we have a problem."

"Here are the things we know," Martin said. "Lucien

approached me about a joint business venture. We had a preliminary meeting to discuss the possibility. I told him I wasn't interested. He asked that I remain open to working with him in the future. That was it." Martin saw the concern in my eyes. "And you're afraid he intends to use you as a pawn or somehow leverage our relationship for his own gains."

"Like I said, we have a problem."

Martin drained the glass. "Let him bring it. I know how to shut him down. If he does anything retaliatory to you, I'll bury him in lawsuits. And despite what he might want you to think, my corporate attorneys are much more skilled at civil proceedings than the legal counsel on his payroll. Furthermore, if it came down to it, I'd buy out your contract. You don't have to work for him." He sighed. "I'm sorry I provided him with a glowing recommendation. You can do much better than Cross Security."

My head pounded, and I rubbed the back of my neck. There were so many things wrong with what Martin just said that it would take the rest of the night to point them all out. He knew that I never wanted to get a job or keep a job because of my connection to him. When Cross hired me, I knew it was because of Martin, even though, at the time, I had no idea Cross was this obsessed. However, under no uncertain terms did I want Martin to fight my battles, nor did I want to be used as a game piece in their battle. And that's what I was to Cross. A piece he could exploit for his own gains, and depending on Martin's actions, I might be nothing more than a prize to be won on the corporate battlefield.

Despite my annoyance with Lucien for putting me in this position, my biggest issue was the worry worming its way through my belly. Someone found my connection to Martin. This time, it was Cross. Next time, it could be anyone with an agenda. But I couldn't act out of fear. That's how I nearly lost Martin the first time. Instead, I had to bury it and hide it. I'd probably end up with an ulcer.

"Alexis," Martin said, drawing my attention to him, "it'll be okay. He can't hurt us. Do you want me to give him a call and clear the air?"

"No."

Martin held up his palms. "Okay." He brushed his thumb against my cheek, knowing that no matter what he said, I still found the situation unacceptable. "What else is bothering you?"

I turned to check the time. Jablonsky was on his way. He'd save me from this, and unlike Martin, he'd fully comprehend the situation. "Kellan betrayed me. Maybe Renner too. I trusted them. Hell, I even liked them. How could I have been so blind?"

He kissed me. "I'm sorry."

I gave him a look, feeling as though he were patronizing me. To Martin, business wasn't personal, but he took the bullshit with Klassi rather personally. Before I could point that out, the intercom buzzed, notifying us Jablonsky was here. At least he saved Martin from a fight I didn't think he'd win.

"I have some calls to make and e-mails to return. I'll be in the bedroom if you need me." Martin took his glass and closed the door behind him while I let Mark inside.

"Twice in two weeks. Clearly, you miss me," Mark said, stepping inside with a bag of takeout. "Hope Chinese is okay. I thought you could use some orange chicken and fried rice."

Even though I wasn't hungry, I thanked him for picking up dinner, and after a brief rant and recap of my dealings with the unsub, Lucien, Martin's view, and the fact that I still didn't know precisely why Lucien was this interested in Martin, we turned the topic of our conversation to cryptocurrencies and Noah Ryder/Ripley. Mark bit into an egg roll, chewing thoughtfully.

"You should hand Klassi over to Heathcliff, and let the detective take care of it."

"I did some digging," I admitted, "but I can't find a connection between Klassi and CryptSpec. It's the same type of cryptocurrency that Noah traded to Don, but that's the beginning and end of it. Don has no obvious ties to anyone at CryptSpec."

"Businessmen tend to travel in the same circles. There might be some overlap but probably not what you're looking for. What about Noah? He's dealing in the same coin." Mark thought for a moment.

"Even if I give Noah to the cops, they won't have anything to charge him with. Don won't come forward."

"Not even for ten million?"

Something told me the answer was no, but I shrugged in response. "I'll keep on it unless it gets to be too much."

"Last night sounded like it was too much. The bastard with the knife connects to Klassi. Have you tried speaking to him about it again?"

"I've left a few messages, but he won't return my calls. The only way I'm going to get answers is to see this through."

"In that case, it sounds like you have everything you need." He blotted the mustard that had fallen onto his shirt with a napkin. "But I don't like it."

"Noah?" I asked.

Mark shook his head. "We don't know much except that he set up these companies and identities years ago. He's a planner. And since the Bureau has no record of him or his scams, he's careful. He won't fall for the usual lines of bullshit. You have to sell yourself as Alexandra Scott. Your background is rock solid, but you need to be on point. Are you?"

"I hope so."

He picked up a container of beef and broccoli and a set of chopsticks. "After you called, I had the boys upstairs do a thorough eval of your entire cover story, including the paperwork on the gallery. Despite Cross losing his shit today, I will admit he did a good job establishing your cover. I don't think Noah will see through it. Hell, our experts couldn't find any loose threads, and they knew it was a plant."

"But that's the crux of the problem."

"I don't follow."

"I can't trust anyone at Cross Security. What if Lucien decides to be vindictive and screw me over? I don't even know what he wants, and after he barged into my office, screaming like a banshee, I kicked him out."

"You should have kicked his ass." Mark put the

container down and slumped back on the couch. "I can't believe Marty's being so cool about this."

"He doesn't understand, and I don't know how to make him understand without sounding like an overprotective, paranoid lunatic."

"That's because you are, but you have your reasons. I know you, Parker. You're freaking out about a million worst case scenarios. Here's the thing. You know the score. You know what this job entails, and deep down, so does Marty. He isn't stupid. He understands Cross better than you think. Hell, you know what my feelings are toward your new boss, but I don't believe he would jeopardize your safety for the very simple reason that it would make him and his precious company look bad. However, the less you rely on him, the better off you'll be." He reached for the container again, digging his chopsticks into it. "Why does Marty think Cross is obsessed with him?"

"It's Martin. Naturally, he assumes everyone wants him."

"He probably thinks he was the subject of Billy Squier's song."

"Probably."

"What do you think?"

"Cross wants to create a line of tactical wear. When I got shot, he actually used that as a way to broach the subject with Martin about taking on a joint endeavor, and that was before he knew we were dating. Just imagine what he'd do now."

Mark frowned, closing the container and putting it back on the table. My words made him lose his appetite. "Before you do anything, you need to find out what's what with your boss. And you need to make it clear that any chance he has at a partnership with Martin will disappear if anything were to happen to you."

"You think he'd stage an accident or attack?" The cold chill traveled down my spine. Until now, I hadn't really considered it, even though I confronted Kellan with that possibility earlier this afternoon. But that was me just lashing out and being bitchy.

"That's the problem, Alex. We have no idea what he's

capable of." Mark began cleaning up. "You need to take control of the situation. He needs your connection to Martin. I suggest you use that to your advantage."

"Except, he's livid that Martin and I are dating. I might have lost my leverage."

"Find a way to reclaim it." He looked at the closed bedroom door. "Or have Marty take care of it." I opened my mouth to voice my obvious annoyance with that idea, but Mark held up a hand. "I know you hate it when other people fight your battles. But this isn't just your fight. It's his too. And I'll tell you what I always do; the most important thing is that you stay safe. Understood?"

"Yeah, okay."

"Contact Noah in the morning and play it by ear. Don't be too easy or too stubborn. And let me know when and where you're meeting. Someone needs to know what the situation is in case things go sideways or if that asshole with the knife shows up again." He gave me a look. "It looks like you're operating on your own again."

"Just the way I like it."

"Yeah, as if that isn't asking for trouble."

SIXTEEN

Noah wanted to meet for dinner to discuss my financial situation and options. He was smooth, selecting a public place. He didn't want to spook me. He explained it was best not to meet at his office until he was sure he could assist me. The way he saw it, there was no reason I should pay for his time if it turned out I couldn't use his services. This was meant to make him more endearing and convince me he wasn't out for the money or to rip me off. However, I couldn't help but wonder if he was still searching for new office space.

I looked up the physical address for R&P. The website and the business cards he gave me only provided a mailbox address. To someone not looking too hard, the address looked just like any other street address. It was only upon closer examination that it became apparent it linked to a mailbox rental. Although, I was sure, if I asked him about it, he would have a logical reason for it, but I had no plans to confront him. He needed to believe that I trusted him.

When I arrived a few minutes late to dinner, he was already seated at a table. He stood, coming around to pull out my chair. "Was it presumptuous to order a bottle of wine?" he asked, returning to his seat.

"I thought this was strictly business. I am a married woman," I tossed him a friendly smile, "which is reason enough to drink."

The waiter returned with a bottle of white, holding it out to Noah, who nodded. After some was poured into a glass, Noah picked it up, swirling it around before taking a quick sniff and a small sip. "That will be fine," he said, waiting for the waiter to fill both glasses and leave the menus.

"Expensive wine," I mused.

Noah remained transfixed by the menu. "Don't worry. I have an expense account." After what felt like five minutes of total silence, he closed the menu and placed it on the edge of the table. "Did you bring the materials I requested?"

Slowly, I closed my menu, as if selecting an entrée was just as important as stealing my husband's millions, and reached for the bag at my feet. "Are you sure you wouldn't prefer to do this somewhere else?"

"I'm sorry, Mrs. Scott. If you feel this is inappropriate or if I'm making you uncomfortable in any way, we will continue this meeting elsewhere." He held up a hand for the waiter, probably to pay for the wine.

"No," I reached across and placed my palm against his forearm, "I didn't mean to be rude. I just figured you had somewhere else to be tonight."

"I'm married to my job, Mrs. Scott. Most nights, I eat dinner at my desk or on the way to meet a client. This is a nice change of pace." He met my eyes. "You said you were free, but if I'm keeping you from other plans, we'll make this brief."

I picked at the corner of the menu, letting my eyes drop. "No plans. Our home is outside the city, but with the gallery showing coming up, I've been staying here to work and paint. Truthfully, I don't have much reason to go home." I reached for my glass of wine, staring daggers into the abyss. "Conrad is using the house to entertain, and the hotel where I'm staying is far from cozy." I took a sip, letting the bitterness eke out of my eyes. "We haven't been happy for quite some time. I should have realized when I turned thirty that he would still want to be with a twenty-something."

"Is it really that bad?"

I brushed my hair back. "I shouldn't complain." Absently, I played with the rings on my finger. "I knew what I was getting into."

Noah finished his assessment just as the waiter brought our dinner. He reached for his silverware, slicing his grilled chicken into thin pieces. I hadn't made a move toward my plate, and he watched as I carefully placed the cloth napkin on my lap and took another sip of wine.

"Based on what you brought, it appears you have liquid assets that could be redistributed, but your husband does not." He popped a piece of meat into his mouth and chewed, waiting for me to pick up my fork and take a bite before he continued. "Most of Conrad's wealth is tied up in investments. Real estate, stocks, property. The usual things. Your resources are more common. Bank accounts, jewelry, things of that nature." He took another sip of wine. "Off the record, how much are you hoping to retain? Most jurisdictions favor a fifty-fifty split."

"As I said before, we have a prenup. I'll be lucky to walk away with the clothes on my back." I narrowed my eyes. "Let's not get into the nasty business of divorce. I don't want to think about that tonight."

"Unfortunately, Mrs. Scott, you have limited options. In good conscience, I can't suggest or condone you taking or hiding what isn't necessarily yours. Even though, the entire situation seems rather unfair."

"It's Alex," I corrected. "Mrs. Scott makes it sound like I belong to him. I am not his property."

Noah leaned in closer. "Okay, Alex." His eyes shifted back and forth, as if making sure no one was eavesdropping. "On the bright side, at this moment in time, you are entitled to all jointly held assets. That includes the house where you live, the gallery, your joint bank accounts, stocks, et cetera. I don't see any reason why you couldn't move some things around, assuming you have the authorization to do so. Maybe you should go on a spending spree." He popped another piece of chicken into his mouth and flipped through the pages again. "Your bank account looks like fair game, as does your control of how business is conducted at the gallery."

"What exactly should I do?"

"I shouldn't say anything. This could get me in trouble." He sat up straight, finishing his wine and refilling both of our glasses. "You probably should seek legal counsel."

"Please," I reached for his hand, "his lawyers will eat mine for breakfast. What can I do?"

He took another gulp of wine. I knew the act. He wanted to appear to be an upstanding guy who followed the rules, but since he was sympathetic to my plight, he was torn. The conversation had invoked a moral dilemma. Should he help the damsel in distress or stick to his principles? His expression and mannerisms were convincing. Too bad he wasn't part of SAG; at least then he might have gotten some type of award.

"I really shouldn't get involved. It's not my place. R&P focuses on alternative investment options. I don't think we can help you."

My face fell. "I understand. I'm sorry I wasted your time." I braced my hands on the edge of the table and pushed my chair backward, but Noah grabbed my hand before I could stand.

"Wait," his golden brown eyes held a shimmer of hope, "don't go. You have to stay for dessert. I reserved the chocolate souffle, and if you leave before it arrives, I'll be stuck eating both of them. I'm not sure my arteries can handle it."

I gave him a completely bewildered and confused look. This was part of his game. He should have been a car dealer. They tried the same tactics except they used the old schtick of *let me see if my manager can give you a better deal* rather than the bribe of a chocolate souffle. But it was the same con. Noah's was just dressed nicer.

For the rest of the meal, we spoke on unrelated topics. Noah wanted to find out what made Alexandra Scott tick, so he asked about my passion for art. He wanted to know what it was like living in Europe for eighteen months, if I'd been to the Louvre, the National Gallery, the Guggenheim, the Musee d'Orsay, and the Vatican Museums, and who my favorite artist was. He'd done his research. I never mentioned those details during our first meeting, but I played the part, happy to talk about something Alexandra Scott loved. This might have been the first time someone paid attention since Conrad turned cold and elusive. And Noah took advantage.

When the chocolate souffles arrived in individual ramekins, Noah ordered a dessert wine. We finished the bottle of white and moved on to a Banyuls, which paired well with anything chocolate, at least according to Martin and several well-known sommeliers. Noah must have done his research on that too or spoke to the waiter before I arrived. Either way, he wanted to impress me with his refinement and knowledge. He also wanted to consume enough alcohol to make me think he was struggling with his decision to help me find ways to hide Conrad's assets before the divorce proceedings.

"That was fantastic. I'm glad you convinced me to stick around." I blotted my lips with the napkin.

Out of the blue, he said, "I have a sister, and I can't help but think if she was in the position you're in, I would want someone to do something to help her." He sighed heavily. "We all make mistakes when we're young and in love. And in this day in age, it isn't wrong to want to find someone who can take care of you. It's not right that Conrad can just pull the rug out from under your feet because he feels like it. You've spent six years with him. It's not right," he said again. "Listen," he reached into his wallet and pulled out a stack of bills, leaving enough to cover our meal plus a hefty gratuity, "I have an idea, but it could get me in a lot of trouble."

"I don't want that to happen." I eyed the cash. He wanted me to know he was generous and rich. For a moment, I considered asking about the expense account but figured he'd say he'd get reimbursed when he turned in the receipt. "You're such a nice man. Maybe if you just point me in the right direction, I can figure it out on my own."

"No, it's okay. Just don't tell my boss I told you this." He leaned forward again as if sharing a secret. "An artist is showing at your gallery, right?"

"Soon."

"Right, and those pieces should sell exceptionally well. How much do you expect to make?"

"We only get a small percentage. The artist actually makes the money."

"I know, but how much do you think he'll make?"

I pretended to do some quick calculations in my head. "Assuming most of it sells, probably close to seven hundred and fifty."

"Thousand?" Noah asked.

"Give or take."

He licked his lips, and I could practically see the dollar signs floating in front of his eyeballs. "How do you normally handle payment? Do you get paid? Or does the money go directly to the artist?"

"We handle the deliveries, so we take payment upon delivery, deduct our cut and expenses, and write the artist a check."

"From a joint account?"

"From the gallery's business account."

Noah flipped through the pages again. "What I'm suggesting is you have Conrad's business manager or accountant pay the artist from some other source. You can say there's been a mix-up or a hold put on the checks. It doesn't matter, just get it done. That way, no one is losing out, except the bastard you married."

I snickered. "That's a lovely thought, but he'll kill me."

"Serve him with papers before he can kill you."

"But he owns the gallery. His name is also on the business account. How is this going to help me?"

"You're not going to deposit the checks into that account. Instead, you'll transfer them into something Conrad can't touch. Something untraceable. Maybe an overseas account or cryptocurrency. Something that he'll never know about or be able to find. Whatever you choose, it has to be something he can't track."

"I don't know," I sounded hesitant. "Isn't that like embezzlement?"

"Not exactly. As long as the artist gets paid and the

customers receive their art, no one gets hurt." Noah shook his head as if dismissing the thought. "Never mind, you probably stand to make more in your divorce settlement."

"You and I both know that isn't true. Honestly, $750,000 is just a drop in the bucket for a man like Conrad. I don't know. I feel like I should be entitled to something. I don't want much, just a little something to fall back on so I can start fresh somewhere else." I flopped back in my chair, as if overwhelmed by the possibility. "Wow. This could really happen."

"It's up to you." Noah glanced at his watch. "But it gives you something to think about."

"Conrad knows people in all sorts of banks. I'd be afraid his banker friends would figure out I opened a new account."

"Like I said, there are alternative options."

"But I don't know anything about cryptocurrency."

He thought for a moment. "Actually, I might have some additional information on it in my car. Why don't we go check before we call it a night?"

"Noah," I pressed my lips together tightly, hoping to fake a slight chin quiver, "thank you."

"I haven't done anything yet." He offered me his arm and led the way to his car.

It was the same vehicle he had driven to the gallery. He leased the black, luxury sedan from a local dealership. I happened to notice the agreement as he dug through an attaché case for additional details on cryptocurrency. While he was occupied, I circled the car, making a mental note of the plate.

"Here it is." He held out the same pamphlet he'd given me the last time we met.

"Unless that's written in a different language, I don't think I'm going to understand this one any better than the last one."

"Oh," he looked sheepish, "sorry about that. It can be complicated. It's an entirely different monetary system. It isn't backed by any one country, so it's protected from things like stock market crashes and economic downturns. A government collapse would probably wipe out the banking system, but this would be safe." He grabbed a pen and scribbled a number on the pamphlet. "That's my personal cell. Why don't you look this over and think about it? If you have any questions, call me. Since my bosses wouldn't be happy with the advice I'm giving you, it'd probably be best if we discuss these things away from the office. Is that okay?"

"Sure. The last thing I want is to get you in trouble. Are you sure you want to help with this? I can probably find stuff on the internet."

He rolled his eyes. "The internet's full of scam artists and trolls."

Takes one to know one. "All right. Let me think about it."

"Oh, wait. I actually have just the thing." He opened the back door and pulled out a beginner's guide to cryptocurrency. "This should help."

I flipped through the pages. "Looks like I know what I'll be doing tonight."

"I'm busy the next couple of days, but if you want to move ahead with this plan, I'll be around this weekend."

"Thanks." I gave him a friendly hug and turned to leave.

"Can I give you a ride?"

"That's okay. My hotel isn't far." I pointed to a tall building a block away. Cross made sure the hotel's computer had a room reservation in Alexandra Scott's name that began three weeks ago and ran until after the alleged art opening. "Oh, and Noah, thanks for dinner. I was getting really sick of eating alone."

"You're welcome."

He waited until I was out of sight before driving away. Even though I felt confident he trusted me, he was careful. He didn't want to risk being followed. I repeated his license plate number a few times on my walk to the hotel parking garage where my car was actually parked. When I got inside, I wrote it down on the notepad in my purse, glanced around, and drove to the office, keeping one eye on my mirrors to make sure I wasn't tailed.

The plate was the same, and I ran it again and identified the dealership where he leased the vehicle. They must have done a credit check, so they should have a home address. I knew the info on his driver's license was bogus, but surely, he'd have to hand over legitimate information to someone at some point. I just had to find the right someone. Leaving the computer search running, I took a deep breath and headed upstairs.

I knocked against Cross's door. His assistant told me he was inside, but he didn't pick up the phone to notify Cross of my impending arrival.

"Enter," Cross called. He looked up from the paperwork. "Alex, how did it go?"

"Perfectly."

"Good." He didn't stop what he was doing. "We still have the matter of James Martin to discuss."

"My personal life is none of your business."

"I can respect that, but you know I have an interest in Martin. Your failure to disclose has put me in a difficult position. I merely want to know how long this has been going on in order to accurately conduct damage control." Unlike yesterday, Cross was back to his normal, diplomatic self.

"That is none of your damn business." Mark's words repeated in my mind. "But you should be aware that Martin takes my safety very seriously. If anything were to happen to me, he would probably hold you responsible."

Cross looked up. "Go on."

"That's it."

"That doesn't sound like it." He put his elbows on the desk and rested his chin in his palm. "Ask your questions, and then I'll ask mine."

"Why are you obsessed with Martin?"

"It's not obsession. It's pragmatism. He's on the leading edge of technological developments, not computer programming or the newest apps or AI, but on creating practical items that impact our lives. His company comes up with amazing innovations. He's done the research on biotextiles. And as soon as he releases that research, every military and defense contractor will be clamoring for it. I want it."

"He said it isn't feasible, and he has no interest in going

into the defense business."

"Maybe not now, but one day." Cross narrowed his eyes. "You were supposed to be my in with him. You worked for him, knew his needs, and what his company and personal security looked like. I figured he'd eventually ask you to do some work for him, and he'd see exactly what benefits Cross Security has to offer."

"You thought he'd see your business as a lucrative way to expand?"

"No, to embark on a joint venture. Neither of us would ever give up control. You must realize that. However, after his recent problems with inappropriate workplace relationships, he's issued several public statements that past mistakes will not be repeated. In other words, he won't mix business and pleasure." Cross narrowed his eyes. "I believe you mentioned having the same philosophy when speaking to Mr. Dey."

My irritation from yesterday returned with a vengeance, but I tamped it down. "For the record, I don't appreciate having my coworkers spy on me."

"Yes, well, it was a good thing Kellan was checking into you. If not, I never would have realized I handicapped myself by hiring you."

"So fire me."

He stared at me for a moment. "If that would solve the problem, I would, but it will only further complicate matters. I don't wish to make him vindictive. How serious is your relationship? Assuming it's just a fling or fizzles away, James might be amiable to a partnership in the future."

"That won't happen."

"The fizzling or the partnership?"

"Both."

Cross frowned. "That's what I wanted to know." He went back to his paperwork.

SEVENTEEN

As with most undercover assignments, there was a time when one had to commit to her undercover persona. Since Noah said he would be busy until the weekend, I wouldn't make contact again until Saturday morning. That gave me a few days to continue my investigation before I'd have to assume the role of Alexandra Scott again.

The car dealership gave me Noah's home address, believing I was calling from his insurance company to verify his vehicle information. Afterward, I spent half the night staked out across the street from his alleged apartment. It was two a.m. when I spotted the luxury sedan pulling up to the curb. He parked, and I ducked down in my seat, watching as he headed inside. The building didn't have a doorman or much in terms of external security. It wouldn't be difficult to get inside, but Noah's schedule was unpredictable. That might cause a problem, so I waited to make a move.

Over the course of the next two days, I ran a thorough check on the apartment owner. It was rented to an older man who was away on an extended business trip. Noah had sublet after finding an ad on an apartment listing website. I couldn't help but wonder if anything in Noah's life was real. For all intents and purposes, he was just a name on a piece of paper. His apartment and his car weren't even his. Maybe he just didn't exist.

The next day, I phoned Jablonsky and asked for a favor. I gave him everything I'd gotten on the con artist, hoping something would shake loose. I was itching to break into Noah's apartment, but it was risky. I should exhaust all other avenues first, so I returned to the office Noah used to scam Klassi.

Cross's forensic experts failed to find anything inside. No prints. No hairs. No evidence of a crime in progress. But maybe they missed something. Maybe Noah hid a stack of passports under a loose floorboard or in a ceiling tile.

I borrowed a chair from the interior designer across the hall and checked the ceiling tiles. Nothing. The floor tiles and baseboards yielded the same results. There was nothing here. Noah didn't leave anything valuable behind.

"Strike two," I murmured. Deciding it was time to leave, I returned the chair, locked the office, and went to Noah's apartment.

The drive didn't take long. It was close. Maybe that was why he chose that office or this apartment. More than likely, it was because he was able to rent both of them without a formal background check or thorough examination of his phony IDs. I circled the block to make sure his car wasn't in sight. Getting caught would be an amateur mistake, and I was no amateur.

I parked at the side of the building in case I needed to make a fast getaway. Luckily, Noah had never seen my vehicle, so it shouldn't arouse suspicion, but if he spotted me, I'd be screwed. I braided my hair and tucked it into my shirt. Then I grabbed a baseball cap and hoodie that I'd brought in preparation for this particular venture and slipped them on. Next, I put on a pair of large, wraparound sunglasses and a pair of leather gloves. My nine millimeter was holstered at my side, and I slipped my lock picks into my pocket.

In the event the building had security cameras, they wouldn't be able to identify me. Hell, maybe I should have been a criminal. I could make a black leather catsuit look good. Of course, I didn't know any criminals who actually wore catsuits, which meant I could start a trend.

Stepping out of my car, I kept my head down as I went up the front steps of the building. The door opened, and I glanced around. The building wasn't anything special. Just another apartment building in the city. A man was leaning across a counter, staring at his phone which was propped against the wall. My guess was he worked here. He grumbled a hello but never looked up. I returned the greeting and continued to the stairwell.

Noah's apartment was on the third floor. I followed the increasing numbers until I found 312. It was difficult to see clearly with the dark glasses. The hallways weren't brightly lit, but I couldn't risk my anonymity by removing them. Instead, I knocked on the door. I had no idea what I would do if someone answered, but I'd come up with an excuse. Thankfully, no one came to the door. I leaned in closer, casting glances to the left and right before removing my lock picks.

Slowly, I turned the knob and stepped inside. I remained at the door, listening for sounds of water running or a TV, but the apartment was quiet. After flipping the lock, I checked all the rooms. It was a two bedroom. One of the bedrooms had been converted into an office, so I started there.

Noah was smart. He didn't keep much out in the open. He had folders neatly placed on the desk. Each one contained a variety of materials and business cards. One of the folders contained the information he had given me. Another contained the brochures and work details he'd handed to Klassi. I photographed the contents of the other two folders. Each one must correlate to a separate con. He knew to mix things up. If he kept the same identity or used the same phony company too long, someone would wise up, and the authorities would be able to track him.

I searched for a computer or tablet but didn't find one. Since that was a necessary tool of his trade, it had to be with him. That piece of hardware might prove crucial to locating Klassi's stolen millions. Without it, I didn't have much to go on.

After completing a thorough examination of the office, I moved into the bedroom. The dresser contained basic items. Everything was plain. No graphic tees or memorabilia. I hoped to find something of substance, even if it was a souvenir tee from the Grand Canyon or a ratty old high school football jersey. But there was nothing.

"Dammit," I hissed. His clothes were solid colors in common brands found at any department store. I opened the closet. He had a couple of suits, dress shirts, slacks, and sports coats. Everything was off the rack. Noah was bland. Nondescript. He didn't stick out or invest in anything that might identify him. He had no watches or jewelry to speak of.

Next, I went into the bathroom, hoping to find a prescription pill bottle. "You've got to be kidding me." He had all the necessary toiletries and nothing else. No little blue pills or painkillers. Not even a box of condoms. I snorted, realizing there wasn't a chance in hell he'd ever take anyone home with him.

I closed the medicine cabinet and looked down at the wastepaper basket. I found some used dental floss, cotton swabs, tissues, and a dry cleaner receipt with gum stuck to the back. I pocketed the disgusting receipt, figuring we'd at least have Noah's DNA if nothing else. I was just about to leave the bathroom when the floor creaked.

Frantically, I looked around for somewhere to hide. Maybe behind the door or in the shower. My options weren't great, so I stepped behind the shower curtain. The creak sounded again, and I held my breath. I needed an escape plan.

After two minutes of complete silence, I edged to the bathroom door and peered out. I didn't see anyone. I held my breath and stepped into the hallway. The bedroom was empty. I continued to the next door, which was the office. The light was on, and I couldn't remember if I turned it off.

I pressed myself against the wall and strained to hear something over the sound of my beating heart. A part of me wanted to run for the door, but that wasn't the best option. Sneaking out as quietly as I snuck in would be best. Making a break for it would alert Noah that someone was inside.

When I failed to hear any noise coming from inside the office, I peered around the corner. No one was there. Idiot, I berated as I blindly hit the light switch. That meant the sound must have come from the kitchen or the living room. The longer I waited, the greater my chance of getting caught. Still, I couldn't go to the front door if Noah was waiting in the living room. He had to be in the kitchen. If not, I was trapped.

The creak sounded again. This time, it was much louder and a lot closer. I spun, expecting to come face to face with Noah. But no one was there.

And then the loud and annoying sound moved from the far right corner of the living room toward me and past me. I looked up at the ceiling. The creaking was coming from above. I ran a hand down my face and let out a lengthy exhale, my heart rate slowing.

Hurry up, Alex, the voice in my head warned. I moved into the kitchen. Noah must have secrets. His entire life, even his name, was a secret. There had to be something here. I opened the cabinets, checking beneath the drawers and under the sink. Nothing was hidden. I checked the fridge, shaking several containers in the hopes of discovering something with a false bottom. I looked in the freezer. Ice trays were commonly used to hide things, but he didn't have any. That would be too easy.

Getting frustrated, I opened the microwave. Also empty. My focus turned to the pantry, but he didn't have much. No canisters of sugar or flour. The usual suspects were out. There must be something here. Something to find. How could someone with ten million dollars stashed away keep it entirely secret?

My eyes fell on the stove. Since Noah didn't have much in the way of foodstuffs or cookware, I doubted he used the oven often. I checked inside. Nothing. Cursing, I slammed the door, hearing the rattle of the drawer beneath. Pulling it open, I found a couple of lids.

I'm not sure what possessed me to remove the drawer. It might have been sheer determination to find something. Taped to the bottom was an envelope. Carefully, I pried it free and opened it. Inside was a Wyoming driver's license, matching passport, and five hundred dollars in twenties. The name didn't match any I was aware of, but the photo was Noah.

For the briefest moment, I thought about taking the envelope with me, but instead, I photographed the documents and flipped through the cash again. It looked real. Still, five hundred dollars wasn't much. He couldn't get too far on that. The ten million must have been hidden in an account he could access from anywhere.

The details Don Klassi gave me on the wire transfer couldn't be traced. He daisy-chained the transfer from bank to bank, all from countries with closed banking policies, ensuring the U.S. government couldn't get a look at it without good reason, and those reasons were limited to matters of national security, not some asshole getting duped by a con artist. With any luck, this new ID would lead to something. It was the only thing I found.

Before giving up entirely, I searched the living room. The furniture was old and worn. There were dried up tortilla chips in the couch cushions, along with lint, cookie crumbs, and random stains that I didn't want to think too hard about.

Well, Noah, your secrets remain secret, I thought. My gaze fell on the front door. I had a new problem, figuring out a way to relock the deadbolt. Noah was clearly persnickety when it came to his privacy. I doubted he'd ever leave the deadbolt unlocked, and if he found it that way, he'd know someone had been here.

I went back into his office in search of tape. Hopefully, the roll of clear tape would be strong enough. After hooking a piece around the lever and folding it over so it wouldn't stick to the door, I let myself out of the apartment, closed the door, and tugged on the tape. The lock slid into place, and I pulled the rest of the tape free from the door. With any luck, it didn't leave sticky residue behind.

I had gone down three steps when I heard someone coming up the stairs. Noah. Shit. I turned around just as he rounded the corner and headed up the next flight. As casually as possible, I jogged up the steps as if I'd been on my way all along. Two flights up, I stopped and waited. He wasn't following, not that he had any reason to.

Someone coughed, and I nearly jumped out of my skin. A man watched me from his doorway. I was glad my appearance was obscured by the glasses, cap, and hood.

"Yo," I said, "I'm looking for Dino's place. I don't remember if he said he lived on four or five. You know him?" I adopted a tough, punk voice, hoping the guy would think I was just some stupid kid.

"You have the wrong floor. I suggest you go."

"Yeah, no problem, pops." I shot him the peace sign and went down the steps.

I kept moving, not turning or stopping. I didn't take another breath until I was outside and rounding the corner. My car was inches away, but I stopped dead in my tracks. The red Pontiac blew past me and was gone by the time I thought to look at the plate. This was no coincidence.

EIGHTEEN

Throwing my car into drive, I floored it. The bastard with the knife wouldn't escape again. He blew through a red light and took a sharp left. I laid into my horn, hoping to stop oncoming traffic as I barreled after him.

My heart leapt into my throat, and I slammed on my brakes. My tires screeched. The acrid smell of burnt rubber filled the air, and my back wheels skidded and jumped against the asphalt.

The woman yanked her young child back onto the sidewalk. She was white as a sheet, but they were okay. Several people yelled profanities and made obscene gestures. Waving them off, I hit the gas. After the extreme braking, my engine was sluggish. It bumped and protested before smoothing out and accelerating. But I didn't take my eyes off the red car.

The driver took a ramp, abandoning the surface streets for the expressway. Dammit. I was seconds away from losing him. By the time I made it to the ramp, he had already merged into traffic. I was stuck waiting for an opening.

Aggravated, I pounded on the steering wheel. I had him. I fucking had him. Grabbing my phone, I dialed Jablonsky.

"I need eyes on the expressway. Westbound," I gave him the nearest exit and mile marker. "The bastard with the knife just made a reappearance."

"Are you sure?"

"Mostly."

"Hang on. I'll see if the police or highway patrol has anyone close." Jablonsky put me on hold, and while I waited, I merged with traffic and darted from lane to lane, searching for signs of the red jalopy. My phone beeped, notifying me of an incoming call, and I looked at the display. It was Noah.

Did he know? Was I caught? It was Friday. He was supposed to be busy. He shouldn't be calling. What if he had surveillance equipment or an alarm system in his apartment? Did I overlook it? Maybe I accidentally tripped it, and he somehow realized it was me.

"No one's near your location, but they have units positioned ten miles away. They'll keep an eye out," Mark said. "Are you sure it's him?"

"He was outside Noah's apartment." My phone beeped again. "He must have followed me. I don't know how, but he did." I thought through the commonalities. "I went to the office Noah rented before the apartment. That's the second time I've been there, and both times this asshole popped up. There might be a connection. Let me call you back."

Talking while zipping in and out of traffic is not recommended, so I stuck with the lane I was in and hit answer. "Hello?" It took every ounce of training to keep my voice neutral and calm.

"Hi. This is Noah Ripley."

"Hey, Noah." I tried to sound friendly. He doesn't know, I told myself. "I was about to call you."

"Really?"

"Yes, someone needs to explain this entire unbacked system of currency to me. I understand the logistics, but I have no idea how it works."

He laughed. "Sure, I'll explain that if you can explain how our monetary system works. And don't tell me it's backed by gold bars kept at Fort Knox because I'm nearly positive that isn't true." He didn't give me time to speak before he said, "I'm just finishing up for the night and wondered if I could drop by the gallery. You did promise me a preview of the artist's upcoming show, and I wouldn't mind having someone to eat with, if you haven't eaten yet."

"Not yet." I had to think quickly. "Actually, I just stepped out to run an errand and order some dinner. It shouldn't take long. Why don't you join me for takeout? It won't be fancy, but I could use the company. Although, I'm a bit of a mess. I've been painting most of the day."

"I'd love to see it."

"It's not ready to be seen," I said, regretting my lie.

"I'm sure it's magnificent. How does seven sound?"

"Yeah, okay."

"I'll see you then."

I bit my lip and continued a few more miles on the expressway, searching for the car. The exits were frequent. When I made it to the waiting patrol car, I knew I lost the bastard. He must have exited somewhere else. I took the next exit and backtracked on the surface streets. I didn't spot his car. He could be anywhere.

Forced to give up my hunt now that I had other plans for the night, I headed for the gallery. A million thoughts went through my mind. The bastard was outside Noah's. Were they working together? Is that why Noah called? He wanted me distracted so his accomplice could escape. Hell, maybe the unsub redirected to the gallery to finish what he started in the alley.

Unsure if I was compromised, I dialed a number for a delivery joint and placed an order for some pizza. It was best to keep up appearances until the last possible minute. It might just confuse my assailant or foster doubt in Noah's mind. But I wasn't an idiot either. I wasn't walking into an ambush unprepared. I ditched my car a few blocks away, tossing the hoodie, cap, and sunglasses into the trunk. I unzipped my jacket and rested my hand against the butt of my nine millimeter. There would be no digging for a weapon tonight.

Keeping my cover intact was tantamount to this investigation, but now I was regretting it. The man in the red car was dangerous. I didn't know who he was, just that he was somehow linked to Don Klassi and possibly the grifter. Klassi insisted he didn't know anything about this guy. And I didn't have any definitive proof to the contrary, but I knew it couldn't be a coincidence. I didn't like that this asshole had picked up my trail on three separate occasions. I didn't even notice I was being followed. How the hell did he tail me without me noticing?

A moment later, Jablonsky called back to tell me highway patrol didn't spot the red car. No kidding.

"Just be careful," Mark warned. "I don't like the idea of you meeting the con man alone."

"I'll be okay, but since you're concerned, do me a favor." I gave him Noah's newest identity to run.

"I'll see what I can dig up, and in the meantime, I'll try to locate your unsub." He would coordinate with local law enforcement to see if they could track the car. I still didn't get a plate, which was entirely my fault. The car was heading straight for me, and I was caught like a deer in headlights. I never froze before, but the sight of the car caught me by surprise.

"Dammit," I hissed. "I should have paid more attention."

"You do what you can, Alex. I'll be in touch." Mark disconnected.

No one jumped me as I walked to the gallery. With a couple hours left until sunset, it would have been stupid to try something in broad daylight. And the only thing I knew about the unsub was he wasn't stupid.

Taking a seat behind the computer, I ran a quick search, hoping to find something. A knock sounded at the door, and I closed the browser window and cleared my internet history. I rushed to the front. Thankfully, it was the pizza guy. I paid him, taking the box and six-pack of beer into the studio. I laid them out on the table beside some art supplies and looked around. I said I'd been painting all day, so I had to do something to make it look real.

I found an already started canvas, propped it up on an easel, and grabbed a palette, squirting paints in a circle on the wood. This was ridiculous. I wasn't an artist. Luckily, this was more of a fancy paint-by-number. Cross had obtained some scrapped canvases through unknown means. I just needed to make it look like they were mine.

Noah would notice if the paint wasn't fresh and drying. He would also expect a certain amount of mess. I'd been in enough art studios to know what the clutter should look like. A working palette, a cup of brushes, some cleaner, a few rags, and possibly a dirty smock. I spread out the rest of my materials, dabbing paint on the canvas.

Since I still didn't know how the unsub fit into any of this, I had to be careful. The best way to do that was by maintaining appearances, and that had to start right now. Alex Parker might be hot on the trail of a grifter and in the midst of tracking a violent offender, but Alexandra Scott had a completely different set of concerns.

When enough of the painting glistened with fresh paint, I smeared some of the paint onto the smock and put it on over my dress shirt. I returned to the front desk and tucked my weapon into the top drawer. My purse went into the bottom locked drawer, just in case Noah did some snooping when I wasn't paying attention.

For a moment, I wondered if he was on his way here to confront me about breaking into his apartment or to silence me for discovering his secrets. Although nothing indicated he was violent, he had ten million reasons to get rid of me. And he might be pals with someone who already tried once.

I was spinning. My mind scattered. My focus shot. However, I didn't try to rein it in or compartmentalize. Alexandra Scott would be just as fragmented. Instead, I blew out a few calming breaths and planned my next move.

Noah arrived a few minutes later. He wore a suit with no tie, as if he'd come straight from work. He had a grocery bag in his hand.

"Is anyone here?" he called, stepping into the lobby.

"Only me." I forced my expression to remain neutral, even though my hand lingered inside the top drawer. "You just missed the artist for next week's showing. He dropped by to add a few new pieces to the collection."

"That's good, right?"

"I guess. Let me lock up, so we won't be disturbed." I tucked the gun behind my back and moved past him, carefully tilting my head to see if he was armed. I didn't spot any bulges, suspicious or otherwise. "How are you?"

"I'm okay. Busy day at work. You aren't the only one who doesn't understand cryptocurrencies. I actually had to give a presentation to our new advisors on how coin works and the steps we take to exchange it for cash." He placed the grocery bag on my desk, and I watched him take out a box of cookies and a pint of ice cream. "I brought dessert."

"You know, don't you?" I let the accusation hang in the air while I analyzed his expression, but he looked genuinely confused. "I have a fridge in the back. You brought ice cream as an excuse to see my work."

"I didn't know you had a fridge," he chuckled, "but I am curious. Ever since you said you had a studio, I wanted to see your art. What's your specialty?"

"The kind that isn't very good and doesn't sell."

He smirked. "Give it time."

"Yeah, well, you know the saying about starving artists." I pointed down the hall, waiting for him to check out the studio so I could stow my gun. "That's part of what made Conrad so appealing. He said he believed in my work, and he wanted to give me a lifestyle that allowed me to create without worrying about anything else." I laughed bitterly. "I was so naïve and stupid. Life isn't a fairy tale."

Noah entered the room just ahead of me. He looked around, taking in every aspect. It looked real, just like the cover story he'd given me. I took the bag from him and placed the ice cream in the mini-fridge.

"Wow, that's amazing." He stood in front of the canvas. "I like the color balance and composition."

"It's rather abstract. I'm not really painting anything."

"Yes, you are." He looked straight at me. "You're painting emotions."

That was a good line, as if he understood my art and what I was going through. It was the kind of line that made him sound deep and thoughtful. "Wow, you get it," I said, even though I couldn't help but think he was full of crap. "No one's ever gotten it before, except Conrad."

"You loved him, didn't you?"

"Of course, I did. He's my husband. I knew who he was and what he was like, what he wanted, but I thought it'd be different. That he would be different with me, but that didn't last."

Noah stepped closer and placed a comforting hand on my shoulder. "I'm sorry."

As if brushing the thought away, I shrugged away from him. "Are you hungry?" I didn't stand on ceremony and instead went to the pizza box. I yanked a piece of paper towel off a nearby roll and removed a slice. I took a seat on one of the various stools in the room and nibbled on the end.

He followed suit, taking a seat and carefully balancing his paper towel plate on his lap while reaching for the six-pack. After taking a slug of beer, he put the bottle down on the table. "Not to be indelicate, but have you given any more thought to my suggestion?"

"I have. Lots." I took another bite, waiting until I swallowed before speaking again. "I did some research online. I never knew I could just pay and have my money transferred into coin."

"It's amazing what you find on the internet."

"I thought the internet was just for shopping and porn." I finished my slice and wiped my hands on the paper towel. "What I don't understand is how Conrad won't be able to trace the transfer of funds. From what I've seen, exchanging one currency for another requires filling out the usual billing forms. He'll know. He'll find out. I don't think this will work."

Noah thought for a moment, helping himself to a second slice in the process. "There are ways around it. You could go through a firm instead of doing it yourself."

"Yes, but it's the same dilemma." I shook my head. "I think this is just a cosmic sign that I shouldn't do it." I looked sadly around the studio. "I hate to give this up, but I guess I should be thankful I had six years to create and manage. It was a dream come true, but it's time I wake up and accept reality."

Noah didn't say anything. We ate in silence. When we

were finished, he stood. "May I see upstairs?"

"Oh," I said, as if remembering why he was here, "right. I promised you a tour." I led the way past the main gallery and to a back staircase. Once we went up the steps, I flipped on the lights. Most of the art was covered in sheets. I removed a few. "This is what's going to be shown next week. I think everything's set. We have invitations and flyers going out. Everyone who's on the list will be notified. I booked the caterers, finalized the menu, found a bartender, ordered the liquor," I ticked the items off as I went, "and rearranged a few of the pieces."

"That's a lot of work. What do you get paid?"

I stared at him. "Nothing."

Noah frowned. "It just doesn't seem fair." He lifted one of the sheets, studying the art. "This reminds me of something."

"Street art," I suggested. "The artist emerged on the scene with his graffiti, but he found an agent and went legit. Crazy how that works for some people."

"Y'know, you shouldn't have to give up. Let me make a few calls."

I gave him a bewildered look. "What are you talking about?"

"Trust me." He headed for the stairs with his phone pressed against his ear.

I followed behind, retaking my seat behind the desk in the lobby. In the event he was calling for reinforcements, I didn't want to be too far from my nine millimeter. Instead, he asked a few questions about a recent transaction R&P had authorized. I listened, knowing that he was either talking to an accomplice or to himself. It wasn't hard to fake a phone call. I'd done it on occasion.

"So it's just sitting there? What does Mr. Rappaport want to do with it?" After a long pause, he said, "I see. Okay. I might have a solution. I'll let you know." He hung up and smiled.

"What?" I returned his grin as if it were infectious, and I wanted to be let in on the joke.

He held up a finger and went back to the studio. A moment later, he returned with the remaining beers and the dessert he brought. He pulled out a spoon, opened the container of cookies and the pint of ice cream, and scooped the ice cream between two cookies, making a sandwich. He held it out, offering it to me, and I took it.

I licked the excess from around the edge. "You just made my night, Mr. Ripley."

"Noah," he corrected automatically, "and you haven't seen anything yet." He pulled a chair closer and perched on the edge. While he scooped more ice cream onto another cookie, he said, "You need a middleman."

"I am a middleman. Middlewoman." But that didn't sound right. "Whatever."

"Yes, you are, but you need someone who can do the same for you. You act like a broker, selling off art in these showings and transferring money from the buyer to the painter. You need that kind of separation."

"I'm not ready to sell my paintings."

"Not your paintings, the funds we talked about. If you give someone else the cash, Conrad will never be able to find it. It'll be untraceable. Then your middleman would take the cash, exchange it for cryptocurrency, and give you the coin. You'd be in the clear."

I frowned. "Except that's a lot of cash to withdraw. If I had that much cash, why would I need cryptocurrency?"

"That's a good point." Noah thought for a moment. "And you're certain you can't convince Conrad or his accountants that they need to pay the artist?"

"I might be able to. I'm not sure."

"Well, if you can, then you'll have the checks from the buyers. You could sign them over to someone else." Noah nodded a few times. "It would be just as good as cash. It could work."

I looked at him. "You're offering to be my middleman?"

"It's just a thought."

"But you said you could get in trouble for even suggesting this."

"That was before." He placed his hand over mine. "We just authorized a transfer for one of our best clients, but at the last minute, he decided he didn't want to do it. Exchanges like that can't be undone, but since he's such a valued customer, my boss returned his money and kept the cryptocurrency. It's only half a million, but it's the best I can do."

"That would be amazing."

"Are you sure?" he sounded hesitant now.

"No," I took a breath, "are you?"

He chuckled. "Not really, but I don't want you to lose this place."

"I'll lose it anyway. It's Conrad's," I reminded him. "But that would be enough to rent a studio somewhere and an apartment, at least for a while."

"Quite a while." He took a big bite of his ice cream sandwich. "What do you say, Alex? I'm game if you are."

I waited a long moment, carefully mulling over the possible ramifications. "You're sure we won't get caught? Conrad already has it out for me, but I don't want you to lose your job. You've been so nice. Not many people even bothered returning my calls or answering my e-mails. I just don't want this to bite you in the ass."

"We regret the things we don't do more than the things we do. I want to help in any way I can. I'll be okay. Actually, my boss will be thrilled to unload the coin we have. What do you say?"

"Can I think about it?"

"Sure," he leaned back, "but you need to decide before the gallery showing and before my boss unloads the coin somewhere else."

NINETEEN

"He wants you," Mark said. "Honestly, he sounds pretty desperate for a payday."

"The greedy get greedier," I remarked.

Jablonsky chewed on his bottom lip. "For a man that just made ten million dollars, what's another half a million really worth? He shouldn't be this pushy. It doesn't make sense."

"It might not be about the money. It could be the game. The challenge. The rush."

Mark rolled his eyes. "You think he's some kind of adrenaline junkie who enjoys flipping the bird at the aristocracy?"

"I don't know what his motivation is. It'd be easier to figure that out if we knew who Noah really was." I jerked my chin at the files laid out on the coffee table. "Based on what I found inside his apartment, he's running at least four con jobs. It blows my mind how he can keep the facts straight."

"All of his IDs are for a Noah R. That probably helps cut down on some of the confusion, but I hear you."

"Except the hidden ID. That was for Dale Billings. Any hits on that name?"

"He has no financial history. We found a Wyoming birth certificate and not much else. He doesn't own a car or a house or a cell phone. He's never paid a utility bill. It looks like another fictitious persona."

"See what else you can dig up on Billings. That might be his real identity." I sighed. "Did you find anything on the unsub?"

"That's what you're calling the asshole now? I thought you were going with dickhead."

"Yes, but since that describes so many, it might get confusing." I knew Mark well enough to know he was stalling.

"Traffic cams in the area spotted the car exiting the expressway. We have a partial plate, Charlie Echo Niner Whiskey."

"Are those the first four? Last four?"

"Something in the middle," he said. "We think it's registered out of state."

"Great. What state?"

"We don't know." He removed the phone from his pocket and tapped on the screen a few times before passing it to me. "That's all we got."

"Damn." The plate was covered in a thick layer of mud. "Any idea where he came from or where he went?"

"I was hoping you could tell me. Have you figured out if he followed you?"

That was the question I'd been asking myself. Since the unsub initially found me at Cross Security, it wasn't beyond the realm of possibility to assume he followed me from the office to Noah's apartment. But I didn't spot the car, and that car stood out. "I don't think so."

"He wasn't parked or waiting when you arrived at Noah's. You said Klassi recognized the vehicle. Have you tried asking him about it again?"

"He says he doesn't know anything, and he won't tell me about his acquaintances. I have people checking, but I can't force Don to cooperate."

"You could refuse to work his case."

"Even if I did, Cross would find someone else to do it, and Klassi threatened to take down Martin if I don't behave."

"I doubt he has dirt on Marty."

"It seems like a stretch, but I don't want to chance it. Plus, the best way to ID the unsub is to work the case."

"True, but he was outside Noah's. And he might have been surveilling the office space Noah rented the first time he picked up your trail. It stands to reason they might also have a connection."

"They can't be working together, or Noah wouldn't continue the con."

"Yeah, well, victim doesn't make a lot of sense. If the unsub had a ton of money, he wouldn't drive a shitty car."

"Unless he had to sell everything after Noah stole his fortune."

"Okay, I'll buy that. But why attack you? Sun Tzu, the enemy of my enemy." Mark raised his brow in challenge. "You and the unsub should be on the same side. And when he cornered you in the alley, you hadn't even met Noah or confronted him. So it's not like he made a mistake. He waited for you, Alex, and it had nothing to do with Noah. My money's on a connection to good ol' Donnie boy. The unsub was watching him too, outside that bar and outside Klassi's apartment. We need to figure this out fast," Mark warned. "You don't need any surprises."

"Tell me about it." My eyes went to the doorway. Normally, I wouldn't have invited Mark to Cross Security to discuss these matters, but a part of me wanted to push Cross's buttons. The other part wanted to make it clear that I didn't need Lucien or this job, and Mark was the best way to do it.

"Did you handle the situation with Cross?"

"I don't know. Cross says he hoped to convince Martin to sign with Cross Security and from there convince him to work on developing body armor."

Mark snorted. "Except you and I both know Marty avoids projects that have military applications. He'd never agree to that. And unlike some people, he's smart enough not to get in bed with Lucien Cross."

I ignored the comment. "Yeah, well, I'm just waiting for Cross to decide what he's going to do."

"About what?"

"He hired me for access to Martin, but now he realizes it's a handicap. He'd fire me if he wasn't afraid that would make Martin even less apt to work with him."

"Well, good. Lucien finally fucked himself. It's about time." He shrugged into his jacket. "Just make sure he doesn't fuck you in the process."

*   *   *

I rolled over and grabbed the ringing phone. "Hello?" I mumbled. No one in their right mind would call this early on a Saturday.

"Alex, hey," Noah said, "I'm glad I caught you."

"What's up?"

"I was just wondering if we could meet for breakfast."

"When and where?"

"Your hotel."

Shit. I climbed out of bed, ignoring the questioning look Martin was giving me. "Yeah, um...I have a confession to make." I pulled on a pair of jeans and a t-shirt. "You woke me up."

Noah didn't speak for a moment. "I'm sorry. I'm used to keeping business hours. I wasn't thinking."

"No, no, it's fine." I grabbed a rolling suitcase from the hall closet and emptied one of my drawers into it. "I just need some time. Can I call you back?"

"Sure, no problem."

"Thanks, Noah. Bye." I disconnected, scrambling to get packed. I should have planned this out. I should have realized he might have wanted to see the hotel. Going into the bathroom, I hurried to get ready, skipping the shower. I was tossing my toiletries into a bag when Martin appeared in the doorway.

"Where are you going?"

"A hotel."

The question formed on his lips, but I went around him before he could ask. I made sure there weren't any luggage tags or identifying marks on the suitcase. Digging through my purse, I found the engagement ring and wedding band

and slipped them on.

"You're supposed to take off your wedding ring when you go to a hotel, not the other way around," Martin remarked.

"No wonder I haven't been able to lure a man back to my room." I grabbed my gun, checked the safety, and tossed it into my purse. "I'll see you later." I gave him a quick kiss and headed for the door.

"Are you coming back?"

"Hopefully." I pulled the door closed behind me.

When I arrived at the hotel, I kept my head on a swivel. Cross had taken precautions and made sure I had a backdated reservation just in case. However, stopping at the front desk to pick up the key and check in would tip off the scammer that he was getting played. Luckily, I didn't spot Noah or the red car.

Dragging my bag behind me, I went to my room. It was a standard hotel room. Nothing special about it. I shoved some of my clothing into the drawers and hung a few items in the closet. I left some things in the suitcase and left it open on the luggage stand.

I entered the bathroom, turned the water to hot, and let the shower run while I placed my toiletries on the vanity and along the ledge. I unwrapped a few of the plastic cups, made a pot of coffee, tossed some tissues and wrappers into the trash can, and turned off the water. I wiped the inside of the shower curtain with a towel, so it would appear used and hung it on the back of the door.

Checking the time, I called Noah back and gave him my room number. I looked around, realizing the bed was pristine. I pulled down the covers, tossed one of the pillows on the floor, and rolled around on the sheets. Now, I was ready for company.

While I waited for him to arrive, I read the room service menu, familiarizing myself with the options. Was it weird he wanted to meet for breakfast? He probably wanted an answer, and I couldn't drag my feet much longer. If I kept this up, he'd find another mark. I had to commit. I glanced down at the ring on my finger. Talk about commitment.

A knock sounded at the door. It was showtime. "You

always walk around with grocery bags?"

Noah laughed. "Well, I didn't know what you might like for breakfast, so I bought a little bit of everything."

"I figured we'd get room service."

"Aren't you tired of it by now?"

"You know me so well."

He went to the table and put down the bag, pulling out paper plates, an assortment of bakery items, and a container of fresh fruit. "Do you have coffee?" he asked.

"Is the Pope Catholic?" I filled two cups and carried them to the table. "Seriously, Noah, what's going on?"

He looked a little embarrassed. "Is it wrong to say I enjoy your company?"

That was unexpected. I didn't think he planned to play the con this way, but he didn't have the same timeframe he had with Don Klassi, particularly when Alexandra Scott's money would be in motion in less than a week. "I like hanging out with you too. It's nice to have someone to talk to."

"My life's been work for so long. It's not often I meet someone like you."

"Like me?" I asked.

"Someone willing to fight for what they want. My clients are great, but they get everything so easily. And you're about to lose everything. It's refreshing to see someone face an actual struggle with such grace and strength."

"Conrad didn't leave me much choice." I rested my chin in my hands. "I don't know what I should do. Most of the time, I'm just angry. Why should he get everything? Didn't our life together mean anything? But then I think about the mistakes I made, knowing how many times he'd been married before, aware he was a cheater." I stared into my cup. "He actually cheated on his last wife with me, and now, he's cheating on me with whoever will come next. I should have known. It's stupid to think someone will change."

"You wanted to see the best in him." Noah reached for a muffin.

"And other times," I smiled at a memory, "he was so sweet. He encouraged my art. He bought the gallery and those paintings because they made me happy. I still love that man, but I don't know what happened to him. He's been so cold. So distant. He hates me now, and I don't know why." I met Noah's eyes. "If I take his money, he'll always hate me. We'll never be able to go back."

"Do you think that's even possible?"

I licked my lips. "No, but I wish it was." I looked up. "I have to do this. If I don't, he'll toss me aside. I found out from an acquaintance that his first ex-wife just got evicted from her home because she couldn't pay her rent. He ruined her life. She was an educated woman, but she never entered the job market. She never had a career, and when he dumped her, she could only find menial jobs. When the divorce settlement ran out, she couldn't make ends meet. I don't want the same thing to happen to me."

Noah reached for my hand and gave it a squeeze. "I won't let that happen."

"Okay, I'll do it. No turning back now."

He was professional enough to keep the elated smile off his face, but I saw the satisfaction in his eyes. He thought he tricked me. He thought he'd just hooked another significant payday. The plans were already in motion. Too bad he didn't' realize I had him by the short and curlies.

TWENTY

Everything was set. Noah agreed to a small transfer, so I could test the waters and make sure Conrad wouldn't catch on. Assuming it went smoothly, which I was sure it would, Noah and I would meet tomorrow, and I'd transfer half a million to him. We never met at his office. He didn't want anyone to see what was happening just in case Conrad tracked the transfer or came looking for the culprit. Instead, we did the deed in my hotel room.

To maintain appearances, Cross arranged an actual showing at the gallery, just in case Noah dropped by uninvited. It was catered with fifty guests. I didn't know who any of the people were, but it didn't matter. No one actually tried to buy a painting. They just ate the food, drank their cocktails, and called it a night. The number of cars outside ensured everyone knew there was a party. I had to hand it to my boss; he actually did a few things right.

"Do you need anything else?" Cross asked as the caterers left.

"Were you able to trace the funds once they went into Noah's account?"

"My people are on it. We'll get him."

"Is that a no?"

Cross gave me an icy look. "It's a not yet. It will be fine. I know what I'm doing."

Earlier, I authorized a transfer of $5000 into Noah's private numbered account. Supposedly, Alexandra quoted her husband the excess amount as an expense for the gallery showing. Noah then converted the dollars into coin and gave me a zip drive with the cryptocurrency. I checked it immediately, then passed the USB off to the experts at Cross Security. The cryptocurrency was the same type of worthless coin Noah had given to Klassi. The same worthless coin Klassi desperately wanted. I still didn't know what his obsession was, but I'd find out soon enough.

We were scheduled to complete the final transaction tomorrow afternoon, except there would be no final transaction. I just had to string Noah along until Cross received the information he needed to recover Don Klassi's millions.

"Fine, but if Noah outsmarts you, it's not my fault. And it better not come out of my paycheck."

Cross gave me a look. "I have no intention of losing any money on this venture."

"That makes one of us."

He pressed his lips together. "When are you supposed to make the next exchange?"

"Tomorrow afternoon. He's going to meet me at the gallery. I should have collected the checks by then."

"No office?"

"No. I imagine he couldn't find a new one on such short notice. But I'll find some way to delay him."

"You better. We don't have half a million, so be prepared for anything."

"Yes, sir."

Things were finally falling into place. Cross had a surefire and probably illegal way of tracking the transferred funds. We'd find out where they went. I just wasn't certain it would lead to Klassi's money. Something about the situation felt wrong. Don's unwillingness to explain why he wouldn't go to the authorities didn't ease my suspicions. He must have done some shady dealings, possibly with the unsub who hated my involvement and wanted it put to an end.

"What if he has as many accounts as he does aliases?" I asked.

"That's also a possibility." Cross studied me. "Are you sure you haven't tipped him off? You seem nervous."

"I don't think so. Still, we can't discount the possibility that the driver of the red car is somehow connected to the grifter."

"I'll put someone on Noah's apartment. If he tries to skip town, I'll make sure we're there to stop him. And if the car comes back again, we'll follow it."

"Thanks."

That night, I went home feeling antsy. The annoying twinge in the back of my mind hadn't stopped since the party at the gallery. Perhaps my subconscious was protesting my alliance with Cross. I didn't know exactly what was bothering me, but I couldn't get comfortable.

I spent a few hours prowling the apartment like a jungle cat. Martin was working late. He had several back-to-back teleconferences, so he wasn't around to distract me. The situation with Klassi stunk to high heaven, but it didn't matter. By this time tomorrow, it would be over. Klassi would get his money back, minus Cross's cut, and I would insist that Don tell me everything he knows about the asshole with the knife. I would have the leverage needed to force the answers out of him. This time, I wasn't taking no for an answer.

When Martin came home, he found me wearing my dress from the gallery. The pins were still in my hair. "You look beautiful. Is this for me?"

"Sure, handsome." I crumpled into his arms. "Run away with me."

He smirked, bending down for a kiss. "Rough night?"

"I don't know."

Carefully, he pulled the pins from my hair, letting the tendrils fall in messy curls. He ran his fingers through it, gently so as not to tug on any knots. "Why are you all dressed up?"

"Cocktail party."

"Without me?" His fingertips traced the straps of my dress. "You know I love a good cocktail party."

"Cross was there."

"So it was a rough night." He brushed his thumb along my cheek and kissed me long and slow. "Let me see if I can make it better."

*   *   *

I shot up in bed. My heart raced, and my breath came in ragged gasps. Martin reached for me. The gentle brush of his fingers against my bare skin made me jump.

"Sweetheart, what is it?"

I recalled the nightmare. "My car exploded."

"What?" He sat up.

I shook my head. "In my dream." I took a deep breath. So much for a peaceful night's sleep. "I got into my car, turned the key, and ka-boom." My skin felt insanely hot, as if I actually had been inside the inferno. I kicked off the covers, wiping at the beads of sweat that dripped down my lower back.

He gathered my hair, lifting the damp locks off my neck and wrapping the long brown strands around his hand a few times. He blew gently against my overheated skin, making me shiver.

"Stop that," I hissed, turning to face him.

"We need to talk."

"It's five a.m. And those are the four worst words anyone can ever say."

"Says who?" Martin asked.

"You."

He thought for a moment. "Regardless, I want to know what's going on with you."

"You didn't seem to care a few hours ago."

"I did. I still do." His green eyes stared into my soul. "I will always care about you. Nothing will ever change that." He swallowed. "You've been having a lot of nightmares again. That means something's wrong, and you're afraid to talk to me about it."

I tugged my hair free from his grip and tied it in a messy knot. "Nothing's wrong. Can I please go back to sleep?"

I flipped my pillow over and pressed my cheek into the first cool spot I found. My thoughts went to car bombings and one of my early private sector cases. I'd been double-crossed by a friend. Mark's warning about Cross reverberated in my mind. Could I trust my boss? What about the rest of his employees? Kellan betrayed me. And yet, I had to put my trust in them in order to work Klassi's case. What if somebody sold me out? Nothing ever turned up concerning the red car or its driver, but the possibilities were endless.

"I don't know what's wrong. I just know something is," I admitted. "I haven't been myself since Stuart Gifford died in front of me, but I don't think it's about that."

Martin sighed, his warm breath caressing my skin. "Are you scared?"

"Of what?" I turned around to face him.

"Us." He struggled to figure out a better way to phrase it. "That Friday, when you came to my office, you were terrified. I could see the trajectory of your thoughts. I knew where your mind was."

"I don't want to lose you. But more than that, I don't want you to die."

"I know. Me too."

"Well, you are rather fond of yourself."

"You know what I mean." His expression sobered. "Someone attacked you. It's not the first time, and I'm not naïve enough to think it'll be the last. I thought you would have...I don't know."

"Found the guy? Kicked his ass? Had him arrested?"

"All of the above." Martin settled down on the pillow beside me. "Are there any leads?"

"We have a partial out of state plate. Mark's expanded the search, but he thinks the plates were stolen or expired. This bastard connects to Don Klassi's case, but we don't know how. He could be working with the grifter, or he could be connected to Don."

Martin squinted. "What can I do?"

"The same as me. Nothing."

"But it bothers you that this prick is out there."

"Yeah, but what am I supposed to do? Freak out and hide away from the world?" Martin didn't answer immediately, so I continued. "Been there, done that. Honestly, that scares me more than whatever asshole is hiding in the shadows." I saw the look that came over him. "You want me to hide."

"That's not it. I don't want you to be afraid." He licked his lips. "Selfishly, I hoped you'd take a break. Too many close calls in a short amount of time is worrisome. The last time that happened, things didn't end well for us."

"It's different this time. The situation is different. I'm different. Please believe that."

He outlined my ear with his pointer finger. "Just don't disappear on me or push me away again. My heart can't take it, Alex. And I see the writing on the wall. The way you're obsessing over this case. The way you dash out of here. The late nights. This is how it always starts."

"You're wrong. I'm just busy. I'm not hiding." I stroked his jaw. "I promise I won't leave you."

He grabbed my hand, his thumb tracing the diamond engagement ring that I forgot to take off. "Why are you still wearing this?"

"It's Cross's stupid ring. I couldn't get it off."

Martin flicked on the light in order to see it better. "Mine's bigger."

"Size doesn't matter."

"Trust me, Alex. Size matters. The width, the height, the weight."

The double entendre was not lost on me. "You sound sure of yourself."

"I've been around. I hear things."

"Women aren't obsessed with size."

"Less fortunate women would disagree." Since I dismissed his attempt at a serious conversation, he was ready to play. He gave the ring a dismissive look. "Since size doesn't matter to you, what does?"

"Taste." I crinkled my nose playfully. "Personal preference."

He grinned mischievously, his green eyes teasing me. "I

have exquisite taste. Some might even say I'm downright delicious. And I damn well better be your personal preference." He held my hand gently in his. "Can I try to take it off?"

I nodded, and he took my finger between his lips, working his tongue around the band before latching his teeth around the metal and gently tugging the ring past my knuckle. He released my finger from his mouth and slid the ring the rest of the way off. He wiped it on his shirt and held the diamond up to the light for a more careful examination.

"Like I said, mine's bigger. The clarity and cut are better. And the color too." For the briefest moment, he considered pulling my engagement ring out of the dresser drawer but decided against it.

When we broke up, I gave him back his ring. But Martin knew the truth; I wasn't ready. We weren't ready. Proposing again, especially now, would do nothing more than prove he feared I'd pull another vanishing act. He said he trusted me, but I knew he had doubts. It was rare that people changed, but Martin had faith in me. Or so he said.

Normally, he'd try to tighten the reins, which would cause me to freak and pull away even harder. But I'd grown. I wasn't going to disappear, regardless of how hairy a case got.

"Here," he held out Cross's ring, "just don't drop it. It's so small that you'll never be able to find it."

"I don't call two carats small."

"And you said size didn't matter. Ha."

We stared at each other for a long time. Neither of us could go back to sleep. My mind was turning around Noah and ways of keeping him at bay until Cross tracked his account information. And Martin was trying to figure out what I was thinking. At six a.m., he shut off the alarm.

"Get dressed," he said. "I want to show you something."

I took a quick shower and threw on something I could wear to meet Noah later. I didn't know what Martin wanted to show me, but since he had to be at work by eight, we didn't have a lot of time.

His driver picked us up outside the building, and Martin

kept me distracted so I wouldn't pay too much attention to where we were going. When the car turned onto the private road, I knew where we were. My posture stiffened. Marcal drove the car into the garage and parked in the usual spot at the end of the row.

"We won't be long," Martin said. His expression was tight. He was afraid I would bolt or breakdown. To be honest, so was I. "Come inside. I need to grab something upstairs."

I stepped out of the car and into the familiar surroundings. It felt the same and yet so different. We moved through the garage, past his home gym. The boxing ring remained in the center with his free weights against the wall. I stared longingly at his treadmill and punching bag, remembering the hours I spent on both of them.

We took the stairs up to the second level. The living room looked the same, and I wandered into the kitchen. "You still have that sadistic coffeemaker."

He laughed. "The one you bought is under the cabinet. Do you want to make some coffee?"

"Are you trying to ply me with caffeine?"

"Is it working?"

I grinned. "You think you're so smart."

"That's because I am." He went to the back staircase. "I'll be right back. Stay here."

While I waited for the coffee to brew, I wandered through the kitchen and living room. This used to be my home. I remembered vividly standing on the doorstep; Martin refused to let me inside. He kicked me out. Now he brought me back. He wanted to know my opinion on selling the house, but it was his house. It wasn't my call.

A lot happened in this house. The first time we kissed. The first time we hooked up. The first time I told him I loved him. I moved down the hallway, wanting to see what had become of the guest suite he'd converted into my workspace. At one point, my furniture had been moved inside, but that was before. He probably turned it back into a guestroom.

I pushed open the door and stopped in my tracks. It looked like a war zone. A golf club was propped against the wall. The furniture, Martin's expensive furniture, was practically obliterated. Even the walls were destroyed. Drywall and dust covered the surfaces, and I examined the nearest hole. What the hell happened here?

"You weren't supposed to see this," Martin said. "I wanted to explain first."

Understanding nearly knocked me to the floor. "You did this." My gaze swept the destruction, seeing the anger and pain that motivated it.

"I hope you know I would never hurt you. This was a moment of weakness. It happened after you left me. I just...I forgot. I woke up one night, wanting it to be a nightmare. When I opened the door, I thought I'd find your things. But they were gone. You were gone. I just lost it."

I stared at him. "I caused this."

"Alex," he reached for me, but I stepped back, "sweetheart, please." He looked embarrassed and ashamed.

"My god." I moved to the golf club, which was dented and mangled. It was covered in a layer of dust, just like everything else. Realization hit hard. Why did it take me so long to have this epiphany? I should have known. He said it so easily and so often, but I didn't believe it because I spent my life broken. He was James Martin. He was worshipped, wanted, desired. He chose me, but I never comprehended the depth of his love until now. Even when we were broken up, I didn't see this. He showed me the civilized, tamed version. But this was raw emotion. He had a capacity for violence, though he rarely exhibited it. I should have been appalled or afraid. A normal woman would have been, but I understood the rage and the anguish. For the first time since I met James Martin, I realized we were both fully invested in each other. One couldn't live without the other; we would merely exist. "You did this?" I repeated, overwhelmed.

"I was drunk and lost. I missed you. It was stupid, but I just...I didn't care." He waited anxiously for me to say something. To make this better or worse. To convey some kind of emotion. "Say something," he begged.

"Fix the walls." My circuits were so overloaded that I

couldn't think to say anything else. I wasn't good at processing emotions or reacting to them, but I finally knew the truth. He needed me as much as I needed him. We were on an even keel. I could trust him not to hurt me again because it would kill him.

He just stared at me, dumbfounded. "Yeah, okay."

He gave me space, afraid the property damage had done irreparable harm to not just the walls but to us too. We didn't speak much the rest of the morning. We barely talked about the floorplans and photographs he wanted to show me for the other homes he was considering. We were both too frazzled.

When he dropped me off at work, I saw the confusion in his eyes. He had no idea what I was thinking. I wanted to reassure him, but I couldn't condense my thoughts into words. I grabbed his face and kissed him. Once the shock wore off, I'd tell him what he wanted to hear. I'd tell him everything he wanted to hear.

TWENTY-ONE

"Alex, are you okay?" Noah asked.

I blinked. "You're risking so much, and you don't even know me. I didn't think good people still existed, and then I met you."

"Hey, what's going on? You know you can tell me anything."

"Conrad called this morning to ask how the showing went. He wanted to know how many pieces we sold. We talked mostly about business. His accountant authorized the transfer, so I guess he must have bought my story about the delayed checks, but he had a few other questions."

"Are you having second thoughts?"

"It isn't that. I'm just afraid he knows something's up. He's always been great at reading me. What if he knows what I'm about to do? What if he set a trap?"

Noah put his hands on my shoulders and stared into my eyes. "Easy there. He doesn't know." But I saw the calculated look in Noah's eyes. "Would you feel better if we postpone?"

"We can't wait. We normally have the paintings delivered within three days and pay the artist within five."

It was important the delay be Noah's idea. I just had to manipulate him into making that decision.

"So we can wait a couple more days, if you want." He stared at me. "Whatever you think is best. He's your husband. You know him better than anyone."

I snorted. "That'll be the day." I forced my mind to stay away from thoughts of Martin. "What do you think?"

Noah glanced at his watch. "I have to get back to work, but how about I swing by afterward and we figure this out?"

"That sounds good."

"You'll be here?"

"I should be. If I'm not at the desk, I'll be painting in the back."

Noah leaned closer and kissed my cheek. "I'll see you later."

After he was gone, I sent a text to Cross. Noah might rabbit. The point wasn't to spook him, just delay him, but I wasn't sure how confident he was that Alexandra Scott wouldn't chicken out or tip off her husband. My phone beeped, and I read the message. Lucien wanted to wait and see how this plays out.

Cross was close to locating the funds. His forensic accountants and financial experts discovered where the five grand was deposited. Noah liked to do things old school and used a Swiss bank account. However, Cross was having difficulty determining if this was Noah's only account or if there were others. He was tracking the transfers but had been inundated with red tape. My boss would get access, even though his methods probably violated international law. But that wasn't my problem. My job was to stop Noah from skipping town until after we reclaimed Don's money, so I had to play my part and see this through.

Since I had several hours to kill, I replayed the last two weeks. Reaching for the phone, I decided it wouldn't hurt to get an update on Heathcliff's progress and offer to hand over my client as soon as Cross Security was paid. I was halfway through dialing when the alarm blared. I dropped my phone on the desk and swiveled around to check the security system. The side and rear doors didn't show a breach, but the motion sensors picked up movement in the main showroom.

Tucking my gun at the small of my back, I got up from the desk and entered the gallery showroom. There was only one way into the room. There were no exterior doors or windows. I checked the sensors for cracks or signs of tampering, but they were intact. The laser grid was active, but no one was inside.

After checking each of the art displays to make sure the pressure sensors weren't acting up, I went back to my desk and reset the system. It must have been a glitch. I rifled through the desk drawers for the user manual. According to the troubleshooting section, there could be dust on one of the sensors or the power fluctuated.

"Stupid security system," I muttered. The warning sounded again, and I flipped through the surveillance feed. No one was inside the room. I gave the glass doors a dirty look and turned off the motion sensors.

Just to be on the safe side, I checked upstairs and the studio in the back. Nothing had been disturbed. When I returned to the main room, I checked the exterior cameras and took a peek outside.

Finding nothing out of place, I went back inside. Out of sheer paranoia, I rewound the recorded footage and watched it play through. No one approached from the outside, and I was the only person inside. Maybe the gallery had a mouse.

Returning to what I had been doing before the interruption, I called Heathcliff and left a message. With little else to do, I keyed in a news search on the CryptSpec shooting. The press always took photos, normally after the fact, but someone might have caught sight of the red car near the scene of the crime. I was in the midst of dialing Heathcliff a second time when Noah called back. He only left four hours ago. It was too soon for him to be calling, unless something went wrong.

"Hello?"

"Alex," he sounded out of breath, "I've been thinking. If Conrad's suspicious, it might be best if you transfer the money now while you still can. If he locks you out of the account, you'll be stuck. I won't be able to do anything to help you."

"I hadn't thought of that." I sighed. Noah had reached the wrong conclusion. He was supposed to insist we wait, not move up the timeframe. I didn't expect him to be this desperate. He shouldn't need the money, unless he couldn't get to Klassi's right away and planned to skip town immediately. Had Cross's tracker been discovered? Had Noah grown suspicious of me?

"Are we doing this?" he asked. "Never mind, I'm parking now. I'll see you in a sec." Noah ran up the front steps, shooting a glance behind him before stepping inside. He looked pale and sweaty, as if he'd just outrun an alligator. He mopped the sweat off his brow with his pocket square and glanced back at the front door.

"What's wrong?" I got to my feet. My hand lingered outside the drawer where I'd stowed my nine millimeter.

"I had visions of Conrad storming in here with the police and having you removed from the premises."

"My husband isn't that dramatic." I gave Noah a wary look. "Are you okay?"

"Fine. The air conditioner in my car stopped working, and I've been sitting in traffic for the last forty-five minutes. According to the weatherman, today is the hottest day of the year."

"Shouldn't you be at the office?"

"My four o'clock appointment cancelled at the last minute." He looked around. "Would you mind getting me some water?"

I didn't want to leave him alone in the main room, particularly after I'd spent most of my time researching Gifford's murder and hadn't cleared my browser history. "Why don't you grab something from the fridge while I lock up? It's always cooler in there, and we can talk."

"Sure, that sounds good."

As soon as he was out of sight, I checked the surveillance feed, but no one was lurking outside. Everything appeared just like it had the last time I looked. I locked the front door, flipped the sign to closed, and followed Noah into the studio.

Noah paced back and forth. He already consumed half a bottle of water. He looked nervous. He was anxious to get this done.

"What's going on?"

He smiled, doing his best to convince me he was relaxed. "You tell me." He stopped in front of my painting. "Do you want to lose all of this?" He put the water down. "That's what's going to happen if you don't stand up for yourself."

"I know. I'm just afraid. What we're planning is illegal. I don't want to get caught and go to jail."

He resisted the urge to roll his eyes. That was desperation. He was determined to get the money. He wasn't willing to wait any longer. "You won't. The money technically belongs to you and Conrad. Worst case scenario, Conrad finds out and goes to the cops. As long as the artist gets paid, you haven't committed any crimes. And honestly, even if you didn't pay the artist for his paintings, that's civil, not criminal. You wouldn't go to jail, just to court."

"You're a lawyer now?"

He snorted. "I've sat through enough business law lectures to grasp the ins and outs of things."

"Excuse me for not knowing that. I never had any reason to. I don't do things like this. I'm a good girl." He gave me a look, but he didn't voice what was on his mind. "Why the hell are you so pushy all of a sudden?" I challenged.

He blew out a breath, put his water down, and approached me. "I'm tired of this. I had a terrible day at work. One of my clients went ballistic over something stupid. My boss chewed me out. And I found myself wondering what's the point. You do what you love. I do what I do to get paid. I want to chase my passion too." He leaned in. His nose brushed against mine. I waited just a moment, practically feeling his lips on mine, before turning my head. He exhaled against my cheek. "I want this for you. For us."

"Noah," I swallowed, "I'm still married. Conrad may be

a cheater, but I'm not. Until the divorce is finalized, I can't."

He gave me a tight nod. "I'm sorry. I shouldn't be here. I should never have given you false hope or stuck my nose in where it didn't belong. If you aren't ready, you aren't ready." He wanted me to argue, to beg, for his help. He thought this was the best way to goad me into transferring the money, but I didn't budge. "I'll see myself out."

"I'm sorry." I followed him down the hallway and to the lobby. Suddenly, the lights dimmed, and the alarm sounded. I looked up. The two of us were alone in the building. No one had entered. I would have noticed, but I had to make sure. Turning around, I clicked through the security footage. No one else was here.

"What is that?" Noah's head swiveled back and forth on his neck; his hasty retreat forgotten. He looked like he wanted to bolt upstairs and hide.

"The fire alarm." According to the computer readout, there was a fire in the main gallery. "It must be another glitch."

"Shouldn't you check it out?" He sounded afraid, which set off the warning bell in my head. "You do own the building and those paintings. It wouldn't look good if something happened on your watch."

"You're right." I moved away from the desk, heading through the glass doors. If there was an actual fire, the fire suppression system would activate. Noah followed a few steps behind. The display panel was on the side wall, and I examined the readout. According to the screen, the entire place was ablaze. "Stupid computer. The system's acting up today." I entered the disarm code, but it beeped angrily. I tried again with the same result. "It's not accepting my commands."

"Do you have a manual?"

"It's at my desk." I tried to move past him, but he put his hand up.

"I'll grab it."

"It's right on top. You can't miss it."

A new alarm sounded, and I turned back to the display to see what was wrong now. It didn't make any sense. I'd been at the gallery several times in the last week, and this was the first day there'd been a problem. It wasn't a coincidence.

That's when I heard the gun being cocked. Slowly, I turned. Noah was standing between me and the showroom doors. His hands were raised in surrender. The second warning claxon sounded shrilly in my ear, drowning out their voices.

"Who are you?" Noah asked, the gun aimed at him. He took a step back, away from the attacker. The man was dressed head to toe in black.

I didn't move. I wasn't sure if he'd seen me yet. I looked around, searching for a weapon. My gun was at my desk. There was no way to get to it without going past them.

A new sound deafened me. It was a warning that the doors were about to seal. Safeguards were supposed to prevent the fire suppression system from activating, but those measures were connected to the motion sensors. And I had disabled them.

The man aimed the gun at me. "Don't move," came the barely coherent growl.

I froze in place and raised my palms. Noah cowered, and the gunman turned the weapon on him, forcing him out of the showroom and into the foyer. I inched forward again. The alert was growing louder, more urgent. The doors would seal at any moment, and I'd be trapped inside. If the gunman didn't kill me, the fire suppression system would.

I kept moving, determined to get out. Staying was an obvious death sentence. Maybe he was a lousy shot. I'd survived gunshots before. I could do it again. I was almost out of the main gallery when he fired at me. I dove to the side. The bullet tore through the edge of the wall I was hiding behind. Okay, so he wasn't a lousy shot.

Before I could do anything else, a sudden whooshing filled my ears as the automated system kicked in. The doors swung shut, locking in place. I was sealed inside. I ran at the glass, pounding my fists against it.

"Let me out." The sound of the fans sent a jolt of adrenaline into my system. Any minute now, the room would become devoid of oxygen. It was the safest way of extinguishing fires without harming priceless art. "I'll die in here." Although, that was probably the shooter's hope all along.

Frantically, I pounded against the emergency button, but it didn't stop the fans. I searched for something to break the glass. The master switch was behind my desk. Maybe a bullet would work. I screamed at the asshole with the gun, but he didn't fire again.

Noah was on his knees now, facing me. The man held the gun to the back of his head. I didn't want to see the con man get executed.

The force of the oxygen being displaced caused a breeze that whipped at my hair. I didn't have time for this. "What do you want?" I screamed, finally distracting the man. Hopefully, he could hear me. "My husband has money, influence, power. Whatever you want, I can get it for you. But you have to let me out."

I gasped. My lungs ached in their fight to hold on to what little oxygen was left. This wasn't working. I dashed back to the panel, entering the unlock codes, the emergency release code, and anything else I could think of. The panel didn't respond.

"She's no one. She's my mark," Noah said, his voice muffled by the fans and the impenetrable barrier. "She'll get you what I owe you. Let her go. Let me go."

The shooter considered his words, and I raced back to the barrier. "The switch. Behind the desk." I gasped again. "Hurry."

He edged backward, disappearing from my line of sight. Noah didn't move, so I assumed the gun was still trained on him. In the meantime, I had to do something. I grabbed the closest thing I could find, a potted plant, and heaved the ceramic pot at the thick glass. It bounced off. Shit, it was shatterproof. My lungs were burning now. No matter how forcefully I inhaled, I wasn't getting enough oxygen. Breathing actually made it worse. I held my breath. My vision blurred. I couldn't stand. I went down, barely able to see through the encroaching darkness.

Noah pounded against the glass on his side. Bullets

flew. I heard the recoil, muted through the cacophony. My body convulsed. I couldn't hold my breath for another second. My lungs fought to obtain the last few molecules of oxygen but found none.

The tunnel vision got worse as everything turned black. I saw movement behind Noah. A figure. A man, maybe. Noah was on his knees again. Bursts of light fired from beneath my eyelids. I blinked and saw Martin, sheer disappointment on his face. And then there was nothing.

TWENTY-TWO

Nothing existed but the darkness. Were my eyes even open? I tried to blink, unaware if I was doing it. Total blackness surrounded me, pressed against me, suffocated me. I was dead, and there was nothing. Panic took over, and I whimpered. No. This couldn't be. Pain shot through my chest. Did the dead feel pain? I forced a breath into my lungs. The air scraped against the raw tissue, and the blinding headache set in. No, I wasn't dead, unless this was hell.

I reached out my left hand. It made contact with something solid. I ran my palm along the flat, scratchy surface. I knew that texture, but I couldn't place it. It wasn't as abrasive as sandpaper, but it was coarse and itchy. I followed it as far as I could reach. It was at a ninety degree angle to the surface I was lying on. It had the same texture.

I tried to sit up and instantly hit my head. I put a hand in front of my face, feeling a solid flat surface above me. Unlike the bottom and sides, it was smooth. Oh god, I was in a box. Was I buried alive? I extended my right hand to the side, coming into contact with a new texture. It was softer.

"You're awake."

I screamed and yanked my hand away, twisting away from the voice and hitting my face against the side of the box.

"Shh," Noah said, "it's me." His voice sounded weak. "When he threw you in beside me, I thought you were dead. I tried to give you CPR, but I didn't think it worked."

"He?"

Noah didn't answer.

It was hot, and the air felt thin. I was having trouble recalling how I ended up here. "What happened to us? The last thing I remember, we were in the studio." I fought against the blur. "The alarm went off in the gallery." Martin. "What happened to the other guy?"

"What other guy? The asshole who threw us in here?"

"No, there was another man. Is he okay? Where is he?"

"Alex, it was just us."

I ran my hand against the rough wall again. The box bounced, and I practically collided with the top. "We're moving."

"We're in a trunk."

That was the texture. I knew I recognized it. My eyes sought the slightest hint of light against the solid black. "What about emergency releases? Have you seen one? Or felt it? They glow in the dark."

"There isn't one."

"Taillights." I reached out again, tracing the side. I was on the outside, which meant I should be against the taillights. Why couldn't I feel or see them? Slowly, I felt along the side, finding a smoother surface against the scratchy carpeting. I ran my fingers along it, but it wasn't a light. Something was covering where the light should be. I dug my nails into the smooth surface and punched against it, but it didn't give. "Who did this? Who took us? Why?"

"I don't know."

"What do you mean you don't know?"

"I don't know."

My instincts were to fight, protest, and point out that he was the con artist, but I kept my mouth shut. For all I knew, this was part of the con. It seemed real. Noah's fear and reaction seemed real, but he lied for a living. I took another breath, unable to get enough air. "How long have we been locked in here?"

"Hours." He let out a ragged exhale, shuddering beside me.

"Noah?"

It took almost a minute before he responded. "Yeah, I'm here."

It was hot, making the air even harder to breathe. No wonder my head hurt. We hit another bump, and I tried to think of an attack plan. I tried to swallow. My throat was dry, and I was becoming increasingly aware of my motion sickness. It was too hot. The air was too thin. The bile rose, and I barely managed to force it back down. I lifted my hips and felt beneath me for a flap, but the trunk didn't have a hidden compartment. "What about a tire iron or a jack? Something we can use as a weapon."

"There's nothing."

I curled on my side, blindly feeling for a way out of the trunk or a way to get light and air inside. Who took us? Why? "Noah?"

He didn't answer. I could hear his labored breaths. Fear gripped my insides. I didn't want to suffocate. Not again. I couldn't go through that again. Tears welled in my eyes, and in my panicked state brought about by the dark and the circumstances, I didn't have the energy to keep them from falling.

Calm down, Parker. You'll figure it out, but you need to stay calm. At least one of the voices in my head was rational. I gasped, sending razors into my lungs. The pain gave my fraying nerves and fractured psyche something else to focus on. I calmed. Rational thinking would get me out of this. At some point, the car would stop. And when that happened, I needed to be ready. I needed a plan.

Without a weapon, I had to rely on the element of surprise. Noah thought I was dead when I was tossed in beside him. Hopefully, whoever took us thought the same thing. As soon as he opened the trunk, I'd attack. I'd only have a few seconds. He would have a weapon, probably the gun. I'd get it away from him and get out of this mess. Simple. The best plans were always the simplest ones.

I felt myself drifting. The heat was unbearable. It had to be over a hundred degrees. We'd been taken hours ago. Someone would realize I was gone. Cross. Jablonsky. Martin.

My eyes closed, or maybe they remained open. It didn't make a bit of difference. There was nothing to see. Was Martin at the gallery? It made no sense that he would have been there, but I remembered seeing him. Or did I? Things were blurring. Someone came in behind Noah. How did he get inside? Cross had a key. My thoughts scrambled. My head drooped forward, coming into contact with the side of the trunk, and I blinked back to consciousness.

We stopped. Now was my chance. I had to ready myself. The key scraped in the lock. This was it.

The lid lifted, and I was blinded by the sun. Wincing, I hoisted myself up and out, crashing onto gravel. I tried to scramble up, but something knocked me onto my back. A foot pushed down on my chest, keeping me on the ground.

My eyes were still adjusting, but I saw a scuffed black boot before I was roughly flipped over. The gravel scraped against my cheek and elbows. My hands were bound behind me. Then I was lifted into the air and tossed over someone's shoulder. My stomach couldn't take it anymore, and I heaved, leaving a trail of vomit behind us. I tried to look up, catching a glimpse of the rear bumper. It was a red car, doused with mud and dust. CE9W. Fuck.

The ground crunched beneath his feet. The gravel turned into dirt, then stone. It was dark. The air got cooler, and we went down some steps. He dropped me onto a paper thin mattress. My head was swimming. I couldn't focus. Breathe. Just breathe. I inhaled deep breaths, hoping to clear away the black bubbles and confusion. Slowly, I sat up.

I was in a windowless room. The walls were a drab grey. The floor was painted the same color and covered in a layer of grime. I edged off the mattress. It was less than six inches thick, old and worn. The stains on it turned my stomach, but there was nothing left to expel.

I struggled against the restraints. The metal bit into my wrists. This was not good. I searched for a weapon. There were chains and a metal cage in the room. I managed to stand but had to lean against the wall to steady myself. I was woozy. Did I have brain damage? Was I suffering from heat stroke? I couldn't be sure. But I knew I had to get out of here.

Steps led up to the door, and I moved toward them. I'd get out of here and get help. I took another step, and the door opened. A man dressed entirely in black dragged Noah into the room. He shot a look in my direction and pointed at me with his finger. He didn't speak, but I understood. He wanted me to sit down and stay put. When I didn't budge, he removed a gun from behind his back and aimed at me.

"Yeah, okay." I eased onto my knees.

He kept an eye on me as he dragged Noah into the cage and secured the door. He picked up the chains and came closer. He grabbed my wrists, unhooking the cuffs before encasing my forearms in heavy metal shackles. He bound the two shackles together with a long metal chain and threaded the ends through a metal loop in the floor. He fastened them together with a padlock and gave it a tug to make sure it was secure.

"Who are you? What do you want?" I asked.

He didn't answer. He turned around and went up the steps, returning with two small items. He placed a bottle of water and a meal replacement shake on the floor beside me. I didn't make a move toward them, even though every cell in my body begged for water. He went to the cage, sliding open a slot and tossing the same items inside with Noah.

Immediately, Noah grabbed the water and chugged it down. The man looked at me. He went to the corner of the room and dragged a portable toilet within range of my chain.

"What? No toilet paper?" I retorted.

He stared daggers at me. The plastic bottle in Noah's hand popped, and I turned at the noise. The man in black went up the steps and secured the hatch. The lock clicked into place. We were trapped, but at least it wasn't inside a trunk.

TWENTY-THREE

I lay on the cold, hard floor. Despite being overheated earlier, I was shivering now. The bottle of water and the nutrition shake remained untouched beside the mattress. I stared at the bottles. It took every ounce of self-control I had not to gulp down the water. My headache had gotten increasingly worse, and I could only assume it was from dehydration. But I was more afraid of being drugged and raped than turning into a prune, even though that would kill me first.

"Noah, are you okay?" Since he drank the water, he was my guinea pig. If he was okay, I'd drink. How long had we been here? Without any windows or clocks, there was no way to determine time of day. And I wasn't coherent enough to make a reliable estimate.

He pulled himself off the floor and leaned against the side of the cage, so he could face me. "I don't know, are you?"

That was good enough for me. I sat up, struggling to twist off the cap. It was difficult with my wrists bound by such thick shackles. Bringing the bottle to my lips, I drank. Nothing in this world had ever tasted better, but I allowed myself only a few small swallows before I put it down.

"I'm not sure. Is the room spinning?" I asked.

"It might be."

I leaned against the wall. It was just as grimy as the floor. "Where the hell are we?"

"I wish I knew."

I narrowed my eyes. "Who is he?"

"I don't know." Noah rested his forehead against the cage, the tip of his nose poking out through the crisscrossed metal.

I blinked through the fog, taking another small sip of water. "Are you sure about that? You have a nice little abode. No shackles." I scanned the interior of the cage. It was furnished with a mattress and portable toilet, but he wasn't chained to the floor. And the cage had been set up before we were even taken. If the man had planned to abduct me, I would be in the cage. The cage was for Noah. My appearance and abduction were just an afterthought. "What makes you so special? Were you a hamster in a previous life?"

"It's a Faraday cage."

I stared at him. "Is your name Faraday?"

Noah laughed, probably out of nerves. "It blocks electromagnetic signals. It'll keep electronics functioning in the event of an EMP or prevent signals from getting in and out." He surveyed the room. "This is a bomb shelter, isn't it? Probably built in the 1950s when people were terrified of Communists dropping an A-bomb."

"How do you know so much about where we are?"

"Look around."

I finished the water, wishing there was more. Noah was right. This did look like a bomb shelter, but I doubted it was far enough below ground to withstand a nuclear attack. The room was lined with shelves. Unlabeled cans covered one wall. I studied the meal replacement shake. It was starting to make sense.

"If that's for electronics, is there anything in there we can use? Do you have your phone? We need to call for help."

"He took everything before he put me in the trunk. My phone. My wallet. It's all gone." Noah climbed to his feet and carefully checked the interior. "I found a flashlight." He picked it up, examining it oddly. It had a hand crank. "That's not useful."

"Actually, it is if you run out of batteries." I stood on wobbly legs and walked the half circle. Nothing was within my reach. This side of the room was empty. No cans. No flashlights. Nothing.

The stained mattress, the shackles, and the nutrition shake confirmed one thing. The man in black, who drove the red car, wanted to keep us alive, at least for a while. He had enough supplies saved up to last months, if not years. I shivered again. I would die before I stayed locked in this hellhole for years.

I slid down the wall and followed the chain to the metal hook in the floor. It was cemented into the ground. There was no way to tear it free, but that didn't stop me from tugging on the chain as hard as I could. It didn't budge, but I was determined. I yanked and pulled until my arms ached. My eyes fell upon the padlock, and I carefully lifted it. No keyhole. It was a combination lock.

My thoughts went to what brought us here. This man, our abductor, attacked me in the alleyway. That night, he would have killed me, so why didn't he do it already? Something told me I wasn't his target. But I must have been. He attacked me before I ever met Noah. Why didn't this make sense?

"Oh god," Noah screeched, standing and rattling the metal mesh, "let us out." He rattled the cage again, screaming to be set free. He begged for mercy and freedom and offered anything and everything in return. Until now, I thought he had been keeping it together, but I realized he'd been in shock. Reality hit him hard. He continued to panic and thrash. I tried to stop him, but he ignored me. He threw himself against the cage over and over. He wailed and cried. Eventually, he ran out of steam and curled onto his bed and wept.

"Stop," I growled.

I had enough trouble concentrating without listening to a grown man cry. I slumped onto my side and stared at Noah's back. His sobs turned into sniffles. Eventually, his breathing normalized, and he fell asleep.

It had been a long day. So long. But I fought to keep my eyes open. I needed to stay awake and alert. Now that Noah had grown quiet, I loathed the silence. It was hard to focus and think. My priority was an escape plan, but I didn't think it was possible. I stared at the shackles. They were locked around my wrists and forearms. The metal encased at least four inches of my arm, maybe more. And they were heavy. The chain was the weak link. The stress had me snickering at the pun.

My best chance of escaping had passed. When the trunk opened, I should have fought harder or run. Dammit. Our captor would be back at some point. Ideally, I wanted to be in a position to overpower him. Since that didn't appear possible, we'd have to negotiate. That meant I had to determine who he was and what he wanted. It was our one shot at survival.

I wracked my brain for clues I might have missed. The attack in the alleyway was planned. That would indicate I was the target. The unsub waited for me. He attacked me. He followed me. He tried to escape from me at the sex club, outside Noah's, and outside Don's. Was this retaliation for something? Who was he? What did he want?

As my thoughts continued to spiral, I remembered the frantic tone in Noah's voice when he called and the way he was sweating when he showed up at the gallery. The unsub was chasing him. Noah led him right to us.

The unsub held a gun to Noah's head, but he didn't pull the trigger. That could only mean one thing — he needed Noah alive. He fired at me. If I didn't dive out of the way, he would have shot me dead. Why the change of heart? Why did he take me too? He could have left me sealed inside the gallery. My murder would have looked like an accident. *Woman suffocated to death after security system mishap, details at eleven.*

Except, he shot at me. He had to get inside the gallery showroom to recover the bullet. And leaving a body behind would have resulted in a lot of unnecessary attention. Assuming he did a decent job cleaning up his mess, the authorities wouldn't think much of a missing woman. He'd have twenty-four hours before the cops came knocking, except I wasn't just any woman. I questioned whether he realized that, but I didn't have an answer.

Martin would know something was wrong when I didn't come home. He'd have every law enforcement agency scouring the city for me, unless he thought I was running from him. Dammit, why didn't I say anything to him this morning? I shuddered, curling tighter into a ball. What if I never got to tell him all the things I wanted to say?

Swallowing the tightness in my throat, I mulled over other possibilities. Mark was searching for the car. He would come through. He would find me. It was just a matter of time. Cross would notice my absence. He would go to the gallery, realize something had happened, and determine where we were. He might not like me, but he wanted that million dollar payday. I just had to stall until someone found me or I figured out how to get the hell out of here.

While I ran through everything I remembered about the first attack in the alley, I let my eyes close. The answers were here; I just needed to find them. I needed this headache to go away in order to think clearly. My body needed water and sleep. Food would be nice too, but too much adrenaline was coursing through my system for me to feel anything but nausea.

My thoughts drifted. The obvious answer was staring me in the face, but I didn't see it. Unable to come up with a solution, I allowed myself to sleep.

The door slammed, and my muscles tensed. I remained curled on the floor. Maybe he wouldn't notice I was awake. My eyes followed the heavy black boots as they descended the wooden steps. He opened the metal slot on Noah's cage and tossed in another bottle of water and a shake. Then he crossed the room to me.

He stopped inches from where I lay. I didn't move, so he nudged me with the toe of his shoe. I looked up at him. He was clad entirely in black. Without a word, he pointed at the mattress.

"No," I said. My eyes narrowed. I'd kill him or die trying before I let him have his way with me. It might be smarter to live to fight another day, but I wasn't wired to accept that.

He stared at me for another moment before picking up my empty water bottle and replacing it with a fresh one. He reached for the shake, finding it unopened. He held it out. I didn't take the gesture as a peace offering, more like a command.

"I'm not hungry."

He twisted off the top and held it out.

"What do you want?" I asked.

I sat up, assessing him and considering possible strategies. Without the combination to the lock or a method of freeing myself, taking him down wouldn't solve my problem. And at the moment, he was the only person who knew we were here. If I killed him, I'd be signing our death warrants. And dying of dehydration wasn't the way I wanted to go. Not to mention, it was unlikely I'd be able to kill him under current conditions.

He grabbed my hair and yanked my head back. He shoved the bottle in front of my face. "Drink."

"Fuck you." I batted it away with my bound arms, watching the contents splash across the floor.

He jerked my head back and punched me. He flexed his hand, fighting to remain in control. Temper flared in his eyes. He wanted to hit me again, but instead, he let go, satisfied when I crumpled to the floor. My eye teared, and my cheek swelled. He put another shake down beside my water and stormed away. I wasn't sure what to make of that, but I knew this was just the tip of the iceberg. He had a short fuse. I had to get out of here before he put an end to my insolence.

TWENTY-FOUR

He returned a few minutes later. I didn't move. I stayed still, hoping to make myself as small as possible. He wanted to control me. He had the power. It was up to him whether I lived or died. I didn't care for that arrangement, but I was smart enough not to provoke him. At least not yet.

He unlocked Noah's cage and stepped inside. Noah's begging started out subdued and quiet, but as the man dragged him out of the cage, it became more frantic. He kicked and screamed, reaching out for whatever he could grab on to.

"Don't hurt me," Noah begged. "I'll get you what you want. Just don't hurt me. Please." The man in black dragged Noah up the steps. "I can get it. I said I'd get it." The hatch slammed closed, and I strained to hear the muffled pleas.

I wasn't sure what our abductor had in store for Noah, but Noah was terrified. I had to get out of here. Noah needed help. I tugged on the chain, but the metal loop had no give. I focused on the lock. It could be broken off with bolt cutters or something heavy.

Scanning my surroundings, I didn't find anything in

reach. The only items at my disposal were the portable toilet, nutrition shake, and water bottle. I tugged again, my eyes stopping on the thick shackles. I tucked the excess chain under my foot to keep it out of the way, raised my arm, and slammed it down against the lock.

The impact reverberated painfully up my arm and through my shoulder, but the lock didn't give. I repositioned the lock, hoping to hit it at a better angle to break it off, and tried again. Gritting my teeth against the pain, which made my cheek throb more, I repeated this another dozen times until I no longer had the strength to raise my arms.

My muscles ached from hefting the heavy chains and banging against the lock. There had to be some way to break it. I tried sliding the shackle up or down my arm, but it had no give. It was too narrow to move up my forearm or over my hand. I studied it, wondering if I dislocated my thumb if I'd be able to slide free, but it felt too tight.

I stretched the chain as far as it would go and leaned back, tugging with all of my might. I pushed off the floor with the heels of my shoes, hoping to exploit a weak link or tug my arm free, but neither of those things happened. This wasn't working.

I regrouped, scouring the vicinity for something I could use to free myself. Even the items not within reach looked useless. The asshole planned this out. He was careful. Hell, he barely even spoke, probably on the off chance that I'd be able to identify him from his voice. Did I know him? Or was he actually a doomsday planner, figuring that a worst case scenario would mean I was rescued and in a position to identify my captor?

"Who the hell are you?" I snarled, sliding the mattress away from the wall to see if anything was behind it. The sound of metal scraped against the floor, and I froze. My eyes went back to the door, but the asshole wasn't returning. With my hands bound so close together, I couldn't lift the mattress, but I reached beneath it. My fingers curled around a thin, flat, metal object.

I opened my hand and inspected the spoon, wondering if the last person he'd chained up had hidden it. It wasn't sharpened into a shiv. It just looked like a regular spoon.

"Great," I growled, manipulating it around to see if the flat end was thin enough to wedge into the seam of my shackles. It was too thick, and I cursed. I heard a faint scream coming from above. It had to be Noah.

That's when clarity struck. This wasn't about me. It was about Noah. Either this was part of the grift, or Noah scammed the wrong man. The red car had been outside Noah's apartment. The man followed Noah to the art gallery. The attack in the alleyway didn't fit with the facts, but maybe, somehow, that was unrelated, just like our encounters at the sex club and near Don's apartment building.

I took the spoon and positioned myself next to the hook in the floor. If inmates could dig their way out of prison cells with nothing but a spoon, I could dig this metal hook out of the ground. I might still be chained, but I'd be mobile. That would make escape possible. I scraped and scraped as blisters formed on my hands, but I didn't stop. I had to get free.

The door opened, and I slid the spoon beneath my thigh. I'd scratched away some of the grime and grey paint, but the floor remained rock solid. The damage I'd done wasn't noticeable, but our captor couldn't say the same. The man dragged Noah to the cage and shoved him inside. After he refastened the door, he gave me a cold, threatening look and went back up the steps.

Noah wasn't moving. He remained where he'd fallen. His face was covered in blood, but I couldn't see the wound. He held his stomach, and I knew he'd been beaten.

"Who is he? What does he want?" I asked.

"Money," Noah managed. "He wants money."

I tucked the spoon beneath the mattress and picked up the nutrition shake. I couldn't exactly reach the cage, but I loosened the cap and slid it over to Noah. The bottle was too large to fit through the crisscrossed metal, but the spout was small enough that he might be able to drink it.

"You'll need your energy," I said.

Gingerly, he sat up. He stuck his fingers through the holes of the cage and lifted the shake off the ground. He knocked off the cap, and with some serious dexterity, he tilted it far enough to drink. "Thanks."

"Who is he?" I asked again when Noah finished and let the bottle drop to the floor.

"I told you I don't know."

"Don't lie to me." I didn't want to stick with the charade of being Alexandra Scott, but on the off chance they were working together, I couldn't break cover. Even now, with blood covering his face, I didn't trust Noah. "When you showed up at the gallery, you were scared. You were out of breath. You were panicked. You knew he was looking for you. Who is he?"

"I. Don't. Know."

"What does he want?"

"Money." Noah wiped the blood out of his eyes, blotting his face with his shirt. He'd been struck near the temple. He had a deep laceration along his scalp that was bleeding everywhere. Finally, he took off his shirt, revealing burn marks and bruises, and held it against his head. "Lots of money."

"So give it to him."

He gave me an incredulous look. "I don't have that kind of money."

"Bullshit."

He stared at me, suddenly suspicious. "I don't. Unlike you, I didn't marry rich."

"You're a financial consultant. You deal with money all the time. Surely, you must have a way to access what he wants."

"I don't."

"How much does he want?" I asked.

"It doesn't matter."

Ransom amounts varied drastically. It actually depended on a lot of factors, but since Noah stole ten million, someone threatening his life should ask for millions in exchange for letting Noah live. "Did you rip this guy off or something?"

Noah wiped his face and sunk against the side of the cage. "I don't know. It's possible, I guess."

It was more than possible, but arguing that point would

be fruitless. "What does he want with me? Why did he take me? Why didn't he just leave me in the gallery?"

Noah's eyes were full of sincerity. "I'm sorry. I told him you would pay, so he would let you out of the gallery. I didn't want you to die. This is my fault."

"We'll fix this. We'll figure it out."

He licked his lips, which were just as dry and chapped as mine. Neither of us would survive much longer. "He didn't even care. He thought you were dead. I don't think he wanted to leave witnesses or evidence. After you blacked out, he waited to make sure you were done before he opened the door."

"He went back for the bullet."

Noah nodded. "I couldn't leave you there like that. I crawled over to you and started chest compressions. He knocked me away, but..."

I rubbed a hand over my sternum, acknowledging the ache. It was a wonder he didn't break my ribs. "But what?"

"I guess he changed his mind because he tossed you into the trunk."

I looked down at my hands. That asshole took the diamond ring. Too bad Cross didn't install a tracker inside of it. This was about money. Noah had gotten caught, and this was revenge.

"What about the paintings?" I asked.

"He took those too."

They were forgeries. If he tried to fence them, he would realize they were fakes. At least the diamond was real. Still, that put us on a clock, if we weren't already on one. "Where did he take you?"

Noah cringed. "The hatch lets out into some kind of barn or shed."

"Did you see anything?"

"Just some shitty wooden walls and the farm tools he used to work me over."

"What about outside? Is it morning? Night? Any windows?"

"Just one. There was daylight, and a whole hell of a lot of trees." He pressed his lips together and wrapped one arm tighter around his middle. "I think we left the city."

Intellectually, I already knew that, but hearing the words squelched what little hope I had. It would be that much harder for Mark to find me. It would take longer to contact other FBI field offices, get approval, and catch a flight or make the drive. Still, I knew Jablonsky would do everything in his power. I just didn't know if he was aware he should be looking.

By now, Martin would know something was wrong. It had been at least twenty-four hours, maybe more. He said he trusted me. If he meant it, then he knew I wouldn't leave him again. I promised him I wouldn't. He would have called Mark first thing. They were already searching. They had to be. I had to hold on to that thought and believe in that possibility. If not, the despair would eat me alive.

TWENTY-FIVE

Hours went by. Maybe days. I did nothing but dig at the floor surrounding the metal loop. My body was getting weaker. Perhaps I'd die of starvation instead of dehydration. For whatever the reason, I couldn't stomach the shakes. I tried taking a sip, which resulted in an immediate and violent reaction.

I couldn't afford to lose any more fluid. When I recovered somewhat, I went back to digging. I loosened the cement around the metal ring, creating a dusty crater around it. No matter how much progress I made, the metal remained deeply rooted in the floor. This wasn't working. This may never work. I was losing hope.

The sound of the lock scraping against the hatch alerted me of our captor's return, and I brushed the bits of concrete and dust back into the crater and patted it down, hoping he wouldn't notice. The floor was too filthy for the dust to be noticed, but the hole would be obvious.

When the unsub stepped inside, I could sense the shift in him. He had grown tired of torture. He stormed to the cage. His rage barely contained. Even if I couldn't see his face, I knew he intended to slaughter Noah.

Noah must have realized the increased danger because

he hunkered against the far back wall. He wasn't bound. He could fight. He should fight. I told him as much when we were alone, but we both knew he didn't stand a chance. Still, I urged him to run. To try to escape. All he had to do was make it past the man in black and up the steps. If he made it that far, he'd have a chance. Help was out there. But he was too afraid.

For a professional criminal, he should have been prepared for the worst. Hell, he talked a good game. Why couldn't he talk his way out of this? But I knew the answer to that. He'd already spun a web of lies. Nothing he said at this point, even if true, would be believed.

The man didn't even wait to get Noah out of the cage before he thrashed him. He wore brass knuckles over his black leather gloves, and the sight of Noah's blood covering the cage and spraying the floor behind it was something I could never unsee. I didn't have a choice. I had to break the pattern. If I didn't, we'd both be dead.

"Hey, asshole," I bellowed, "leave him alone. I'll get you your fucking money."

Slowly, the man turned. I imagined the glee on his face, even though it was concealed by the mask. He glanced back at Noah, who was unconscious, perhaps dead, and stepped out of the cage, kicking the door closed. He towered over me, waiting for cash to materialize out of thin air.

I stuck with my cover story. If he realized I was the same woman from the alleyway, that decision might be my death sentence. "My husband will give you whatever you want in exchange for my safe return."

The man assessed me, as if trying to decide if he should believe me. Without a word, he went up the steps to the hatch. He left it open, and I wondered what this meant. Was he getting a chainsaw to hack us to bits? A shovel to dig a hole to bury our bodies? I cast a quick glance in Noah's direction. He wasn't moving. I couldn't tell from this distance if he was breathing. It might have already been too late. I might have waited too long. I tried bargaining with our captor before, but he was never receptive to my pleas. But now that changed. He was unpredictable, and that made him dangerous.

A minute later, he returned. He left the hatch open and remained on the steps, not fully committed to entering the bomb shelter. He had a phone in his hand. "Number," he barked.

I could give him any number. He was desperate enough to trust that I wouldn't double-cross him, which was precisely what I planned, but everyone I knew in law enforcement was in the habit of identifying themselves when answering the phone. Even Cross and my fellow private eyes answered the same way. He'd have to call Martin. There was no other choice. I didn't know what time it was or even what day. If Martin was at work, it might go to voicemail, and I'd be done. The only other option was the emergency burner Martin kept. I was the only one with the number. It was always charged, but he never carried it, unless he had reason to.

It was the safest bet since it didn't have voicemail. I just didn't know if he'd answer. Reluctantly, I gave the bastard the number, regretting it the moment it was done. I might have just signed Martin's death sentence too. The man dialed, and I held my breath. Would Martin be smart enough to play along? I didn't know what to expect, but I was out of time and options.

The man sat on the top step, staring down at me. "Mr. Scott, I have your wife."

I cringed. How did he know my cover identity? How much did Noah tell him about me? I looked at the cage from the corner of my eye. The grifter hadn't moved. I felt dizzy and sick.

"Two hundred and fifty thousand," the abductor said. It was the most he'd spoken in my presence, and even now, he kept the conversation short. "I'll send a location." His cold eyes flicked to mine as he stood. I knew that look. "It'll be worse if you don't."

He hung up, slamming the hatch closed before barreling down the steps. The call didn't last long enough for a trace. It was twenty seconds at most. What did Martin say? Did he even speak to Martin? Or was this some kind of charade? A sadistic means of torture before he painted the floor with my blood too?

He stormed toward me, and I backed against the wall. There was no defensible position. He crouched down in front of me and toyed with a limp, greasy strand of my hair.

"You'll get your money," I said with complete certainty. "He'll pay." I swear I thought I saw him smile, despite the mask.

"So will you."

He went for my throat, wrapping his hands around my neck. Despite being bound, I reacted the only way I knew how. I slid onto my left hip, bringing my right leg over to the left side, between us. With every ounce of strength I had, I drove the ball of my foot into his right side. It was enough to cause his grip around my neck to loosen, and I used the momentum of my kick to propel myself around him.

Hooking both of my feet around his upper thighs, I clung to his back. My arms were around his shoulders, and I wedged the excess chain into the bend of my right elbow. I pulled back on the right side with all my might. The heavy metal sunk into his neck, and I held on as he fought and bucked.

This wasn't the best angle for choking someone out, but I couldn't risk attempting to reposition. I wound the chain around my right hand, pulling harder. He jerked from side to side, hoping to throw me, but we were tangled together. Unexpectedly, he stood, lifting me entirely off the ground in the process. I clung to his back. My arm started to shake. My muscles burned under the weight of the chain and his continuous attempts to free himself.

My fingers went numb, my grip slipping. He threw his right elbow back, catching me beneath the ribs. My legs fell from his thighs, and he swiveled around. The chain skimmed against the back of his neck, but he didn't care. He let out an inhuman snarl and slammed me against the wall.

The moment I hit the ground, he was on top of me. The first hit glanced off my cheek, but with the brass knuckles, it set my face on fire. After that, the rest of the hits seemed to land at once. His jabs felt like knives slicing into me, ripping me apart. He didn't need me anymore, so he would kill me. But as quickly as it started, it stopped. My mind couldn't process anything but the pain.

He rubbed his neck, glared down at me, and went up the steps. The hatch slammed, and the lock clicked into place. I needed to get up. To get out of here. I rolled onto my side, tried to boost myself off the floor with my hand, screamed in agony, and collapsed.

I didn't know how much time passed. Reality was a fickle bitch. Death and destruction surrounded me. There was nothing but pain and misery.

*   *   *

A million tiny knives thrust into me, and I screamed. Freezing cold water tore into my flesh. I lifted my head, and the spray from the pressure hose nearly blinded me. Water shot into my mouth and nose, and I sputtered and choked. I turned my face away as the spray continued. There was no escaping it.

Eventually, it stopped, and I stared at the reddish brown puddles as they crept toward the drain in the center of the room, just to the right of the cage. Why hadn't I noticed that before? I struggled to sit up, realizing my arms were no longer shackled. The asshole lugged the hose up the steps and closed the hatch.

Two bottles of water rested on top of the now soppy mattress. My head throbbed. Several of my teeth felt loose, and I forced my tongue away from them. I didn't want to lose my teeth. It seemed like a stupid thing to worry about, but it was the only thing I could think about as I assessed the bleeding cuts, thick welts, and bruises that covered my body.

I reached for the water, seeing the stark contrast of the dark marks against my pale arms. "I have to get out of here," I murmured, my eyes drawn to the hatch. Apparently, after I assaulted that asshole, he got wise to the dangers of the lengthy chain and instead bound one of my ankles to the floor. The chain was barely six inches, just enough for me to stand.

I didn't have time to wait around to be rescued. I had to

get out of here now. Assuming the two bottles meant I'd been unconscious for two days, Martin must have negotiated a trade by now. It was probably why the man in black came in and hosed me off. Or he wanted to eliminate the evidence. It would take more than a little water to wash away his crimes.

The crumbles of concrete and dust that I refilled the hole with were now softer, like wet sand. I dug it out with my fingers, figuring the spoon must have washed out of reach. The high-pressure hose had penetrated pretty deep. Maybe the water loosened the concrete dust or whatever the hell the floor of the shelter was made of.

A few puddles remained, but most of the water had drained away. Visually, I searched the inside of the cage, but Noah's body was gone. His remains were probably dumped somewhere, or he was being tortured in another location. I should have felt something — sorrow, remorse, sadness. But my mind was numb. I'd worry about Noah later.

After clearing away as much of the concrete as possible, I pressed my heel against the metal loop and put all of my weight on it. Did it give, even a little? I wasn't sure, so I repeated the process over and over, scooting around to the other side and trying to move it in the other direction. The metal ring seemed to wobble, probably less than my teeth, but wobble nonetheless. I grabbed one of the precious bottles of water and poured some of it into the crevice. Maybe it would help. Maybe it wouldn't, but I had to try. Then I drank the rest.

I heard a noise from above, and I froze. There was no way to cover the hole again. If that asshole saw what I was doing, he wouldn't restrain himself from killing me this time. The noise sounded again. Were those car doors?

Thoughts of a possible exchange came to mind. What if Martin negotiated my release? What if he was outside? I wanted my freedom more than anything, but it wasn't safe here. I didn't want Martin anywhere near this psychopath. The asshole would kill him as soon as he got the money.

I kicked ferociously at the metal loop holding me captive. I had to get out. I had to get free. I climbed to my feet, pressing sideways against the metal that held the chain in place. Under my weight, it bent, and I nearly toppled to the floor. Unfortunately, it didn't break. Now what was I going to do?

I studied the bent metal, finding a thin separation. It was narrow. Too narrow to be of much use in its current state, but it was a defect I could enlarge. I pressed against the top of the loop with all my might. My foot slipped, and I sliced the back of my calf open on the protruding metal. It stung, but I didn't care. I tried again and again. Finally, the loop looked less like a solid circle and more like a cane.

Slipping the chain that bound my ankle free from the metal ring, I breathed a sigh of relief. The length of chain hung ineffectually from my ankle; the bulky lock remained fastened at the end. I wrapped the chain around my ankle a second time to limit its length, hoping to avoid tripping over it. I didn't have time to do anything about the lock. I needed to move.

Impossibly quick, I checked the rest of the shelter, but the bastard was clever. He didn't leave any weapons or tools inside. Even the flashlight Noah found was gone. With nothing but the dripping wet clothes on my back, I made my way up the steps, wondering how I'd get the hatch open.

TWENTY-SIX

By some miracle, the asshole didn't slide the lock into place. After a bit of cajoling and manipulation, I inched the weathered, wooden door upward. It opened into a wooden shed with a dirt floor. No one was in sight as I slipped out of the hole.

Remnants of improvised torture took up the rear of the building. A chair, chains, cables, and a car battery. That asshole liked the tried and true torture techniques. I shivered, hating to think what he had in store for me.

I found a hatchet. Clinging to it, I edged to the door and peered out. It was the middle of the afternoon, judging by the shadows and the sun's position. The gravel path led to a makeshift driveway, but the red car was gone.

Opening the door wider, I studied my surroundings and realized I had no idea where I was. This wasn't farmland, like Noah thought. This wasn't a suburban neighborhood. This was a cabin in the middle of the fucking woods. Didn't they make horror movies about such things?

The cabin was off to the side. It might contain weapons or a way to call for help. I had to check it out. Inching along, I swallowed the cry that threatened to burst from my lips when one of those nasty welts came into contact with a protruding nail. My desire to escape outmatched the pain and kept me moving, but it was an unpleasant reminder that I wasn't okay. In fact, I was pretty far from it.

Scurrying toward the house, I made it to the front door, but it was locked. I maintained the death grip on the hatchet, knowing it was my only line of defense. I couldn't get the door to budge, so I went to the nearest window. If he was inside, he'd hear me, but I had to risk it.

I broke the window and waited, poised to run. When no one came to investigate, I ran the hatchet along the jagged edges and hoisted myself inside. The cabin was sparse. I went to the phone on the wall, but it didn't have a ringtone. I hung up the receiver and tried again, but it was dead.

I didn't have time for a thorough search, but I did my best. I didn't find a gun or a cell phone. The fridge contained bottles of water that I gulped down. And the couch had a blanket thrown over the back. Despite the hot summer day, I wrapped it around my soaking wet body. I couldn't stay here. He'd be back any minute. With the hatchet in hand, I went out the front door.

The gravel road must lead to an actual road. If I followed it, it would lead to civilization. Unfortunately, when he returned, it would be via the gravel road. I couldn't risk getting caught again. So I took to the woods.

It was slow going. I hated the outdoors. I was a city girl through and through. My only guide was the gravel road, and I'd periodically have to leave the cover of the trees to make sure I was still heading in the right direction. My body ached, and I shed the protection the blanket offered when I couldn't carry it any longer. The sun burned my skin. I was so thirsty. And dizzy. I stumbled but kept going.

By the time the sun set, I wished for the blanket, food, water, and enough painkillers to put down a tyrannosaurus. Headlights caught my attention, and I froze. They were coming toward me. Was I deep enough in the woods not to be spotted? I dropped onto my stomach, wincing. The car continued on its path up the gravel road. As it passed, I recognized the red jalopy.

As soon as the psychopath got back to the cabin, he would know I escaped. And he'd come looking for me. I counted to ten and cautioned a glance behind me. The taillights disappeared from sight, and I struggled to get back on my feet.

Run, my mind screamed, and my body did its best to comply. The branches whipped at my hair and face. I ducked my head and continued running. I didn't know where I was going. All I knew was I had to get as far away as possible. The dark made it impossible to see the path, and I tripped and stumbled. But I kept going.

The roar of an engine caught my attention. How the hell could he have backtracked this quickly? I dashed deeper into the woods. I propelled myself forward with everything I had.

In the distance, I heard dogs. Was he tracking me? From what I learned during basic survival classes at Quantico, it was hard to track in water. But where the hell was I going to find a lake or river? Maybe I should climb a tree. Or was that for bears?

Keep moving. Keep one step ahead, the voice in my head ordered.

My legs were shaking now. My muscles cramping. My pace slowed, and no matter how hard I pushed, my body didn't have anything else to give. A sudden surge of pain erupted from beneath my ribcage, knocking the wind out of me. I staggered forward, the ground uneven, and I tripped over a branch.

I couldn't stop the scream that ripped through me as I rolled down an embankment, losing the hatchet somewhere in the process. I had to get up. I had to keep moving. The engine rumbled, as if idling. He must be right behind me. I didn't turn around to look. Instead, I pulled myself against the trunk of the nearest tree and hoped he wouldn't see me.

A car door slammed. I tried to camouflage myself in mud and leaves, but the ground was dry. There were no leaves. No cover. Steeling myself for the inevitable, I cautioned a glance around the tree.

Headlights shone straight ahead. They caught a reflector on the road. A real road, not that gravel and dirt bullshit. I heard a soft padding sound. Footsteps. A light shone in my direction, and I shielded my eyes. The light grew brighter. He was coming closer. He was right on top of me.

"Stay back," I warned in a final act of defiance.

"Dammit, Parker. You're going to give me a heart attack." A sigh of relief was followed by a few more curses as Jablonsky lowered the flashlight. He held the radio to his lips. "I found her. Continue the search for the suspect." He crouched beside me. "I thought you hated camping."

I hugged him, hissing at the pain but refusing to let go. "You came looking for me."

"I'll always come looking for you." His voice cracked, and he returned the hug. "Marty and I have been frantically searching for days. We put surveillance on the car. We needed him to take us to you."

"Where's Martin?"

"He's waiting." He pointed the light at me. "Let's get out of here." He noticed the bloodstains on my clothes. "Can you walk?"

"I'm not sure."

He slipped underneath my arm and helped me stand. "It's just a few steps. I've got you."

When we emerged from the woods, the door of the SUV sprung open. Martin had me in his arms before Mark even let go. He carried me into the SUV and laid me down on the back seat. I blinked up at him. Since when did Jablonsky allow a civilian to tag along on what probably would have been a raid? It didn't make sense. Neither did the tactical vest securely fastened around Martin's torso or the nine millimeter holstered at his hip. No, I thought sadly, this is just another delusion, probably a result of the trauma or dehydration.

The hope fizzled away. This wasn't real. Tears welled in my eyes. It was another dream or hallucination. I'd been having enough of those lately. I was probably still trapped in that bomb shelter or unconscious at the bottom of the embankment. My mind was playing cruel tricks, imagining escapes and happy endings. I shuddered. Of course, it felt real. The pain was real, but nothing else was.

"Sweetheart, you need to drink," Martin insisted, holding my head up as he pressed a bottle of water to my lips.

I swallowed a few mouthfuls.

The radio chirped. "Jablonsky, we found someone. Another victim. He's in bad shape."

"Reroute the ambulance to your location. I'll take Parker myself. Stay on top of the search. I want this son of a bitch in custody by the end of the night." Jablonsky glanced back at us. "She's in rough shape. We should go now." He flipped on the lights and hit the siren.

"Alexis," Martin said softly, "you'll be okay. It's not far. Just stay with me, okay?"

"I wanted to tell you how much I love you," I said, "but I didn't get the chance. I probably never will. Wherever you are, I hope you know that. I'm sorry I didn't say it more."

"Alex, hey, I'm here. I'm right here. You'll have plenty of time. You're going to be okay. I promise."

I closed my eyes. I wasn't a quitter, but this time, I was ready to give up. Noah was dead. I was trapped in some godforsaken hellhole with no chance of escape. And my mind was creating the perfect delusion, which should have thrilled me but instead broke my heart and spirit. My own psyche was far more damaging and dangerous than anything that sick bastard could do to me.

"Do you know where he went? Where he might go?" Mark asked, but I didn't respond. "Parker, hey, focus. The man who took you, the one with the red car, do you know where he might be? Where he might hide?" My hallucination of Mark was just as dogged and demanding as the real Mark.

"I don't know. I don't know who he is or where we are." I rubbed my hand against the seat upholstery, aggravating my blisters. "He had me in the trunk. I tried to escape, but I failed. He kept me chained in the bomb shelter. I didn't see much. When I got free, I went into the cabin. There might be something there. I don't know. I had to leave before he came back."

Mark relayed the details over the radio as the SUV took a sharp turn and stopped. Suddenly, bright overhead lights disturbed the dark. I was moving quickly but not under my own power. Questions. So many questions. Voices. I blinked against the too bright lights. Martin was beside me, jogging to keep up.

"Sir, family only."

"She's my wife."

Yeah, definitely hallucinating, I decided. Well, there was no reason I couldn't try to enjoy it. I turned my head and saw the determined look on Martin's face. Truthfully, he didn't look so bad in tactical gear. It must have been a memory from when I watched him run through the HRT training course, except I didn't recall the dark circles under his eyes or the beginnings of a beard. Those were probably products of my imagination. A result of the cabin and woods.

"Is she allergic to anything?" a nurse asked.

Martin said something that I missed while I wondered what he'd look like as a lumberjack. Flannel and plaid did not suit him. Not at all. He did pull off a convincing tuxedo, and I focused on that, wondering if hallucinations worked like lucid dreams. If so, I should be able to control things. After all, it was my mind.

My head lolled back, and I noticed the tubing in my arm. Whatever they pumped into my veins was nice. Everything stopped — the pain, the thirst, the fear. It was gone. All gone.

When I opened my eyes again, I felt okay for the first time in as long as I could remember. The hard concrete floor was replaced with a soft bed. My skin wasn't sticky with sweat, and even my hair felt clean. Something rubbed against the inside of my forearm, and I turned to see Martin gently rubbing arnica gel over my skin.

"Am I dreaming?" I asked.

"No." He leaned down and pressed his lips against my forehead. "The doctors said you were lucky. They believe you'll make a full recovery as long as you get plenty of fluids and the proper amount of rest."

"I'm not lucky."

Anguish burned in his green eyes. "No, you're not. But it could have been worse. They bandaged what they could. Your rib was dislocated, but they popped it back into place." He leaned close, gently brushing my hair back. "Are you in any pain?"

"Not right now." I looked around the room. "Where's Mark?"

"He's leading the search for the fucker who did this to you. I swear, we'll find him, and when we do..." He bit his lip and moved to stand, but I grabbed his arm.

"Don't go."

"Never." He repositioned the tray table and moved his chair closer. "I'm not letting you out of my sight ever again."

I reached for the cup of water, and he held it so I could sip from the straw. "I heard what you said to the nurse last night."

Martin smirked. "Did you? You weren't making a lot of sense at the time. I distinctly recall you asking where my tuxedo was." He chuckled. "That was a pretty high dose of morphine they gave you."

I winced, feeling the bandage along my cheek. After checking to see if my teeth were still in my mouth, I asked, "Did we get married?"

"Don't worry. You didn't do anything that crazy. I just said that because they wanted to kick me out, and I wasn't letting you go. The lie was easier than waiting for actual documentation to be faxed over. You know how inept administrators can be. It's not like we're home with the paperwork on file at the hospital. I hope I didn't freak you out. I didn't mean it, Alex."

"Are you sure? We could get married. Find a chaplain."

His gaze shifted to the bag hanging above the bed. "Yeah, okay. Those are the painkillers talking, but whatever you say. I'll do anything you want."

The questions continued to come to mind. There was no stopping them. "Where are we?"

"About three hundred miles from civilization."

I stared at him. Thoughts of Noah ran through my mind. Mark was searching for the man responsible. We must have crossed state lines for this to be FBI jurisdiction, or he called in some favors. "Idiot."

Martin frowned. "What?"

I shook my head. "Me. I'm the idiot. It was an

abduction. That makes it an FBI case." Another thought formed. "Did you pay the ransom?"

"Let's not talk about this now. You need to rest."

"Did you?" I repeated.

"Yes," he squeezed his eyes closed as if in pain, "it should have gone smoother. I did what he asked. He shouldn't have hurt you." A harsh breath escaped his lips, and he stared out the window. "That's why I was in the car, how we knew to follow him, how we found you."

I turned and looked out the window, seeing far too much tree and sky. "I want to go home."

Martin nodded, already expecting that request. "I'm working on it. Just as soon as Cross's medical team arrives, we'll go to the airport. My jet's waiting."

"Cross's team?"

"It's a short flight, but I don't want to take any more chances." He kissed my knuckles. "Lucien has a stellar trauma team on his payroll. They'll accompany us home. It's the least he can do."

"How long was I missing?"

From the look on Martin's face, I knew he didn't want to have this conversation, but he answered anyway. "Four days."

In a lot of ways, it felt longer. "I was afraid what you'd think. That morning at your house, I should have told you I understood." I cracked a teasing, playful smile, ignoring the pain in my cheek. "You're invested. You can't lose me." My face fell, seeing the pain in his eyes. I'd gone through hell, but so had he. "Shit. I'm sorry."

"Don't you dare be sorry. I love you, and I'll shoulder whatever burdens are a part of that."

TWENTY-SEVEN

The constant dull throb was turning back into a stabbing pain. The painkillers were wearing off again, but I didn't want any more pills. I'd been in a pleasant fog since the hospital. It was time to face reality. My mind needed to clear.

I reached for Martin, hoping to find comfort in his arms. Despite the fact he'd been keeping his distance, it was the middle of the night. He should be asleep beside me. However, he wasn't there, and I opened my eyes. Resisting the urge to jerk upright and search for him, remembering what a bad idea that had been when I'd done it earlier, I slowly rolled onto my back until the heating pad was beneath me and turned it on. Most of the swelling had gone down, so the heat soothed my aches and pains.

Martin was sitting in a chair at the foot of the bed. His elbows dug into his knees, and he stared at me with an intensity I usually only saw when we were fighting or making love. I groaned, and he physically flinched at the sound.

"He shouldn't have hurt you," Martin said, his voice rough. "I gave him what he wanted. He wasn't supposed to hurt you."

"What did you expect from a sadistic piece of shit?" I retorted with my usual level of sarcasm.

"As soon as I realized you weren't coming home, I called your cell. You didn't answer, so I called your office. Lucien gave me the address and met me at the gallery. I don't know why he did that."

"I have an idea."

Martin didn't hear my comment or chose to ignore it. "I should have tried calling you sooner. I should have realized something was wrong. Maybe we would have gotten to you faster. Maybe this asshole would be in custody or dead by now."

"You were there when it mattered."

His features contorted, and he looked away. "I should have acted quicker."

"This isn't your fault."

"I've never been able to protect you. I wanted that to change. I thought it would be different now." He rocked back in the chair. "I would do anything to keep you safe." He let out a cynical laugh. "I just keep thinking of the terrible things I said to you. The way I treated you when you took extreme measures to protect me. I'm a fool. All the time we wasted. Three months. We could have had another three months. That's time we'll never get back." The last few days had made him rethink, revisit, and spin out.

"No, you were right to be angry. But we're so far beyond that now. It's ancient history. I don't want to think about that. You shouldn't either."

"So what should I think about? The bullet hole in the wall of the gallery? The video footage of you trapped inside? Watching that animal drag you away?"

"There's footage?"

"Cross recovered the data. Most of it was corrupted when the drive was destroyed, but some of it was backed up on the server. It recorded the changes that were made to the security and fire suppression system. It caught bits and pieces, enough that we knew what happened." Martin worked his jaw. "I called Mark and Heathcliff and everyone else you know. They searched for you, for signs of what might have happened. Since he took the paintings, Jabber figured this was about money. We expected a ransom. I was ready."

"Did you let the FBI conduct the negotiation?"

Martin scowled. "I know their recovery rates. I tried calling Mercer, but the number was disconnected."

For a moment, I wished Julian had manned the negotiation. I knew how the former SAS operative worked. The asshole responsible would be dead now. "He tosses his gear after every mission." Martin didn't know the other methods of getting in touch with the K&R specialist, and it wasn't important that I tell him now.

"I would have hired someone else, but without a ransom, I had to wait. And Mark thought it was a bad idea to have private contractors involved. He was afraid they'd botch it. So when the call came, I followed the instructions to the letter." Martin sighed heavily and rubbed his face. "That bastard knew I'd give him whatever he wanted on the condition that you not be harmed. I don't understand why he would risk everything by violating the terms." Martin frowned. "I told him I'd pay."

That asshole's words repeated through my mind. *So will you.* "Fuck."

"What is it?" Martin asked, already on his feet and beside me.

I waved him off. "He knew. All along, he knew who I was. That's why he made sure I was trapped in the gallery, so I couldn't interfere. I would have tried something, and he knew it. That's why he never tortured me for information or money. It's why he kept me chained to the floor with those ridiculous restraints. He couldn't let me wander freely in a cage." I cursed my own stupidity. "He fucking knew." I reached for the phone. "I have to call Mark."

Mark didn't return home with us. He was leading the search. Every inch of the property had been scoured for evidence. The surrounding woods were still being explored for clues or hints to the unsub's whereabouts. Somehow, the asshole gave us the slip. The cover of night and the unfamiliar surroundings gave him a clear advantage. One of the teams found tracks which led to a dirt path. The bastard had an escape route planned.

I looked at the clock. It was a little after three a.m. "You're still out there?" I asked. The teams had been searching nonstop for over a day.

"I'm heading back in the morning." Mark sounded defeated. "We're working the last of the grid tonight. Everything we collected is being processed. I won't lie to you. What we've found is disturbing. I will be damned if he gets away with this."

"How's Noah?" The grifter had been discovered unconscious a few hundred feet from the shed. I didn't know the specifics, but I knew it was under dire conditions.

"Out of surgery, but he's still critical. He hasn't woken up. They don't know if he will. The locals assigned a protection detail, but they aren't equipped to handle this situation. As soon as he's stable, I'll have him transported back to the city." Someone said something, and Jablonsky barked a response. "I have to go, and you need to get your beauty sleep. The docs said you were battling exhaustion on top of the extreme dehydration."

"Yeah, yeah. Call me when you get back."

"I will. Night, Alex."

"What is it?" Martin asked.

"Mark didn't say much. The asshole's in the wind." I propped myself up a little higher and swung my legs over the side of the bed.

"Whoa, where do you think you're going?"

"To get soup. I'm starving."

"I'll get it for you." He returned a minute later, trading the mug for the phone in my hand. I drank, wishing for something a bit more substantial. But this would do for now.

"Aren't you tired, handsome?"

Martin didn't answer. He ran his fingers through my hair. "You think he knows you." He examined the self-inflicted bruises on my forearm from my failed attempt to break the padlock. "Jablonsky said it's the same man who attacked you outside Cross Security. Is that what you meant?"

"Tell me about the phone call and the ransom demand. He called you Mr. Scott, right?"

Martin rubbed his temple. "Yeah, I think so. I didn't give a shit what he called me."

"Alexandra Scott was my cover identity for dealing with Noah, the con artist."

"Yeah, I know. I remember the rings." He smirked ever so briefly before the magnitude of the situation weighed him down once more. "What does that have to do with any of this?"

"Alexandra was a trophy wife with a rich husband. Noah owed this guy money but couldn't pay. He took Noah because of money. It's why he took the paintings from the gallery and the rings." I bit my lip and reached for the phone again, but Martin grabbed my hand instead. "I need to call Jablonsky or Cross. Someone needs to track the paintings. If they get fenced, we'll find the guy."

"They know, sweetheart. They scoured every inch of the gallery. They know what's missing. They're already on it."

"Right." I finished my broth, far from satiated but too tired to ask for another cup. "My point is, if this son of a bitch believed I was Alexandra Scott, he would have gone for the easy payday. Instead, he ignored the possibility completely. It was only after he nearly killed Noah that I promised him the money, and he called you."

Martin followed along very well for someone who probably hadn't slept in nearly a week. "He didn't believe you had the money. He didn't believe your cover. And since he attacked you outside Cross Security before this shit went down, you're guessing he knows precisely who you are."

I shivered, and Martin climbed into bed beside me. Our apartment building had top of the line security, but the possibility that the abductor might try to finish what he started left me unsettled. I wasn't safe, and neither was Martin. We wouldn't be safe until this bastard was behind bars or in the ground. Too bad we still didn't have any idea who he was or where he was. He was careful. Meticulous. Possibly versed in evidence collection.

"He's not getting near you again," Martin insisted. "Bruiser and Marcal are going to stay close, at least until you're back in fighting shape." I opened my mouth to protest, but he put his finger to my lips. "I'll hire additional security to watch my back, but I want people I trust guarding you."

"Marcal isn't a bodyguard. He's your valet."

"You say valet. I say he's my go-to for anything and everything. That includes watching over you. If I'm not around, he will be."

"Martin," I tried to protest.

"Don't fight me on this. You will lose, Alex. It's not because I don't believe you can take care of yourself. Hell, you fucking proved you're more than capable. If Mark and I hadn't shown up when we did, you would have flagged down the next car, gotten yourself to the nearest hospital or police station, and told them what happened. You didn't need us to rescue you. You did a fine job on your own."

I snorted. Considering the circumstances, he had a lot of faith in me. I wasn't even that confident myself. "Then why?"

"I need the peace of mind."

"You have to go to work." It wasn't a question. It was a statement because I knew he'd do all he could to move things around and work from home, but he needed to go to the office. He needed some semblance of normalcy. This was hitting him hard; so hard, in fact, that I was more concerned about how he was handling it than I was. He wasn't eating or sleeping, which I'd been doing almost religiously since he found me. "Remember what you told me years ago? You can't let the bastard win, so you don't let him dictate the terms of your life. Despite this little hiccup, you have a company to run."

"Yeah, okay." He moved to get out of bed, and I gripped him tighter.

"It's the middle of the night. I know you have some crazy workaholic tendencies, but it can wait until morning. I need to get some sleep, doctor's orders, but I can only do that if you're beside me."

"Then we'll talk about this in the morning."

I pressed a kiss to his chest. "Yes, we will."

TWENTY-EIGHT

"It's nice to see you up and around," Jablonsky said, nodding at the couch in his office. "Where's your shadow?"

"At work."

He swiveled his chair around to face me. "I didn't expect that."

"Neither did he, but it's important he goes through the motions. You know how he gets."

"Go easy on him. And go easy on yourself. We will hunt this shithead down. It's just a matter of time."

"You didn't find anything, did you?"

"We found plenty. Just not him." Mark blew out a breath and gulped down some coffee. He only landed a couple of hours ago, and from the dark bags beneath his eyes, it was obvious he hadn't slept in days. "We found some prints in the cabin, but they aren't in the system. I've never seen anyone this careful or lucky. Are you sure you never spotted any identifying marks?"

I thought about every interaction. "None. He was always covered head to toe. Even the ski mask he wore covered his mouth. He barely spoke. Almost as if he feared I'd recognize his voice."

Mark thought for a moment. "You must know who he is.

Just take a minute to think about it."

I'd done nothing but think about it since the attack in the alley. If I knew who the bastard was, I couldn't place him. "He's familiar with evidence collection and the way I'd react in volatile situations. He could be on the job."

"That would explain how he's managed to stay one step ahead and give us the slip." Jablonsky scribbled a note.

"Marty spoke to him several times." Mark reached for the phone and requested copies of the recorded conversations to review again. "I'll see what I can find, but I probably will have to talk to Martin again."

"I'm sure he'll make himself available."

Mark kept his thoughts to himself. "How are you feeling?"

"We should probably move on. Next question."

He picked up the phone and barked at one of the agents to bring a bottle of water to his office. He knew I could only stomach clear liquids. When it arrived, he twisted off the cap and placed it on the edge of his desk, nearest to me. As I settled back with my beverage, we went over the statements I made. This was now an FBI matter. The local field offices were conducting a nationwide manhunt for the psycho who abducted me. So far, they had no leads.

"We searched the shed and bomb shelter. There was no sign of him. He must have realized he was being followed and got spooked. He rabbited. Drove down that dirt path and pulled onto a service road. From there, he could have gone anywhere. We're searching DOT cams in the vicinity, but it's unlikely we'll get a hit. We issued a BOLO on the vehicle and a statement asking the public for help."

"Surely, someone will spot the car. It stands out like a sore thumb."

Mark leaned back in his chair. "You miss being an agent, don't you?"

"Right now, I miss solid food." I gave him a hard look. "What about the property records?"

Mark steepled his fingers together and pointed them at me. "That's where we run into problems." He glanced around, probably realizing he wasn't supposed to be telling me these things. But his loyalty to me ran deeper than his loyalty to the job. I wasn't sure when it happened, but we became family. Blood was thicker than water. Thoughts of the last time I saw Noah went through my head, and I cringed. "You sure you're okay?"

"Fine. The property records," I nudged.

He pulled a sheet of paper out of the blue file on top of his desk and held it out to me. "Property belongs to a Gideon Steinman. The cabin, the shed, and the car all belong to the octogenarian who's been living in a nursing home for the last six years."

I rubbed my temples. "Dammit."

"We're running down the usual suspects, checking with family and friends. Whoever decided to use Steinman's car and cabin must have known the man. Maybe a grandson or nephew. Hell, even a home health aide or caretaker." He chewed on his thumbnail. "Anything you remember might be of use."

"I don't know." I thought about everything I knew, afraid my memory was skewed on account of the unsub being the bogeyman of my nightmares. "Do you think our unsub could have an accomplice? Gideon or one of his caretakers could have given someone else a run of the property and keys to the car."

"Like I said, I'm looking into it."

"Noah sublet his apartment and rented the office under a fictitious name. Maybe he was working with the unsub. They had a falling out, and I got caught in the middle. It would explain why the unsub attacked me and also showed up outside Noah's apartment. Assuming they were on the outs, the unsub wouldn't have warned the con man about me, and when he found us together, it was kismet."

Mark got up and took a seat beside me. "Good theory. I'll do some more digging." He remained quiet for a time, internally debating what to say. I knew it was best to wait him out. Eventually, he said, "The search team found Noah a couple hundred feet from the cabin. In the middle of the woods, the ground had been cleared. He was partially buried, lying beside a pile of freshly dug dirt. We found a second grave beside his. It was empty."

"It was intended for me."

"That would be my guess. At the drop, the unsub left GPS coordinates which led to a diner a few towns over. We suspected it was a hoax. The agents positioned nearby managed to track him despite the deserted area, and once he turned onto the gravel road, we used aerial images to determine the most likely location. But if we hadn't," Mark shrugged, "well, it wouldn't have mattered. You already escaped."

"I was only able to do that because he went to pick up the money." It made sense now why he had hosed me down. He was cleaning up after himself, knowing he'd be leaving soon. Hell, the only reason he didn't kill me before he left was on the off chance the money wasn't in the bag. He might have needed to provide another proof of life before getting his payday. That was the only reason I survived.

"Yeah, well, after we found two graves, I thought there might be more. Cadaver dogs and those fancy scanners searched every inch of the woods. He's done this before."

"The mattress." I recalled the stains. "He kept others inside that bomb shelter. The mattress he gave me to sleep on was stained."

Jablonsky reached for another folder on his desk. It fell to the floor, revealing a stack of glossy crime scene photos. He bent down to pick up the items and held up a photo. "This mattress?" I nodded. "Yeah, the lab's testing it. Preliminary results show blood from four different people." He picked up the rest of the photos, stopping on a shot of the canned items. "You said he had meal replacement shakes and bottled water. He had no intention of letting you die before he was ready, but he wanted you weak."

"Yeah, well, I don't always follow the rules."

"I'm not complaining this time." He closed the folder. "We'll know more once the results come back from the lab."

"You should check into missing persons reports and unsolved abduction cases," I suggested.

"Already on it."

I didn't like what was going through my mind. "Noah could be in on it." I had days to think about it, and I couldn't shake a few glaringly obvious discrepancies. "He was dragged out of the cage several times and taken away. He came back bloody and beaten, but I never knew exactly what happened. Noah wouldn't fight back, and he didn't try to escape. The only time he tried to fight back was the last time I ever saw him. It was too little, too late. I tried to intervene by offering up the money, but I don't even know if it made a difference." I rubbed a hand over my chest, remembering the trunk, Noah's words, and the kidnapper's knowledge of my cover identity. "I need to check some things with Cross."

"Go. I've sent teams to scout all of Noah's known locations. We impounded the car he leased. But I was hoping to send a team back to the gallery to conduct a more thorough search. We rushed it the first time. As soon as Marty told me you were missing, he called Cross. I don't know what he might have collected or destroyed before we got there, but I'd like to find out."

"I'll get him to play ball."

Mark nodded. "Just in case you were wondering, I performed a quick check on Lucien and the rest of your coworkers. They look clean, but given the givens, we should assume the man who abducted you has some sort of law enforcement training or an obsession with police procedure. Cross knows a lot of people who fit that description."

"Do you really think he'd do this to me?"

"I don't know what to think. He wants Marty, and you already confronted him about that. Furthermore, I heard a little something about a seven-figure payday. If you're not around, he wouldn't have to split it with you. Until I'm positive his financials are clean, I'm keeping an eye on him, but if I honestly believed he was responsible, I wouldn't let you near him."

"Cross has money," I pointed out. "Lots of it. He wouldn't care about a quarter of a million. Plus, he was in the city. He helped search. It would have taken hours to make the trek back and forth."

"Yeah, but what if there's more than one unsub?" Mark offered a hand and helped me off the couch. "Just don't go anywhere alone with him or anyone else, including your buddies at the police department."

"Don't worry. Martin has assigned me a team of babysitters." I went to the door. "Call if there's any news."

"You do the same."

TWENTY-NINE

I left Mark's office and took a brief detour to see Dr. Weiler, one of the FBI shrinks. I hated psychobabble, but extreme times called for extreme measures. After getting a recommendation for one of the retired shrinks who specialized in PTSD and emotional trauma, I left the federal building.

Marcal and Bruiser were waiting out front. Bruiser stood like a statue beside the rear door. He didn't move, but I knew he was watching everything. He opened the door when I approached. Normally, I'd have something to say about that, but for now, I was grateful to stretch out in the back of the town car and not worry about walking any further than was absolutely necessary.

"Ready to go home, Miss Parker?" Marcal asked. Martin wasn't pleased I was venturing out and made that clear to his staff.

"We have one more stop to make. I need to speak to Cross."

"Very well."

"I'll accompany you inside," Bruiser said, catching my eye. He expected a protest, but I didn't give him one.

The drive didn't take long, and I stared pensively at the

looming office building. "I'm not sure how long I'll be. You can park in the garage."

Marcal winked at me from the rear view mirror. "I'll be waiting right here. Take your time."

"Thank you."

The lengthy elevator ride messed with my equilibrium, and I stumbled out of the elevator car on the thirtieth floor. Bruiser grasped my arm to steady me, and I gasped as his strong grip closed around my black bruises.

The receptionist stood. "Are you okay?"

"I'm great," I said sarcastically. I wasn't going up another two floors. "I need to see the boss."

"Yes, Miss Parker, right away." Wow, people were bending over backward for me. At least there were a few perks to nearly dying. "He's on his way." She stared at me uncertainly. "Would you be more comfortable in your office or one of the conference rooms?"

"Office."

I went down the hall and pushed open my office door. Amazingly, Cross hadn't hired someone to replace me yet. The intel I gathered remained pinned to the walls, and I dropped onto the couch and stared at it. Bruiser took an unobtrusive spot in the corner and waited.

A moment later, Cross quietly cleared his throat. "You should be in the hospital."

"People die in hospitals. Would you like me to drop dead?"

"Not in the least." He entered the room and nodded at Bruiser, as if this was a commonplace occurrence. "My medical team apprised me of your condition, Alex. Despite their report, you appear to be bouncing back."

"Well, dehydration isn't that hard to fix, assuming one has access to enough drinkable water."

"And the rest?"

"Should stop hurting eventually." I hated to ask. I didn't have the energy for a fight, but I had my argument prepared. "I need a favor. I need you to give Jablonsky everything we've collected on Don Klassi's case and complete access to the gallery and whatever you found there. I think it'd be best if the FBI takes over searching for

Noah's financial assets."

"Have they located the grifter?"

"Yes."

Lucien worked his jaw for a moment. "Not to discount the government's fine work," he said with a degree of venom and sarcasm I rarely heard, "but this is an area in which I excel. If you want to find out what's really going on, you'll tell them to let me stay the course."

"Lucien," I said, seeing a fire in his eyes, "is this about the ten million?"

Cross glanced at Bruiser. "This is confidential. Will you please wait outside?"

Bruiser looked at me, and I nodded. I saw the irritated look in the bodyguard's eyes, but he did as I asked and stood outside, refusing to completely close the door.

"There is no ten million," Cross said. "Klassi played us."

"Are you positive? Maybe you just haven't found it yet."

"I haven't found it because it doesn't exist." He reined in his snippiness. "Tell Jablonsky to send a request, and I'll see that he gets what he wants. You want to give him Noah's financials and Klassi's case, that's your call. Autonomy, right?" The word left a bitter taste in his mouth.

I thought for a moment. "Has anyone tried to hock the paintings or the engagement ring? It might lead to the asshole we're hunting."

"I already have people on it. Nothing has surfaced so far." He looked at the notes hanging on the wall. "At the risk of overstepping and violating your autonomous status, I took the liberty of researching some of the details you failed to share with me. I'm not sure it's important, but I did find several interesting pieces of information." He went to my desk and picked up the phone. "Make copies and have them brought to Parker's office."

"What did you find?"

"Nothing you need to concern yourself with today. Take them home. Read them at your leisure, and let me know what you think." He was practically throwing me out of my own office. His assistant brought the files down, and Lucien handed them to me.

"What are we doing about Don Klassi?" I asked.

"That's up to you, but I'd be more than happy to confront the lying sack of shit. You aren't in any condition to deal with more irritation, and you don't have to." He assessed me from head to toe. "A dislocated rib hurts like hell, almost worse than a broken one. And that's not even taking into account the bone bruises you sustained." He studied my cheek. "Are they sure that's not fractured?"

"Don't you trust your people to do their jobs?"

He smirked. "I do." Nodding down at the files, he said, "I'm interested to see what you think. In the meantime, I'll assist the FBI in any way I can." His face pinched together as if he'd been sucking on a lemon.

"Thanks." I slid off the couch and headed for the door.

"And Alex, you were right."

"About what?"

"James."

Bruiser took the files from me as soon as I exited the office. "Are you ready to go home now?"

"Do I have a choice?"

He hid his amusement well. "Not really."

"I guess I'll go home then."

On the drive back, I phoned Mark and told him Lucien was amenable to working together. In the time it took to leave the federal building and speak to Cross, the FBI had already made progress on the case. They located the red Pontiac, just not its driver.

"What about the car?" I repeated, cringing against the static.

"We found it abandoned on the side of the interstate. He didn't even make an effort to conceal it. He wanted us to find it. He's thumbing his nose at us. When I get my hands on this guy, he's going to regret everything he's ever done."

"He wants you to stop looking. He thinks he's clever."

"Unfortunately, he is."

"Yeah, well, that doesn't matter. I'm going to find that motherfucker." I licked my lips. "I have to. He's done it before. If we don't stop him, he'll do it again. And I won't let this happen to someone else."

"Parker, I know it's personal for all of us, but you should step back and let me handle this."

"Is that what Martin asked you to say?"

"No, but it's clear the unsub has a bone to pick with you. You don't need to piss him off, especially when you're on the mend."

"You're right." But I didn't always make the best decisions.

THIRTY

Detective Heathcliff was waiting in the lobby when I returned to the apartment. Upon seeing me and my entourage, he stood. Nodding his thanks to the concierge, he fell into step beside me.

"Jones. Marcal." Derek acknowledged each of them in turn before focusing on me. "Parker," his eyes narrowed on my cheekbone, "good to have you back in mostly one piece. Does that feel like it looks?"

We stepped into the elevator. "I don't know. Let me find some brass knuckles, and you can tell me." It was a bitchy remark, but I was tired and achy. "What are you doing here?" No one had been to the apartment Martin and I shared except Jablonsky. No one even knew about it.

"I phoned Martin. He said you'd be here." Derek glanced back at the boys. "After the ordeal you went through, I didn't think you'd be galivanting around town. Shouldn't you be in bed?"

"I spent the last two days doing nothing but sleeping and eating. Since my strength's returning, a field trip was in order." I led the way into the apartment, hoping to get a little privacy. The only way to do that was to send my bodyguards on a few errands. After asking Marcal to pick up some groceries, he left the apartment. Bruiser was easier to ditch. I simply asked him to wait in the lobby, which he interpreted to mean just outside our front door, probably with his ear pressed against it.

I sprawled out on the couch, wincing. Derek took a seat across from me. "God, Alex, I am so sorry this happened to you."

"Thanks."

He assessed me carefully. "For what it's worth, you've looked worse."

"Just what a girl likes to hear."

"Can I do anything? Get you anything?"

"No."

He removed the notepad from his pocket and clicked his pen a few times, a habitual act he performed when nervous or deep in thought. We had been at odds over his case, and I could tell he regretted that now. So did I. "Was it the same man from the alley?"

"That's the working theory. The man who abducted me and the one who attacked me drove the same vehicle. Same plate. Dressed the same. So we're assuming it's the same guy. The FBI's on it."

"I'm aware. SSA Jablonsky's spoken to me several times. But you and me, we're thick as thieves. I'm not letting this go." He held up his palm before I could speak. "I won't get in their way. Actually, I'm wondering if this connects to my murder investigation. We discussed it before, but I thought maybe now you might be more forthcoming."

"CryptSpec?" I asked.

"Yeah."

"You still haven't solved that? Sheesh. It's not like you had anything else to do." I shot him a playful smile. "Seriously, is this visit just an excuse to ask for my help? My consulting rate has skyrocketed since I signed on at Cross Security, but I'd be willing to give you the friends and family discount since we're thick as thieves."

He chuckled. "I wish it were that simple." He blew out a breath. "Would you mind answering some questions, and we'll take it from there."

"We'll see."

It was basic follow-up. Jablonsky, several other agents, and LEOs had already asked me the same questions. I didn't have anything new to say, but it wouldn't hurt to have someone else's input. Perhaps Heathcliff could offer a new perspective or gain some type of insight that no one else had. After all, he was coming at this mess from a different angle.

His theory was, and still remained, that the unsub was connected to Stuart Gifford and CryptSpec. The type of cryptocurrency Noah was dealing linked my investigation with Heathcliff's, even though I still wasn't sure how. The unsub probably wanted to scare me away from Klassi's case, and when that failed, he escalated to what would have culminated in murder had I not escaped. Derek closed the notepad and tucked it into his breast pocket.

"Gideon Steinman," he said. "It's a start. And you're sure he's not responsible?"

"He isn't. Jablonsky even checked with the nursing home. The man didn't escape."

"Has anyone questioned him yet?"

"You'd have to ask Jablonsky."

"That's probably the first place he looked." Heathcliff stood. "I'll look again and cross-reference his name with CryptSpec's employee database."

"How is the case coming?"

Derek scratched his head and found something interesting to stare at in the kitchen. "You mind if I have a cup of coffee?"

"Help yourself, but don't ask me how to make it because that's Martin's job."

He trudged into the kitchen, and I wondered if he planned to flip through the files on the counter when I wasn't looking. Honestly, I didn't care if he did. After searching the cabinets for a mug and coffee, he waited in the kitchen for the coffee to brew. "I looked into Don Klassi. You were right. He did have an alibi for the time of Stuart Gifford's murder. But Martin clued me in on Don's questionable dealings. He thought they might connect to whoever took you."

"And?"

"It's all one big question mark." He removed the mug from beneath the brewer and returned to the living room.

"Does the FBI have any leads? Hell, Parker, do you have any leads or a workable profile for this bastard?"

"Not really, but he's smooth. He doesn't leave prints, and if he does, they aren't in the system. It makes it impossible to determine who he is. But he's killed before. The search team found four bodies buried in the woods. It would have been six, but he forgot to lock the door. As far as I can tell, that's the only mistake he's made. He knows what he's doing. Jablonsky thinks he might be on the job."

Derek mulled it over. "Sounds plausible, but in that case, he'd have to know how risky it would be to make a move on you. He would need a really strong motive to even consider attempting it, and aside from sex and money, the only one left is to cover up another crime."

"Like another murder or a ten million dollar scam?"

"Sounds like you have a theory."

"I'm borrowing it from you. Honestly, I don't know what to think. This asshole is obsessively careful. Jablonsky's considered every possibility, but given what we know, I'm guessing this slimeball is a career criminal who's never been caught, which is what the evidence indicates. He's got to be a true psychopath. Intelligent, methodical, and lucky as hell."

"That's comforting." Derek finished his coffee. "Do you think he's smart enough to cut his losses and go to ground?"

"He's smart," I admitted. "And careful." But dumping the car on the side of the road was a taunt. He could have left it in a parking garage, drove it into the river, or found some less obvious way of disposing of it. "He's not done yet. He fucked up. He left two witnesses alive. Now we know he exists. He can't continue to anonymously kill, abduct, or whatever it is he does. We know he's out there. And we're not going to stop looking."

"Are you going to be okay?"

"I'll be fine."

"You need me, you call. Got it?" He considered giving me a hug but thought better of it. "I'll have patrols beefed up in the area. He's not getting near you again."

"Martin already hired additional security."

"Can't say that I blame him." Derek reached for the door, finding Bruiser on the other side. "And the fact that you're going along with it says a lot."

"Shut up."

Heathcliff gave me one last look and shook hands with Bruiser. "Make sure you keep her safe. And good luck. She can be a handful."

Bruiser snickered. "Yes, sir."

Instead of feeling empowered by the progress that had been made, I was overwhelmed. Everyone was working on this. Jablonsky mostly. But my pals at the precinct weren't going to drop the ball either. The only one I wasn't sure about was Cross. And honestly, I didn't want him involved. I didn't trust him. He had my back in the past, but his convoluted motives muddied the issue now.

"Hey, Jones," I said, and Bruiser closed the fridge door and turned around to face me, "I want to know what happened."

"Ma'am?" He tried to play dumb.

"I'm not in the mood. Spill."

He poured two glasses of water and brought them into the living room. He handed me one and sat in the chair Heathcliff vacated. "Martin doesn't want me discussing this. He's already going to be upset when he learns you went out, disobeying the doctor's orders for a week's worth of bed rest. I don't want to cause him any more problems."

"He's unraveling. I don't like seeing him suffer. I need to know what happened, so I can do something to fix it."

Bruiser sipped his water but chose not to comment. "He mentioned you saw the damage at his compound."

"Yeah." I wondered where this was going.

"He didn't know how to fix that situation, so he had to find a release valve."

"It wasn't his to fix."

"And this isn't yours," Bruiser said with wisdom not many possessed. "He has to come to terms with the way things went down. He's used to exercising a certain level of power and influence. He's never been able to do that with you. I imagine you could say the same about him. It's why the two of you work as a couple."

"I didn't know you had a psychology degree."

His eyes crinkled at the corners. "He believed he could negotiate and reason with someone unreasonable. From what I've seen, he's always believed that if push came to shove, he could pull enough strings and exude enough influence to keep you safe. Despite his best efforts, things did not go as planned."

"It wasn't his fault. He did everything he could." This situation mirrored so many that I had faced. Intimately, I knew the feelings of despair and helplessness. I'd felt them when Martin was shot, and no matter how much progress I made, they never completely went away. I doubted they ever would, and I knew this was what he was staring down every time he looked at me. "If he hadn't gone to the exchange, if he didn't agree to pay, I probably wouldn't be sitting here right now. But the rest was beyond his control."

"He won't stop until he figures that out." A sound at the front door had Bruiser tensed, his gun aimed at the doorway even as he maneuvered around the sofa to put himself between me and whoever was about to enter.

Marcal lugged several grocery bags into the apartment, and Bruiser's gun vanished just as seamlessly as it materialized. The bodyguard secured the front door and returned to his seat. We didn't speak of it again.

When Martin came home a few minutes later, cutting his workday short, he frowned at the files on the counter. "Did Detective Heathcliff leave these?"

"No." I pulled myself off the couch and went to grab the files, but Martin brought them to the coffee table and politely dismissed Marcal and Bruiser before taking a seat beside me. "You're not supposed to lift anything heavy."

"They're just files."

"Metaphorically speaking, they weigh a ton. You're going to need someone to help you with the heavy lifting, at least for a little while." He separated the files into different piles based on color. "Where do we begin?"

"Martin." But one look silenced my protest. He needed this. "We should start with the progress Mark's made." I pointed to a stack. "Hand me those."

"Okay."

I spread the pages out between us. "We need to simplify things." I grabbed the notepad off the side table and explained what I wanted to do.

Martin took off his jacket, loosened his tie, and settled back with pen and paper. We worked for hours sorting through the data and building a profile. We made lists of facts and items found in the bomb shelter and the cabin. We detailed everything there was to know about the car. Martin pulled information off the internet for that particular make and model. I wrote down what I remembered from being locked in the trunk.

He searched for details on the bomb shelter, finding out when it was built and who built it. He pulled the company details and called to see if they were still in business after almost seventy years. Since bomb shelters were no longer a hot commodity, predictably, the company went under decades ago. Still, he continued on that path. He made a list of the owners and the workers, figuring it couldn't hurt to check into their offspring.

"We need more details on the car. There must be purchase records."

I held out a page. "Is that what you want?"

He skimmed it. "Yep." He found the dealership and name of the salesman who sold Gideon Steinman the vehicle. "They're still in business. Perhaps Steinman brought someone with him when he made the purchase. A relative or friend." He bit his lip. "What do we know about Steinman?"

"He's old."

"Don't be an ageist."

I sighed. "He isn't responsible."

"But he's our best bet of finding the asshole who is. I want to talk to him."

Truthfully, so did I. "Jablonsky called dibs."

"He can't do that."

"He can actually. This is an official investigation. Any interference could be considered obstruction of justice. He could arrest us."

"Well, he wouldn't," Martin said. A pain shot through me, and I nearly doubled over. "Alex? What is it?"

"I'm okay."

"No, you're not. Maybe you should take a break. I can continue working on this."

"How about some lunch first? I'm famished."

"You haven't eaten? No wonder your stomach hurts. You should have eaten hours ago." He went to heat some broth. While he was in the kitchen, he skimmed my discharge papers. "Hey, do you want to try some soft foods? You've been doing the clear liquid thing long enough. I think we have some applesauce." He opened the pantry and peered inside. "You weren't supposed to go out. Did you go shopping?"

"Marcal did."

He took the steaming mug out of the microwave. "You should have told him to get applesauce." He reached for his phone. "I'm sure he won't mind making another trip."

"I don't like applesauce." I took the offered mug and blew on the rising steam.

"I could puree some vegetables. Carrots or something. Soft, overcooked fruits and vegetables should be easy to digest. You like carrots, right? I can boil some carrots. Maybe add them to the broth. Hell, you're just a few vegetables away from a hearty soup. It should be easy on your stomach. I should make some."

I grasped his hand. "Make yourself a drink and sit down."

Martin laughed. "You've never said that to me before. Normally, you say the opposite."

"Special circumstances."

He didn't make a move for the liquor cabinet, but he did sit beside me. "It's not even happy hour yet."

"It's five o'clock somewhere." I looked at his crumpled suit jacket hanging haphazardly off the back of the sofa. "And Mr. Armani would be crushed to see what you did to his masterpiece." I put my mug down and undid the buttons on his vest. When I was finished, I tugged on his tie. "This is usually the first thing you take off when you get home. Unless you're going back to the office, you need to take this off. Now."

"Next, you're going to tell me I should strip."

I grinned. "I wouldn't be opposed to a striptease."

"Oh, really?" He tried to play it off with that sexy, cool attitude that came naturally to him, but his words were hollow. He wasn't in a playful mood. His libido was inextricably linked to my well-being. "I'll make you a deal, sweetheart. As soon as this is behind us," he gestured at the papers and files, "I'll perform the hottest striptease of your life."

"With an offer like that, how can I refuse?"

I finished my cup of broth, and we went back to work. Martin picked up the phone, and before I could stop him, he was discussing the octogenarian with Mark. At least it gave Mark an opportunity to follow up with Martin, like he wanted. I sat back and surveyed the progress we made. I'd already begun this research at Cross Security, but maybe starting fresh with new facts would make a difference.

"Alex," Martin held out the phone, "Jablonsky wants to speak to you. It's about Noah."

THIRTY-ONE

"How is he?" Jablonsky asked.

"Remarkably well for someone who's gone through what he has." The doctor flipped through the chart. "We do have him on high doses of pain medication, so he isn't entirely lucid. But you can try to talk to him."

"Thanks."

The doctor glanced at me and touched his own cheek. "You might want to get someone to look at that."

"Someone already did." I waited for Mark to flash his credentials at the protection detail guarding Noah's room. "Do you want me to take lead?"

"You're not an agent, Parker," Jablonsky reminded me. He scratched the back of his head. "But seeing you might get him to open up. Just limit what you say. If you screw up, it's on me."

"In that case, you better be nice to me." I entered the room. "Hey, Noah."

Noah turned at the sound of my voice. "Alex? You're alive?"

"It looks that way." I moved closer and stood beside the bed, doing my best to block his view of Mark. "The last time I saw you, I thought...I'm glad you survived."

"Barely. The last thing I remember was you telling that sick fuck to leave me alone. Everything's fuzzy after that." He winced. "God, my head hurts." He tried to massage his temples but found his hand stuck to the rail. He stared at the metal bracelet, confused why it was there.

"Do you mind if I talk to you?" I asked gently.

Slowly, he turned back to look at me. "Talk to me all you want." He licked his lips. "I should have done something," he said quietly.

Resisting the urge to say I told you so, I went with the next best thing. "We're safe now. But I don't understand what happened. Who was that guy? Why did he want $250,000?"

Noah closed his eyes, sinking deeper into the pillow. The bandage around his skull matched the pillowcase. "Did you pay?"

"Yes."

"Good," he eked out. "He got what he wanted. He'll leave us alone now." His eyes closed, but I wanted answers.

"It can't be that simple. He tortured and buried you alive. He's killed before. I don't think he's finished with us." I shook his shoulder. "Noah, he nearly beat me to death. You owe me an explanation."

His eyes blinked open, but I wasn't sure if he was still coherent. "Huh?"

"When I woke up in the trunk, I thought I was dead. For a moment, I thought I had been buried alive. It was terrible. I can't imagine what the real thing must have been like. I'm so sorry."

He swallowed, fighting back tears. "I'm just glad someone found me. How did they find us?" He looked at Jablonsky before turning back to me. "Who are you?"

"You know who I am."

He shook his head, attempting to gather strength. "Under the circumstances, I have a hard time believing the police would let an art gallery owner in to see me." He jangled the handcuff on the bedrail. "Am I right?"

"I'm not a cop, if that's what you think, but I have friends who are. That's the only reason they found you before it was too late. They just want to help, but you have to let them."

"She's right," Jablonsky said. He put a hand on my shoulder, and I took a seat in the chair beside Noah's bed.

"So why am I a prisoner?" Noah asked. "I haven't done anything wrong."

"We have a strong case against you, Mr. Billings, but it doesn't have to be that way. My interest isn't in arresting you. It's in stopping a serial killer. I believe you know who he is, and if you cooperate, you'll be free to go as soon as the hospital clears you."

"It's Ripley," Noah insisted.

Jablonsky nodded. "Right, Ripley, that's what you were calling yourself when you tried to convince Alex to fall for your scheme."

"There was no scheme."

"Actually, we have evidence of your four latest con jobs. We've spoken to several of your marks. You're facing multiple counts of identity theft and fraud. And we're just getting started. But no one's been physically harmed by your actions. Am I right?" Mark asked.

"I don't hurt people." Noah appeared to be on the brink of passing out. Questioning him like this wasn't fair, but with a psycho on the loose, we didn't have a choice.

"I've spoken to the U.S. Attorney's office, and they're willing to make a deal if you provide us with intel that leads to the arrest of the violent criminal who nearly killed you and Alex."

Noah let out a wheeze. "I don't know who he is."

I took his hand. "You know plenty. Just think for a second. He focused on you. We need to know what he wanted. Was this about money? How much did he want? Did you rip him off?"

"I don't know who he is. I never saw his face. He wanted the coin. He wanted to know where I got it. How much there was."

"The cryptocurrency?" Mark asked.

Noah squinted and groaned. "Yes."

"Are you sure you don't know who he is?" Mark asked.

"He was always covered head to toe." Noah looked to me for affirmation, and I nodded. Suddenly, his eyes fluttered, and one of the machines beeped. He started convulsing, and a nurse rushed into the room.

"Get out," she yelled at us while a team of medical professionals raced inside.

Watching that brought back a lot of bad memories, and I dropped into a chair in the waiting room. Noah was a lot of things, but he didn't deserve this. No one did. "I don't want him to die."

"That's not up to us." Jablonsky rubbed my shoulder. "Do you believe that he doesn't know who did this to him?"

"After everything that he's been through, I don't see why he would protect that asshole."

Finally, a doctor came out, saying Noah was being moved back into the ICU. His condition was precarious. They didn't know if he'd make it, but obviously, speaking to him again was out of the question. Jablonsky offered me his arm for support as we went back to the car.

"This has to do with the cryptocurrency," I said. "It's worthless. I don't see why anyone would want it. It doesn't make any sense."

Mark blew out a breath. "That doesn't explain why the unsub has it out for you. It's personal for him. How the hell could you and Noah have pissed off the same man without even realizing it? You don't have anyone in common."

"Except Don Klassi."

Mark swore and reached for the phone.

*   *   *

"We've got one guy with a million identities and another guy with no identity." I paced in front of the couch, each step a reminder of running through the woods, the impact of my footfalls jarring the rest of my body. Pain shot through me, and I stopped moving. "They're connected somehow, but since we don't have names or basic facts, we can't determine how."

Martin flipped through the pages of notes he made and the intel he printed. "I don't understand why Noah didn't cooperate."

"It's not his fault. He's not in any condition to think

clearly or answer questions. I'm not even sure if he'll make it through the night."

"Dammit." Martin's jaw clenched. "He isn't innocent. For all I know, he's the reason you were taken."

"It's more complicated than that."

"Sweetheart, he stole ten million dollars. That's the reason Don approached you. It's the reason for all of this. Don't forget that."

I lowered to the floor, searching for the files Cross had given me. According to Lucien, Don never lost ten million dollars. "Everything tracks back to Don. He's the connection. The unsub knows him. He's been watching him. That's why I picked up his trail outside the bar and near Don's neighborhood."

"I wish I never let you speak to him. I should never have allowed shareholders to have seats on the board." He went to the liquor cabinet, poured two fingers, and knocked it back in a single swallow. "You didn't even want to go to that dinner party." His face contorted, and he swore. "I did this."

"Martin, no."

He fought the tremor that went through him. "I'm the reason Cross has been assigning you to these cases. And I fucked up the negotiation. Y'know, maybe you've been right all along, and we aren't good for each other."

"Come here."

"Alex," Martin didn't move from his spot, "I did this."

"You know that isn't true. It's not any truer than every time I've taken responsibility for your safety."

"This is different."

"The hell it is. Deep down, you know it's exactly the same. Our roles are reversed, but that doesn't change anything. I'm here because you intervened. Maybe it wasn't some heroic and chivalrous feat, but you got the job done. So I need you to pull it together because I can't do this by myself."

He poured another shot and swallowed it. "I said I'd do anything for you, and I meant it."

"Good. Why don't you start by helping me up?"

He knelt beside me, and I wrapped my arms around his

neck. He stood, and I crushed myself against him. He hugged me back, and we just held each other for what felt like hours. It was what we both needed. When I released him, he seemed steadier. More in control. More like the Martin I knew.

"Grab that folder." I pointed down at the table. "Lucien might be on to something."

I moved to the island counter and took a seat on one of the stools. Martin placed the folder in front of me, and I skimmed the pages as I laid them out. Cross Security had done a deep dive into Don Klassi's financial history. Most of Don's money was tied up in developing properties. It wasn't liquid, and it definitely wasn't hiding in some offshore account.

"Are those tax returns?" Martin asked, horrified and impressed.

"Yeah."

"How did Lucien get these?"

"I don't think we want to know."

Don said most of his money was offshore. I figured that was to avoid paying taxes, and based on what he reported to the IRS, he never paid taxes on the alleged ten million. Klassi was a partner in a real estate business with an estimated worth of twenty-two million, but that was for the entire business. Klassi wasn't sole owner. He wasn't worth that much. Honestly, according to what I was reading, he wasn't even worth ten million. And it looked like his partners wanted to buy him out.

Martin took the tax returns and a calculator and began running numbers while I examined the rest of the intel Cross collected. Klassi had several foreign bank accounts, but they equaled less than five million. These were the bank account numbers Klassi gave us when we promised to track the transfers and get back his money. Cross included lists of transactions into and out of the accounts. The most Klassi ever possessed was four million dollars.

"Don lied. He never gave Noah ten million. According to the transaction history, over the course of their relationship, he gave Noah $100,000." Even though it was written in black and white, I wasn't sure what to believe.

Noah had a system of names and accounts; he was a grifter, a known liar. Cross traced the $100,000 to a numbered Swiss account which belonged to Noah which currently had $168,590 in it. "This doesn't make any sense. Don hired me to recover the money. Why would he do that if there was no ten million? He could have just hired me to recover the hundred grand. He must realize we can't recover money that doesn't exist."

Martin jotted down a few numbers and pounded away at the keys. "He could sue Cross for failing to fulfill the contract to try to make up the difference. Or maybe Don figured since Noah conned him, he must have conned a lot of other people. First come, first served."

"Except he didn't want the money. He wanted the ten million in cryptocurrency that he claimed Noah owed him." I snorted. "Now who's the con artist?" I glanced at Martin. "What are you doing?"

He held up a finger, indicating I should wait. "I don't know. There's something screwy with these numbers. Don's assets don't add up."

"Yeah, well, he lied to us. He probably lied to the IRS too."

"I get that, but that's not the problem. Just give me some time to get this sorted."

Relieved Martin had something to work on that didn't involve planning a tactical assault on a nursing home or hospital room, I gave Cross's notes a more thorough readthrough. To summarize, he believed Don was on the verge of being pushed out of his company. Don didn't have the cash needed to prevent his two partners from taking over. They had already offered him a healthy severance and stock options which he turned down. They tried again, upping the offer. It was clear they wanted him out. They wanted to demolish several of the properties to rebuild and rebrand. The project required a lot of capital, but Don didn't have it. Since he was outvoted, he had to put in an equal share or bow out.

I rubbed my eyes and returned to the couch. Don was sleazy; I knew it the moment we met. I wasn't surprised his business associates wanted him gone. Hell, we all wanted him gone. Maybe Klassi thought he could collect an eight-figure payday by convincing me he'd been swindled by a charlatan. However, no matter how I twisted and turned the facts, it didn't answer the biggest question. Who abducted me?

"Noah didn't have that much money," I mused. "I wonder how much worthless coin he has."

"Probably not enough." Martin snorted. "Are you sure he's that great of a con man?"

I dug through the FBI files. Finding what I was looking for, I read the report. Noah's documents, the driver's licenses, social security cards, and birth certificates were infallible. They passed muster. Even the scan strips on the back coordinated with state DOTs.

"He actually had these issued by the government. They aren't fakes. They're copies." From my research into the phony names, I knew the men he impersonated existed. "He must have gone to these places to have the photo IDs made. It would have taken a lot of time and effort. Maybe there are other accounts in other names that we just haven't found."

"Then why didn't Noah offer to pay the guy? Agents found him buried. Surely, he must have realized he'd be killed. It's not like he could take it with him."

"That shithead would have killed us either way. After you gave him the money, he had no intention of bringing me to you. The reason he went back to the cabin was to kill me and clean up the mess."

"I know."

I looked at him. "You saved my life."

"Guess we're even, huh?" Martin said, his tone flat and cynical.

"Guess so." Another thought came to mind. "How did you pay the ransom?"

"Cash, nonsequential bills, nothing larger than a twenty. No trackers. No dye packs."

"Really?"

Martin scowled. "It was your life on the line. I only cared about you, not the money."

"I'll pay you back. It'll take some time, but I'll find a

way."

"No."

"Martin, it's a quarter of a million dollars."

"So what? I'd rather be bankrupt and have you than have all the money in the world and no you." He cracked a smile. "I just won't buy another Ferrari. It's not that big of a deal."

By all accounts, Noah was a coward. He would have done anything to save his own neck. He knew the unsub was coming for him. It's why he was so desperate for Alexandra Scott to fork over the money. He needed it to pay the bastard back or to finance his escape. But how could he owe money and not know who he owed? Why didn't any of this make sense?

THIRTY-TWO

"You're assuming the motive is monetary," Jablonsky said. "Psychopaths have their own reasoning, but it's usually not that simple."

"What if he isn't a psychopath?" I asked, and Mark gave me a look. "Yeah, okay, he's definitely a psycho, but maybe he's muscle. Someone could have hired him to take care of the problem. Perhaps he doesn't have skin in the game or a beef with Noah. Maybe he just does it for sport. For the thrill. He obviously enjoys killing. Maybe he just wanted Noah out of the picture."

"Noah and you."

A chill went through me. "Did anything come back on the blood found inside the bomb shelter? Have we identified any of the other victims? Dental records shouldn't take this long." I swallowed, predicting the answer to my next question.

"Parker, this is an active investigation."

"Just tell me."

"The remains are in advanced stages of decomposition. No prints. Initial exam suggests they're at least five years old. We'll know more after the lab processes everything. He knocked out their teeth, so we can't run dental records. The techs are hoping to do some computer modeling and facial reconstruction based on the bones and what flesh remains."

"Have you tried speaking to Noah again?"

"Hospital won't allow it. He's taken a turn. His brain is swelling. It might be an infection. We're waiting to see."

"Keep the protection detail on him."

"I intend to. Speaking of protection," Mark said.

"Don't worry. Martin and I are well-versed in the birds and the bees. We're always safe."

"Parker," he growled.

"Like I said, Martin has it covered."

"Now that image is burned in my mind."

I laughed. "Sorry, that one was unintentional. Heathcliff upped patrols, and Bruiser and Marcal are sticking around me. Martin hired a secondary team to shadow him."

"Cross's guys?"

"No. Bruiser's navy buddies. We've used them before on occasion. Didn't you vet them?"

"Yeah, but Marty didn't tell me why he wanted them. I was afraid it might have been a tactical breach or some other hairbrained black ops rescue mission."

"Is that why you let him have a gun and wear a vest?"

"He knows how to shoot, and he insisted on making the drop. I had no choice but to let him tag along. The least I could do was make sure he was protected. Damn, there's that image again. You make any more progress on figuring out how Don Klassi fits into this?"

"I'm working on it."

"Same here. I'm hoping to get a peek at his phone records to see who he's been in contact with."

"Call Heathcliff. After I was attacked in the alley, the detective thought it might be linked to Stuart Gifford's murder. He's investigating Don in relation to that on the off chance they are connected."

Mark snorted. "It's a long shot, but if we can convince a judge that it's a real possibility, I might just get that warrant. Thanks, Parker."

"I got you covered."

"Ugh. I'm going to soak my brain in vodka now."

Chuckling, I put the phone back on the table. Martin gave me a cock-eyed look. "You haven't laughed much since I got you back. I missed that sound." He rubbed his eyes and put the documents down. "Do you want to let me in on the joke? I could use a laugh."

I laughed harder which caused a sharp pain in my side. I did my best to hide that from Martin and fought to regain my breath. "Mark's just having some very dirty thoughts."

"Oh, really? And he told you about them?"

"Well, he didn't have much of a choice. They were about you."

Martin gave me a look. "Should I be worried?"

"No, I told him you always use protection." I did my best to fight off the fit of giggles that threatened to rip my insides apart. "Forget it. It made sense in context."

"I'm sure it did." He gave my pill bottle a look, contemplating if I'd been self-medicating when he wasn't paying attention. "You should get some sleep," he concluded. "You weren't even supposed to get out of bed today, and you've been traipsing across town, conducting interrogations, and answering questions. You need to rest."

"In a few minutes. I just want to finish this." I looked at the growing number of pages in front of him. "Are you still working on Don Klassi's financials?"

"Yeah, I'm almost done."

Martin continued to work, and I read through the rest of the FBI reports and updated the information to reflect the newest details. I laid back against the couch. The ache in my back and ribs subsided as the couch cushions took the strain off my knotted muscles and bruised bones. I turned my head to see Martin still hard at work. I didn't know what he hoped to find, but he was determined to figure out how Don was connected to the unsub. He wanted to know the psycho's identity just as badly as I did. I closed my eyes and listened to the click of the keys.

Like Mark said, this case was personal. The abductor attacked me for a reason. Why did he want me to pay? Why did he want to punish me? What did I do to him? How did he know Noah and I would both be at the gallery? He followed Noah; I was positive of that. But how would he have known I'd be there too?

Who knew where I'd be? I ran through the possibilities, not liking the answers. I had no idea what my coworkers were capable of. Kellan proved that by investigating and selling me out to Lucien. Well, turnabout was fair play. I snatched my laptop off the table, but I wasn't sure where to start. Jablonsky investigated everyone at Cross Security and said they were clean. But something stunk, and it tracked back to the office. The first attack was right outside. The second was at Cross's gallery. Cross was the common denominator.

*   *   *

The next day, I went to the office, feeling more jittery than usual. Bruiser followed me inside and closed the door. I stared at the walls. Everything I had on my three cases was here. The intel on CryptSpec, details about the attack in the alley, and Don Klassi's case. Someone could have come in here, looked at it, and decided to make a move. And the few people with access to my office had the skills necessary to conceal a crime.

"Are you sure this is a good idea?" Bruiser took a seat in my chair and placed his firearm on top of the desk.

"Nervous?"

"No, but Mr. Martin would not be happy about this."

"Yeah, well, not much has been making him happy lately. I'd hate to break the pattern." Letting out a lengthy sigh, I picked up the phone. "Is Mr. Cross in?"

"No, would you like to leave a message?" his assistant asked.

"No, that's okay." I put the phone down. "Guess I won't be confronting the bastard after all."

Bruiser eyed me skeptically, not believing I would give up that easily. In truth, I knew I wouldn't be able to handle a confrontation. And every fiber in my body said this was wrong.

It was lunchtime. I knew there was a good chance Cross wouldn't be in the office. That meant I could either wait him out or let Jablonsky handle it. I knew which choice I should make. Jablonsky phoned this morning. Crime techs found Cross's business card inside the abandoned red car, and after taking a look at Don Klassi's phone records, Mark reached the same startling conclusion I did last night. He wanted to have a chat with Lucien, and I wanted to clear out before he did.

Kellan's office was dark. He wasn't around either. I didn't like the thoughts going through my head, but all signs pointed to it, even if my gut disagreed. It wrapped up nicely, but we had to be sure. Mark would make sure. Lucien Cross was not a man who took kindly to accusations, but he wasn't exactly the cooperative, transparent type either. Cross left us no choice.

After removing the intel from my walls, I tucked the files under my arm and gave the office a final look. Until this was sorted, I wouldn't be back. It wasn't safe. I cursed myself for allowing Lucien to discover the connection between Martin and me. If my boss was dangerous, I didn't want to think about what might happen.

When I arrived home, Martin was gone. Fear gripped me, but I was assured he was safe at work. He hadn't slept the night before. Evidence of his insomnia covered every flat surface in our apartment. He was right. We needed a bigger place.

I put the files down on a stool and looked around. Our apartment was starting to resemble the inside of my brain. Fighting back the overwhelming desire to tidy up, I checked my messages. Jablonsky was supposed to call, and until he did, there wasn't much I could do.

A pot of soup simmered on the stove, and I lifted the lid. "He's insane." I ladled out a bowl. "When did he have time to make soup? Did he even change his clothes this morning?"

"Love makes men crazy," Bruiser said.

"Do you want some?" I asked, taking the bowl and clearing off a spot on the couch.

He shook his head and checked the balcony door. I just finished eating when the intercom buzzed. Marcal pressed the button.

"Miss Parker, there's a delivery. Office supplies. Mr.

Martin said they would be arriving this afternoon," the doorman said.

"Send them up," Marcal said, knowing more about what was going on than I did.

Bruiser gave me a look. "Go in the bedroom and close the door." He had his gun out.

"You're joking."

His eyes went hard. "Now. Don't come out until I tell you it's safe."

Payback's a bitch, I thought as I closed myself into the bedroom. How many times had I used that line with someone else? Hell, how many times had I said something along those lines to Martin? And when exactly did he order office supplies?

I kicked off my shoes and pulled down the covers, desperate to lie down for a few seconds. The bed hadn't been slept in. I had fallen asleep on the couch while Martin apparently did my job, his job, cooked, went shopping, and saved the entire free world. At this point, he had to be running on fumes. He had barely slept since he found me in the woods, and I doubted he slept much the prior four days. He was going to hit the wall hard. He couldn't keep this up. It was time I climb back into the driver's seat. With any luck, this would all be over soon. Maybe I could convince him to take a nap when he got home. Frankly, I wasn't opposed to the idea.

"Clear," Bruiser said from the other side of the door.

So much for my nap. Stepping out of the bedroom, I spotted three free-standing magnetic whiteboards taking up every spare inch of space in the living room. Obviously, this was a cosmic sign that I should get to work. Last night, we laid the groundwork. Today, I'd build a profile.

I knew things about the man who abducted me. First and foremost, he was a killer. He had at least four prior victims and had been intent on adding two more. He worked in seclusion. He was prepared to keep his victims indefinitely before executing them. I wasn't sure how long the others had been held captive, or even if they had been, but he had enough supplies and privacy in that bomb shelter to keep his prisoners alive for years.

Cringing at the thought, I grabbed a handful of clip magnets and stuck photographs of the cabin and the bomb shelter on the board. Next to that, I placed a map of the area and an aerial shot. The unsub knew he wouldn't be found. He also had a short fuse but was capable of exercising extreme control when necessary. He was obsessed with control.

He was also prepared. The trunk had been outfitted to prevent escape, and the car was old enough not to have the modern safety features. Even though it was old, it had once been a common vehicle. People didn't notice it, except when he set off the alarm. He knew how to distract and bide his time. He wasn't in a rush.

Two things stuck out. The quarter of a million dollars and his desire to make me pay. Those details would lead to his identity since nothing else would. He was always covered head to toe. He rarely spoke. He didn't demonstrate any nervous habits or tics. He could be anyone, even Lucien Cross.

I stuck photos of the red car on the board. The FBI techs photographed everything. Predictably, the interior was clean, except for the business card beneath the seat. Lucien Cross's business card. That couldn't be a coincidence. Leaving the car behind was a dare. A challenge. He was taunting us, demonstrating that he knew just how good he was. He was an egomaniac, confident in his abilities, just like Cross.

Who are you? I scribbled on the board. The unsub knew me and how I would react. He knew to neutralize me. Despite his ego, he knew it was best not to face me in a fair fight. Aside from the gun he used to garner Noah's compliance and keep me at bay, he never brought a weapon into the bomb shelter, except for the brass knuckles. Another thing he never brought inside was his phone. He was afraid they could be used against him. Did he fear me?

While I was contemplating that unlikely possibility, the phone rang. After glancing at the caller ID, I answered. "What happened?" I asked.

"Cross is in custody. Unless he confesses or something

solid turns up in the next couple of hours, we're gonna have to kick him. He has an alibi for the time of the assault and abduction, but I'll follow up with the two women and motel manager to make sure he's not lying. After that, I'm going to take a crack at him. His card was in that car for a reason."

"Women?"

"At the approximate time you were assaulted in the alleyway, Cross was with two women. They were checked into a motel. The clerk at the desk saw them enter, and they didn't leave until after eleven."

"He came back to the office as the police were finishing up. It was 11:30, maybe. It sounds like his story tracks."

"Yeah, but it's possible he could have slipped out. There weren't any surveillance cameras aside from the one at the desk. Lucien could have left through a different exit and came back in without anyone noticing, but with three people saying he was there, it'll be hard to disprove."

"If he is involved, he has an accomplice. Cross was with Martin at the gallery while I was locked in the trunk. He couldn't have been in two places at once."

"Great way to establish his innocence, by getting your boyfriend to be his alibi. It's genius."

"It's also farfetched."

"Maybe, but Cross knows more than he's letting on. I'll get him to crack," Mark said, and I wondered if his judgment was clouded by his disdain for Lucien. "During those four days you were held, there were a dozen calls back and forth from Lucien to Klassi. It's suspicious as fuck."

I looked back at the profile I made. Every one of my bullet points accurately described Cross.

Mark sighed. "I know it sounds crazy, Parker, but Lucien Cross is the only person I can think of who would have known where you'd be, when you'd be there, and what you were working on. He had the codes to the gallery. He could have remotely caused the alarm to go off, which forced you to deactivate the motion sensors, and then he triggered the fire suppression system. Who else could have done that? Who else even knew you were there?"

"Shit."

"Cross knows procedure. He understands crime scenes. He knows how to avoid getting caught. And," I heard Mark swallow, "he was angry at you over Marty. Maybe he figured he'd get some payback, or he just wanted you out of the way. You said the unsub wanted you to pay, and we already discussed the possibility he's just hired muscle. Cross could have hired him. You said it yourself; he has money and the means to get away with it."

My stomach twisted in knots, and I regretted eating the soup. It fit. All of it fit. But I wasn't convinced it was true.

THIRTY-THREE

"You're enjoying this." Cross sipped the sludge that passed for coffee inside the federal building. "I hope it's worth it, Jablonsky. By the time my attorneys finish with you, you'll be lucky not to be facing charges of your own. And you should kiss your pension goodbye."

Mark chuckled. "That's a new one. Look," he held out his hand, "I'm shaking."

"Obviously, you have nothing better to do with your time. However, I can't say the same."

"Have more people to abduct?"

Cross put the cup down. His eyes grew sharp and cold. "What did you say?"

"You heard me."

Cross stared at the glass, searching for some way to verify what he suspected. "You think I kidnapped Alexis Parker? Have you lost your fucking mind? I've been nothing but cooperative. I helped you find her. I was at the gallery while she was being driven across the state."

"It makes you look innocent, but it doesn't mean you are."

"That's thin, even for you." Cross sneered. "Show me the evidence. What's my motive?"

"I'm asking the questions."

"Funny, I didn't think you knew how."

Jablonsky stood. "When did you meet Noah Ripley?"

Cross turned his head and snickered. "Seriously, that's what this is about?" His gaze settled on the mirror. "It's true. I set up a meeting with Noah before Parker did. After signing Don Klassi as a client, I had my computer experts investigate. They found Noah almost immediately. He had several phony internet IDs, presumably to find additional marks to scam. Within thirty minutes of leaving a message, Noah reached out."

"Why so quickly?"

"Probably because he knew I wanted to move six figures that same day."

"Where did you meet him?"

"We met in the lobby of an office building known for having several prestigious accounting firms. He wasn't renting a space there, but he wanted me to believe he was associated with these reputable businesses." Cross picked up a pen and wrote down the address. "I'm sure you'll want to know precisely where."

"How about when?"

Cross pulled out his phone and looked at the calendar, giving Mark the exact time and date. It was after Klassi left the office but before I went to dinner with Kellan. Cross stared at me through the glass. "I want to speak to her."

"Who?"

Cross rolled his eyes. "Parker. I'm sure she's watching. I want to speak to her. Now."

"Too bad." Mark flipped through a folder. I didn't know what he was looking at, but Cross appeared to be interested in it. "Why would you meet with the target of an investigation without informing the primary investigator?"

"She doesn't like it when I interfere, but I wanted to check things out. This case was going to require a significant investment by my firm with the possibility of a large payday. But it was a gamble. I don't like gambling, unless the odds are in my favor."

"Significant investment." Mark rubbed his mouth. "You wanted James Martin to invest with you, right?"

"That is irrelevant."

"Not when it goes to motive. Parker's dating him. You didn't like that because it screwed with your plans. You couldn't control what their relationship meant for your business ventures. Initially, you must have thought hiring her would get you in with Martin, but it didn't. And you didn't know why. So you had one of your investigators look into it because you were too inept at doing it yourself."

"Careful, Jablonsky," Cross growled.

Mark didn't falter; instead, he turned up the heat. "Maybe you wanted her out of the way since she was ruining your chances. You couldn't fire her. That would look bad. But if she disappeared, well, you could play that just right. You could lead an investigation that would drag on indefinitely. Given their relationship, Martin would practically insist upon it. And you figured eventually he'd weaken. He'd see the error of his ways and decide to partner with you. That's what you thought, right?"

Cross gave him a deadly smile. "You're right. She did fuck me over. But that was my fault. Did it make me mad? You bet. It made me furious at myself for not getting the details straight before I hired her. But I wouldn't hurt her." The smile dropped, and he stared into the glass. "I respect her. I value her."

My stomach flipped again. It might have been stupid, but I believed him. That was the point of the show though. Lucien knew I was here. Maybe that's why he didn't bother having Mr. Almeada, his attorney, sit in on the interrogation. He figured I'd call it off.

"Respect her?" Mark scoffed. "You had Kellan Dey befriend her just to get close to her. That isn't respect."

"Have you spoken to Mr. Dey?"

"Not yet, but I'll get to him soon enough."

Cross cleared his throat. "I'll save you the trouble. Kellan informed me he and Alex were going to dinner that evening. I was aware of what time they left and her plans to return to the office afterward."

"So you could have attacked her in the alleyway?"

"No. You know where I was at that point. That's been asked and answered, or are you too senile to remember?"

"That doesn't mean you weren't working with someone else. How did your business card get inside the unsub's car?"

"How the hell should I know?"

"The attacker knows Alex or at least some basic things about her. And he had your business card. That can't be a coincidence. You must know who he is. Now's the time to tell me. The longer you wait, the worse it'll be on you."

"I can't tell you what I don't know."

Mark flipped to another page. "Do you deny that you knew Alex was at the gallery or that you possess the know-how and skill necessary to cause the malfunctions in the alarm system and activate the fire suppression system?"

"I knew where she was. We spoke about it earlier that morning. And I could have easily accessed the gallery's security system. My people installed it, but you already know this. You also know I was busy at the time. Had I not been in a meeting, I would have been notified of the malfunction and conducted a diagnostic. Unfortunately, I wasn't around to prevent what happened. Like I told you before, I believe the system was hacked. What did your investigation turn up on that matter?"

"The breach was seamless. The person who did it knew exactly what to do. Maybe you had one of your experts do it for you?"

Cross slammed the mug down. "I wasn't there. I'm not responsible. My people are not responsible."

"How can you be sure?"

"I trust the people who work for me."

"Fine," Jablonsky said, "but you know plenty of shady individuals. You could have paid an outsider, just so you wouldn't be implicated."

"You're a moron if you think that."

"So give me access to your phone records and financial statements."

"Get a fucking warrant." His fists clenched, and he blew out a breath. "Let me talk to her." Mark didn't respond, so Cross tried another approach. "Either I speak to her now, or I'll speak to her as soon as I'm released. You have no evidence. How long do you think you'll be able to keep me before my attorneys cite you for abuse of power?"

Mark took a seat and stared at Cross. "You've been speaking a lot to Don Klassi lately."

"He's a client. Alex's client."

"Probably goes back to your obsession with James Martin." Mark continued to stare. "The two of you spoke often over the course of this week, at least a dozen times. What were you discussing?"

Lucien's expression soured. He was fed up. "His case."

"That included details about the scammer, right?"

"If it was relevant."

Mark nodded. "And you knew Noah had been abducted from the gallery at the same time Parker was."

"I gave you the footage."

"Right. Did you share that information with Klassi?"

"Do you think he's involved?" Lucien asked.

"Anything's possible." Mark snorted. "Were you working together?"

Lucien neatly folded his hands. "This conversation is over. I am invoking my right to legal counsel."

Hoping to avoid Mark getting into trouble, I left the observation room and opened the door to interrogation. Mark glared at me. *Get out*, he mouthed, but I entered anyway.

Cross sat up straight and offered the empty chair across from him. "Turn off the recording equipment."

"There is no privilege here. She's not your lawyer," Mark snarled. "Hell, she shouldn't even be here. Whatever you say to her is staying on the record. So make it quick. I do have better things to do."

Cross snorted and tuned out Mark. "Miss Parker, I told you that I didn't require your trust or loyalty, but I need it now." He swallowed. "I didn't do this, Alex. You know that. Call off the dogs. You're wasting time and resources. He designed it this way. He wants you to be confused. It'll buy him time to figure out his next move. He's smart enough to know he should move on, but I don't believe he's done. There's more at play here. I just don't know what it is."

"Who is he?" I asked.

Cross shrugged. "I don't know. But I can tell you,

whoever he is, he isn't in this room."

"What about Noah? Why did you meet with him? Did you make an exchange?"

"You were right about me. I am a micromanaging prick. That's why I met with him behind your back. You wanted autonomy, but I had to see for myself what was what. I gave Noah fifty thousand dollars," Cross said, "half of what I promised during our internet exchange. Amir ran the trace. When you transferred the five grand to Noah, it went into the same account. It never branched. It wasn't withdrawn. It just sat there. I had the transactions run, along with an account history. There was never ten million. Klassi never transferred that much to Noah. It was a lie."

"What about other accounts? Noah must have more than one."

"Check the notes I gave you. Klassi is using my firm for something insidious. I don't know what. I was trying to determine that when Jablonsky decided to arrest the wrong man." Cross leaned back in the chair. "Do you believe me, Alex?"

I sat there, unsure what to think. Cross admitted he could have done it or had someone else do it for him. He'd gone behind my back before. He manipulated and controlled people.

"It doesn't matter what she thinks," Jablonsky said. "It's my case. My call. Since you denied my request for access to your financial history and phone records, you can wait in a holding cell until the warrant comes through."

"I'll be out a lot sooner than that," Cross warned. Another agent came in to escort him from the room. "Parker, find out what's going on."

The door closed, and Mark blew out a breath. "Lucien's right. The man who attacked you and abducted you isn't in this room."

"Lucien's going to bury you," I said.

"Well, at least he didn't bury you." Mark sighed. "What do you think? He admitted he's an asshole. He could be involved. He could have hired the unsub."

I watched the red light blink out on the camera. "By his own admission, he could have pulled it off, but it doesn't feel right. He's lobbing softballs. He could have shut down the interrogation the moment you stepped inside, but he didn't. He's cooperating, trying to help."

"That's cooperation?" There was too much bad blood between the two. "He could be doing it to screw with your head."

I thought for a moment. Memories of other cases came to mind. Cross saved my life. He tried to protect me. To do a complete one-eighty was unlikely. "Lucien's right. This is about Don."

"I'll figure it out. In the meantime, you should go home. There's nothing else you can do here," Mark insisted. "Check those notes he mentioned and get back to me."

"Yep."

THIRTY-FOUR

"Where's my fucking money?" Don Klassi screeched in my ear. I pulled the phone away and hit the speaker button, hoping to avoid hearing loss. "Lucien phoned last week and said you were close to tracking my stolen money. He said you made contact with Noah, that you were going to trace everything back to his account. When Cross called again, he said he was taking over my case and promised to have information by the end of the week. I've been calling him all day, but he won't return my calls. His secretary won't tell me where he is, just that he's out. I want answers. I hired you, not Cross. Have you forgotten our arrangement? I held up my end. I'm waiting for you to hold up yours. I want to know what's going on."

Martin, who was in the kitchen, glared daggers at the phone. He opened his mouth, but I held up my hand to keep him quiet. He looked like he was about to rip Don a new one.

"There's been a snag," I said.

"What kind of snag?"

I silently communicated the question to Martin. I had to be sure. He nodded, and I prepared for another shrieking onslaught.

"Oh, I don't know, Don. The kind that would indicate you never gave ten million dollars to Noah Ryder."

He went eerily quiet. "Are you trying to rip me off? Is that what Noah told you? You know I transferred money to him in exchange for coin. I showed you my bank account and the coin I received. You know I gave him money."

"Yeah, in exchange for worthless cryptocurrency. I'm not saying he didn't screw you. He's a con artist, that's his job. But stop pretending this is bigger than it really is. You showed me what you gave him and what you received in return. That was it. $100,000. There were no other transfers. We checked. You never gave him ten million."

"Are you calling me a liar? Is this how you conduct business? I hired you to recover the coin he failed to provide, and now you're telling me there is no money. Either you're hiding it, or you're too incompetent to find it. I'll sue Cross Security."

"You do that." I expected him to hang up, but he didn't.

"Come on, I need it. I don't have time for this. At least give me what you recovered. It's mine. You can't keep it."

"I haven't recovered anything."

"You bitch."

Martin bristled, stabbing the contents of the slow cooker. I put my hand over his, afraid he might burst out of the apartment in a homicidal rage and slaughter Don Klassi with the meat fork.

Don continued yammering. "The USBs with the verified coin amounted to over a hundred thousand dollars. You can't deny that. You can't say that money didn't exist or that I didn't give it to Noah. If that damn drive he gave me with the ten million wasn't corrupted, you'd be singing a different tune." He blew out an agitated breath. "Since you're telling me the coin is worthless, get me the cash. Cross said he located Noah's account. So reverse the transfers. Give me whatever was in his account."

"It's not that simple. Maybe we should get the authorities involved. They might be able to clear this up faster," I reminded him.

"I held up my end. I sold my shares of MT. You have to follow through, or," he struggled to come up with a decent threat, "I'll expose you and James."

"Too late, but thanks for playing."

Don was becoming increasingly belligerent. "Just get me what you can as soon as you can." He hung up, and I turned off the speakerphone.

Martin shredded the rest of the brisket, probably wishing it was Don he was tearing to pieces. "He's desperate."

"You caught on to that too?"

He smirked. "Based on his upside-down finances, I'd say he owes someone money."

"A lot of money." I glanced at the whiteboard Martin had covered in Klassi's financial statements. "Any idea who?"

"No, but I bet that's the real reason he wanted to unload the MT stock so quickly. It would have been suspicious had you not insisted upon it since he just received his seat on the board." He finished with the meat and placed it in a glass container. "Let me take a look at Cross's notes, and I'll see if I can make heads or tails out of what's going on."

I already read through them twice before contacting Don. They weren't the smoking gun Lucien indicated they would be. I maneuvered around the counter and took Martin's face in my hands. "Later. Right now, you need some sleep. You're running on fumes. And since you're only working half days, you don't have an excuse not to take a nap."

"I'm fine."

He was just as stubborn as I was. "I know you're Superman, but I'm not. It's the middle of the afternoon, but I'm achy and sore. I can't sleep on the couch again, and I can't sleep without you. Is there anything I can do to convince you to lie down with me for a few hours?"

"I know what you're doing." He pressed his lips to my temple. "You hate it when I'm clingy."

"Yeah, but you love it when I am."

"Does Jabber really believe Cross is responsible?"

"He fits the profile, but I don't think either of us believes it. He just doesn't want to take any chances."

Martin thought for a moment. "Does Don have an

alibi?"

"Yes, but Lucien believes he's involved. The one thing we know is the psychopath has an axe to grind with Noah and me. And so far, we only know of two people we have in common, Lucien Cross and Don Klassi."

"Why isn't Don in custody?" Martin asked, climbing into bed beside me.

"Klassi has no criminal record and an alibi. Mark can't touch him, but Heathcliff's working on it."

"What can the detective do?"

"I'm not sure." An uneasiness wormed its way through my gut. Klassi was committed to his lie, assuming it was a lie. Of course, that would mean Noah, the professional liar, had told the truth about the ten million. That was even less likely. This was a mess.

Both Cross and Martin insisted Klassi never had enough capital to lose ten million. Sure, it was possible he had foreign accounts and hidden assets we didn't know about, but in the last five years, Don never earned anywhere near that amount. An inheritance or insurance payout would have been flagged by the IRS. And his investments didn't generate much of anything. Most of what he earned went back into the company.

I could only see two possible explanations. Klassi never had the money and wanted to scam the scammer, which was my initial thought. Or Klassi borrowed a substantial amount from someone questionable, and the loan came due. There was a third man.

Martin jerked. He thrashed for a moment, but before I could wake him, he rolled closer and settled beside me. He wrapped an arm around me, and I bit back the hiss as I carefully slipped my arm beneath his to cushion my ribs. He tangled one of his legs with mine and let his head loll onto my pillow. No wonder he hadn't slept in days. It was the only way he could be sure to keep his distance. Asleep, he always gravitated toward me.

Since there was no way I could slip out of bed and search for the third man, I leaned against him, putting a little more space between his arm and my ribs, and tried to sleep. My phone buzzed, but it wasn't loud enough to wake him. I watched the display light up and the device jitter in place. From this angle, I couldn't see who was calling, and I didn't really care. It stopped, and I closed my eyes.

Gasping, I awoke. My heart was racing. My eyes darted back and forth, but I had no idea what had spooked me. The usual nightmares hadn't surfaced, at least not to any panic-inducing degree.

"Alex?" Martin was still wrapped around me. "I'm here. I'm right here. What is it?"

"Nothing. I'm okay. Go back to sleep." I fought the urge to curl into a quivering ball.

He tried to pull away, but I grabbed his hand and linked my fingers with his. "I'm hurting you. I shouldn't have fallen asleep."

"No, you're not. And don't you dare say that. The only thing we're good at is sleeping together. If we can't do that right, we might as well give up now."

He kissed my neck. "That's not true. We're great at other things."

"Individually, yes. As a couple, not so much," I teased.

Before he could list the things at which we excelled, my phone buzzed again. I wondered how many times it did that while we were passed out. I didn't make a move for the offending device. A voice in my head warned against it.

"Aren't you going to—"

"No," I said quickly.

When it stopped ringing, I settled back against him, but his posture remained rigid. Before he could ask why I was avoiding the late night call, his phone rang.

"Shit. Shit. Shit," I cursed. The world was about to come crashing down.

Martin freed himself from my grip and grabbed his phone. "It's Heathcliff."

I wasn't expecting that. "Answer it." I reached over and checked my missed calls. Three came in over the last seven hours, all from Heathcliff. At least we actually got some sleep, even if I didn't feel particularly rested.

"Detective," Martin said, "yes. That's right." He scrubbed his face. "Yeah, okay, I'll make myself available. Just text a list of what you need." He looked at me and pointed at the phone. "Alex? I'll see." He covered the mouthpiece. "He wants to talk to you."

I took the phone. "Hey, what's up?"

"Screening your calls?" Heathcliff asked.

"Try too tired to answer." I watched Martin climb out of bed and stretch. His back and shoulders popped, and he dropped to the floor to do a few dozen sit-ups and push-ups. With the craziness of our lives, he'd been missing his workouts, not that he had the energy for such things. "Do you mind cutting to the chase?"

"Earlier this afternoon, I responded to a homicide."

"Okay." I glanced at Martin, huffing out reps as he bounced from leg to leg as he did his push-ups. "Who was killed?"

"Don Klassi. He took two bullets to the chest. Ballistics matched the weapon to the one used to kill Stuart Gifford. The cases are connected, like I told you."

"Dammit. What do you know so far?"

"The doorman spotted an unfamiliar vehicle parked near the apartment building and remembered it had out of state plates. The man who got into the car was dressed entirely in black. He didn't see his face."

"Did he get the plate number?"

"No."

"That's not much to go on." I thought for a moment. "Who called it in?"

"Klassi."

"He reported his own murder?"

"He has one of those virtual assistants. He instructed it to dial 911, probably as soon as the guy broke in. The operator heard the gunshots and sent a unit to investigate."

I remembered the first time the phone rang. It was minutes after Don and I had spoken. Had the killer been there while we were on the phone? Was that why Don had been so desperate to get his money? Was that the reason he was killed?

"You're sure it was a break-in?"

"The deadbolt on the front door was broken. Looks like someone bumped the lock. You know what I'm thinking?" Heathcliff asked.

"Martin was here all night," I said, regretting the joke as soon as I said it.

Heathcliff snorted. "I think Don knew who took you, and since I brought him in for questioning, the killer feared Don would crack and spill the beans. He's tying up loose ends."

"Yeah, he planned to eliminate Noah and me at the cabin, but it didn't happen."

"He'll try again."

"I know." I was resigned to this reality, even though I hoped it wasn't true.

"Anyway, that's not why I called Martin. Until two weeks ago, Klassi was on the board at MT. I'll need additional information since we're checking into everything. And I know you've done a lot of research on Don and the bastard in black. It looks like you're interfering in another one of my cases."

"I wish I wasn't."

"Get everything together and bring it to the precinct. I have some questions. And tell Cross to do the same. He hasn't answered my calls either, and if he doesn't comply, I'll have to pay him a visit."

"He's not going to answer. Jablonsky arrested him this afternoon." Of course, if the man who killed Klassi was the same man who took me, it looked like Lucien had yet another airtight alibi. "I think he owed someone money."

"Cross?"

"No, Klassi. Actually, it might be easier if you came to us, Detective. Everything you should see is in our apartment."

THIRTY-FIVE

"Under different circumstances, you'd be my prime suspect," Heathcliff said. He hadn't taken his eyes off the whiteboard. "You mean to tell me, with all of this, you still have no idea who wanted to murder Klassi or how he connects to CryptSpec."

"Off the record, I wouldn't have minded taking a shot at him." Martin flipped to another page. "Klassi never possessed ten million, unless it was physical currency. According to my calculations, Klassi was under water, but he didn't have any outstanding debts or late payments. His credit history is pristine. However, his spending rate far exceeds his earning potential. Lucien made a note of it. So who was paying the bills?"

"Did Cross have any theories?" Heathcliff asked. I leaned over Martin's shoulder, but Lucien only made a note of the oddity. He didn't speculate. Heathcliff watched as we flipped through the pages. "Do I want to know how you came to possess Klassi's tax records and private account information?"

"Nope." I reached for my mug and took a sip.

"Is that why Cross was arrested?" the detective asked.

I chuckled. "Let's work on one crime at a time."

"How can we? They're interconnected." Heathcliff dialed a number. "We're going to need a court order for Klassi's bank account, phone records, his utilities, credit cards, the works." He looked at me. "Anything else?"

"Property records," Martin said.

Heathcliff nodded. "And property records. Put a rush on this. Wake up a few judges if you have to." He hung up and uncapped a marker. "May I?" Martin nodded at the board, and Derek took to writing. "The slugs we pulled out of Stuart Gifford, the civil engineer, matched the bullets used on Don Klassi. It's the same murder weapon. More than likely, we're looking at the same killer. The witness said he dressed entirely in black. Mask over his face, gloves, the whole kit and kaboodle."

"It's the same guy who attacked me," I said. "How did he get into Klassi's building? There's a doorman."

"We're wondering the same thing," Heathcliff said. "I pulled security footage, but every camera in the building went out. We have no footage for thirty minutes before or after Klassi's murder. The doorman is working with a sketch artist to describe every deliveryman and guest that came to the building, but it wasn't a small number. I don't expect he'll remember them all. This would be easier if we could show him some photos and let him pick someone out of a lineup, but I need to know where to start."

Derek took a step back, turning to read the psychopath's profile on the adjacent board. "All right, the answer is in the overlap." He drew a Venn diagram. "Stuart Gifford and Don Klassi. These are our points of interest. Whoever was in both of their orbits killed them."

"Good luck. I tried the same thing using Noah and me, and it only led to Cross and Klassi," I said.

Heathcliff wrote my name and Lucien Cross between Stuart and Don. "You aren't a central point, but you are a connection. However, I don't think you killed them." He spun toward Martin. "You knew Klassi. Did he know Stuart Gifford or have any connection to CryptSpec?"

"I have no idea. We weren't exactly friends." Martin keyed in an internet search and read through the controlling names at CryptSpec. "Klassi must have a list of contacts on his phone or computer. Hell, maybe his assistant kept up with that stuff, but if he knew one of them, that should answer your question."

"Everything's in evidence. Techs are processing Klassi's phone and computer and pulling his files. I'm going to speak to his assistant and his business partners first thing in the morning, but I wanted to get a jump on everything tonight. Considering how much intel you've gathered, it's a shame it isn't what we need," Heathcliff said.

"Just wanted to rub salt in the wound?" I asked. "Or did you stop by because you're worried this psycho is going to make another run at me?"

Heathcliff didn't answer. Instead, he picked through the files, selecting the ones he wanted to take with him. "I'll read Jablonsky in on the situation and see if he's made any progress. This guy knows how to get away with murder, but I think you're wrong." Derek pointed to the note I made concerning the unsub having law enforcement experience. "At that range, he wouldn't have killed Klassi using a rifle, and his grouping would have been different."

"How can you be sure?" Martin asked.

"Call it a hunch." Heathcliff gave us each another look. "You keep your eyes open and your heads down. I won't waste my breath telling you to stay away from this, but whenever you find something, I better be the first call you make."

"Yes, sir." I watched as he took a few of the photos off the board and tucked them into an envelope. "Anything else you want?"

"Answers." He let himself out, and Martin locked the door behind him.

"Don's dead." I dropped into a chair and rubbed my eyes. "That's why he was so frantic on the phone. The killer must have been standing right there while we spoke. It fits the timeline. I'm guessing the killer came to collect, and Klassi didn't have the money. So he called me, hoping I could buy him some time. That's what happened to Noah too."

"So this is about money." Martin rubbed his chin. "Ten million to be precise. Don didn't even spend anywhere near that amount."

"Did you figure in interest?"

Martin flipped through some pages. Heathcliff didn't touch any of the financial forms. The detective liked to stay on the right side of things, but with a killer prowling the city, I didn't have the same hang-up. "The last big investment Don made was six months ago. It was a little over three million. Do you think this psychopath is a loan shark because I didn't realize they had that much to lend?"

"Not a loan shark, but something similar."

CryptSpec originally mined currency, which is how the start-up got off the ground. By the time the currency went bust, they had become a lucrative tech firm. But if they never had that initial investment, they wouldn't have made it. Klassi possessed the same currency CryptSpec mined, but I didn't see how that connected Klassi to Stuart Gifford or CryptSpec. Don got his coin from Noah. That fact was never in doubt. So how did Noah get it?

"The killer wanted Noah's coin," Martin said. "And Don wanted ten million in the cryptocurrency. Don and the unsub were after the same thing."

"It would appear that way." I blew out a breath. "Dammit."

"What?"

"I hate to say it, but I wish Cross was here. We need to know if Stuart Gifford possessed any of the coin. That could be the connection."

"Do you think Stuart was another of Noah's victims?" Martin asked.

Noah had at least four scams running based on what I found inside his apartment, so I couldn't dismiss that theory. Unfortunately, I didn't have access to Gifford's records, and with Noah out cold, I couldn't ask him either. "That could be, but what if we're looking at this wrong."

"Meaning?" Martin went to the coffeepot, unsure if he should be having coffee or making a drink since sleeping most of the day had confused his internal clock. Deciding on neither, he peeled a banana and took a bite. He eyed me, silently asking if I wanted anything, and I held out my empty mug which he refilled with soup and put in the microwave.

"I assumed Noah had been caught scamming the unsub, and that's why the man wanted money from him. But maybe Noah borrowed money and couldn't pay it back." Another disconcerting thought came to mind. "Or the killer wanted to get to me and decided to use Klassi to do it, except when Klassi begged me to give him whatever we found, I didn't offer to meet up and hand over the money immediately. So the unsub ended him. The killer's going to make another run at me. It's just a matter of time."

Martin scrubbed a hand over his brow. "We need a vacation. A real one. How about I book a suite at a luxury resort. I'm thinking Monaco. You'll love it."

"You're joking. We can't go away right now."

"Why the fuck not? You don't need to be here. This guy is crazy. Your client is dead. This isn't about a case. Hell, you don't have a case. Heathcliff and Jabber are investigating. Your boss has been arrested. You hate your coworkers. So why do you want to stay?"

I didn't have an answer. "You think leaving is a solution?"

"Yes."

"Okay."

Surprised by my response, he took a step back. "Okay," he repeated.

"But I'd be remiss if I didn't point out the two obvious flaws in your brilliant plan. First, if Don really owed ten million dollars, don't you think this bastard must have a lot more stashed somewhere. He can travel just as easily as we can. So how is leaving going to make us safe? Second, what happens if Mark and Derek don't find him? How long are you prepared to stay on vacation? When we went to Spain, you barely lasted a full day."

Martin took my mug out of the microwave and put it on the counter. "I can't sit back and let him hurt you again. What am I supposed to do?"

"Nothing. You're supposed to do nothing." I pointed at the boards. "I shouldn't have let you help. I shouldn't have given him your number to call with the ransom. This...this isn't what we do. This is what I do. I keep you away from it for a reason."

"You've never been able to separate this stuff from me. Not really." He bowed his head and stared at the floor for a moment. When he looked up, his expression showed newfound resolve. "It's a part of you, and when you're hurt, it hurts me. So here's the deal. As long as you're staying on this, so am I. It's your choice. All in, remember?"

I scooped my mug off the counter and kissed him. "Let's see what Heathcliff finds first." I turned on my heel and headed for the bedroom. "I have to talk to Mark in the morning." That gave me eight hours to figure everything out. I just didn't know if that would be enough time.

THIRTY-SIX

The sun wasn't even up when the first call came in. I rolled over, grabbing the phone and regretting the stretch almost immediately. Something popped that shouldn't have. Martin wasn't beside me or hovering at the foot of the bed. While I wondered where he was, I answered the phone.

"Get this," Heathcliff said, "Don Klassi was also a victim of ransomware. The techs are trying to bypass it without erasing his data. We need to get a look at that code, but we haven't been able to crack it yet. However, that gives Klassi something in common with Stuart Gifford. Someone at CryptSpec is responsible, so I'm reinterviewing the employees. Cross sent over his files."

"Cross?"

"Jablonsky kicked him late last night."

"Oh, boy."

"We cleared Ian Barber as a suspect in Gifford's murder, but he hates you. Hell, he hates all of Cross Security. The guy's a certified genius, and from his evaluation forms, we know he has a bad attitude and a short temper."

"That combo tends to go together."

"Yeah, but something's not right with this guy. You've seen his financials. He's got some money saved, and I found several suspicious calls from his phone prior to Gifford's murder. They went to unregistered burners. He never explained that, said they were wrong numbers, but wrong numbers don't last twenty minutes a call. Did I mention Don Klassi had Barber's number stored on his phone? They had several conversations and exchanged a few vague texts a few weeks ago, around the same time Barber placed the suspicious calls to the unknown numbers."

"When exactly did this happen?"

"The bulk of it was Thursday, the day before Barber got the boot and Gifford got killed."

Could Ian Barber have contracted a hit? "Have you asked Barber about his connection to Don Klassi?"

"I will as soon as he's brought in."

"Do you think this is still about ransomware?"

"It might be. Klassi was a victim, and given my theory that Barber is behind the ransomware scheme, he'd probably be the man to contact to get it removed."

"Except he never removed it from Klassi's computer since it's still locked," I pointed out. "

Heathcliff thought for a moment. "Once we examine the programming on Klassi's computer, we'll know for sure who's responsible. Did you know coding is identifiable, almost like handwriting?"

"I'm guessing Ian Barber is about to have a very bad day." I rolled my neck from side to side. "But installing ransomware doesn't make you a killer."

"Are you sure? Two of the ransomware victims are dead." Someone shouted to him. "I've gotta go."

"Thanks for the update. And Derek, thanks for assigning the patrol car to keep watch last night."

"Yeah, well, it was the least I could do."

Carefully, I stretched, feeling the muscles in my back tighten in protest. My rib popped again, ever so slightly, and I pressed my palm against it. Hopefully, it was back in alignment again, but I knew better than to try that a second time. When the pain subsided, I ventured out of the bedroom.

I slept for half the day yesterday and most of the night,

and yet, I wouldn't have minded getting another eight hours of sleep. The doctors said I was suffering from exhaustion and needed my rest. Obviously, they got it right for once.

"Martin?" I called, stepping into the living room. I was surprised not to find him working on the case. Maybe he listened when I told him he should stay away from it, but I doubted it. As a rule, he did what he wanted. And he wanted the man responsible as much as I did, maybe more. However, he'd rather have me safe, hence his newfound obsession with going on vacation.

Some coffee remained in the pot, and I poured it into a mug. It was dark, but it should still count as a clear liquid. I drank a few sips, finding it cold. Maybe Martin went to the office early to make up for all the days he missed.

I settled onto the couch and stared at the whiteboards while I tried to wake up. Ian Barber. That was Heathcliff's brilliant lead, and admittedly, I found Barber to be unpleasant and shady. But that didn't make him a killer, even if he knew two homicide victims. Then again, Jablonsky always taught me there was no such thing as coincidence.

My phone rang again, almost at the same instant the intercom chimed. "Seriously?" I read the caller ID as I pushed the button on the wall.

"Miss Parker, Mr. Cross is here to see you," the doorman said.

"Funny," I muttered, ignoring my ringing phone. "Send him up."

I went into the bedroom, tugged on a pair of jeans, and pulled my hair back in a messy ponytail. Grabbing my nine millimeter, I loaded a round into the chamber and returned to the living room. A few seconds later, a key slid into the lock, followed by the doorknob turning. Lucien sauntered inside while Bruiser clocked his every move.

"Is James here?" Cross asked, noting the gun I placed beside me on the counter.

"Why does that matter?" I asked.

Cross surveyed the room, stopping in front of the boards. "I noticed you cleared out your office. Are you planning on returning to work?"

"I have a doctor's note."

He turned around, jerking on the hem of his jacket. Based on his appearance, he hadn't changed since being released from federal custody. He rubbed a hand over his face, contemplating a shave while he assessed me. "Did you have me arrested?" He cocked his head to the side. "Are you afraid I might have come here to get revenge?" His eyes flicked to my gun. "Or do you honestly believe that I'm responsible?" He spun around and pointed to the profile I created. "Describes me to a T, doesn't it? Too bad it's wrong."

"Your business card was found in the abandoned car. We had to be sure."

"We being you and Jablonsky?" He chuckled. "No, Alex. It wasn't we. It was him. He held me out of spite. It was an abuse of power." He shook his head. "No matter. That's not why I'm here." He moved to the next board. "I see you read my notes. Whoever's responsible has plenty of money to manipulate and pull strings. This is about the cryptocurrency and ten million dollars. Don Klassi wants that amount for a reason, and he expects me to get it for him."

"Not anymore."

Cross spun. "What do you mean?"

"Klassi was murdered last night."

"Shit. Do they know who did it?"

"Who do you think?" I asked sarcastically.

Cross removed a few pages from beneath one of the magnets and flipped through them. "He was collecting as much as he could. His debt was coming due. He thought Noah had that kind of money, and we'd be stupid enough to hand it over to him. He bought time by selling his shares of Martin Tech and several other stocks. The last time we spoke, he begged for what little we found in Noah's account."

"Don said the same to me. We spoke last night, probably minutes before he was shot. Any idea who the debt collector might be?"

Cross ignored me, moving past to the island counter

where he put the pages down and grabbed a pen from his jacket pocket. He circled dates of transactions from Klassi's accounts. "He was making payments regularly. These cash withdrawals happened every week. Not a significant enough amount to warrant much attention, but I think that's what they are. Payments toward his loan."

"Maybe he was just a big tipper," I suggested.

Cross snorted. "While you were away," which was the more pleasant way of saying chained to the floor in a psycho's bomb shelter, "I bumped into Joshua Standish and another of Klassi's business associates. Eight months ago, they were phasing him out of their company. He was opposed to sinking more revenue into their current endeavors. He just wanted to maintain the status quo. He didn't understand that he had to spend money to make money. But a couple months later, things changed. He came up with the money. But when the project grew even larger, he went back to his previous stance. He tried to pull out of the project, but his investment had been spent. He wouldn't see a dime until the project was completed and turning a profit."

"And he didn't have any more to spend in order to make that happen."

"No, and from what we've seen, he didn't have it before that either, but he spent it anyway. I dug into his associates. They're clean. They didn't lend him money, and they aren't responsible for the other unfortunate side effects of this case." He rubbed the grit from his eyes.

From the dark shadows on his face, I knew he'd been up all night, probably working on identifying the real murderer before he got hauled in for another round of questioning. I reset the coffeemaker and took a seat beside him while it sputtered and hissed.

"When Don first approached me, he said Noah Ryder stole ten million dollars. When I asked why he couldn't go to the police, he said it was complicated. And since the unsub demanded $250,000 for my release, I thought it was about money. But the unsub didn't want money from Noah; he wanted the cryptocurrency. But it's worthless. None of this makes any sense."

"Maybe Noah borrowed money from the unsub, just like Klassi, and couldn't pay it back. Perhaps Noah and Klassi conspired to convince the unsub that the cryptocurrency was valuable, and he fell for it. Maybe that's why Klassi and the unsub were both desperate to get their hands on it."

"Because the unsub thinks it has value, and Klassi figured it was an easy and free way of paying back his debt?" I asked. "Okay, let's say you're right. But what I can't figure out is why the unsub would introduce Don to Noah. That's where everything falls apart." I filled a mug and handed it to Cross.

He inhaled deeply and took a sip. "The only thing Don could get from Noah was worthless cryptocurrency, which is why he came to us. The unsub wants the coin. Maybe he figured Don would get it for him."

That just left one question; why did the unsub want that particular worthless type of cryptocurrency? "The currency was created by CryptSpec. This goes back to Stuart Gifford's murder. It's connected somehow. Detective Heathcliff said you handed over our files and interview tapes. I didn't realize the two of you were best friends."

Cross practically choked. Glaring at me, he wiped his mouth and the droplets of coffee with a napkin. "I'm not sure anything I gave the police will be of use, but I am certain of one thing. Klassi intended to use my firm to get that ten million. I'm just not entirely sure how."

"Detective Heathcliff said Klassi was a victim of ransomware, just like Stuart Gifford."

"Where was Klassi killed?"

"In his home."

Abruptly, Cross stood. "I forgot I have a client meeting. Stay safe, Alex." Without another word, he strode out of the apartment.

Bruiser gave me a questioning look. "That was odd."

"I agree." Cross knew something, but he wasn't sharing it with me. Bewildered, I dumped the rest of his coffee down the drain and put the mug in the dishwasher. When I turned around, Bruiser was at the balcony door. The bodyguard gave me a polite nod and left the apartment. "Wow, I sure know how to clear a room."

The curtain moved, and I nearly jumped out of my skin. Martin stepped inside from the balcony and gave me a look. "Cross was here?" he asked.

"I thought you left for work."

He pointed to the Bluetooth stuck to his ear. "I've been working since five a.m. International calls. I'm supposed to go into the office this afternoon." He watched me fidget with my holster. "You didn't answer my question."

"What's the point? You already know the answer."

"I don't like it. Did you invite him?"

"You're joking." Before I could say anything else, the phone rang again.

Martin sighed. "Why are you up so early? You look tired."

"I am tired, but the phone hasn't stopped ringing." I reached the device at the same time he did, but he plucked it out of my hand.

"You didn't seem to care about that yesterday."

"And someone was dead. Answering might be important." I held out my palm. "Who is it?"

"Jabber." He handed me the phone. "Vacation, sweetheart. I'm serious. We can leave tonight."

"Hey, what's up?" I asked, turning my back on the frustratingly determined look Martin was giving me.

"I see Lucien paid you a visit. What did he want?" Mark asked.

"Oh my god. Did he tweet about it or send out a smoke signal or something?" I went to the window and peered out the blinds at the street below. From this height, I couldn't be sure. "Are you following him?"

"No, but I just happened to see him leaving your apartment building when I pulled up. I've found something that you should probably see, and I have a few questions that need answering. Thought it'd be easiest, given your condition, if I picked you up."

"My condition?" I bristled.

"Just meet me downstairs."

Martin watched me collect my things and holster my weapon. "When you get back, we're going to finish our discussion concerning Monaco." He leaned in close and kissed me. "You should know I might even have a PowerPoint presentation prepared to support my argument with plenty of bullet points. You know how much I love to argue my case."

"I can't wait."

After convincing Bruiser that I didn't need a bodyguard, I stepped out of the building and spotted Mark's SUV. As I opened the door, I saw a figure in black. He stood across the street, watching. A car went past, and he was gone.

THIRTY-SEVEN

Police and FBI units canvassed the area and patrolled the streets. No one saw the figure in black. No one spotted any suspicious vehicles with out of state plates. Not even Mark or the police officers keeping watch noticed, but I knew what I saw. At least, I thought I did.

No matter how hard I tried, I couldn't shake it. That feeling that someone was out there, waiting, watching. A police cruiser remained outside the apartment building. Surely, they would have seen him. And if they missed him, the doorman would have noticed a sinister figure stationed across the street. Still, it didn't stop me from requesting a detail be placed in the lobby and turning the outside of my apartment building into a circus. If the killer had been waiting, he was gone now. I texted Bruiser and asked him to be vigilant. Mark circled around a few more times, but no one was there.

"It's normal to be spooked after what you went through," Jablonsky said as he merged onto the interstate. "Dr. Weiler told me you asked for a recommendation. Have you made an appointment yet?"

I let out a displeased growl. "I'm not sure it'll be necessary. We'll see."

"How are you handling everything?"

"So far, so good. I've been too tired and achy to dream much, and aside from this morning's hallucination, I've been reasonably okay. Martin's another story. He's the reason I asked for the recommendation. I'm worried about him. I finally convinced him to sleep yesterday, but now he's got this crazy notion that we should go to Monaco."

"You should. Remember that detour we made in Monte Carlo when we were working that case overseas?"

"I don't have the same fond memories from that trip that you do. I just remember the fancy casinos, ridiculously expensive hotels, and wanting to get back in the field."

"Speaking of casinos, that's actually why we're going on this little excursion."

"You have a compelling need to gamble?" I cocked a confused eyebrow in his direction. "They have support groups for that."

"I already hit the jackpot with Gideon Steinman."

That piqued my interest. "What did you discover? Do we have any leads? What about the bodies?"

He shook his head. "I guess I should have said Steinman hit the jackpot. Fifteen years ago, he spent a weekend in Atlantic City and literally won the jackpot. Ten million dollars."

"Ten?" That couldn't be a coincidence.

"Yep. He returned home the next day and went to work like nothing happened. Everyone I've spoken to had no idea he won any money whatsoever. But his winnings were reported to the IRS, and he paid taxes on them. Never put the money in the bank and continued going about his life like nothing happened. Six months later, he retired and took a bunch of trips to his family's cabin to hide away from the world and fish. At least that's what he told his neighbors. Steinman was a total loner. No living family, few friends. It was just him and the great outdoors." Mark pulled to a stop outside a house with a shiny new for sale sign in the yard. "Now his bills are starting to come due. Until three months ago, he was getting regular deposits in his bank account, but when they stopped, he stopped paying for his care. The nursing home threatened to take his house. The realtor put up the sign this morning, but no one's been inside except a team of agents."

I stepped out of the car and looked at the small, suburban home. "Who's been paying his bills this whole time? And why wasn't he using his winnings?"

Mark jerked his head at the door. "Come on." He led the way inside. Sheets covered what furniture remained. A few photographs dotted the mantle. Mounted hunting trophies lined one wall. He led me through the house and to a staircase that led to the basement. "We're lucky the realtor didn't have time to clear the place out before we found out about Gideon and his cabin." Mark flipped on the light.

Descending a wooden staircase into a cold, dark, concrete structure wasn't how I wanted to spend my day. I shivered. The rear wall was covered in canned foods, bottled water, and emergency rations.

"What the hell is wrong with this guy?" I asked. "Are you sure he isn't a serial killer working with a protégé?"

"The bodies were too fresh." He glanced back at me. "It's not a crime to be prepared for the apocalypse." He led me to a closet in the rear and tugged on the cord. A light came on inside, and I stared at a large gun cabinet filled with a vast assortment of hunting gear, handguns, shotguns, rifles, and knives. "The weapons are registered. We found all of them except two — a handgun and a rifle."

"The killer was here. This is where he got his toys." A small metal object caught my eye, and I knelt down to examine it. "Who's taking care of the house while Steinman's in the nursing home?"

"We're not sure. Gideon suffered a stroke and has trouble speaking and remembering things. The nursing home staff mentioned a nephew, Nicky, but that doesn't track. Gideon didn't have any siblings."

"Are you sure it wasn't Noah?"

"Could be."

"Maybe it was a friend's kid." I held up a bullet. "This isn't helpful."

"I had a team search the house. We didn't find anything, but I thought you should take a look. Maybe you'd recognize something the killer had or some similarity to the bomb shelter. Anything to lead us to the killer."

"Where do you think the ten million went?"

"Your guess is as good as mine."

I pointed at the shelves. "That's the same setup from the bomb shelter." I shrugged. "I don't know. Let me look around upstairs." I wanted out of the basement as quickly as possible. "Did you dust for prints?"

"We found a few sets. Four or five, but we didn't get any hits in IAFIS."

"Every print we've ever found isn't in the system. Why would that change now?"

We went up the steps while I continued to pepper Jablonsky with questions about the four bodies and Gideon Steinman and who had access. A team of agents performed their due diligence by questioning Gideon's former coworkers, neighbors, colleagues, nursing home staff, and volunteers. One of them had to be the killer or know who was.

I stopped in the bedroom, wondering if Gideon hid the money in the mattress. Of course, that was the first place Jablonsky checked. While searching through Gideon's closet, I caught movement in the mirror. I turned, seeing only myself.

"Mark?" I called.

"Out here." He was searching the linen closet to see if he could find any blankets similar to the one I found at the cabin. "What's wrong?"

I looked back at the mirror, but I was the only one here. "Nothing. I thought you came into the room." Backing against the wall, I removed my gun and looked around. The bedroom was empty. Taking a few steps to the side, I checked the bathroom. It was also empty. I returned to the bedroom and stared at the mirror. It was on a wall between the closet door and the bedroom door.

I stared at my reflection for a moment, seeing a thinner, frightened version of what I normally saw. Maybe I should call the shrink. Turning, I went back to searching the closet. When I didn't find anything, I stepped back into the bedroom and gave the mirror another look.

"That's weird." The wall was as thick as the closet, but

the interior of the closet ended three inches from the doorjamb. There were at least two feet of unaccounted for space behind the mirror.

Removing the floor length mirror from the wall required lifting, which I wasn't supposed to do. "Shit." I doubled over and fell against the side of the bed just as a bullet tore through the window behind me. Glass showered down around me, and I yanked my gun free. A barrage of gunfire pinned me against the floor.

Mark rushed to me, but I told him to stay back. "He's outside. I'll distract him. Go." I fired a few shots out the window, but no return fire followed. Biting my lip to keep from screaming, I rolled onto my side and pushed up on one hand. Crawling to the window, I waited a beat before peering outside.

Jablonsky barked orders into his phone, requesting a perimeter and back-up units. "Son of a bitch. He's gone."

Using the window sill for support, I climbed to my feet. "Get in here. I found something."

I ripped pieces of the damaged wall away, revealing a hidden compartment. Obviously, there was another way to access this, but I'd just been shot at. I didn't feel like looking for the door. A metal box sat on the floor, and I crouched down in front of it.

"Are you okay?" Mark asked, keeping one eye out the window.

"I've been worse." I flipped the latches on the box and opened it. Inside were dozens of USB drives, brochures, and several pamphlets. I picked them up, recognizing them as the materials I'd found in Noah's apartment. "How much you want to bet these are loaded with worthless cryptocurrency?" I asked, holding up one of the drives.

Sirens blared, and Mark went outside, holding up his credentials. After informing the responding officers to maintain a perimeter and canvass the area, he returned inside. "Noah's still in the hospital. He hasn't gone anywhere, so he can't be the shooter. But if you're right, he must have been here at some point to stock up on the coin, and the shooter is probably his accomplice. The asshole's been lying to us all along. We never should have trusted a con man."

"Did you get a look at the shooter?" I asked.

"No. He vanished by the time I got outside." Jablonsky blew out an angry breath and slammed his palm against the wall, knocking bits of drywall loose. "I already have people checking nearby traffic cams. A silver SUV with rental plates blew through a red light. We're running it now, and the police have set up traffic stops."

"He'll slip through. He always does."

Jablonsky swore. "How did he know we'd be here?"

"He followed us. Well, me." I rubbed my cheek. It was still sore. "He was outside Martin's apartment this morning. I don't care that no one else saw him or the search turned up empty. He was there." I dialed Bruiser. Depending on how smart the killer was, he might target Martin.

"He must really hate you," Mark mused as FBI techs arrived and entered the house. "Any idea why?"

"Heathcliff thinks I ruined his life."

"Who?"

"Ian Barber."

"You think he's the killer?"

"Derek does, even though Barber has an alibi for the time of Stuart Gifford's murder. But Derek's a professional. Let's see if he's right."

Jablonsky narrowed his eyes, watching as I detoured away from the exit and into the kitchen. With shaky hands, I opened the drawers and held up a spoon. "Same flatware I used to dig myself free. This is definitely the right place."

"I thought the bullets through the window would have tipped you off."

Growling out a creative obscenity, I walked out of the house. Visually, I swept the area, but the shooter was long gone.

THIRTY-EIGHT

Ian Barber was inside an interrogation room while someone shot at me. In fact, several of CryptSpec's more questionable employees had alibis for the time in question. Surprisingly, most of them were cooperating, and Heathcliff had collected a number of fingerprints. So far, none of them matched the unknowns found at the cabin or in Steinman's home.

"Hey," Heathcliff said, stepping out of the interrogation to speak to me, "remember that theory you had that the killer had law enforcement experience? It turns out CryptSpec's been designing simulation training modules. One of them deals specifically with evidence collection."

"Great," Jablonsky said, nonplussed. "Let me guess; they have another one on how to shoot."

"I wouldn't doubt it," Heathcliff said. "I don't suppose that means anything, but I figured you might want to know."

I stared at Barber through the glass. "I heard he admitted to the ransomware scheme. Why would he do that?"

"Prosecutor cut him a deal due to the murders. The AG's office would prefer collaring a serial killer with four known victims, rather than a cyberterrorist who's only targeted a couple of the city's professionals."

"That's how it goes," Jablonsky said.

"Nonviolent crime trumps violent crime every day," Derek said. "It's a federal matter anyway. I'm just trying to figure out who killed Gifford and Klassi."

"Has Barber said anything useful?" I asked.

"Just that Mr. Mansfield knew about the ransomware scheme and wanted it stopped. Barber says Mansfield didn't want anyone to know about the weakness in CryptSpec's latest app, so Mansfield lied about the corporate espionage to cast aspersions and hired Cross Security to investigate."

"Do you believe that?" Jablonsky asked.

"I don't know," Heathcliff said. "But Barber admitted to targeting Don Klassi with the malware. According to Barber, Klassi and Mansfield were tight. They were best friends or something, so Barber thought that would be a great way to stick it to his boss."

"Have you spoken to Mansfield yet?" Jablonsky asked.

"Not today. We tried calling, but his assistant said he was in a lunch meeting and couldn't be disturbed. He's probably getting the bandages removed from his plastic surgery." Derek rolled his eyes. "Uniforms are at the office, waiting for him to return."

Jablonsky snorted. "If I were you, kid, I'd disturb his lunch meeting."

Turning away from the men with the badges, I fished my phone out of my bag and called Cross. He spent the most time with Mansfield. Perhaps the owner of the start-up had confided in Cross, and that's why the investigation had been reopened after I completed my analysis.

I only asked Lucien the most basic of questions, knowing that Jablonsky would want to point out that Lucien's visit to my apartment this morning provided the perfect opportunity to stake out the place, follow us, and shoot at me, but I didn't think Cross was the killer. And when in doubt, I knew to trust my gut. Since my boss was playing ball, I told him about the pamphlets and cryptocurrency we found hidden in Steinman's house.

Hanging up, I turned back to Mark. The killer didn't target me because I fit his obsession. He targeted me because he feared what I knew. That meant there was only one other person he would lash out against since he couldn't get to me.

"We need to get to Noah before our killer does," I said.

*　　*　　*

When we arrived at the hospital, Lucien was seated in the waiting room. I stared, horrified, at him. My gut said the killer would come to the hospital to end Noah since the trail from Steinman's home led back to the grifter. Cross's appearance couldn't have been an accident, and I never mentioned I was coming here.

"What the hell are you doing here?" I asked as the sick feeling twisted my insides tighter.

"He's begging to get arrested again," Jablonsky offered from a few steps behind me. "What do you know about Gideon Steinman?"

Cross ignored the question. "I have to speak to Noah. It's urgent."

"You're not getting near him," Mark growled. "And it's mighty convenient that you show up now, right after someone tried to kill Alex." Jablonsky gestured to the police officers stationed at the door.

"What happened?" Cross asked.

"As if you don't already know," Mark snapped.

"I don't." Cross stared at me. "Parker?"

"What did you find on CryptSpec and Mansfield?" I asked. Mark gestured for one of the officers to check on Noah, and the other two flanked Cross.

"Barber wasn't lying. There was no corporate espionage, just the ransomware scheme. It was a security issue with CryptSpec's latest app that allowed for the backdoor into the system. It was a weakness the programmers knew about and some chose to exploit. Detective Heathcliff was right; that's why Mansfield hired us," Cross said.

"Did you know all along?" I asked.

"No." Cross glanced in the direction of Noah's room. "I

have to see him."

"You know who the killer is," I said.

"I have a hunch but no proof." Cross licked his lips. "I need to know where Noah got the coin. How he got it. It shouldn't be in circulation. It was something Mansfield created that launched his company. Only a few people came to possess it, and most trashed it when it tanked. Mansfield started CryptSpec with several close friends, but when the company became profitable, they took payouts and abandoned ship. It makes no sense. Why did Steinman have a closet full of it, and how did Noah get so much of it?"

"You think Noah got the cryptocurrency from one of them?" Jablonsky asked.

Suddenly, it clicked. "Did Mansfield know Steinman?" I asked. Both men shrugged. "Mansfield doesn't have a criminal record, but we need his prints."

"His address might be better," Lucien retorted.

"What does that mean?" I asked.

"I'll tell you later."

I peered into Noah's room, but he was unconscious with a breathing tube down his throat. The swelling in his brain hadn't completely subsided. We wouldn't be able to talk to him. "We need guards stationed at his door. No one except hospital staff in or out."

Mark smiled. "I knew you missed being an agent."

We reconvened at Cross Security since it was faster to get intel without the hassle of court orders and warrants. Plus, Lucien already had a case file started on CryptSpec and its founder. Kellan and Bennett joined us in the conference room, and we poured over the information, searching for a completely different set of clues.

Mansfield knew there was no corporate espionage and his programmers were responsible for the ransomware scheme. He just didn't know exactly who was responsible, so he hired Cross Security to detect the problem under the guise of corporate espionage. The suspicious payments tipped me off to Ian Barber, who I then turned over to Mansfield.

"Stuart Gifford knew of the app's weakness. He was one

of the first victims," Heathcliff said, arriving just as Kellan and Bennett called it a day. "That's why he was killed. He threatened to expose them and the entire CryptSpec operation. He spoke to several of the programmers and Mansfield. Gifford was going to go to the press. A reporter was going to meet him that afternoon."

"You're sure?" I asked.

Derek nodded. "I arrested Gifford's killer an hour ago. He was just a hitman for hire. He alibied out for the time of the abduction and for Klassi's murder. He's not our unsub, but our unsub contracted him, probably in order to ensure he had an alibi. The hitman was paid anonymously to take out Gifford. He was supposed to do it outside Gifford's office, but it was too busy there. So he followed him and popped him outside CryptSpec."

"How did you find the hitman?" Jablonsky asked.

Heathcliff nodded at Cross. "Those two female eyewitnesses you pointed me to."

Jablonsky narrowed his eyes at Lucien. "Why didn't you tell me you found two eyewitnesses to the shooting?"

"You're not a homicide detective, and I don't investigate murders," Cross retorted. "Plus, they didn't want to come forward, and you would have spooked them. I had to meet with them in a motel several times to convince them it was in their best interest to cooperate with the police."

"Guess something you said or did persuaded them. Anyway, we traced the hitman's financials, but he didn't get paid with the usual wire transfer. Want to guess how he got paid for the hit?" Heathcliff asked.

"Cash at a dead drop," I said. "Two hundred and fifty thousand."

Heathcliff pointed at me. "Bingo."

"Did you check surveillance footage of the area?" Jablonsky asked.

"Yep," Heathcliff said. "Want to guess who left the money and picked up a rifle?"

"The man in black." I blew out a breath. "It's Mansfield. It has to be. He must have given the hitman Steinman's rifle to use in the commission of the crime and to hold as collateral until the contract was paid in full. I bet the bodies buried in the woods are a match to the four people who helped start CryptSpec. Mansfield was afraid the unnecessary attention from the ransomware scheme would lead to someone digging around in CryptSpec's background and discovering how he really took control of the company, by killing off his partners."

"He probably didn't have a choice. The five of them committed fraud," Lucien said. "The coin they mined was always fake. It didn't lose value. It never had any, but they figured if people believed it had worth, then at some point, it might. They perpetuated the lie in order to make a name for themselves."

"They distributed flyers and printed materials to make the coin appear legitimate, but they never had any takers. The concept was new. No one trusted it," I said.

"And then they found the perfect mark," Jablonsky said. "Gideon Steinman. Mansfield or one of his partners convinced Gideon to invest his winnings. The monthly payments Gideon received were dividends from CryptSpec, but after the ransomware scheme caused the company to come under extreme scrutiny, the payments stopped. Mansfield was afraid we'd discover the truth."

"Great," I sighed, "so how do we prove some techie is a psycho killer?"

THIRTY-NINE

Heathcliff hauled Nicholas Mansfield down to the precinct for questioning. Jablonsky, Cross, and I waited impatiently in the interrogation room. The first thing I noticed about Mansfield was the faint yellowing around his eyes. During Heathcliff's earlier interviews, Mansfield told the detective he had a procedure done to remove the bags from beneath his eyes, and he bandaged the area well enough that Derek didn't realize Mansfield's nose had been broken.

"Did you get a look at his medical records?" I asked.

Cross let out a snarl. "He went to the plastic surgeon. He's too smart not to cover his tracks."

"Dammit." I stared at the glass, wanting to carve that smug look off Mansfield's face.

As predicted, Mansfield claimed to have no knowledge of Gideon Steinman. However, due to the questionable nature of the cryptocurrency he financed his company with, along with the two recent murders, we had gotten a warrant. While Derek spoke to Mansfield, police and FBI agents were searching Mansfield's home, phone and business records, financial records, and CryptSpec for evidence.

"Unless we get something that directly links Mansfield to Steinman, we've got nothing." Jablonsky cursed.

"The actual smoking gun would be nice," Cross muttered.

"What about the shares of CryptSpec?" I asked.

"Circumstantial. Everything is fucking circumstantial," Mark said.

"Not coincidental?" Cross enjoyed putting the screws to Mark.

"Where were you last week?" Heathcliff asked, staring at Mansfield. "You refused to come in to answer questions, and you weren't at CryptSpec either."

"Recovering from surgery, like I said," Mansfield replied. "I'd be happy to show you my discharge papers and care instructions, Detective. I'm sure my doorman can vouch for my whereabouts."

"He's not going to crack," Jablonsky said. "Without some sort of corroboration or proof that he sold worthless coin to Gideon Steinman, we can't make the fraud charges stick either."

"What about the ransomware?" I asked.

"He's already denied knowing about it, and even when things come to light, he'll claim he hired us to sort through the mess," Lucien said.

I watched Heathcliff. I'd seen him conduct enough interrogations to know he was frustrated. The situation seemed hopeless. Mansfield's attorney wasn't allowing his client to answer anything that might be damning or could be used to link Mansfield to another crime. The only thing Mansfield admitted to was being friends with Don Klassi and residing in the same apartment building. Acquaintances was the term he used. He said they only spoke about possible properties for CryptSpec's inevitable expansion.

"All right, so we do this the hard way," I said.

Mark stared at me. "No. You are not going in there to confront him."

"Of course not," I said. "This is a police matter, and I promised Heathcliff I'd stay away from his case." But I had to do something.

"You have no evidence against my client. Mr. Mansfield is a respected member of the community. We've been nothing but cooperative." The attorney stood. "This interview is over."

"Not so fast," Heathcliff snapped.

The attorney stared at Derek for a long moment. "Then charge him."

"I'm sure I will soon enough." Heathcliff gestured to the medic to conduct a blood draw. The warrant also included a blood sample, and I was confident it would match the drops left by my attacker in the alleyway.

Mansfield's eyes went ice cold, and he glowered at the medic as the tube filled. He knew he was caught. It was just a matter of time.

"He knows he's dead to rights. He'll run," I said.

"I'll put a surveillance team on him," Jablonsky promised. "I'm sure the police will do the same. He won't escape."

"You have no grounds yet to detain him," Cross said. "How exactly do you plan on stopping him from fleeing?"

"Don't worry about how I do my job," Mark growled.

I stared through the glass, watching Mansfield roll down his sleeve and put on his jacket. He lived in Klassi's building, which explained how he gained easy access to Don's apartment and slipped away after the gunshots without being seen. And since he was a programmer, he knew how to hack into security feeds, deactivate cameras, and even how to screw with the security system at the gallery. Still, I couldn't help but wonder how he managed to slip in and out of his apartment building without anyone noticing.

"Where the hell is he hiding the handgun and rifle?" I asked.

"We'll find them," Jablonsky said as Mansfield walked out of interrogation with his lawyer in tow.

Before anyone could say or do anything, Cross stepped out of the observation room. "I'm not doing your job for you," Cross bellowed. "Get your own evidence." He stormed down the hallway in a huff.

"What the hell was that about?" Heathcliff asked,

stepping inside as a bewildered Mansfield continued in the opposite direction, toward the front entrance. Jablonsky raised an eyebrow and folded his arms over his chest and stared at me, waiting for an answer.

"I don't know, but I think Cross has a plan." I grabbed my bag off the table. "I'm going to find out what it is."

"Alex," Jablonsky warned, but I pushed past him.

"Parker?" Heathcliff called after me.

"Maintain eyes on Mansfield. Do not let him slip away," I called over my shoulder.

Finally, I caught up to Cross at the back stairwell. He concluded a call and put his phone back in his pocket. He looked behind me, spotting Mark watching us from the other end of the hall.

"You should go home. I'll assign a security team for your protection," Cross offered.

"Did you know Mansfield was a killer?" Cross didn't answer, so I pushed harder. "Did you know he was behind the attack? That he trapped me in that room, hoping to kill me?"

"Watch yourself."

"How long have you known?"

"I didn't know," Cross bit out. "I still don't. I have people looking into the four other men who started CryptSpec. It could be one of them. Right now, nothing concrete points to Mansfield."

I scoffed. "Are you that stubborn that you can't admit coincidences don't exist? Or is this because you're too arrogant to accept you were working for a psychopath?" I saw something in his eyes. "Tell me the truth."

"I overlooked him as a possibility until you told me Don Klassi was killed at home." Lucien rubbed a hand over his mouth and stared at the wall.

"Guess what," Jablonsky said, joining us, "we all missed it." Mark blew out a breath. "Agents are going to show Mansfield's photo to the nursing home staff and see if he might be Steinman's nephew Nicky. I have a few calls in to see if we can get a warrant to ping his phone and track his movement for the last few weeks. I'm just waiting to hear back."

Cross bit his lip, the wheels turning in his head. "I should go. Obviously, you know what you're doing. And as a rule, I don't involve myself in murder investigations." He nodded at me. "I'll have a team placed outside your apartment building. Let me know when Mansfield is apprehended."

Mark watched him leave. "I still don't trust him."

"That makes two of us."

*　　*　　*

Ditching the protection detail wasn't difficult, but the same couldn't be said for Bruiser and Marcal. Martin was at the office, probably setting plans in motion to work remotely for the foreseeable future, so in his absence, his bodyguards were sticking to me like glitter to glue. I paced back and forth inside our tiny apartment, feeling caged and helpless. It wasn't a good feeling, particularly after enduring four days of hell locked in that bomb shelter. I could feel the panic starting to bubble closer to the surface.

"I need air," I said.

Bruiser studied me, recognizing the signs. "I'll open the balcony door."

"No." I shook my head vehemently. "Heights. Pigeons. Bad idea." I exhaled. "I need to get out of here."

We went for a drive. The entire time, my mind remained on Mansfield and the investigation. We were so close, but blood evidence took time to process. And even with a rush order, it would still take hours, probably days, before anything definitive surfaced. Jablonsky hadn't called back with news regarding the nursing home staff, but even if they IDed Mansfield, it wouldn't prove anything. Any halfway decent defense attorney would point that out. We needed the weapons. Hell, we just needed proof.

"I need to check something at the office."

Marcal glanced in the rear view mirror and eyed me. "Yes, Miss Parker."

When we arrived at Cross Security, Bruiser accompanied me to my office. Marcal remained illegally parked out front. I keyed in a few searches and dug through the filing cabinet for additional information on the CryptSpec case. Heathcliff had been right all along to think they were connected. I should have trusted him and told him about Don Klassi sooner. Perhaps if I did, the man would still be alive and none of this shit would have happened.

"I messed up." The sick feeling returned. "I'm gonna use the bathroom. I'll be right back."

Bruiser gave me an uncertain look, but surprisingly, he didn't follow me to the ladies' room. After splashing some water on my face, I detoured to the elevator and went up to Cross's office. His assistant announced my presence and ushered me inside. From the blueprints spread across the desk, I knew Cross was on to something.

"I was just on my way to meet with Detective Heathcliff," Lucien said. "You should go home."

"You found something."

"I might have figured out how Mansfield got in and out of his apartment building undetected and perhaps where he's been stowing his black clothing and weapons. Right now, it's just a guess. I have to be certain before I share it with the authorities."

"You're helping them?"

Cross stared at me for a moment. "It's not like you've given me much choice. When this is over, we need to modify our arrangement because it's not working for me."

"Me neither." I noticed a wire poking out from the top of his collar. "I'm coming with you."

He eyed me for a moment, seeing the nine millimeter holstered at my side. "Fine. Let's go."

We took the elevator down to the garage, and I wondered how long it would take before Bruiser realized I ditched him. To be on the safe side, I told the receptionist to tell Bruiser I was following up on a lead with Cross and would be back soon. Hopefully, the bodyguard wouldn't call in a rescue team or order an airstrike.

Cross parked half a block from Don Klassi's apartment building. The neighborhood looked just like I remembered it, except now I spotted Jablonsky and a team of FBI agents stationed near the rear door and Heathcliff and several police officers at the front. They remained concealed in their surveillance vehicles, but I knew what to look for. They must be waiting for confirmation before raiding the building and apprehending Mansfield.

The bastard who tried to kill me was somewhere inside, probably masterminding his escape. During my time at CryptSpec, Mansfield had remained aloof and unreadable. He was cool, never giving any indication he was a serial killer with a violent temper. No wonder it had taken years before anyone realized what he had done.

"This way," Cross said, drawing me out of my reverie. He went around the side of the neighboring building and opened a door labeled maintenance.

"This is the wrong building."

"We'll see." He flipped on a light switch. At the other end of the room was another door. "That should lead to the generator room in Mansfield's building."

I opened the door and found a second door. It should have been locked, but I could tell it had been tampered with. The door wouldn't even stay closed. The lock had been bumped. Slowly, I entered. The room was small, holding the generator and not much else. We branched out to begin the search.

Cross picked through some discarded cardboard boxes and supplies, stopping to study something on the wall. "We need to hurry."

I spotted the strap of a duffel bag hidden beneath a cardboard box in the corner. Slipping on a pair of gloves, I crouched down and moved the box. "Lucien, I found it."

I looked up to find Cross's weapon aimed in my direction. I let go of the box and reached for my gun, but someone grabbed me from behind. I felt the edge of a blade press into my neck.

"I won't hesitate this time," Mansfield hissed in my ear.

Cross's finger flexed on the trigger. He needed to take the shot. Mansfield would kill me if he didn't. Lucien's eyes darted from me to Mansfield, and I had to decide just how much I trusted my boss. "Don't do it, Mr. Mansfield. We're both businessmen. This doesn't have to get ugly, but if you try to kill my employee, I'll put a bullet in you and bury you in the woods next to your former business partners."

Mansfield's eyes grew cold. "You shouldn't threaten me." He kept the knife against my neck, but with his other hand, he jabbed into my injured rib, knowing exactly where he previously inflicted the most damage.

I screamed, unable to stop my body from folding forward. The blade cut into my neck, and I jerked backward. Mansfield removed the gun from my holster and aimed at Lucien, knowing he had complete control of me and my boss.

"It's not a threat. It's a guarantee," Lucien said. He reached into his jacket, and Mansfield edged backward, dragging me with him. "Easy, sparky, I'm getting my wallet. This isn't the Wild West. How much will it take to get you to back off? You can invest it, shove it up your ass, whatever gets you off. But I need assurances that you're done with Parker and you will stay the hell away from my firm." He tossed the wallet at Mansfield's feet.

Mansfield let out an ugly laugh. "I don't want your money. I want your silence." He pulled the knife away from my neck and ran the tip down the side of my face. It might have been a brazen move if I wasn't in so much pain that I could barely even stand, let alone fight.

I hissed when he pressed against my bruised cheekbone. Since Cross was taking his sweet time, I had to do something. "You thought you were so clever, hacking into the security system at the art gallery. Too bad you left a digital trail," I said.

Cross caught on to my play, remaining cool and detached, even as I frantically fought to keep still to avoid being cut. "Oh, you didn't realize the safeguards I have in place, did you, Nicholas? You probably figured since you run a tech company and I just run an investigation firm that I would have no idea what to do with cybercrimes." Cross grinned. "Oh, wait, that's one of my specialties." He stared at Mansfield. "Isn't that why you freaked out and decided to silence Parker? She knew what you had done, how you started your company, the deal you made with Don Klassi." He snorted. "Your best friend betrayed you, and you were afraid of what he told her. That's why you attacked her and killed Don."

"And since the two of you are here, I can put all of this behind me right now," Mansfield said.

"It won't end here," Cross warned. "I have contingencies in place. Should anything happen to me, evidence will be released against you. Now put down the weapons."

"If that were true, the cops would have arrested me." Mansfield didn't lower the knife; instead, he held it against my throat, preparing to cut me open.

"The only reason you're still free is because of my obvious dislike for law enforcement and my reputation. I won't let my bias stand in the way again. If you refuse my terms, I will go to the police and the FBI, and you'll be fucked up the ass."

"Do it," Mansfield said, calling Cross's bluff, "but she'll be dead. And so will you."

Cross pulled out his phone. He hit speed dial and put it on speakerphone. "Justin, prepare the files for release. I want copies sent to the local FBI field office and the PD."

"What about the witness to Don Klassi's murder? Are we disclosing that information as well?" Justin asked.

"Yes, and make a few extra copies of the footage from the hidden video surveillance camera from Don's apartment, just in case we—"

Mansfield fired at Cross. The bullet whizzed past him, just to the left of Lucien's ear. "I changed my mind. Hang up," Mansfield ordered.

"On second thought, that might not be necessary. I'll call you back." Cross ended the call. "Did you think I was bluffing?" He rolled his eyes at the gun. "There's no need to point that peashooter at me."

Mansfield fired again, hitting Lucien center mass. He squeezed off two more shots, and Lucien dove to the right. I jerked my head back and knocked into Mansfield's chin. The edge of the knife nicked me, but the move surprised him. Reflexively, he threw up his hands, lifting the knife away from my throat.

"Down," Lucien bellowed, and I dropped to the floor. He fired, and Mansfield staggered backward, falling to the ground.

I lunged for the gun, but Mansfield wasn't down for the count. Despite the bullet in his shoulder, he was determined to see me perish. We fought over control of the gun. It skittered across the floor, and I reached it just as he grabbed the knife. He held the blade high, intent on plunging it into me. He stabbed at my stomach, and I narrowly managed to roll to the side just as the door behind Mansfield burst open.

"Drop the knife," Heathcliff bellowed.

It clattered to the floor just as Jablonsky and a team of agents burst into the room from the door Lucien and I used to enter. "Parker, are you okay?" Jablonsky asked.

Mansfield fell to the floor, and I scooted away from him, but my gun didn't waver. If he twitched, I'd shoot him. The psychopath looked up at me, uncontained rage burning in his eyes.

"Give me a reason," I said.

He let out a huff. "I should have killed you."

"Yep."

The thought went through his head. The gravity of the situation set in. He was caught. There was no escape. He stared at the knife, inches from his fingers.

"It's never too late," he said.

"Don't even think about it." Heathcliff kicked the knife away and cuffed him. "Clear." Heathcliff eyed me. "It's okay. We got him, Alex."

I held out my gun for one of the officers to take and glared at Mansfield. "You fucking asshole." I got to my feet and kicked him. None of the police or FBI agents tried to stop me, and I would have kept kicking him if Cross didn't grab me by the hips and pull me away. I made another attempt to get to Mansfield, and Lucien pulled me into his chest, flinching as I struggled against him.

"It's over, Alex. It's done," Cross said.

I watched Jablonsky drag Mansfield to his feet, knocking him hard against the doorframe on the way out of the room. By the time the bastard was booked, he'd probably have a concussion to go along with the bullet wound. Maybe it would knock some compassion into the cold-blooded killer.

"What the hell took you so long?" Cross released me and tugged off his shirt before pulling at the Velcro straps on his vest. Beneath that, he wore a wire, which he plucked off his already bruising skin and handed to one of the cops.

"We couldn't find the access point into the room." Heathcliff knelt beside the cardboard box, lifting it up to find the guns and dark clothing Mansfield used during the commission of his crimes, along with a set of car keys. "I thought you were going to confront him inside his apartment."

"I had a hunch," Cross retorted, "and Parker wanted to tag along." He sneered at the police. "You're welcome."

Derek turned to me, seeing the new cuts. He pulled a handkerchief from his pocket and wiped the trickle of blood off my neck, checking to see how serious the injury was. "You'll be okay. It's just a scratch."

I cradled my side. "Yeah, well, I'm not going to refuse an ambulance if you're offering."

"No problem." He radioed it in and gave me a look. "Cross said he had this handled. What are you even doing here?"

"Closing a case."

Heathcliff grinned. "Me too."

*   *   *

Over the next couple of weeks, everything came to light. One of CryptSpec's co-founders was Ashley Billings, a nobody from Wyoming who lived in utter obscurity until he discovered his first computer at the local library. Soon after, he started coding and programming, practically building machines from scratch. That's when his life inevitably changed. He moved across the country, found several like-minded individuals, and dreamed of starting a tech company.

Noah Ryder, born Dale Billings, was Ashley's brother. The two had always been close, and Ashley had told Noah all about his new friends, the computer geniuses. They wanted to create a tech start-up, and one of the five found Steinman. He was a lonely old man who lived a simple life.

He was sitting on a fortune and had no idea what to do with it, so they convinced him to invest in CryptSpec.

But Mansfield didn't want a nobody owning his company or dictating terms. He convinced Steinman that cryptocurrency was money of the future, and they were just exchanging the cash hidden in the secret wall of his bedroom for something just as practical.

Inevitably, Mansfield feared the fraud he and his partners committed would come to light, and on a weekend trip to Steinman's cabin, something happened. Mansfield must have snapped, or one of his partners suddenly grew a conscience. Mansfield held his partners hostage for months, forced their signatures, and had them cut ties with their family and friends before killing them and burying the bodies. Then he took sole control of CryptSpec.

Before that happened, Ashley had given his brother some of the bogus cryptocurrency and the flyers, perhaps as a joke or because he wanted to confide in someone. When Ashley disappeared, Dale decided to find the truth. For five years, Dale searched for Ashley. When money ran tight, he decided to use his own variation on the fraud scheme, and that inevitably caught Mansfield's attention. But Mansfield couldn't risk confronting Dale, a.k.a. Noah, on his own, so he monitored Noah from a distance, waiting for the perfect opportunity.

Don Klassi idolized Mansfield since the tech genius created something from nothing and a company was born out of it. Don wanted nothing more than to emulate Mansfield. Eventually, that friendship led to Don asking for a loan to get out of his own messy business problems. But that loan came at a price. At the same time Don was getting himself in deeper with a killer, his constant calls and proximity to Mansfield caught the attention of Ian Barber, who figured Klassi was another big fish he could gouge with his ransomware scheme and indirectly stick it to the boss all at the same time. However, Don didn't care about the ransomware. He had bigger problems.

When Don couldn't repay the loan, Mansfield led Don right to Noah. Mansfield either wanted his cash back or all of Noah's cryptocurrency. Having no idea how much the grifter possessed, Mansfield knew the maximum amount of coin couldn't exceed ten million, so he decided he wouldn't settle for anything less. But when Don couldn't get ten million, the threats began.

Fearing for his life, Don hired me to persuade Noah to give up the cryptocurrency. When that backfired, Don tried to buy himself some time by insisting I knew the truth about CryptSpec and Noah was helping me.

Mansfield was a killer. He wore nice suits and blended in with society, but he always had the darkness within him. Maybe slaughtering his business partners made him lust for blood. Or it was just another way the arrogant egomaniac could demonstrate he was the smartest man in the room. He was never caught. No one suspected him of a crime, be it murder or fraud.

So when problems arose half a decade later, Mansfield figured he could solve them. And he almost did. Only he knew about Steinman's cabin and car. So he came up with a plan to eliminate Noah and me, but it failed. And since he hadn't paid the rest of the hitman's contract, he thought Martin's unmarked money would be perfect. In the event the cash was being tracked, it would link to Gifford's killer and not to Mansfield. But that also backfired.

It was over now. Mansfield was facing multiple life sentences. Noah could finally lay his brother to rest, and my life could go back to normal.

"So where did we land on that vacation?" Martin asked, rubbing his thumb against my cheek.

"You missed doing that."

"I like you better when you aren't bruised." He stole a kiss. "So vacation?"

"The only place I want to go is home."

He gave me a confused look. "Okay, I'll give you a ride to your apartment."

"That's not home. Our home. Have you fixed the walls yet?"

He sat on the edge of the bed and stared at me, fighting to keep the smile off his face. "Are you serious? You want to move back in with me?"

"As soon as the walls are fixed."

"I'll have someone start on that tomorrow." He looked utterly content. "I'm proud of you. You kept your word. You didn't pull away or try to send me to Monaco without you. I guess I better keep my word too. I believe I owe you a striptease." He winked. "Be right back." He returned with the remote to the stereo and keyed the music. "I hope you have plenty of singles. You're going to need them."

DON'T MISS THE NEXT NOVEL IN THE
ALEXIS PARKER SERIES.

SIGN-UP TO BE NOTIFIED OF THE LATEST
RELEASE.

http://www.alexisparkerseries.com/newsletter

ABOUT THE AUTHOR

G.K. Parks is the author of the Alexis Parker series. The first novel, *Likely Suspects,* tells the story of Alexis' first foray into the private sector.

G.K. Parks received a Bachelor of Arts in Political Science and History. After spending some time in law school, G.K. changed paths and earned a Master of Arts in Criminology/Criminal Justice. Now all that education is being put to use creating a fictional world based upon years of study and research.

You can find additional information on G.K. Parks and the Alexis Parker series by visiting our website at
www.alexisparkerseries.com

Made in the USA
Middletown, DE
02 February 2021